"Critical Mass," by Douglas Clark. ISBN 978-1-62137-301-8 (softcover) 978-1-62137-302-5 (hardcover) 978-1-62137-303-2 (ebook).

Library of Congress Control Number: 2013910377

Published 2013 by Virtualbookworm.com Publishing Inc., P.O. Box 9949, College Station, TX 77842, US. ©2013, Douglas Clark. All rights reserved. No part of this publication may be reproduced, stored in a retrieval system, or transmitted in any form or by any means, electronic, mechanical, recording or otherwise, without the prior written permission of Douglas Clark.

Manufactured in the United States of America.

Also by Douglas Clark

To Josie for her editing contributions and faithful support.

DOUGLAS CLARK

CRITICAL MASS

A Novel

❦ *It was the best of times, it was the worst of times, it was the age of wisdom, it was the age of foolishness, it was the epoch of belief, it was the epoch of incredulity, it was the season of Light, it was the season of Darkness, it was the spring of hope, it was the winter of despair, we had everything before us, we had nothing before us, we were all going direct to Heaven, we were all going direct the other way.* ❦

Charles Dickens, 1859, *A Tale of Two Cities*

ACKNOWLEDGEMENTS

Extensive research went into the creation of *Critical Mass*. The history of the United States' effort to develop an atomic bomb during World War Two has been the subject of a wide body of published works. To any historical novel, the author is not only obligated to get the facts right, but to offer the reader a sense of that time in history. While the Internet is an indispensible tool for the modern researcher, printed word publications still occupy the central repository for exploring detail. The following books provided not only a wealth of that detail, but views of these historical events from differing perspectives. My gratitude for the invaluable contributions provided by Richard Rhodes, *The Making of the Atomic Bomb*, 1986, and *Dark Sun*, 1995; Robert S. Norris, *Racing for the Bomb*, 2002; General Leslie M. Groves, *Now It Can Be Told*, 1962; Gregg Herken, *Brotherhood of the Bomb*, 2002; Kai Bird & Martin J. Sherwin, *American Prometheus*, 2005; Jennet Conant, *109 East Palace*, 2005; Jim Baggott, *The First War of Physics*, 2010; Cynthia C. Kelly, *The Manhattan Project*, 2007; Robert Serber, *The Los Alamos Primer*, 1992; Nigel West, *Mortal Crimes*, 2004; Christopher Andrew & Vasili Mitrokhin, *The Sword and the Shield*, 1999; Herbert Romerstein & Eric Breindel, *The Venona Secrets*, 2001; Ferenc Morton Szasz, *The Day the Sun Rose Twice*, 1984; David Holloway, *Stalin and the Bomb*, 1994; David Halberstam, *The Fifties*; 1993, Richard P. Feynman, *Surely You're Joking Mr. Feynman*, 1985 and *The Pleasure of Finding Things Out*, 1999.

i

FOREWORD

While this is a work of fiction, I have attempted to portray the historical events as accurately as possible. The chronology of these events is accurate. The science that led to making the atomic bomb is accurate, albeit explained from a layman's perspective. The exclusion of the Soviet Union from participation in the Manhattan Project is historical fact as were their efforts to penetrate the program through espionage under the code name ENORMOZ. The principle characters of Mikhail Voronin, Elena Obolensky, the Ramazanovs, and Victoria Prescott are however entirely fictional. Any resemblance to actual historical persons is unintended and entirely coincidental.

Many of the characters in this work of fiction were real people involved with these events. Every attempt has been made to portray them in accordance with the accepted historical record. Most of the dialog attributed to these people is of course purely fictional. I have however attempted to remain consistent in the portrayal of their personalities as commonly ascribed in historical accounts and by their own comments. Admittedly, I have taken liberties in fictionalizing the interaction of these real people with the fictional characters.

Most of the real people associated with the Manhattan Project are now deceased. I believe I have avoided unfair treatment by their fictionalized involvement in this novel, or through the construct of fictional dialogue. I apologize to any heirs that might feel otherwise.

Klaus Fuchs, George Koval, Theodore Hall, and David Greenglass were actual spies for the Soviet Union during World War Two. They all had access to sensitive material within the Manhattan Project. However, with the exception of Klaus Fuchs, the other known spies had only fragmented or narrowly specific information. Fuchs was the only known spy within the upper echelon of scientists at Los Alamos. In succeeding decades, others have fallen under suspicion from that period. It is commonly believed that espionage activities allowed the Soviet Union to advance their own nuclear weapons program by years. That is increasingly difficult to assess with the passage of time. However, the collective espionage of these known Soviet spies would not have come close to that of the fictional Mikhail Voronin with his access to essentially everything. Had there been such a highly placed spy, arguably the success of the Soviet Union's nuclear weapons program within only four years of the first U.S. test could clearly be attributed to Soviet espionage.

Regardless of the truth or the fiction of how the Soviet Union gained nuclear weapons parity with the United States, the second half of the twentieth century was dominated by the stand-off of mutually assured destruction. Had the Soviet Union acquired nuclear weapons much later than 1949, and a thermonuclear weapon later than 1955, then the shape of Eastern Europe and the Middle East might well have been very different.

The history of the Manhattan Project involved a great many people. The additional fictional characters appearing in *Critical Mass* makes for a long list of characters that is unavoidable given the scope of the story. To assist the reader, the appendix at the end of the book provides the backgrounds of those real people that appear in the novel, along with their place in history. Brief biographies of the fictional characters are listed as well, fitting them into the chronology of the actual history.

Douglas Clark

CHAPTER 1

VICTORIA PRESCOTT WOULD otherwise be feeling foolish had it not been for the excitement of meeting her quarry after years of research. Her obsession was about to see fulfillment. She had been sitting in a rental car parked on a quiet tree-lined street in the small California city of Claremont. It was a quaint university town in eastern Los Angeles County. The San Gabriel Mountains just to the north sported snow down to 4000 feet, yet it was sunny with a temperature in the sixties on this early December day.

She had been watching the house in a modest neighborhood of older homes for nearly two hours. Several people out walking had viewed her a little suspiciously. One woman had returned for what might have been a second pass of surveillance. If the police were called, she would have to contrive some cover story. Damn. Where was he? She was not a trained investigator. This was probably a bad idea but she had no other way of confronting him.

After deciding to allow only fifteen more minutes before aborting, an old BMW sedan pulled into the driveway of the house. An elderly man exited. Prescott walked briskly from across the other side of the street as the man was removing a bag of groceries from the trunk.

"Mr. Voronin?" she called out.

The man turned toward her but did not answer.

"Are you Mikhail Voronin?"

"And who are you?" the man answered. His voice was strong and direct. He was thin, of medium height, glasses, with hair now gone white.

"My name is Victoria Prescott."

"Ah, the persistent Ms. Prescott. I would have thought that my lack of response to your letters would indicate that I have no interest in participating in your project. There have been countless books written on the subject. I've read most of them. I would have nothing to add that hasn't been discussed by others."

"Well if you've read the many books on the Manhattan Project, I'm sure you would not agree with all of the different opinions and characterizations, even from some of the direct participants. You could add some new clarifications. I'm intimately familiar with those same books. My career has been largely concerned with the Manhattan Project. I did my doctorial thesis on the subject. Most of the central figures are know all deceased. You were so central to everything and yet no one has interviewed you that I can find. Your recollections could be most enlightening."

The man set down the grocery bag on the steps of the landing to the side door.

"And at my age, I will soon be joining those others from that time. I can see why you would like to interview me, but there is nothing I can add to the historical record. It was a difficult time for all of us who participated. Difficult from emotional factors you cannot appreciate unless you were there at the time. It was the defining event in most of our lives. As for me, I have tried to create a life since my involvement with nuclear weapons. I must still decline helping you, Ms. Prescott. I'm sorry. Goodbye."

The man picked up his groceries and proceeded to insert the key into the door.

Prescott said, "Mr. Voronin. Before you reject helping me, I would like you to read these materials."

The man turned to face her.

"I've tried to be polite, Ms. Prescott. I'm not interested. If you don't leave me alone I will make a complaint to the police."

"I don't believe you will, Mr. Voronin after you have read what I have here."

She handed him a sealed envelope. He did not reach out to take it from her.

"I assure you, I'm not a process server," Prescott said. "As I told you, I'm an historian. In the envelope are materials that will explain why your assistance is vital to my project. I think perhaps you will also find reason to change your mind about participating. My mobile telephone number is in there. I'm staying in Southern California until Sunday. I'll expect your call."

The man took the envelope but said nothing. Prescott turned and walked back toward her car. She did not appear angry, and surely not defeated. She was fairly certain he *would* call her after he opened the envelope.

Voronin entered his house. The grocery bag was deposited on the kitchen countertop. He sat down at the dining room table. Before she showed up it was an otherwise idyllic day. The sun streamed in through the north-facing window with the snow-capped mountains framing a postcard scene. Persistent arrogant bitch. Bile rose in his stomach as dread gripped him over the unknown contents of the envelope. He suspected what might be in there. After a few moments he tore open the envelope.

Hours later he was still sitting at the table. The initial shock had only slightly subsided. It was the worst of all his fears comes true. Why now after all these years? He passed quickly through the initial denial phase at what he had just read. For some time he just contemplated a swirl of possible damage control ideas. But there was no clear option to mitigate the situation. This Prescott woman's material could not be brushed aside.

Once the initial shock eventually abated, he started to deal with the problem in earnest. Voronin was a pragmatist. The rest of the night he devoted to trying to develop a strategy. At the least he needed to find a way to wrest the initiative from Prescott to provide some sort of maneuvering room. It took a couple of Scotches to finally get some rest for the night. He would call Prescott the following morning.

The night's sleep, although fitful and interrupted, did afford him a more objective view of his options the following day. By the time he dialed Victoria Prescott at noon, he had formed a rough plan.

Prescott arrived an hour after taking his call. After Voronin opened the front door, neither exchanged any words for several moments. Both just stared at the other like two boxers sizing up each other before the bell.

Breaking the silence, Voronin finally said, "Come in. We can talk in the dining room."

"Please sit down, Ms. Prescott. Coffee?"

"No thank you."

"Are you sure? I'm having some. Probably drink too much coffee, but it's one of my last remaining vices."

"Then sure, I'll take some. Just black thank you."

Voronin returned with two mugs and sat down. "I agreed to talk with you to convince you that your suspicions about me are all wrong. Your allegations are frankly insulting. I don't need you smearing my reputation. I'm an old man. I just want peace for the little time I have left. Your premise in the letter is flawed, Ms. Prescott. Your evidence is wholly circumstantial. It's extremely thin at best. Sounds like a conspiracy theory looking for a scapegoat. Not the sort of scholarship I'd expect from a Stanford history professor."

Within the package she had left Voronin, Prescott included background information on herself. Voronin needed to understand that she was a reputable, accredited historian, not some journalist out for a headline. Prescott had thought a lot about how to approach Voronin. The opportunity to confront him with the details and debate the conclusions would be invaluable. At the least, she wanted to afford him the opportunity to refute her conclusions.

"You're right about the need for credible scholarship, Mr. Voronin. But you're mistaken about the depth of my evidence. I've done some unique research. The evidence is conclusive I assure you. There's much more than what was included in the package. I'm willing to share those details and give you the opportunity to explain, or refute for that matter. I'd like you to expand on my material from your own first-hand perspective. More as a collaborator than just the interview subject. It would change the level of the book's impact. So I have a selfish motive for seeking your collaboration. But make no mistake, Mr. Voronin, I will publish my findings even without your participation."

"After all these years to be accused of such a thing." Voronin shook his head with an expression of disgust. "That whole time was fraught with allegations of loyalty. Worse right after World War Two with the beginning of the Cold War. Communism was the new enemy. Look what happened to Oppenheimer himself. There's nothing new here, Ms. Prescott. I'm just an old man and one of the few remaining people from the tens of thousands that worked on the Project. Why are you pursuing this ridiculous conspiracy theory? You're looking for ghosts."

Prescott shook her head emphatically.

"No I'm not. That I'm sure of. Let me lay out what this is about. First is the opportunity afforded by your position. You were an Army officer and a key member of General Groves' staff. You joined his staff at the inception of the Manhattan Project. More than that, outside of Groves himself, you may have known more about the entire scope of the project other than the most senior scientists. You had access to all the technical work at every location of the Project. After all, it was your job to spend time at the various Project sites and write detailed reports for Groves and other senior Army staff. You had access to the most sensitive information. You personally interacted with all the top scientists."

Voronin was silent for a few moments. "And there is of course the fact of my ethnic background. Does that add weight to your argument?"

"That may be a factor in some way. But my research did not uncover anything specific about your parents being Russian. At best your parents were anti-Tsarist before the Revolution and their immigration to the United States. No record of any Communist activities during the twenty years they lived here. You have no siblings. Obviously you weren't a Communist."

"You're implying that I leaked atomic bomb secrets to the Soviet Union. Yet you don't suggest how I did this, or why. So what specifically are you alleging, Ms. Prescott?"

"I'm saying you spied for the Soviets, not leaked information as you put it. That you were undoubtedly a more vital source than Fuchs, Hall, or Greenglass with your breadth of access. That you were the most senior spy, speculated for decades to be either Oppenheimer or one of the other senior scientists. That you could circumvent the rigorous security measures surrounding the Manhattan Project because you moved above the security blanket. You were a trusted Army officer. You simply had the keys to everything. And why can I be so certain? Simply that you were intimately connected with people that I can conclusively prove were trained Soviet intelligence agents. Agents that were assigned to penetrate the United States nuclear weapons development program, the Manhattan Project. Agents who were apparently successful in that mission. The evidence I have is conclusive, Mr. Voronin. The *why* I don't know. That's what I hope you will explain."

Prescott caught her breath. Voronin said nothing but a facial tic suggested she had made an impression. He rose from his chair and went into the kitchen. Had she gone too far? Would he have a gun? Her aggressive makeup may have caused her to overlook an obvious danger. If he was a former Soviet spy, as she was sure he was, then would he not be potentially dangerous if forced into a corner? In his eighties, though? What difference does that make if he has a gun? Murder-suicide would not be a farfetched result of her naivety. Stupid to have confronted him like this.

Voronin returned with the carafe of coffee. "More?" he asked. Her eyes may have belied her anxiety.

"More coffee, Ms. Prescott?"

She simply nodded.

"If I'm guilty of your accusations, then you must harbor some strong feelings about me personally. I would be a traitor. I'm no lawyer but there probably is no statute of limitations on espionage. Innocent or guilty, I see no benefit in helping you. What is it you realistically expect of me, Ms. Prescott?"

She had not constructed a particular mental image of what it would be like to finally confront the result of her breakthrough research. But still, this poised old man was unexpected. He was dressed in gray wool slacks with a neatly pressed white shirt, glasses, and although his hairline was receding, his white hair was still thick. Stylish glasses. In every way a professorial impression. He could have been a senior academic, yet he was a traitor to his country. Perhaps a key factor in creating the Cold War. The answer to his question was she simply wanted his participation regardless wherever it led, even if she was forced to counter his denials with her evidence. At the least, he would put the flesh of reality to the skeleton of her story since he was there at the time.

"As I said, to participate. Fill in details. Confirm, deny, debate my findings. Suggest alternative conclusions. I know the history as well as any historian. I've lived my personal and professional life against the backdrop of the Manhattan Project. My grandfather was a scientist at Los Alamos. A chemical engineer. His name was Aron Zielinski. The only person that can fill in the gaps is you. There is simply no one as senior as you still alive. I've interviewed Teller but he is still hung up on Oppenheimer's culpability as a security leak. Nichols provided some helpful general background but he was always at Oak Ridge until after the War. He spoke highly of you by the way. Of course I was careful to suggest nothing about you being a spy. So you're the only one left. And of course, you were a Soviet spy. You're the central player."

She finished the last comment with a slight smile.

Voronin did not respond in kind. Letting out a sigh, he said, "So you expect me to defend myself? You will still publish your assertion that I was a Soviet agent no matter what I say. You have the benefit of years of documented research. I have only a failing memory of events over fifty years ago. What does my participation do for me?'

"I would think that everyone would want the opportunity to tell their version of important events. If nothing else, the opportunity to refute my allegations for the record."

Voronin grunted as a way of dismissing her trite response. The reality of his situation was clear. This woman was not only smart but aggressively determined. She had the academic stature to give her research credibility. What she already revealed to him was sufficiently incriminating. He had to assume she had even more evidence. What she had would bring about an FBI investigation. It would bring the media. His fate had been determined the day he received Prescott's first letter. There was no way out of the inevitable result of all this. He knew that when he arrived at his decision that morning. This conversation was just verbal jousting. He could only try to manage the process.

"And if I'm guilty of spying for the Soviets fifty years ago, why should I confess to a stranger now? Simply unburden myself of the guilt? Atonement? Make peace with my soul before I die?"

Prescott was uncertain where this was headed. Voronin remained defiant. He certainly did not appear trapped. Perhaps this entire conversation was simply to assess her as an adversary. In the end he could simply retreat without comment after she published. Her research was sound but there would still be a media fight that might reflect poorly on her academic scholarship. At best it was a risk. If he participated, even denying everything, the work would have a balanced journalistic cover.

"Mr. Voronin. I would not pretend to know your personal reasons for working with me any more than I know why you spied for the Soviets. I do however believe that in a practical sense of being faced with imminent exposure of your past, you have more to gain by collaborating."

"I'm sure you know a great deal about me. Since I'm eighty-four, I'm obviously in the twilight of my life," Voronin said. He had placed his elbows on the dining table and leaned forward toward Prescott. "I believe there is one thing you do not know however." He coughed successively several times and covered his mouth with a handkerchief. "As if on cue."

"Are you all right?" Prescott asked.

"No. I don't believe I am. You see, I have lung cancer. Well advanced. Too many years of smoking. It's terminal. Not all that much time left I'm told."

Prescott hardly knew how to respond. She instantly started to calculate the impact of that information on her project, but offered the expected empathy of, "Oh God. I'm so sorry. Are you undergoing treatment?"

"Just a drug regimen. The more aggressive treatments can be more debilitating than the disease. It's a quality of life decision at my age. So now you're wondering how this changes things."

Prescott fumbled for the right expression that would keep her in the game. "Well ….. with that looming ….."

"With my mortality immediately looming you would expect me to tell you to go to hell. And part of me says I should. But I will make a bargain with you instead. I'll tell you everything I can about those times. In exchange you must promise not to make your story, your history, in whatever form, public until after my death."

"Well sure. I guess I could agree to that," Prescott said. She was a little unsettled with this turn of events. How long might that be?

"But of course you want some time frame before committing. The doctors give me only six to twelve months. That's a statistical mean. You'll be taking some gamble that I might be in the more optimistic percentile."

"I can agree to those terms, Mr. Voronin. Perhaps you will even find the experience of our collaboration important to you in your own way."

Voronin coughed some more. "We shall see. At any rate to insure our deal, I will arrange for you to receive unspecified documents upon my death. These will greatly validate your work and establish a solid base of scholarship. These materials will be worth the wait. Not that I don't trust you, Ms. Prescott, but there is no reason I should is there? I know nothing about you. The best arrangements are made on a basis of mutual benefit. Just like mutually assured destruction. These documents will make your career, I assure you. They're worth waiting for me to die."

That was an unexpected benefit. Circumstances had turned from nothing to exceeding all her expectations. She could wait until he died.

"Tell me this, Mr. Voronin. Why the change of mind about working with me?"

"You were right about two things, Ms. Prescott. First, we all want to tell our version of our own story. Secondly, *I did spy for the Soviets.*"

Voronin's outright admission stunned her. She had expected him to continue his denials. Beyond his admission, he was also offering to be interviewed. This was the mother lode.

"Just like that you're admitting you spied for the Soviets?"

"It may seem like that, Miss Prescott, but this day has been feared for most of my adult life. There were countless times that I expected to be exposed. During the Second World War and especially afterwards during the era of McCarthyism and the beginnings of the Cold War with the Soviet Union. Even during the last few years since the collapse of the Soviet Union in 1991. I feared Soviet intelligence archives might become public and implicate me. There were reasons to explain why I was never discovered, but like most circumstances in life, chance played the major factor."

"Were you a Communist, Mr. Voronin?"

His dark blue eyes flashed and his cheek muscles tighten in an expression of anger. But the reaction passed within a moment.

"No. I was not a Communist. Communism is a failed concept. Stalin's Communism was simply a contrived political structure to control power. I hold views that are left-leaning, even Socialist, but not Communist. My parents were Communists by the way, original Bolsheviks even, but I didn't embrace that dogma."

That was interesting. The parents were academics with no documented evidence of involvement with the American Communist Party. Nothing damaging was discovered in the Army's background check when Voronin was issued a security clearance in 1942. Yet they were Bolsheviks?

"Most of the World War Two Soviet spies that were identified were Communists, or avowed sympathizers. Why then did you end up spying for the Soviets?" She hoped it was not something as venal as money.

"You only know the surface truth somehow pieced together from your research. There is no simple answer to that question. I'll attempt to explain as I tell you my story. However, before we get into that, I would like to know about you. You are changing what remains of my life. I'd like to understand how a young academic discovered this buried secret from fifty years ago."

CHAPTER 2

VICTORIA PRESCOTT SPENT the afternoon relating the particulars of her professional life to Voronin. Told from the dry biographical facts, it did not explain how she had succeeded in discovering this great secret from fifty years ago.

Central to Victoria Prescott's career were the two most important men in her life, her father, Hamilton Prescott and her maternal grandfather, Aron Zielinski. Hers was a family of high achievers. She had two older siblings, both brothers. The older brother was a surgeon. The other followed their mother's profession into international business law.

Prescott's father served eleven years as a senior State department official during the Reagan and Bush administrations. Having earned a PhD in political science from Columbia University in 1963, he escaped the Vietnam era draft by obtaining a job in the State Department. His academic expertise was the Soviet Union. He spoke and read fluently in Russian. After five years of government service, he joined the faculty at Columbia. In 1981 he was recruited again by the State Department for an Undersecretary position, serving until 1992. He then returned to Columbia as a professor of political science.

Her grandfather had the professional distinction of having worked at Los Alamos on the Manhattan Project during World

War Two. Specifically he was a key scientist working on the implosion team tasked with creating the detonation mechanism for the plutonium design bomb. Beyond that, Victoria was his only granddaughter and the two spent much time together even during her high school and college years. The making of the atomic bomb and the sheer magnitude of the effort always fascinated her. She could experience the history firsthand with her grandfather's recounting of his personal experiences. And like all historians, some particular time in history tends to grab their interest.

To carve out her own intellectual niche from this family, Victoria chose history. Bearing the influence of family, she did her master's thesis on the organizational aspects of the Manhattan Project, and her PhD dissertation on the broader geopolitical impact of nuclear weapons. Like her father, she became fluent in Russian. Her father was pleased with her daughter's pursuit of a career so closely paralleling his own field of expertise. Her unbounded confidence backed by an outsized intellect made her both a challenge and a delight. Of his three children, she was the strongest personality. Easy to see why she was unmarried.

"Interesting family I'm sure, Miss Prescott. But I'd like to hear how your career path to a Stanford history professor has now led you to this investigative coup."

"That will become somewhat involved. It will take some time in the telling," she said. Her stomach was demanding food. She never ate breakfast and today she missed lunch with her immediate response to Voronin's telephone call. "Are you perhaps getting hungry? I know I am."

"Perhaps. Not sure sometimes. The medication. Maybe too much coffee. Afraid I can't offer much in the way of food. I just keep some very basic items around. Not much of a cook anyhow."

"Do you have a favorite restaurant nearby?" Prescott asked.

"No favorite, but there's a number of restaurants a few blocks from here in quaint area called Claremont Village. Haven't been to dinner with a pretty woman for decades."

She felt awkward and a bit silly. Christ she was talking pleasantries with ..... what did she think of this old man? He was an admitted spy, a traitor, clearly a villain. She had been looking for him in musty archives and volumes of historical documents for years. She had pieced together an impossible puzzle with most of the pieces missing. There were all sorts of emotions having arrived at this point. Animosity, much less revulsion, was not among them though. This was just an old man with an extraordinary story. She didn't want to leave their discussion yet but they needed a break.

"Then let's go. I'll drive," she said.

Dining with Voronin at a small Italian restaurant added to the surrealism. She ordered a glass of wine for each of them. Voronin was intelligent in full possession of his faculties. A lot like her grandfather who was also born in 1914.

"Does anyone other than you know of me?" What you've discovered I mean?"

"Know? My grandfather may suspect since I asked a lot questions about Los Alamos. He was surprised that I knew so much about so many of the people involved during the war-years, even military personnel. He knew what I was looking for. We talked at length over the years. At the end of my research, when I already knew, I quizzed him at some length about you. He knew you of course. Do you remember him?"

"The name yes. Can't place the face though. He worked on George Kistiakowsky's team. You haven't confided in your father either?"

"No. He knows about my research but I haven't told him specifically about you." That was a lie but no need to spook Voronin.

"Why wouldn't you have told either of your parents? They're your confidents, kindred intellectuals, much respected as you've told me. I'd have thought you wouldn't be able to contain yourself."

"Just a secretive bitch I guess," she said.

She regretted the vulgar comment. Might be offensive to someone of Voronin's era.

"Perhaps you just wanted to be sure before you claimed success. Which would mean you harbored doubts until I confirmed your conclusions?"

Nothing wrong with Voronin's mind. She hoped his memory was just as good.

"No, I was sure it was you. The evidence is as solid as you get when researching historical events decades old. It would have been good enough to warrant a criminal investigation had I gone that route. I didn't want to announce it until I had advanced the project further. Even to family. That's where you came in. At the least, I hoped to clarify some things, or even get your denials. At any rate, there was no reason to jump the gun."

In relating her bio data for Voronin, Prescott did not mention her current personal situation, and Voronin was polite enough not to ask. Truth was she had told someone. This was a major professional accomplishment. The product of hard work and ingenuity. She was going to Los Angeles to confront her quarry. Everyone wanted to impress in the eyes of their significant other. For Victoria Prescott that was her live-in companion of two years, Phillip Baxter.

They shared a townhouse in the Telegraph Hill neighborhood of San Francisco. It was a ninety minute commute to the Stanford campus depending upon traffic. Phil Baxter was a fellow Stanford professor. Tenured. PhD in computer science. A recognized expert in advanced computer security, working from one defense grant to the next. He was an alpha male in the information technology field and often an arrogant shit in his personal sphere. Still, the relationship lasted longer than Prescott's others. She suspected he may harbor the same view of her. Too much ego both sides, but the sex was good.

"Jesus, Vicky, do you know what you're doing?" Baxter asked when she told him what she planned. "It's a bad idea to confront him personally."

"You know the evidence, Phil. He's guilty. I've got him cold." Why wasn't he excited about her triumph? Why couldn't the sonofabitch be a bit more supportive?

"Could be dangerous," he said. "Couldn't he react violently? Maybe he's gone senile. Obviously he's ignoring your letters. At the least he's just going to tell you to get lost."

"Phil, if he's got anything to say, I've got to try. After all, I'm going to expose him as a traitor. It will end his life badly. Media, FBI. Just like those former Nazis war criminals being exposed."

"Nobody's going to give a shit about this. It happened fifty years ago. It's only academic masturbation."

"What the fuck are you saying? That this history is worthless? My work is worthless? Not like your cutting edge computer shit where you can change the world like a bunch of adolescent gamers. Not your avant-garde world of geeks," she said.

Unfortunately, their career differences highlighted basic philosophical differences. He was technology, she was ideas. Combined with high intellect and ego, it created minefields. What kept them together? Fundamentally they both loved the intellect of the other. In public they were always considerate of the other. Quick to compliment. They had genuine affection for each other, each realizing the other was uniquely interesting. Their lovemaking was good because they both wanted to please the other. That had once been a source of balance to counter the emotional bruising they inflicted on each other. Since returning from Russia, she knew it was no longer enough. Why were they still together? Because they both knew they were difficult?

Prescott and Voronin finished their pastas and ordered more wine.

Voronin said, "That was very good. The wine too. I don't eat many good meals anymore. So it was PUPPETEER and TRAVELER. They were the key weren't they? Without them you had nothing but conjecture about me."

"Yes. PUPPETEER was of course the link. The mention of that code name was the key. With his connection to you, you were either a spy yourself or an unwitting dupe. The historical evidence suggests you could not have been duped."

"So please do me the courtesy of telling me how a historian did this extraordinary investigative work."

"Alright, I'll tell you how I discovered PUPPETEER and TRAVELER. Once I did that, you became the obvious candidate for my spy. Do you recall the media reporting of the defection of a Soviet cipher clerk in Ottawa, Canada in 1946?"

"Yes, of course. Everything about Soviet espionage was of personal interest. But I didn't attach much significance to the event since it occurred in Canada after the War," Voronin said.

"Well, this clerk by the name of Igor Sergeyevich Gouzenko learned he was to be sent back to the Soviet Union in 1945. Gouzenko had a taste of the better life in the West. The homeland was still under Stalin's rule. Life in Soviet intelligence could be tenuous. The easier choice was to defect and stay in Canada. He took with him 109 GRU, the Soviet military intelligence organ, documents. Among other things, the documents, along with Gouzenko's testimony, outlined Soviet efforts to penetrate the Manhattan Project in the United States. His testimony even contributed to the successful prosecution of Klaus Fuchs."

"And you were able to examine these Soviet documents?" Voronin asked.

"Yes. With some string-pulling in 1992. Even then, I only looked at a censored version of the documents with sections still redacted. But within them was an agent list with code names and their undercover legends. It's from there that my hunt really started, but I didn't know that at the time. It was just another piece of the historical record to absorb. Let me try to explain."

For the next hour, Prescott recounted the research journey that led her to him.

The Manhattan Project had always been a personal historical event. Her grandfather arrived at Los Alamos in 1943. He was a brilliant student, earning a PhD in chemical engineering from the Massachusetts Institute of Technology before the war broke out. He was recruited by the Monsanto Corporation to work at their newly acquired research and development laboratory in Dayton, Ohio. He started working on Monsanto's styrene monomer project as a key ingredient in synthetic rubber. Eventually the site would become known as the Dayton Project working on development of the atomic bomb neutron trigger. Robert Oppenheimer personally recruited Aron Zielinski for the Los Alamos team.

Victoria Prescott explained that her fascination with the Manhattan Project originally derived in large part from the first-hand accounts from her grandfather. Later as her career aspirations became centered on history, the atomic bomb project took on even more interest. All this led to her master's thesis with the academically slanted title, *The Political Dynamics of the Manhattan Project and the Legacy Effects for Military & Foreign Policy*. She also acquired an obsession with Soviet espionage penetration of the United States program to develop a nuclear weapon.

Like others, she assumed there were potentially other spies never identified. Unlike some others, she discounted Oppenheimer himself as a possible Soviet source, as well as a number of other of the prominent scientists working on the Project. What she did come to believe was the real probability there was at least one highly placed Soviet source never identified. The consensus of an array of scientists across the span of forty years disputed the Soviet ability to develop their own program so quickly based upon only the known espionage. The materials supplied by Klaus Fuchs and David Greenglass did not account for the compressed time frame for Soviet progress. Even the other spies like David Greenglass, Theodore Hall, and George Koval did not seem to rise to the level of technological access on a scale that would allow the Soviets such quick success. Most of their intelligence was related to bomb design, whereas the real hurdles were more associated with producing quantities of fissile material. It was always a belief held as well by her grandfather which may have accounted for her tenacious pursuit of that historical Holy Grail of nuclear lore. To others in the academic community, her obsession was more like the search for Bigfoot.

To Voronin's more specific question, she explained the list of agents revealed in Gouzenko's stolen GRU documents. Eventually the Canadian RCMP shared the information with the U.S. FBI. Among the agents listed was a husband and wife team of ethnic Russian Jews having immigrating to Canada in the 1920's. They were identified only by the code names of PUPPETEER and TRAVELER. PUPPETEER was a chemical engineer working for a private corporation in Montreal. The location took on some significance in that it coincided with the British relocation of their nuclear research program from Great Britain to Montreal in 1942. It was assumed PUPETEER and TRAVELER were sleeper agents activated in the Soviet effort to penetrate Western nuclear weapons development.

However, even that sparse trail for PUPPETEER and TRAVELER seemingly ends in 1942. Their code names never reappear in the historical record, including the Venona decryptions released in 1995. Gouzenko had no specific knowledge of their identities. He speculated they might have been personally controlled by the Soviet GRU resident for Canada, Colonel Nikolai Zabotin. The RCMP investigation concluded from the documents that PUPPETEER may have resigned from his job in 1942 and left Montreal. The most likely employer was E. I. du Pont.

But this was now 1946 and hundreds of chemical engineers had been employed by DuPont over the years in question, many ethnically Russian. The investigation did not reveal anything conclusive. The FBI theorized that PUPPETEER and TRAVELER might still be in Canada or even the U.S., but there was no other actionable intelligence to further a search. Since the British had just moved their nuclear program to Montreal in 1942, and that was the year PUPPETEER and TRAVELER seemingly left Montreal, it suggested they were probably not active in nuclear technology espionage. In 1946, the Ramazanovs were dead so that trail was only history at best. The prevailing wisdom being PUPETEER and TRAVELER were probably recalled to the USSR. Since they did not defect, that probably meant they were stood against a wall and shot like so many others during Stalin's indiscriminate purges. Without anything further surfacing, the trail simply went cold out of lack of interest.

With no further intelligence, or any means of identification, PUPPETEER and TRAVELER dropped from any active FBI scrutiny. They only reappeared to her in the form of a connection culled from her assembled database. With the programming algorithm developed by her boyfriend, connections achieved *values of interest*. Values of interest could further be tested with a probability calculation based upon a weighted hierarchical matrix she provided for the program. It was a cutting edge approach to historical detective work. She understood the underlying conditions. Her computer whiz boyfriend understood how to program her assumptions to suggest statistical based conclusions that might otherwise not be recognized.

"I'm not sure I understand," Voronin said. "You're saying a computer program linked these unidentified agents named PUPPETEER and TRAVELER to me? And without any further information since these code names never resurfaced after 1942?"

"It wasn't quite that simple. Remember, I had amassed a comprehensive list of everyone of significance in the Manhattan Project. Thousands of names. And to those I had developed associated names of family, friends, and professional relationships culled from all sorts of sources. To this database, I added the mass of names from intelligence on Soviet espionage efforts for the last fifty years. It became quite a database. So large that it was only useful as a reference until a computer program could provide the ability to mine the data for patterns and associations."

"And the association that connected to me?" Voronin asked.

"The connection was a Russian chemical engineer. That was PUPPETEER from Montreal in 1942. That's all there was about him in Gouzenko's stolen documents. I eventually discovered his real name was Boris Dmytryk. You knew him as Boris Ramazanov," Prescott said.

"That still seems an obscure connection," Voronin said. "Because they were simply both chemical engineers?"

"Just one of many connections actually. Not even the most promising at the onset. However, consider the additional factors. You are ethnically Russian. Your parents returned to the Soviet Union during the Depression. That could mean that they might be committed Communists, or being used as a threat for your assistance. And you had a father-in-law that was a Russian educated chemical engineer with a wife, emigrated from Russia, the same background as these Soviet intelligence operatives named PUPPETEER and TRAVELER. Your in-laws emigrated from Canada to the United States in 1942 making the chronology work. Add to this your unique access to everything related to the Manhattan Project. The computer algorithm weighed all of these individual factors. You were among a small number of others with a comparatively high statistical value. Those others were ones whose loyalties were speculated about for years and generally discounted. You were entirely new, virtually unknown."

Voronin said nothing for a few moments. He was still amazed that his life had come so abruptly to this.

"Even with that lead, there must have been more for you to feel so sure that I was the one you were looking for. You didn't invest your reputation on a statistical probability."

"Oh there certainly is more. I'll be glad to elaborate on those details later on. But we need to get back to the heart of the matter which is your story. You've been interviewing me for the last hour. It's getting late though. How about we resume tomorrow?"

"Yes. I suppose we can."

Prescott paid the bill and got up to leave. Voronin followed her to the front door. Both felt awkward. The accused and the accuser having a civilized discussion. He had taken the plea bargain and now had to deliver his story. For her part, Prescott felt an unanticipated affinity for this old man that most would consider a true villain. She did as well, but that condemnation was difficult to hold onto after spending several hours with Mikhail Voronin.

She drove them back to his house, neither saying anything.

"I will see you tomorrow then," Prescott said. She extended her hand.

Voronin shook her hand and said, "Tomorrow then. Can't say this has actually been a pleasure, but have a good evening, Ms. Prescott."

Grand Coulee Dam construction 1937

CHAPTER 3

GRAND COULEE DAM, WASHINGTON – 1936

I GOT OFF the train in Spokane, Washington. It was 7:00AM on a Tuesday in the middle of June. My luggage consisted of a large duffle bag and a small shoulder bag. Other passengers disembarked, mostly men, all of us stretching and yawning. It had been twenty-four hours since I left Union Station in downtown Los Angeles. Most of the men wore rough work clothes while I wore my only suit. Not sure what I was supposed to wear, but as a recently minted professional on my first job it was important to make a good impression.

At the end of May I received by bachelor's degree in civil engineering from the University of Southern California. It had been a struggle financially. There seemed no end to the Great Depression. I was bright enough to get a modest scholarship that provided the means of surviving my first couple of years. For the last two years I was fortunate enough to get a coveted job with the City of Los Angeles Department of Public Works. One of my professors, Edik Maisky, took an interest in me. Like me, he was ethnically Russian. I provided the rare opportunity for him to interact in Russian. Beyond that, we greatly liked each other. Professor Maisky possessed my father's intellectual bent but with a more jovial manner. More importantly, the Professor was also the chief engineer for Department of Public Works for the City of Los Angeles. That circumstance provided me the opportunity to secure a job over other experienced professionals. Maisky was a mentor on many levels.

Upon graduation, Professor Maisky was instrumental in helping me secure a position with the U.S. Bureau of Reclamation working on the Grand Coulee Dam construction on the Columbia River in eastern Washington.

From Spokane I boarded a bus full of men recruited for work on the dam. Most carried beat-up satchels or cardboard suitcases with little more than a couple of changes of clothes and a shaving kit. Most were weathered manual laborers who would work for the meager wages, much of which they would send back home to hungry families left behind.

As we drove closer to the construction site we passed men in what appeared to be makeshift shanty towns. Many of these men I learned later had been laid off by the prime contractor, Consolidated Builders Incorporated for having union sympathies. The men on the bus were hired from other construction projects. Arguments suggested that CBI was trying to break organized labor's influence at Grand Coulee. These were hard times.

I stepped off the bus at the construction site. The first impression was awe at the scope of the project started several years previously. The Columbia River was a formidable river for man to constrain. The second impression was of a vast military-like base occupying both sides of the River. The town was comprised of inexpensive wood frame barracks and office buildings.

The disembarking point at the site directed new arrivals where to report. Clerks processed the new arrivals. The camps occupying both sides of the River were connected by a bridge. I was assigned to the west bank to the smaller government workers' enclave.

I reported in at the Bureau of Reclamation office to the Construction Engineer for the project, Horace "Happy" Parker. I introduced myself to a clerk at a desk. Parker was talking on the telephone with his office door open.

Overhearing my name he motioned me into the office. "Ah, Voronin. Been expecting you. Ready to get to work?"

"Yes, Sir."

"Not in that outfit I hope. Charlie, take Voronin over to the barracks and get him a hardhat. Get him back here in twenty minutes. We need to get down to the site." Turning back to me he said, "Get your boots and work clothes on and we'll head down to the site. You can relieve Joe Valentine overseeing the concrete pouring. He's been there fourteen hours. I was going to take over for a while myself but now you're here."

My stomach was grumbling having eaten only a sandwich and apple in the last twenty-four hours. Looks like it would be awhile before I could get a regular meal.

I dumped my bag and quickly changed into work clothes and heavy boots. Back at the office I piled into a pickup truck with Parker driving. He handed me a rolled-up stack of blue prints. "Here's the plans for the section were working on. Your job is to make sure everything is proceeding within specifications. Been on big pours before?"

"Some. I worked for the City of Los Angeles. Bridges, flood control channels. Nothing as large as this though. But I understand the technical aspects."

"How's that? From college?" Parker said as he drove. "Listen, the continuous pours we're making here, along with the sheer volume of concrete has an entirely different set of challenges to those things you're used to. So pay attention and read the specifications. You'll get the hang of it, but get up to speed quickly."

And so began two years in the wilds of eastern Washington. The experience was rewarding, but it was hard duty. The workdays were long. Happy Parker was a good boss and professional mentor. The men I worked with were a good bunch but the place was an intellectual wasteland. Nothing to do for entertainment. Remote from any city of size. At least Prohibition had been repealed a few years before. Life at Grand Coulee Dam needed liquor for survival. From an early age I had been introduced to vodka. My father even made his own during the dry years of Prohibition. Both of my parents drank a couple of shots of vodka before the evening meal as a way of preserving some cultural connection. The vodka available from bars at the site was low quality so I often stuck to beer. The best liquor turned out to be homemade 'moonshine' shared by some good old boys from Tennessee.

Within the heavy construction areas, only men were permitted to work. Women were few and deployed in typical 'female' jobs. The largest concentration of unattached females was telephone operators working for the contractor, CBI. The small community of Mason City close to the dam site had a few teachers but few other single women. While the ratio of men to women was extreme, there were also few opportunities or venues for socializing.

Organized square dances on Saturday nights were the principle social functions. The dancing seemed a sweaty exertion, lacking intimate contact with your partner. I did appreciate the fiddle playing since I knew something of the violin. My mother was an accomplished violinist and I inherited a modest talent. Vivaldi and Bach were more to my taste however than bluegrass.

The best memory from Grand Coulee was my first real romance. Before Joanne Cartwright I had the typical high school crushes. Maintaining a full-time job during my college years offered little room for romance. Joanne was from Spokane. She worked as a telephone operator. The best things about Joanne, not necessarily in the order of importance, were that she was attractive, laughed a lot, liked vodka, and liked sex.

We met outside the place holding a square dance one evening in the fall of 1936. I was holding a drink and smoking when she approached.

"Hi. Can I bum a smoke from you?" she said.

She was smiling and looked perfect. I had had a few drinks. She was wearing a tight sweater which accentuated her breasts, drawing my eyes unconsciously. I fumbled for the cigarette pack. "Of course. My pleasure."

"Thanks," she said as I lit a match and cupped my hands to shield the flame. She touched my hand with her own. "My name's Joanne Cartwright."

"I'm Mike Voronin." I shook her extended hand.

"What're you drinking?"

"Vodka."

"Vodka? Did you get that inside?"

"No. I brought it. Only fruit punch and flat beer in there."

"Mind if I have a taste."

"Sure. But it's straight vodka, no mix. Not the best vodka either," I handed her my paper cup.

Joanne took a tentative sip. "Wow! That's powerful but good."

We spent the rest of the evening talking. I went back to my barracks nearby and returned with the bottle of vodka. By the time the dance broke up we were both a little drunk. She left on a bus to return to her own barracks across the river. Before parting she kissed me passionately. We agreed to meet the following day at one o'clock. We both had Sunday off.

That Sunday I lost my virginity to Joanne Cartwright. Upon reflection, I suspect she had lost hers long before. We had packed a picnic lunch then walked into the hills finding a small secluded spot with some trees. It was a warm sunny day. We sat on a blanket and told each other our life stories while sipping warm Cokes.

Joanne initiated the sex by placing my hand over her breast. From there things progressed rapidly. After we were through we dressed quickly as we both begin to chill in the autumn air. Joanne put her panties and skirt on first making sure I continued to look at her naked breasts for as long as possible. The sight of her caused another erection.

"Save that for next time," she said and placed her hand on my crotch. "Let's get back before it gets any colder."

I hold fond memories of Joanne Cartwright even though she was the first to break my heart. She may have been a bimbo and frivolous, but she was an oasis of delight during my stay at Grand Coulee. I was innocent at the time. She was my first love affair. My parents had returned to Russia a year earlier in 1935. My father had held a teaching position at Pomona College in Claremont, California teaching classical literature. The chair had been endowed by a wealthy benefactor. Unfortunately the original endowment eventually ran out and the benefactor was bankrupt after the stock market crash of 1929. Few opportunities existed for a literary academic with no other skills. Mother taught violin to bring in some money. Both flatly forbid my leaving school. They correctly argued that without an education I would be just another in the vast population of unemployed.

Both of my parents held strong feelings for Mother Russia. They held fast to as much of the culture as possible. Fearing the Tsar's secret police, the Okhrana, they fled Russia in 1913. They had been active in Vladimir Lenin's Bolshevik faction of the Russian Social Democratic Party since the failed revolution in 1905. The threat of imprisonment or worse became an increasing threat as the Okhrana infiltrated the Bolshevik cells with informers, or extracted names through torture from those arrested. Although safe from the Tsarist police state, life in the United States was still a difficult transition.

After arriving in Brooklyn, New York, my parents settled into an ethnically Russian neighborhood. It was a difficult struggle. As she did later, my mother gave violin lessons to bring in some money. My father worked the neighborhood for connections amongst the many mostly Jewish ex-patriot Russian intelligencia. Eventually that led to the teaching position in California. Their twenty years in the United States was a struggle that ultimately ended with the prospect of returning to the Motherland.

Although both my parents were committed Communists, they kept their politics hidden. Secretly they felt America was a fertile field for their socialistic ideals. My mother was attracted by the growing women's suffrage movement in the West. Father indulged his social activism by writing editorial copy under a pseudonym supporting organized labor, particularly related to the circumstances of agricultural workers in California. To his dismay, the prosperity of the 1920's and the post-1929 onset of the Great Depression saw a decline in the organized labor movement. There was no leverage during hard times. It was also clear that anti-Communist feelings were becoming more pronounced in America. Maintaining secrecy of their Communist backgrounds would benefit me greatly later on.

After a year, my romance with Joanne ended. She was looking for a husband. I wasn't sure I wanted a family yet. I believe I intellectually intimidated her, while she intimidated me with her sexual aggressiveness. In the end she found someone else. I was emotionally devastated, angry. I now wanted more than ever to leave this godforsaken place in the wilderness.

*Franklin D. Roosevelt at
Grand Coulee Dam, 1937*

CHAPTER 4

GRAND COULEE DAM, WASHINGTON – 1937

I WAS PLAYING chess with Happy Parker on a cold night in early December. It was a few weeks after Joanne announce our breakup. The isolation of the dam site was immediately more depressing without Joanne. I was now reduced to playing chess with old man Parker. Parker liked me and knew I was unhappy. We were huddled over a small table pulled close to the pot bellied stove in Parker's office having just knocked off work. Parker was a pretty good chess player but not in my league.

"Sorry, Happy. Mate," I said as I moved my knight to checkmate him after only eleven moves.

Parker looked at the board in bewilderment. "Well I'll be damned. We've hardly even started. Most pieces are still on the board. I ponder my moves for minutes, but you make your moves almost immediately after mine. You're the best damn player I've ever met, Mike. Who taught you?"

"My father. He was a real chess master. Played tournaments in his younger days. I never could beat him until I got older. Even then, it was rare. I felt I had played well when I could push him to a draw."

"Amazing, truly amazing," Parker muttered, still staring at the pieces. "Let's go over to the saloon and I'll buy you a beer."

The saloon was a Quonset hut-style structure with a rounded corrugated roof sloping down to form the side walls of the utilitarian building. The bar itself was a wide wooden plank "U" shaped affair. Tables were tightly scattered about the rough wooden floor. The only adornment was a few Hollywood pinup photos of starlets in bathing suits. It was a depressing place intended for male drinking. As usual, the place was packed that evening.

Happy Parker ordered a couple beers after finding a place at the bar. We were standing at the bar with one foot on the galvanized pipe that served as a foot-rail. Parker turned and saw a colleague sitting alone at a corner table working on some paperwork.

Parker pulled me along over to the table. "Major, I'd like you meet one of my best engineers, Mike Voronin. Mike, this is Major Reed Jensen of the Army Corp of Engineers. He's the new District Engineering Officer. The Major fancies himself a pretty fair chess player. At least he's better than I am. But I'll wager you can whip him blindfolded."

The Major rose and extended his hand. "Parker's correct about me liking chess. I'd love a game with you. I'll be here for a couple of days. How about tomorrow night? We'll see if Parker has exaggerated your skill. Right now I've got to finish this damn report so you'll have to excuse me."

Back at the bar, Parker said to me, "I did that as a way of introducing you to Jensen. Might be worth talking to him about the Corp of Engineers. It would make a good career for you."

"Career? I thought I had a good start at a career with the Bureau. I've done a good job haven't I?"

"Of course you have. But you're not happy here, Mike. You're a good engineer but I'm not sure building dams is what suits you. If you stay with the Bureau of Reclamation you know it will be mostly dam building projects. I'm suggesting you consider the Army Corp of Engineers. They work on a broader range of projects. You'd be an officer in the Army. Good career move. Good for attracting the ladies. At any rate, play chess with Jensen and feel him out about the prospects."

I took Happy Parker's advice. I talked to Jensen. Got his attention after beating him five games in a row over a two-hour period. Because of both Parker and Jensen, my life set off in a new direction. Within eight months I was a newly minted second lieutenant in the United States Army Corp of Engineers.

Downtown Washington D.C., 1940

CHAPTER 5

WASHINGTON D. C. – 1940

BY 1940, I had served two years with the Army Corps of Engineers. The work was difficult but it was a rewarding time. Parker was right. I not only got out of the dam building business but without knowing it had set myself up for an ideal wartime job. It was becoming clearer that the United States would eventually be entering the war in Europe. Germany had already overrun France and the Low Countries. Great Britain was now threatened. I was well positioned as an officer in the construction wing of the Army. War preparations were underway.

The United States military was already embarked on a massive construction program to provide facilities for a rapidly growing United States military with the newly instituted peacetime draft. The frantic program faced continual problems of delays and spiraling cost overruns. In November, I received orders to report to Washington D.C. I was ordered to join the staff of Colonel Leslie R. Groves. Groves was the newly appointed commander of the Fixed Fee Branch of the Construction Division. He had a reputation as a doer and a driver who got projects done on time and within budget. I had made a mark for myself as a first-rate project manager. As a young first lieutenant, I was flattered to be tapped to join Groves' staff. That euphoria soon dissipated once I came under the Colonel's direct command.

I had met Groves once when he arrived to inspect construction at Fort Bliss in El Paso, Texas. I had been sent to take over the project several months earlier. It was plagued with severe delays and my orders were to get it back on track and meet the completion deadline. For three months I had no days off. I worked at least sixteen hours days. As hard as the work was, I was able to apply my developing project management skills, achieving clear results. In the years following my graduation from USC, I learned that my effectiveness as an engineer was less dependent upon my technical knowledge and more about other skills. The ability to analyze complex situations with many variables was essential. Little attention was devoted to organization and problem solving in the engineering curriculum. No attention at all was devoted to interpersonal skills. How effective one was in manipulating people was the central determinate to achieving a successful project. The Fort Bliss project provided a fertile test of my abilities.

That one time I met Groves should have given me some hint as to his management style.

I saluted as then Major Groves walked up to me next to a newly poured concrete foundation for the last of the buildings I was working on. He was big man with the unmilitary appearance of being overweight.

"Lieutenant. When do you expect completion?" Groves asked as he returned my salute.

"Another five weeks I believe, Sir."

Groves looked around, then said, "Why not less? These are the last buildings. You've already got the foundations poured."

"Just poured two days ago, Sir. Need to get some cure time before we start putting load on the concrete."

"I'm an engineer, Lieutenant. You don't need to educate me on materials properties. Find a way to wrap this up in three weeks."

Groves turned and left leaving my salute unreturned. I was totally deflated. The project was four months behind schedule and over budget when I relieved the former project engineer. I made up two of those months by what I thought was real innovation. Groves didn't even acknowledge my accomplishments.

Groves had moved from the Engineering Corp to take the position of deputy to the Quartermaster General. When I first met Groves he had only been promoted to major a month before. Now he was a full bird colonel only a few months later. Groves was certainly someone to tie yourself to in this man's army.

Groves didn't achieve this rapid rise in rank by being a warm personality. My previous brief encounter should have prepared me for my reception at Groves' office in Washington in December, 1940.

"Voronin. You've been assigned to my staff because you have a record of some success at getting things done. Those were small projects to what we are now facing. We will soon be at war. The United States still isn't anywhere near ready. Things will only become more demanding. Your job will be to visit sites I either can't get to, or sites with problems. I want reports as to the status of the project. Not the normal official crap, but a realistic assessment if the work will be completed on time. If not, I want to know why. Where's the bottleneck, who is responsible, what needs to be changed and how do we do it. I expect solutions. If you identify a problem, I expect you to identify a solution. A real solution, not some bureaucratic platitudes. I expect you to stick your neck out. You up to it, Lieutenant?'

"Yes, Sir."

As time progressed, working for Groves never got any more agreeable. It wasn't personal to him. He treated everyone with a brusque, often rude exchange. I even witnessed him doing the same thing to superior army officers. Some staff thought he just didn't know how to be personable. That was nonsense. Groves simply didn't give a damn what anybody thought as long as he achieved what he wanted. Groves got away with his aggressive manner simply because he always got difficult things done. His intellect and grasp of complex data was astounding. He could analyze a situation quickly and understand what needed to be done intuitively. Human relations were not part of achieving results. The singular exception was his unusual relationship with J. Robert Oppenheimer, but I will get to that later.

From that first meeting in Washington, I got an appreciation for the scope of Groves' responsibilities. Our meeting consisted of me following him down a corridor while he was assaulted with questions and requests from other army officers along the way. He was making million dollar expenditure decisions daily on the fly. It seemed a total madhouse.

I spent the next year traveling the United States. I met Groves only occasionally back in Washington. However, I frequently talked to the Colonel on the telephone. That was rarely a pleasant event. There seemed to always be something lacking. Groves was just that way. He got things done and didn't care about the casualties. Interaction with the Colonel was usually unpleasant for any of his staff.

Even my promotion to captain was couched with a slap from Groves. "You're being promoted to captain, Voronin," Groves said over the telephone after I had been attached to his command for a couple of months. "As a captain, I expect you to exert more pressure when necessary to get things done." No congratulations, just a click of the telephone connection. I was at Fort Custer. It was a cold February day in 1941. I celebrated by myself at a sleazy bar in Battle Creek, Michigan with a bunch of construction workers.

In August, 1941, the "Boss" took over the construction project for the new headquarters for the Army and Navy. It was to be the largest building in the world, covering a footprint of 29 acres. The five-sided design immediately became labeled the Pentagon. Groves got the assignment because his ability to get construction projects done was unmatched. The sheer size of the Pentagon building to be completed within an unrealistic deadline would become a test for even Leslie Groves' unique organizational skills. It would also be the basis for Groves being handed an even larger and more difficult project within a year.

The world changed for everyone in the United States on December 7, 1941. The attack by the Japanese on the United States naval base at Pearl Harbor, Hawaii brought the country into the greatest military conflict in history. The United States declared war on Japan on December 8. Allied with the Japanese, Nazi Germany followed with a declaration of war against the United States on December 11.

CHAPTER 6

Pentagon Building construction, 1942

WASHINGTON D.C. – 1942

FOR COLONEL LESLIE R. Groves, his life changed several months before the attack on Pearl Harbor in December, 1941. He had been offered an attractive overseas assignment. It was exactly what he wanted. While giving testimony before a Congressional committee on Capitol Hill, his boss, General Brehon Somervell pulled him aside in a Capital Building hallway to tell him that he would have to turn down the other offer.

Stunned, Groves asked, "Why?"

"Because the Secretary of War has an important assignment for you," Somervell said. "And the President has agreed. If you do the job right it will win the war."

Groves' spirits dropped even more. He knew the assignment. "Oh, that thing." Groves was aware of the secret project taken over by the Army earlier that summer to use uranium to build an atomic bomb. Theory suggested a weapon of unprecedented power. Groves saw it as a fringe assignment, inferior to his present duties. The project was speculative. The pipe dream of some egghead physicists. It was expected to cost no more than $100 million. Groves currently spent that much in a week. Success was anything but certain. The science was pure theory. Even if such a device was possible, it could conceivably take many years to develop.

Ever the good soldier, Groves eventually resigned himself to the assignment. Ever the opportunist and accomplished infighter, he wangled a promotion to brigadier general for the new assignment on the basis that he would need the rank to garner respect from the high-level scientists. In less than two years he moved up four ranks from captain to one-star general, jumping ahead of officers graduating from West Point up to six years before him.

For all his vaunted intellect, Groves initially misread the importance of the project to develop the bomb. He did not know the full sequence of events of the past several years that led not only to the scientific possibility, but the fact that Nazi Germany had probably already been engaged in a development program. Hitler armed with such a weapon was unimaginable. That possibility, coupled with the advocacy of a number of brilliant scientists brought direct sponsorship of the project by President Roosevelt and his close advisor, secretary of War Henry Stimson. Funding would never be a constraint. The project would rise to the highest level of priority in the War effort. Groves' authority went way beyond his single star. Groves nominally reported to the Chief of Engineers, but his direct line of authority now ran to the Chairman of the Joint Chiefs of Staff General George Marshall, Secretary of War Henry Stimpson, and then directly to the President.

Like its own chain reaction, the combination of escalating events, circumstances, and unique individuals culminated in a project of unprecedented scope. It was purposely given the misleading name of the Manhattan Engineering District, the MED, following the Army Corps of Engineers naming protocol. Unofficially it was known simply as the Manhattan Project.

The fundamentals of nuclear technology, whereby energy could theoretically be released through nuclear fission, or releasing the binding energy by the splitting apart of the nucleus of certain heavy elements, was the subject of much scientific research in the early part of century. In 1933, Hungarian theoretical physicist, Leo Szilard working in England, had a revelation of the possibility of a nuclear chain reaction. In effect this would be the ability of nuclear fission once started to either sustain itself by constantly producing vast amounts of energy in a controlled state, or running out of control in a single discharge of energy in the form of an explosion. Earlier theoretical work, and Einstein's famous $E=mc^2$ equation in particular, suggested the potential for released energy from relatively small amounts of fissile material to be on orders of magnitude almost unimaginable. In 1934, the Italian physicist, Enrico Fermi actually achieved nuclear fission in experiments conducted at the University of Rome. All three of these pioneers in nuclear physics escaped Fascist Europe to eventually work in the United States.

Austrian physicist Lise Meitner and her nephew Otto Frisch were the first to articulate a theory of how the nucleus of a uranium atom could be split into smaller parts forming other lighter elements along with the ejection of neutrons and a large amount of energy. The ejected neutrons would in turn bombard other uranium atoms causing a "chain reaction". Meitner and Frisch also discovered why no stable elements beyond uranium's atomic weight existed naturally. Nuclear research now centered on the unique properties of naturally occurring uranium-238.

Like so many other scientists, Meitner and Frisch's Jewish heritage forced them to also flee Nazi Germany.

The United States and Great Britain increasingly feared that Germany was not only conducting their own development program, but were perhaps years ahead. So many physicists originated from the fascist sphere, all from prestigious universities, that a German nuclear program had to be assumed. And there was in fact a nuclear fission program underway. However, by 1942, the German Wehrmacht determined that the effort to construct a nuclear weapon could not be concluded in time to affect the outcome of the War. Hitler himself never embraced the prospects of nuclear research leading to a viable weapon. From then on, the program became fragmented and underfunded. Early on, German nuclear research had also been irreparably crippled with the emigration of so many top physicists because of their Jewish ancestry.

But the status of German nuclear development was not known to the United States or Great Britain once war broke out in Europe in 1940. What they did know was that Germany had expanded production of 'heavy water' in Nazi occupied Norway. Heavy water was deuterium concentrated in H_2O, or light water, and a possible neutron moderator, an essential component in constructing a nuclear reactor powered by uranium. After invading Czechoslovakia in 1939, Germany ceased any exports of that country's uranium. As they swept across Belgium then into France, they confiscated 3500 tons of high grade uranium mined in the Belgian Congo. Clearly the Nazi regime must be pursuing a nuclear weapon.

Allied bombing in the north of Germany disrupted Nazi research early in the War. Commandos destroyed German heavy water production in occupied Norway. By 1943, there was intelligence suggesting a nuclear reactor was being constructed outside the picturesque town of Haigerloch in southwestern Germany, removed from the threat of Allied aerial attack. The Allies had every reason to fear a Nazi nuclear program and the unimaginable consequences.

In August, 1939, Leo Szilard approached his old friend Albert Einstein to coauthor a letter to President Franklin Roosevelt explaining the real potential of creating nuclear weapons. The letter warned of German scientific efforts and lobbied the President for the United States to counter the threat by embarking upon its own development program. Einstein was already famous and also another refugee from Fascist Germany. The letter struck the right cord of concern with Roosevelt. The President asked Lyman Briggs, director of the National Bureau of Standards, to secretly organize the Briggs Advisory Commit-tee on Uranium.

In 1940, working at the University of Birmingham in the UK, two other refugee scientists from Nazi Germany made another advance in the science that would lead to creating a nuclear weapon. Austrian-born Otto Frisch and German-born Rudolf Peierls were considering the fast-fission properties of the uranium-235 isotope. Less than one percent of naturally occurring uranium was the more fissile U-235 isotope, comingled within the U-238 representing over 99%. They theorized methods for *enriching* U-238 to create higher concentrations of the fast neutron emitting U-235. They further suggested a construction design and method of detonation for a nuclear bomb. This led to another famous memorandum to the British government. As a result, the British created the MAUD Committee, the acronym standing for the bluntly stated Military Application of Uranium Detonation Committee. It was the beginning of the British atomic bomb project, code named *Tube Alloys* to obscure its real purpose. The United Kingdom eventually joined forces with the United States and Tube Alloys was absorbed into the Manhattan Project.

During the same year, the National Defense Research Committee was formed in the United States. At its head was Vannevar Bush who was a close confidant of Harry Hopkins, President Roosevelt's closest adviser. The NDRC essentially reported directly to the President, and Bush became the defacto scientific advisor to the White House. The Government's fission research was taken over by the NDRC.

The NDRC then evolved into the Office of Scientific Research and Development with Bush as director. Uncharacteristically for Washington D.C., it was not bureaucratic. There were few layers between the doers and the President of the United States. The

OSRD would control the Manhattan Project until 1943, when administration was assumed by the Army. Under General Groves, there remained no bureaucracy. The weight of scientific development toward the war effort was so important that two-thirds of all of the physicists in the U.S. were working under the direction of the OSRD. By real measure it became a cabinet level agency of the Executive, reporting directly to the President. Other government entities were angered and jealous, but the function of the military's applied science was efficiently directed.

In the same year, Franz Simon, another German physicist that fled Germany to the UK, reported that more fissile U-235 isotope can be separated from U-238 using gaseous diffusion. Acquiring sufficient quantities of U-235 to produce the necessary critical mass for even one bomb was recognized early on to be the dominate problem. The problem was never fully overcome.

Britain was at war and felt the development of an atomic bomb to be urgent. The United States was not at war. The MAUD reports sent to the Biggs' Uranium Committee in the United States during the prior year had received no response. In reality it had fallen into a bureaucratic hole. In August, 1941, Marcus Oliphant, an Australian physicist working in Great Britain flew to the United States. After personally meeting with top physicists working on uranium research, he successfully pushed the American program into action. On December 6, 1941, Vannevar Bush held a top level meeting circumventing the bureaucratic obstacle and accelerating uranium-235 research. Prophetically, the United States would be at war the following day.

On December 7, 1941, Japan attacked Pearl Harbor. On December 8th the United States was officially at war with Japan. On December 11th the United States was officially at war with Germany. Whatever urgency existed before, was elevated to a higher priority. President Roosevelt formally authorized the development of an atomic weapon. Vannevar Bush's OSRD was placed in charge of the project. A subordinate Executive Committee, designated as S-1, was specifically directed to manage the atomic bomb effort. The Manhattan Engineering District was organized as the Army component of the research effort. The name derived from the Army Corps of Engineers typical organization structure with the label obscuring its real mission.

The Manhattan Project came into being as a perfect storm of the confluence of an array of critical factors. Foremost was the Nazi persecution of Jews which drove out the best scientific minds of Europe. The science suggested not only the possibility but the probability that a weapon of unprecedented destructive power could be created. German successes in the early years of World War Two made the possibility of a nuclear armed Germany unthinkable. Roosevelt's personal sponsorship of the effort caused the U.S. program to rise above other competing military demands. The vision of selecting Vannevar Bush to navigate Washington and the scientific community, then to organize the scientific effort, proved fortuitous. The selection of the organizational genius of Leslie Groves to head the direct developmental effort of the bomb under Army control ultimately proved decisive.

The compelling reality for the United States to develop nuclear weapons first coalesced by convincing the finest scientific minds to sacrifice other work and come together under specifically directed teams. It became the military's highest priority. As such, the Manhattan Project received unlimited funding. Once in place, the only obstacle became the engineering challenges of converting the theoretical physics into a real weapon.

CHAPTER 7

VICTORIA PRESCOTT HAD spent the last five years working on her *project.* Her current live-in boyfriend was inclined to call it an obsession. She knew in a way it was. Early in her academic studies she had resolved making history her career. She loved the rigors of research, the detective work, the analysis, interpreting the past. Her doctorial thesis was titled *The Political Dynamics of the Manhattan Project & the Legacy Effects for Military & Foreign Policy.* The early Cold War era with the USSR became her academic specialty. As any scholar needed to read historical materials in the original language, Prescott acquired reading fluency in Russian, and passable verbal competency.

Prescott's interest in the Manhattan Project was first sparked because of her maternal grandfather. Aron Zielinski was a young chemist when he was recruited to work at Los Alamos. Her father had been a senior official at the State Department during the Regan administrations. That span of history was dominated by nuclear saber rattling of the world's two super powers. With a family steeped in the early decades of the nuclear age, it became a natural specialization for the budding academician.

There was no compelling evidence to make the case for a highly placed, unidentified person that fed nuclear weapons technology secrets to the Soviets during World War Two. Someone with perhaps even greater access than the foremost known spy, Klaus Fuchs. A couple of Venona decryptions may have suggested a high level source but the references were vague. They could be argued as referring to spies already discovered. The defection of Vasili Mitrokhin only a few years ago with his vast archive of KGB files held intriguing speculations, but nothing specific.

The idea of another undiscovered top level spy had taken hold with Victoria Prescott largely because of her grandfather's assertion that there must have been someone else besides Fuchs spying for the Soviets. And her grandfather had some credibility. Besides having been at the very center of things at Los Alamos for the two years, Aron Zielinski remained in the U.S. nuclear weapons program until 1955. He saw the science grow from the first modest weapons dropped on the Japanese, to the thermonuclear fusion devices hundreds of times more powerful. Zielinski made a strong technical argument that the information passed on to the Soviets by Fuchs was not sufficient for them to have made such rapid progress, and particularly their leap into thermonuclear weapons. The Soviets were either extraordinarily talented, or they acquired more U.S. technology than accounted for by the known spies.

Perhaps it was her grandfather's obsession also. At any rate it became her sustaining side project. The principle research she was now doing was to write a book on the early Soviet nuclear weapons development program to the time they achieved thermonuclear parity with the United States. Since the collapse of the Soviet Union in 1991, access to some Soviet files from that era became possible with the right connections. If her quest for an unknown spy from that era did not materialize, the book would still progress as planned. If she did a first rate job it would secure her tenure at Stanford. If she unmasked a previously unidentified high level spy, the book would be a sensation. Her career would rocket.

After five years of research, she still had no potential candidates for this super spy but she did have a body of information that would make for a successful book. At the least, it painted a comprehensive picture of Soviet nuclear espionage. Soviet spying efforts were explained in the context of the convulsions of leadership from an increasingly erratic Joseph Stalin to his successors. The work would reflect good scholarship. If she did find her super spy, it would not be a sensationalized tabloid-like account.

She had amassed an extensive database of names related to the 1940's and 1950's numbering into the thousands. Prescott was intimate with the organizational structure of the Manhattan project since it was the subject of her doctorial thesis. This provided the basis from which she greatly expanded the list of names culled from a lengthy bibliography of sources. She had paid student research assistants to input data culled from all manner of records. The Soviet names from the era were as comprehensive as any outside classified government archives. The amassed names had extensively documented connections to others, affiliations, dates, family backgrounds, places, and any miscellany of interest. Early on she had seen the benefits of being able to sort the database as a means to organizing such a massive body of information with infinite connections.

A year earlier she had met Phillip Baxter, a fellow Stanford faculty member. She felt she had traded up from her previous romantic involvement with a corporate lawyer. Baxter was a full professor. PhD in information technology working on particularly lucrative government grants related to cyber security. He was a high flyer, charming, brilliant, good looking, just two years older than her, and fairly good in bed. Unfortunately he could be an arrogant asshole at times.

Besides occasional outstanding sex, the liaison produced something of even greater use; a sophisticated computer program to query the database and generate statistically quantified results based upon certain algorithms. It was something better than any other historian had access to.

Phillip had introduced her to the underlying structure of the program algorithms. The search construction was far more advanced than the early Internet search engines that had just come on-line in the last couple of years. It took some practice to fully utilize the full potential of Phillips program. Working from her home office, Prescott was glued to her PC for days generating outputs. The program also generated graphically displayed pattern relationships that could be further filtered. Her pile of printouts grew. Some interesting associations emerged, but no revelations. That changed one day as an output drew her interest.

Perhaps it was because the first iteration of this particular query mentioned her grandfather. The connection between a number of people in the database that spilled out in one particular search was that of chemical engineer. There were many hundreds of chemical engineers involved in the Manhattan Project, but this list was much shorter. She was looking for senior scientists with broad access to the nuclear program research. Because of the way she framed subsequently defined queries, the outputs alternated between lengthy to fairly concise. She persisted for no reason other than to exhaust this particular line of inquiry.

The query output that now piqued her attention delivered a short list of fifteen names. Thirteen of the names were chemical engineers working within the Manhattan Project. All had access to sensitive information. One was a military officer working on General Leslie Groves staff. The fifteenth was only a Soviet military foreign intelligence code name of PUPPETEER.

Where did the name PUPPETEER come from? Prescott read the output.

- PUPPETEER: code name for **Soviet GRU** agent operating in Canada
- Soviet control: GRU Colonel Nikolai Zabotin

- Name identified from stolen files from Soviet Embassy, Ottawa, Canada by cipher clerk, Igor Gouzenko, 1945
- Employed as **chemical engineer**, probably for **E. I. du Pont**, Montreal, Canada
- Believed to be of **Russian** ancestry, no other known history
- No GRU records from Ottawa reference PUPPETEER activities after **1942**
- RCMP and FBI investigations did not identify real name among 340 chemical engineers and technicians employed by **E. I. du Pont** in Montreal from 1938 to 1946, 86 being ethnically Russian or East European
- No further investigations to identify PUPPETEER were pursued with ending of WWII
- FBI concluded PUPPETEER most probably recalled to USSR in 1942 since no further references ever surfaced after that time
- No Vernona transcripts reference to PUPPETEER

How did this Army officer make this list? The connecting information was highlighted in bold.

- Voronin, Mikhail
- DOB 3/31/14, Los Angeles, California
- BS degree civil engineering, USC, 1936
- Employed Bureau of Reclamation 1936-38, Grand Coulee Dam
- Father Stefan, professor classical literature, Moscow State University
- Mother, Kira, musician, violinist
- Parents **Russian** immigrants 1913
- No siblings
- Father employed as associate professor, Pomona College, Claremont, California 1915-1934
- Parents returned to Russia 1935
- U.S. Army Corps of Engineers, 1939-1959, retiring rank of colonel
- Scientific Liaison Officer, General L. R. Groves staff, Manhattan Project 1942-46, rank of major
- Special Top secret clearance level

- Married – Elena Obolensky, DOB 8/12/19, **Montreal, Canada**, **Russian** ancestry suggested by surname, parents unknown, raised in orphanage, bachelors degree in political science McGill University
- Known relatives, adoptive parents Boris and Vanya Ramazanov, **Russian** ancestry
- Boris Ramazanov employed as **chemical engineer** with **E. I. du Pont**, New Jersey
- Vanya Ramazanov employed as elementary school teacher
- Ramazanovs immigrated to U.S. from **Canada, 1942**
- Both Ramazanovs naturalized **Canadian** citizens
- Obolensky and both Ramazanovs died in a single accident,1945

Prescott reread the details several times. How was this possible connection overlooked? What kind of laxity was in the background security screening for this Mikhail Voronin? The answer was obvious to her when considering the chronology. This GRU sleeper spy's name only came to light in 1945. The Second World War had ended. The RCMP and FBI found no reference to PUPPETEER after 1942. Boris Ramazanov's name would have come up, but he died in 1945. The intelligence on PUPPETEER was not actionable. It was simply archived into obscurity.

Voronin joined the Army in 1939. He would have been vetted with extensive screening when he was posted to the Manhattan Project in late 1942. But he was not married at the time. When he did marry in 1943, there would have been a screening of his wife and her parents. That security evaluation would find that Elena Obolensky was a low level secretary working in the Office of War Mobilization, although without a security clearance. Her adopted father, Boris Ramazanov, held a Canadian passport, and had years of employment with DuPont in Canada before being transferred to the DuPont plant in Carney's Point, New Jersey in 1943. This DuPont plant soon became engaged in research and development of chemicals in support of the Manhattan Project. Ramazanov held a secret level security clearance so there would be no red flags when his daughter married Voronin. Elena Obolensky's adopted mother was an elementary school teacher. Little reason for General Groves' security staff to probe any deeper into Voronin's new in-laws. No compelling reason for the FBI to investigate the deceased Boris Ramazanov further in 1946, had they even made any connection with an agent code named PUPPETEER.

The fact that Boris Ramazanov held a security clearance dampened Prescott's enthusiasm slightly. But still, looking at the data now with the coincidence of the PUPPETEER and Boris Ramazanov backgrounds connected with so many pieces raised all sorts of flags. This was clearly something new to look into. Voronin was ethnically Russian. His parents returned to Russia before the War. Voronin was certainly highly placed. He had more than just access to all the atomic bomb scientific work since his job was to write briefing reports to Groves himself. This would make Voronin technically conversant in all aspects of the program. Traveling to all the locations that constituted the Manhattan Project, he knew all of the senior staff. He held the highest security clearance possible. Beyond all that, Voronin almost singularly had the easiest ability to pass information secretly because of his mobility. Everyone else highly placed, particularly the scientists, was under the most intense security imaginable. Voronin had no watchers. Boris Ramazanov was more than interesting. If he was PUPPETEER, then Voronin was also a Soviet spy, or an unwitting source. But this was not yet a smoking gun. It might all be just coincidence. But Prescott's instincts said she was on to something.

Prescott couldn't wait to tell Phillip. They would celebrate. She went out to get some steaks for dinner. It was a sunny July day. She lived in a townhouse on Greenwich Street in the Telegraph Hill neighborhood of San Francisco. It was a long commute to the Stanford campus in Palo Alto, but she loved San Francisco. Besides it was her grandfather's place before he moved back east into an assisted living facility after the death of his wife. She could walk to restaurants in the North Beach area and walk to the market as she was doing on this perfect afternoon.

Phillip Baxter arrived home before dark. "Hi. You home?" he called out.

Victoria Prescott came out of the kitchen holding two flutes of champagne. "You bet I'm home."

She was wearing tight jeans with a low cut sweater revealing as much cleavage as possible. See handed him the glass, then gave him a protracted passionate kiss.

"That's very nice. The kiss I mean," Baxter said. "You look pretty good too. Are we celebrating something?"

Prescott looked at him. He was a good looking guy. Modestly handsome, trim physique. Dressed casually in jeans and a sweater with a designer leather jacket, he was clearly not the geek-type suggested by his field of expertise.

"Shit. To hell with the champagne. Let's just fuck instead and drink afterwards."

Prescott put her drink down and kissed him again, this time running her hand over his groin. He responded accordingly.

An hour later they had dressed.

"That was super, Phillip. You're a great lover."

"It's easy with you. You're pretty hot yourself. So what's going on that made you so horny today?"

"Look at these." She handed Baxter several pages of printouts. "It's your program, Phillip. I've discovered something. Something that could be important. Might be what I've been looking for with my obsession as you call it. Look at the data in bold on the last two sheets."

Baxter looked over the printouts. "Ok. I see the connections. What's it mean to you, Vicky?"

"It's obvious. If this Boris Ramazanov is the GRU spy known as PUPPETEER, then he was directly connected to this Major

Voronin. Voronin was on General Groves staff. Highly placed. The highest in terms of access to World War Two nuclear secrets. His wife's pseudo-parents may be spies, perhaps she was too. At any rate that makes Voronin a probable spy."

"That conclusion seems a little premature, Vicky. These connections could easily have a different explanation. This Ramazanov had his own security clearance so the FBI must have checked him out."

"Sure. But he could have covered that easily. Klaus Fuchs had a security clearance too. What if Ramazanov was his real name? He was apparently a real chemical engineer. What if his cover, what the intelligence trade calls a legend, was actually all real? There'd be nothing for a background check to turn up."

"I guess. Seems a little thin though."

"Christ, Phillip, I thought you'd be ecstatic as well. After all, it was your program that unearthed this connection. Otherwise it would be buried forever just like it was for fifty years."

"Easy, easy. I just mean you shouldn't get your hopes up until there's something more to make the case. You couldn't publish this allegation with only this to go on could you?"

He was right of course but she still knew this was something. A real find. At least she hoped so.

"Of course not. But it sets me on a specific direction to pursue it further. Historical research is really detective work."

"Just don't want to see you disappointed that's all," Baxter said. "If this army guy turns out to have been a spy, is it really such a big deal fifty years later?"

"Goddamnit, Phillip. You've never thought my work was important. It's just *history* after all, right? Do you ever read anything but computer science shit?"

"Ease up, Vicky, I didn't mean it that way."

"Then what did you mean?"

"I mean will this be that important? Important to your book?"

Prescott calmed down. She wasn't going to ruin what had started as a wonderful evening.

"More than important. It will make it a best seller with mass popularity. It'll be a scholarly work without it, advance my credentials and satisfy the academic need to publish and all that shit you need for tenure. But the revelation that there was a previously undiscovered spy at the very top would make it a sensation. It would move it outside academia into the mainstream."

"So where do you go from here?"

"To New York to see Dad. Maybe as early as next week. I need his leverage to get me access into some secret stuff."

Hamilton Prescott was a professor of political science at Columbia University. He served eleven years as a senior official with the State Department. He was recruited by Alexander Haig who became Secretary of State under Ronald Reagan's first term. He subsequently served under George Shultz and James Baker until 1992. Prescott was a Soviet specialist still well connected with both Washington and Moscow.

That got Baxter's attention. What the hell was Victoria up to? Nothing illegal he hoped. He had a government security clearance since he worked on classified software development. He wouldn't want his girlfriend raising any security questions.

"What kind of secret stuff?" Baxter asked.

"Soviet Union secret stuff. Stuff I'd find in Moscow. KGB and GRU archives. Old Soviet records going back to the 1917 Revolution. I need to see people that will let me take a look. To do that, I need Daddy's contacts in the Russian government. Maybe a little help with accessing some old World War Two archives in Washington that are still classified."

"Moscow? You're planning on going to Moscow? You think they'll let you look at KGB files? Be realistic, Vicky."

"Actually GRU files, Red Army intelligence. And I am being realistic. The Russian's have already released a lot of material since the Soviet Union dissolved. Besides, I'm interested in much older stuff. Stalinist era material. The age and the historical period should not make it particularly sensitive. The problem is still persuading the record keepers. Government types do not like to give up secrets even ancient ones. The point is I've got to resolve this lead that could make this Voronin my Soviet spy. Boris Ramazanov is that key. Was he the GRU spy PUPPETEER? I can only resolve that question in Moscow. Besides, I've got six weeks before the fall semester starts so the timing is perfect."

Baxter just shook his head and pursed his lips.

"What the fuck does that mean, Phillip?" Prescott said. "You think that's stupid, naïve, unimportant? What?"

"I don't mean anything, Vicky. It's just ..... It seems like you're grasping at straws. You're looking for evidence to support your theory."

"And why not? That's how all research, scientific or otherwise proceeds."

"No. This is obsessive. Your whole academic career starting with graduate school has been shaped by the beginnings of the Cold War. This spy thing is like looking for Bigfoot or UFO's. If you never find evidence, the search just goes on. This coincidence you discovered in your database may be just that, a coincidence. Shit, this is all you talk about, your fucking phantom spy from World War Two."

Baxter regretted his remarks immediately. Prescott was stung deeply. She was thanking him for providing the means to dig out this potential connection with a member of Grove's staff and a known Soviet spy. They'd just had great sex. Now he's pushing an old unresolved argument.

Uncharacteristically, Prescott chose not to elevate the argument any further. She already knew Baxter's views on her work. Dumb idea that this might cause him to acknowledge that there could be something to her theory. To hell with him. Time to focus on resolving this Ramazanov question. Were these connecting points culled from a database just an anomaly or was it historical gold? If it didn't develop into something, would she ever abandon the quest?

CHAPTER 8

IN AUGUST OF 1942, the Manhattan Project was born. It had started out with the title of *Development of Substitute Materials*. General Leslie Groves observed that this was a poor label for security reasons since it invited speculation. He suggested adopting the title Manhattan Engineering District after the Corps of Engineers practice of naming the area of operations after the headquarters' city, initially in this case, New York City.

The district engineer first assigned to the project was Colonel James Marshall. Vannevar Bush, Roosevelt's scientific advisor, had pushed for a stronger officer to take charge. From the onset, Colonel Marshall struggled with understanding the technical challenges. With the War in its early months, his project could not compete for resources with other Army demands. Bush wanted the second in command of the Army Corps of Engineers to run the program. He had to settle for another colonel, Leslie Groves. Bush felt Groves did not have sufficient rank, and although an accomplished project manager, he had a reputation for being tactless and excessively blunt. Groves took care of the rank issue by simply demanding his general's star as necessary for the project's success. His personality would prove to be exactly what *was* needed, but Bush was unhappy with the selection at the time.

Groves moved quickly to ease out Colonel Marshall. Marshall and his deputy Colonel Nichols had successfully located a tract of land in Tennessee for construction of a massive uranium separation facility. Impressed with Nichols, Groves appointed him as District Engineer and moved him to Oak Ridge, Tennessee. Groves took personal charge like a wolf tearing the flesh from a fresh kill. He moved the headquarters from New York to Washington D.C. His staff would be lean, the reporting hierarchy flat, just like it was to his own superiors. And the staff would be handpicked.

In September, I was ordered to Washington D.C. to the New War Department Building on 21st and Virginia Avenue. I was to report to a Lt. Col. Boris Pash who was technically part of the Army's Military Intelligence Service staff. In practical terms, he reported to General Groves. Based upon Groves' style and a free hand with the Manhattan Project, Groves effectively ran his own intelligence service without outside interference. Security clearances were issued according to Groves' criteria. The FBI provided background checks but it was Groves' intelligence group headed by Pash that made all decisions on project access.

I waited my turn for an hour before being ushered into Pash's office. Besides Pash there was another captain present.

"You're here Captain because you're being considered for a special project. It's highly secret. All staff are undergoing extensive additional security screening," Pash said.

"You're of Russian heritage, Captain?"

"Yes, Sir."

"Your parents immigrated here in 1913. I see they returned to the Soviet Union in 1935. Why was that?"

"Economics, Sir. My father and mother are both academics. My father taught classical literature at a college. My father lost his teaching position in California. He had no other skills. The Depression made it impossible to find another position. My mother could only bring in a bit of money teaching violin. My father had kept in contact with academics in Russia over the years. From them he learned of an opening at Moscow State University where he had previously taught."

"Why did he lose his job in California?"

"Like most other people, because of the Depression. The wealthy benefactor that endowed his chair lost everything in '29. The school eventually couldn't afford to keep my father on the faculty."

"What do your parents think of Stalin's Communist regime?"

"They're both apolitical, Sir. They left Russia because of both Tsarist oppression and the Bolsheviks. They experienced the failed revolution of 1905. After that, life in Russia became more difficult. They could see the coming chaos that happened a few years later. I don't believe they favor Joseph Stalin's brand of government, but they saw it as stability. Of course now with the Germans invading, things could not be worse for them."

"Are you still in communication with your parents?"

"Not for well over a year. The last letter I received said things were pretty desperate there. Severe food rationing beyond what we have here. Fear that the Germans will reach Moscow. I'm very worried about how they're doing. I write them but never hear back. Mail over there would understandably be a low priority."

"So what did they say about Stalin's non-aggression pact with Hitler in 1939?"

"They were against it. But they rationalized it as Stalin's way of trying to keep them out of war. Russia wasn't ready. They saw it as no different than Neville Chamberlain's appeasement giving Hitler the Sudetenland region of Czechoslovakia."

"So they never discussed politics?" Pash asked. "Seems they would have had comments as any of us might."

I was wary of where this was going. I was well aware of my parents' early backgrounds. They were part of Vladimir Lenin's Bolshevik faction of the Russian Social Democratic Party before leaving Russia. That made them charter Communists. Fear of arrest by the Tsars' secret police, the Okhrana, was the real reason my parents emigrated. They hid their political leanings rightfully sensing such views would not be welcome in the United States. There were strong socialist movements taking shape in America but all faced equally strong countervailing pressures from the conservative Right. Clearly it was best for a new immigrant to avoid politics altogether. I did not believe there was any trail to my parents' Communist past. Even for the FBI, it was unlikely they could check backgrounds to Tsarist Russia before 1913.

"Yes, Sir. They had opinions of course. They were intellectuals. But they favored discussions of art, literature, history, particularly Russian history. They loved an idealized Russia. A Russia of the past. More than once they expressed contempt for all political ideologies."

"Even American democracy?"

"They certainly appreciated the freedom of speech in America. They welcomed the absence of fear from living in a police state. But they often remarked on the terrible social inequalities that are obvious here in America. They were troubled as a matter of conscience, not of politics. They liked it here."

"Yet they still returned to Russia. To a police state again."

"They had reservations about the political climate. But they thought as academics they could avoid involvement in politics. They also missed their motherland, even after 20 years. It was still difficult for them to leave the United States, especially since I would not be joining them. But the deciding factor became my father's ability work again."

At the end of the interview, Pash shook my hand and dismissed me. I did not know at the time that Pash was also of Russian decent. He had returned with his parents as a boy and eventually fought in the civil war against the Bolsheviks after the 1917 revolution. Coincidentally, Pash had also attended the University of Southern California.

Two days later I was to leave Washington on my first assignment. Pash obviously had approved my joining the staff. Groves himself gave me brief instructions which suggested what my role was to be.

"Captain, I want you to report on progress at the Clinton Works. I want an independent assessment of the construction progress as it relates to a phased-in timing capability to start producing enriched uranium. Not only the building construction, but the status on the equipment as well."

"Excuse me, General, but I'm not sure I'm qualified technically. I don't even know what enriching uranium means."

"Well you'd better get up to speed damn fast. I knew nothing myself of the physics a short time ago either. Here's a bunch of technical briefing papers prepared for non-scientific personnel."

Groves placed a three-inch stack of bound reports on the corner of his desk. All had *TOP SECRET* stamped in red.

"The reports can't leave the building. Return them to Jean when you're done with them."

Mrs. Jean O'Leary was Groves' personal secretary. She had the distinction of knowing where everything was and the only staff member to whom Groves was consistently civil.

Not only was I not a scientist, but even the science for making an atomic bomb was itself mostly still theoretical. The principle task was to enrich the naturally occurring uranium-238 with only trace amounts of the uranium-235 isotope to a level greater than eighty percent uranium-235. It was the uranium-235 that was necessary to produce a bomb.

There were two enrichment methods under consideration in 1942. In typical Groves' style, he made the decision to pursue both methods simultaneously. The Y-12 plant at the Oak Ridge

Clinton Works would pursue electromagnetic means of separating uranium-235 from uranium-238. The K-25 plant would pursue enrichment by means of gaseous diffusion. Both facilities represented what was to become the largest industrial complex in the world. The giant K-25 building covered 44 acres. The Y-12 plant would employ magnetic assemblies larger than anything ever previously constructed. The construction had just commenced and I was to determine when product could be expected from these untried processes using equipment not yet fully designed.

The unsaid but understood part of the Manhattan Project command structure was that it was all about General Leslie Groves. It was a team effort as long as all staff knew that Groves would make all important decisions. Groves would typically know more about everything than any of the staff, yet he expected everyone to keep up. Decisions came rapid fire from the boss. Orders were expected to be executed immediately if not faster. On the positive side, it was exciting if one was up to the task. His staff was kept small. There was little chain of command. Everyone, including Groves himself had more clout than their rank suggested. It was a heady atmosphere.

"Jean will give you the names and locations of people to start talking to. None of them are in Tennessee at the Clinton Works so it's premature to go there first. Unfortunately they're scattered all over the country. You'll need to see Ernest Lawrence at the University of California in Berkley. He's the expert on electromagnetic enrichment. Experimental physicist. Nobel Laureate. The Y-12 plant is based on his cyclotron invention. See Glenn Seaborg when you're at Berkley. He's the scientist that first produced plutonium. It's the man-made element that's of interest along with uranium-235. Next are Leo Szilard and Enrico Fermi at the University of Chicago. Szilard started this whole thing when he and Einstein wrote a letter to Roosevelt about the feasibility of an atomic bomb and scared the hell out of the President if the Germans were to beat us to it. Beyond that are the equipment manufacturers and operators; General Electric, Westinghouse, Allis-Chalmers, Tennessee Eastman, DuPont, and a host of others. You need to see them all and understand the obstacles."

"Yes, Sir," Voronin said. It was overwhelming.

"Your reports. They're to be succinct. I want conclusions supported with facts. Get to the heart of the issues. Cut away the crap. Most of all I want solutions. If you cite a problem give me solutions. That's what you're here for. Get it done. Get it done fast. I'm not concerned how much debris is left in the wake as long as we're successful. Is that understood, Captain?"

"Yes, Sir."

"I'll see you back here in twelve days, Captain."

Groves was making things up as he went along. He attacked this great project of uncertainty like a field commander. Leslie Groves was never a bureaucrat. By October he determined an additional research site would be required to bring the final development work together to achieve the creation of an atomic bomb. Experimental work was being conducted at the Radiation Laboratory at the University of California in Berkley and the Metallurgical Laboratory at the University of Chicago. Oak Ridge, Tennessee would be the site of separating uranium-235 from uranium-238. Hedging his bets for an alternate fissile material, Groves intended to pursue plutonium extraction in Hanford, Washington under a contract with E. I. du Pont. This additional site he had in mind would concentrate all of the theoretical work at one location. Ultimately, it would be the design and assembly location of the bomb. A single purpose site would allow for massing the scientific talent under tight security. It would be known as Site Y.

That is where my role in the Manhattan Project escalated to a new level. On November 14, I returned to Washington from Oak Ridge where I had been reporting on progress of the early construction of what was formally called the Clinton Engineering Works in Tennessee. The next day, I was on a military transport C-47 flying to Albuquerque, New Mexico with General Groves. Groves briefed me that we were to inspect potential sites for a scientific laboratory in the mountains in the Santa Fe area. He did not elaborate as to why I was along.

We spent the night in the officers' barracks at the Albuquerque Army Base. The following morning we were joined by a Major Dudley. Dudley's job was to survey potential locations for Site Y. Groves told me we were waiting for Dr. J. Robert Oppenheimer to fly in from California.

I knew that Oppenheimer had been appointed scientific director of the project by Groves himself. I was excited about meeting the physicist selected to supervise the leading physicists of the world. This was a rarefied atmosphere I was being sucked into.

When Groves met Oppenheimer as he stepped from his plane, a strange event took place. Groves actually smiled and greeted Robert Oppenheimer with uncharacteristic warmth. Not the fearsome General Groves that Dudley and I knew. Even with his own superiors, Groves was professional, but typically blunt and never friendly.

"Good flight, Doctor?" Groves asked.

Oppenheimer was tall and unusually thin to the point of being gaunt. He was wearing an unstylish wide-brimmed fedora. He lit a cigarette, something the rest of us knew not to do around the General.

"Uneventful. The best kind of flight."

"General, this is Dr. Edwin McMillan from the Rad Lab," Oppenheimer said.

Groves shook McMillan's hand and said, "Glad to have you on the team, Doctor."

That was it. No other pleasantries. Groves then turned back to Oppenheimer. "I understand you know these mountains where we're going quite well, Dr. Oppenheimer."

"Very well indeed. I've spent a lot of time there over the years, mostly on horseback. It's magnificent country. More specifically, it should suit our purposes for a number of factors."

The foremost criterion for Site Y was isolation. It would be home to a large number of scientists and technicians. Inhibiting the ability to leave the site was as important as limiting access. An urban location would present impossible security for the ultra-sensitive work. This would be a top security military installation. The civilians working there would have highly restricted freedom of movement. Many of those civilians were Nobel laureates used to academic freedoms, not to mention physical freedom. That remained a difficult sell individually for the newly appointed director, J. Robert Oppenheimer.

Additionally, the population within a 100-mile radius had to be sparse. There must be adequate road and rail access to move substantial amounts of material and personnel. The winter months must still allow for outdoor work. Because of the war, the potential for attack dictated the site be well removed from either sea coast. By those criteria, all of the considered sites eventually narrowed to New Mexico.

"Major Dudley. The place we're visiting?" Groves said

"It's called Jemez Springs, Sir. Less than a two-hour drive from here. It's west of Santa Fe."

"Do you know the place, Doctor?" Groves asked Oppenheimer.

"I believe so. It has been some time so I can't comment on its suitability until we see it. I recall it's actually a canyon. Am I correct, Major?"

"Yes, Sir. It's surrounded by mountains rising above the location. Good roads leading into the site. It appears to fit the requirements very well."

"We'll see, Major," Groves said. "Voronin, you ride with Dudley. I'll go with Dr. Oppenheimer and Dr. McMillan in the second car.

We arrived in the place known as Jemez Springs. Upon exiting the army staff car, Oppenheimer immediately remarked, "This might not be adequate, General."

"Why not?"

As Dudley said, it was enclosed by mountains all around, enclosing what amounted to a narrow valley. Oppenheimer commented, "It's somewhat claustrophobic. We're going to have to entice scientists to work and live here for some duration. This place just makes that more difficult. Ed, what do you think?"

McMillan said, "Might be an issue. But on a more pragmatic level, I don't believe it's large enough. We're not sure what might be required, but at the very least it would be cramped from the onset."

Groves did not like the site either. "I concur. This won't do. Major. What about other options in these mountains?"

Dudley was deflated. He thought this was an excellent site. "Well, there's one other called Otowi. I had thought it inferior to this site for a number of reasons. It's east of here. We backtrack and go north out of Santa Fe then west into the mountains."

"Dr. Oppenheimer. Do you have any suggestions since you know these mountains?"

Oppenheimer was into his third cigarette since arriving. "I believe I might have a possibility. The Major's right, Otowi wouldn't do. But continuing on west on the same road from Otowi is a place called Los Alamos. There's a boy's school located there with a large lodge building and a collection of cabins. Beautiful place. Lots of space. Grand views."

"I'm familiar with Los Alamos, General," Dudley said. "I've been there. I felt the water supply would be inadequate. The road's also narrow and winding."

"Nevertheless, we'll still take a look. Major, did you have the foresight to bring food and water?" Groves asked.

"Yes, Sir. I'll have our drivers lay out lunch. We have coffee too."

Dudley did better than that. He had the two sergeants pull out folding tables and chairs from the car trucks. The temperature was brisk but the sun was warm. Groves even paid a compliment to Dudley on the fine lunch of sandwiches and fruit, followed by a selection of donuts. Seems that Dudley knew of Groves' proclivity for sweets. Evidenced by his considerable girth, General Groves did not miss many meals.

Passing through Santa Fe, they headed north then cut west on a narrow dirt road. They first pasted through Otowi. All agreed that it was unacceptable. Here they crossed the Rio Grande River on a one-lane bridge. The road into Los Alamos was a bone-shaker. However, the ride proved worth it.

Oppenheimer had this location in mind for some time. He knew it well. Unlike the valley of Jemez Springs, Los Alamos sat on a high plateau, populated with pine, offering a broad vista of the surrounding mountains. Instead of confining, the surrounding Sangre de Cristo and Jemez Mountains painted a breathtaking landscape. A light snow had fallen during the night but the teachers and students at the Los Alamos Ranch School were on the playing fields in shorts enjoying a sunny day in November. Oppenheimer commented that the surrounding views would provide an inspiring work environment for the scientists. Practically, the school's main building could be used to house the initial compliment of scientists until new accommodations could be constructed.

In Santa Fe that night at dinner, Groves declared, "I agree on the selection of Los Alamos for Site Y. Dr. Oppenheimer and Dr. McMillan, I would like for you to return next week to Los Alamos with Dr. Lawrence. Re-evaluate the suitability of the site. Dudley, you'll work with Dr. Oppenheimer. In the mean time I will start the process of acquiring the site. The War Department will condemn the property pursuant to its purchase for military purposes."

Dr. Ernest Lawrence headed the Radiation Laboratory at the University of California. He was a Nobel laureate and inventor of the cyclotron. His laboratory was doing advanced experimental physics in atomic research. It was an integral arm of the ever expanding network of facilities comprising the Manhattan Project.

Groves continued to dictate orders. "Captain Voronin, you will remain here and work with Major Dudley. I will expect you back in Washington next Friday with a fully detailed report. The report needs to analyze the key suitability factors and incorporate Doctors Oppenheimer, McMillan, and Lawrence's conclusions. Your report is to cover the initial site preparation tasks with start dates and durations. Layout the construction project. The duration of the tasks is to be the fastest possible. No padding the lead times. Be creative. If something requires three months, find a way to do it in one."

"Dr. Oppenheimer. You now have your research facility. You need to start to assemble your Site Y team. I assume that those you need will rise to the occasion and do their patriotic duty. If necessary, we can always invoke the draft."

"I'm sure all of the senior scientists I have in mind will participate," Oppenheimer said. "I've talked to most already. The hardest part will be the isolation. These are intellectual people with wide ranging interests and associations. Security will be the hardest part for us to maintain. But I assure you, that the threat of Nazi Germany achieving an atomic bomb weighs heavily on the scientific community. So many of those scientists were forced to flee Fascism. They need no further motivation."

Even the rarefied intellectual elite were accorded no deferential treatment from General Leslie Groves. To watch Groves in action was an awesome spectacle, provided of course you were a spectator and not the focus of his attention, much less his displeasure. His command of volumes of complex data was encyclopedic. His ability to reduce complex problems to their basic elements allowed for decisive decision making where most others would hesitate. He calculated the risks against the expected gains and made a decision accordingly. He did not agonize after making the decision, but was quick to remedy a course of action that was not working. With Groves it was not inflated ego. It was just an abiding personal confidence in his intellectual capabilities which he knew to be superior. That was combined with a single-mindedness to accomplish whatever the assignment with little regard for interpersonal debris. He always got the job done his way. He was brilliant and exercised that brilliance indiscriminately.

Major General Leslie R. Groves

CHAPTER 9

WASHINGTON D.C. – 1942

A S ONE TOP level Groves' aide once remarked, "General Groves planned the project, ran his own construction, his own science, his own Army, his own State Department, and his own Treasury Department." It was a fairly accurate assessment.

Before actually taking charge of the Manhattan Project and his promotion to brigadier general, Groves ordered the immediate purchase of the Tennessee site. He ordered Colonel Nichols to buy 1200 tons of Belgian owned high-grade uranium already in the United States. Additional purchases for Belgian Congo ore were transacted to provide the vital natural resource for this new project.

Groves had to also contend with the matter of procurement priority ratings. With the War just started, every conceivable military project had to compete for resources. In characteristic style, Groves demanded a meeting with the head of the War Production Board, Donald Nelson. The project had already been assigned the comparatively high priority rating of AA-3. Groves wanted an AAA rating. If this questionable project had any chance of succeeding, he needed access to resources without restriction.

At their one meeting in Nelson's office, Nelson initially refused. Not getting what he wanted, Groves rose from his chair and made to leave.

Somewhat surprised that Groves did not argue further, Nelson asked, "What action are you now going to take, Colonel Groves?"

Groves said, "Recommend to the Secretary of War that the Project be abandoned on the grounds that Mr. Nelson refuses to carry out the wishes of the President."

Nelson blanched. He suggested Groves sit down to discuss the matter further. Before leaving Nelson office, Groves produced a prepared letter for Nelson's signature authorizing the AAA rating to be invoked as Groves saw necessary.

All this took place within just days from Groves accepting command of the project and before he actually took over. Our trip to New Mexico for the selection of Site Y and Groves on the spot decision to locate it at Los Alamos was characteristic of how the Manhattan Project was to operate.

I returned to Washington D.C. from my initial field inspection trip within the allotted twelve days Groves had ordered. During that time I consulted with Dr. Oppenheimer who provided not only his thoughts on the key phases of developing the project, but who I should consult. I spent most of those twelve days in Berkley, California and Chicago. At the University of California, Ernest Lawrence explained the function of his cyclotron in producing high energy particles required for atomic disintegration. What that meant, or its importance, was something of which I had only a vague understanding.

In Chicago, Fermi personally showed me around his Chicago Pile-1, the first nuclear reactor. Fermi had achieved the first self-sustaining nuclear chain reaction in December with his massive pile of graphite blocks and uranium. He demonstrated for me the energy creation with the audible output on a Geiger counter as the adjusting rods regulated the amount of fission. The demonstration took the science out of the theoretical realm and gave it a physical face.

My last day was spent at the Radiation Laboratory at MIT. By this time I had enough understanding of the basics to ask intelligent questions to the theorists there. The trip was a crash course in the developing science of nuclear physics. Much was beyond my understanding but I had a good technical mind so I was able to grasp the concepts. It was a good enough grounding in the science to allow me to produce a cohesive report.

Surviving on only a couple of hours sleep each night, I was exhausted when I arrived back in Washington getting only some fitful sleep on the train down from my last stop in Cambridge, Massachusetts. That entire first night back in Washington was spent typing my report. Fortified with lots of coffee, I still looked blurry-eyed when I reported to General Groves early the following morning at the New War Department Building.

Groves' office was on the fifth floor, room 5120. It was innocuous and unlabeled. The outer office consisted of gray steel desks occupied by several secretaries and junior army officers. The General's office was through the next door. It consisted of two desks, his and his secretary, Jean O'Leary's, a conference table, and a few leather chairs.

After handing Groves my report, he immediately started to read it without suggesting I take a seat. Even though Groves was a fast reader, it must have been twenty minutes before he said anything.

"Appears to be thorough work. Some interesting conclusions you raise, Captain. Still a little short on solutions but I expect you'll improve on that. Do so quickly. The success of this mission rests on time as much as on science. You understand me, Captain?"

"Yes, Sir."

"This is your new assignment, Voronin. If I can't be somewhere, you will be. You'll be an extension of my eyes and ears. I don't want more problems, I need solutions. I expect you to apply pressure where necessary, but you need to develop good working relationships with the scientists. Your role will often be the good guy to smooth out the rough patches that I will inevitably create. I expect you to be accepted within their social environment. However, never forget you're working for me."

"Yes, Sir. I understand." Sounded like an impossible task.

"Since you'll be dealing with these eggheads, you will need more stature to gain their respect. Therefore, effective immediately, you are promoted to major. They'll see you as a mid-level rather than a junior officer."

I was stunned. Immediately I braced to attention. "Thank you, Sir."

Groves ignored my thanks. "I want you back out to Los Alamos. It is essential that Site Y become operational as soon as possible. Oppenheimer is gathering his scientists. Tough enough persuading these prima donnas to commit to the Project, but they're going to have to live in that wilderness. Your first job is to make sure we're providing sufficient amenities to ease their transition. Personally, I would prefer we run it like the army base that it is. But I'm persuaded that would be counterproductive. So you can see this will be your first balancing act, Major."

In February, 1943, the Los Alamos Ranch School closed. Soon after, the scientists began to arrive. The School's lodge and faculty houses provided the first accommodations. Construction was commencing at an accelerated pace. Problems arose from the onset.

Groves indeed saw this as a military reservation. One with the highest level of security possible. That security was more about containing the information and the movement of the scientists working there than preventing unauthorized access. Groves had institutionalized the security concept of compartmentalization. The concept meant that everyone need know only what was necessary for their specific work and nothing else. That was not how science was done. It was not how the civilian scientists worked.

The first base commander ran the place like a prison. Frictions with the scientific staff became a problem from the first day. Oppenheimer's special assistant for managing the day to day administrative tasks, a noted physicist selected by Groves himself, resigned in disgust after six weeks because of the abnormal security. Mail was censored, travel outside Site Y was heavily restricted, technical discussion was prohibited outside one's designated area of work.

It was to this contentious atmosphere that I was supposed to work. Not only contentious but chaos personified. Everything was in a state of development. Everything was make-shift until space became available and equipment arrived. New people arrived continually. Therefore everything was in constant state of flux. The broader Project scope was complex, vastly complex. Much of the theoretical work was not fully developed, yet the design for the manufacturing processes to produce fissile fuel was already underway. No one was better suited than the organizational genius of Leslie Groves. But my earliest observation was that Dr. Oppenheimer's task was perhaps even more daunting.

Oppenheimer was charged with first persuading the foremost scientists in the U.S. to come work in this beautiful, but primitive remote camp. Away from friends, away from their academic environments, to live in nothing better than army barracks-like housing. And to live as virtual prisoners. They were to then force the science to convert developing theoretical work into practical application. All this stood under the shadow of an undetermined deadline to achieve an atomic bomb before Nazi Germany. Unlike Groves, Oppenheimer could not achieve the objective through blunt force, or throwing unlimited resources at the effort.

Groves had personally selected Robert Oppenheimer to head the Project as Scientific Director. Oppenheimer was a seemingly odd choice that came under initial criticism. Not that Groves cared. He had his own pragmatic reasons for the selection. Groves' had absolute confidence in his own analytical skills that crowded out doubt once he made a decision.

Oppenheimer was an internationally respected physicist. But he was theoretical rather than experimental as were other leading nuclear physicists such as Enrico Fermi and Ernest Lawrence who ran the two principle research laboratories. This task of building an atomic bomb was appearing more to be an experimentally driven project resting on advanced engineering. Oppenheimer had little background in administration. While highly regarded by the scientific community, he had never been awarded a Nobel Prize. With a great many Nobel laureates working under his direction, there was concern this could diminish his stature.

Oppenheimer's own personality might also suggest he was a poor choice. He was a mix of extremes. He had the reputation of being arrogant. When he disagreed, he could destroy a person with his caustic remarks. He was a clumsy experimentalist. His theoretical work was brilliant, but typically left unfilled as he moved on to other problems prematurely. He had an eclectic range of intellectual interests beyond theoretical physics. Personally wealthy, some accused him of being elitist. This was balanced with extreme generosity to those close to him.

Oppenheim was painfully thin, perhaps because of a diminished appetite from his chain smoking. Yet he loved the outdoors. For years he owned a remote property in the mountains of northern New Mexico not far from Los Alamos. Many a guest was exhausted by the long, difficult horseback rides that seemed to invigorate him.

Only those close to Julius Robert Oppenheimer considered him friendly. All considered him brilliant. To anyone except the insightful Leslie Groves, Oppenheimer seemed the most unlikely of choices to organize this unique laboratory.

Add to all that the very real concern of Oppenheimer's politics. The day after my promotion, I was approached by the Project's head of security, Lt. Col. Pash.

Pash ushered me into his office and closed the door.

"The Boss has told me about your new assignment. You've met Dr. Oppenheimer I believe?" Pash said.

"Yes, Sir. When the General settled on Los Alamos as Site Y."

"Know anything about Oppenheimer?"

"Not much, Sir. Brilliant I'm told. Seemed like a fairly pleasant guy when we met."

"I'm not talking about that, Voronin. I'm talking about his politics. Let's just say that the good doctor is about as far left as possible without holding a Communist Party membership card. More than that, he has friends that are believed to be Communists. His wife was even a former Communist, and probably his brother too."

"And the General knows all this?"

"Of course. I've expressed by reservations about Oppenheimer. So has Col. Lansdale, chief of counter-intelligence. Lansdale shares my view that Oppenheimer is a security risk. But the Boss overruled us. Ordered that Oppenheimer be issued a security clearance on his authority. He believes that Oppenheimer is loyal. I don't share that view. General Groves also believes that Oppenheimer's high profile will place him under the tightest of scrutiny and leave little room for ....." Pash grouped for the right word.

"You're not suggesting Oppenheimer might pass information to the enemy are you, Sir?"

"The enemy? And who do you suppose that might be, Major? I'm not suggesting the Germans for Christsakes. I'm suggesting the Communists, the Soviets."

Pash was getting worked up. I chose to say nothing and let him get to wherever he was leading.

"Perhaps you are not aware, but I'm also Russian. I was born here in the United States but I returned as a young man with my parents to Russia before World War One. After the Revolution, I fought with the *Whites* against the Bolsheviks. Obviously that cause was lost and I returned to the United States. I hate the Communist ideology. Stalin himself has no ideology. He's simply a dictator. Stalin is no friend of the United States. His alliance with us is just a convenience no different than his non-aggression pact with Hitler in '39. Stalin with an atomic bomb would be just as bad as Hitler."

I swallowed hard. To think my parents were early Bolsheviks, now sympathizers with the Soviet regime gave me pause to wonder if my background was buried deeply enough.

"I'm asking that you keep your eyes open," Pash said. "You'll be working alongside these scientists. In a social environment, they may reveal certain sympathies. Frankly I don't trust the politics of many of them. I expect you to report anything of even remote interest to me directly."

Did that mean bypassing Groves? I was not going to ask either Pash or Groves for clarification. My job was becoming ever more complex. Developing a rapport with the scientists was essential to my being successful. I had no intention of passing along gossip to Col. Pash.

J. Robert Oppenheimer

CHAPTER 10

LOS ALAMOS, NEW MEXICO – 1943

THE RANCH SCHOOL was vacated in February. It was now early April. Oppenheimer and some staff had already arrived. They had been working out of Santa Fe until construction at the site had advanced. I also arrived in Santa Fe in March, this time by train. It was a two day journey that allowed some rest before launching into my new assignment. The closest rail station was ten miles to the south of the city at a flyspeck place called Lamy. The rail station consisted of one small building housing a waiting room and the station master's office. Nothing else was around. It looked like a throwback to the old west of the last century. Two young men in civilian suits disembarked the train with me.

One man, the younger one in his twenties, said to the other, "My God. This is where we're supposed to work? What happened to the majestic West? This is more like the armpit of the West."

"I'm sure they'll have a proper place for us to work," the older of the two said with the tinge of a European accent.

All three of us stood there for ten minutes looking around. There was no one else about even though it was nine o'clock in the morning. A brown army sedan soon drove up, slamming to a halt in a cloud of dust. A young private jumped out.

Running up to me, the soldier saluted and said, "Sorry I'm late, Major. Had a flat tire. The road's real bad going up the mountain. Let me take your bag, Sir. Are these the other guys I'm to pick up?"

"I don't know, soldier," I said. "You'd better ask them."

The soldier walked over to the two men, "Mr. Wilson and Mr. Fine?"

"That's us," The younger man said. He obviously had a mischievous side. "Not sure which of us is who though."

We were all headed to the same place. I had been told that the scientists all travelled under assumed names. I shook hands with Mr. Wilson and Mr. Fine, and then we piled into the car.

Twenty minutes later we arrived at 109 East Palace Avenue in the quaint town of Santa Fe, New Mexico. As much of a backwater as Santa Fe was, it would be nothing like the austerity I suspected Los Alamos to be. General Groves was a no-frills guy used to constructing functional army facilities. Mr. Wilson and Mr. Fine shouldn't get their hopes up by the agreeable impression of Santa Fe.

109 East Palace was the gateway to Los Alamos thirty-five miles away. There was no official notification on the door. It was here that security passes to Los Alamos were issued. The reception office was staffed by Dorothy McKibbon, a charming woman in her forties. Not only was McKibbon the first person to greet all new workers and visitors to Site Y, but eventually she would became a confident and fixer of all manner of personal problems. McKibbon was Oppenheimer's great find. Everyone eventually loved this pleasant energetic woman.

Armed with our photo-identity badges, we bundled back into the car for the drive to the site.

"Since we're all going to the same place are we allowed to introduce ourselves with our real names, Major?" Mr. Fine asked.

"Not sure since I'm not involved with security. But I don't know what the private here is cleared for so it's probably best to observe the rules," I said.

The photo security badges contained only a letter and a number with apparently no correlation to the name. Once at Los Alamos, I learned my companion's real names. Richard Feynman, aka Fine held identification number I-11. Victor Weisskopf, aka Wilson was O-9.

The ride took more than an hour over unpaved Highway 4 after it left the main highway north of Santa Fe. The road was pocked with continuous ruts so the ride was uncomfortable. As a civil engineer I wondered about the practical difficulties of supplying this remote outpost over this road. Constrained by security rules, there was little conversation. I could see the two scientists were not happy about the prospects of where they were going.

As we pulled up to the small building at the main gate to Site Y, Mr. Fine said, "Looks like a prison compound." He was more right than he knew. A prison still under construction.

There were a couple of hundred construction workers working over several acres. A sea of tents occupied an area in the distance. I assumed these were for the construction workers, hoping we would have something more hospitable. March at this elevation of 7000 feet brought very cold nights. I recalled from my initial visit that the former school had a number of buildings. I assumed they would be used for accommodations for the initial scientific staff. Commuting the difficult thirty-five miles to Santa Fe was not a workable option.

At the main gate we all entered the small guard building. Once the duty sergeant signed us in he instructed our driver to take us to the Director's house.

The former Los Alamos Ranch School Arts and Crafts Building was a spacious single story building that made an elegant house. Oppenheimer had adopted it as his residence, particularly since it was large enough to provide intimate social gatherings. Oppenheimer knew that the social element would be critical to developing a functioning team given the remoteness of Los Alamos. Oppenheimer himself opened the door and greeted us effusively.

He remembered me. "Major. Good to see you again. And congratulations on your new assignment with us. Good to have you. General Groves apparently thinks highly of you."

Turning to the scientists and shaking their hands as he ushered us in, Oppenheimer said, "Dr. Weisskopf. Good to meet you. I'm familiar with your work in quantum electrodynamics. Some ground-breaking material you've hit upon. I want to discuss some thoughts as soon as we can."

Turning to the young Feynman, "And Dr. Feynman. For someone so young, you're already making a mark in this same area. I read your work, *The Principle of Least Action in Quantum Mechanics*. Impressive work. I welcome you both to our club."

"You'll stay for lunch. We were expecting you. Kitty, come greet our newest colleagues."

Oppenheimer could be the most gracious of hosts. When he wanted to charm, he was irresistible. He held each of the scientists with the gaze of his intense blue eyes conveying the sense that each was warmly regarded. Women swooned, men felt exalted.

A maid, Native American by her dark complexion, was setting the dining room table.

A petite brunette in an angora sweater and tailored slacks came out of the kitchen. "Hi. I'm Kitty." She shook everyone's hand. "Please come sit down. Robert you're over there. Mary's prepared an excellent venison stew. The plentiful wild game makes for an interesting cuisine. By the way, where is Hans, Robert?"

A fire blazed in the fireplace of the large living room. The house was tastefully decorated. The thought of working in the wilderness was at least momentarily dispelled for Weisskopf and Feynman.

As Kitty Oppenheimer asked, there was a knock at the door. The maid answered. In walked Hans Bethe, recognizable to the two new scientists with his distinctive, impossibly high forehead accentuated by a receding hair line. He was a large man in a rumpled suit with his tie slightly askew. In German-accented English he said, "Excuse me for being late, Kitty."

Hans Bethe was a noted German scientist that escaped the Nazis in 1933. Among the international community of physicists, he was held in high esteem. Well liked by his colleagues, Oppenheimer picked him to head the crucial Theoretical Physics Division for the Project.

The new arrivals were suitably impressed, as was I being in such exalted presence. But with lunch over, it was down to work for the rest of the day.

"Hans will see that you get set up with some place to stay. It's a little cramped right now until the new dormitories are completed, but you'll make do," Oppenheimer said. "He'll introduce you to the rest of the team. Tomorrow, Robert Serber will give his first in a series of lectures. It will layout the scope of the project. The science as we know it right now, the challenges, how we're to go about creating this thing."

Our driver dropped me off at the base commander's office and then took the scientists to their temporary quarters in one of the ranch school cabins. Since this was a military post, I was obligated to check in. Technically I should have done that first thing upon arrival.

Colonel John Harman took my salute and offered his hand.

"Welcome, Major. Have a seat. From your orders, I understand you'll be in and out of here frequently. At least you will get some reprieve from this nuthouse."

"It's certainly a little unusual, Colonel. An army base full of civilians."

"Groves wanted to put all of these scientists in uniform but that went over like a fart in church. Oppenheimer was ok with the idea but everyone else raised a shit-storm. The problem is we're expected to keep these monkeys locked away here. They're not allowed to send correspondence out with their real names. Everyone has the same address; P.O. Box 1663, Santa Fe. Trips to Santa Fe are infrequent. But the wives are the worse. Every day is a parade of them with complaints. And there's only a few of them right now. I'm told many more are coming along, and with children to boot. I'll be running a fucking town with the highest security level anywhere."

I had little to offer in the way of consolation. The Colonel sounded a bit overwhelmed and his command was only a few months old. I would be expected to report my observations and my recommendations to Groves. What kind of officer could handle this job anyway? Obviously the interactions of the civilians and the military would be vital to the Project's success.

"The biggest issue is about how the scientists go about their work. I don't need to tell you about Groves' idea of strict compartmentalization for security," Harman said. "He's adamant about it. Wanted every scientist to confine himself to only his area of expertise. No sharing of information with others from different technical areas. The scientists said that would not work, or they didn't intend to work like that at any rate. Oppenheimer himself said they couldn't work under such restrictions if they were to get the job done. He and I went round and round on the subject. But Oppenheimer doesn't work for me. I finally told him to take it up with Groves himself."

"So who won?" I asked.

"Oppenheimer. Groves ultimately had little choice unless he replaced Oppenheimer. That of course would not be possible without risking wholesales rebellion among the scientists. Oppenheimer's not only respected but well liked. Groves is not happy about it. So he's leaned on me to make sure that whatever goes on here stays here. Makes for a difficult situation with civilians."

Even with Harman's office door closed we were distracted by a female raising her voice in the outer office. "Sergeant, I need to see the Colonel."

"Mrs. Serber, the Colonel is in a meeting at the moment. Perhaps I can help," the duty sergeant said.

Colonel Harman responded with a sigh. "Christ. It's that bitch again, Charlotte Serber. She's got an acid tongue and a complaint about everything. She's the self-appointed spokeswoman for all the wives. This is what I'm talking about. So I'll leave you to get on with your duties, Major, while I see what's on her mind this time."

Later on, I became good friends with Charlotte Serber and her physicist husband, Robert, a protégée of Robert Oppenheimer. I was intent on doing my part to bridge the animosity between the civilians and the Army. My report to Groves recommended that Col. Harman be replaced immediately.

The following day I shared breakfast in a mess tent. The tent was drafty but the early spring cold was tempered by heaters strategically spaced around the tent. I sat next to young Feynman who was working on a plate of eggs and bacon.

"Well, Dr. Feynman, what do you think about this place?" I said.

"The food's pretty good. But I was right, it really is a prison. Seems escape from here is on a highly limited and controlled basis," Feynman said.

"Other than spectacular scenery, there's not much close by anyway, Doctor. Santa Fe sure isn't much of place," I said. "Are you married?"

"Oh, yes. Two years now."

"Will your wife be joining you here at Los Alamos?"

Feynman paused and set down his coffee mug. "I'm afraid not. You see, my wife Arline has tuberculosis. We're thinking about her coming out to Albuquerque so we can see each other at least occasionally. The doctors believe the dry high desert air will be good for her. But Los Alamos would be out of the question for fear of contagion."

"I'm very sorry to hear that, Doctor. I hope the climate helps her. Certainly makes your sacrifice locked away up here all the more difficult."

I actually new about Feynman's wife but didn't want to be associated as part of military security. I had been given a list of the scientists currently at Los Alamos. It briefly listed their essential personal information of date of birth, marital status, educational background and their latest area of work. Two facts stuck out. The senior scientists were in their thirties, with a few in their early forties. The majority however were younger. It pointed to the birth of modern-day theoretical physics with the pioneering work of Max Planck and Albert Einstein in the early part of the century. Most of the Los Alamos senior scientists were born between 1900 and 1909. Richard Feynman was the exception at age 25, more the age of the recent doctorial students recruited to the Project.

The second startling fact was the ethnic background of these scientists that represented the best minds in physics internationally. The majority of them were from Europe. Most had received their doctorates at the German Universities of Göttingen, Berlin, Munich, or Leipzig. All had been forced to leave in the early thirties with the rise of Adolf Hitler's Nazi Party. All of them came from Jewish backgrounds. The realization struck me that had

Hitler not pursued a genocidal obsession against Jews, these scientists would still be under Nazi control. There would be no viable U.S. effort to develop an atomic bomb. Hitler would clearly beat us to it. Even others such as Albert Einstein and Leo Szilard, who drafted the famous letter to President Roosevelt, were European Jews. Enrico Fermi, the brilliant experiment physicist heading the work in Chicago, was forced to leave fascist Italy since his wife came from a Jewish background.

Even now, there was serious concern that Nazi Germany may be substantially ahead of the U.S. in developing the bomb. Still in Germany were the towering intellects of quantum physics, Werner Heisenberg and Wolfgang Pauli. Many of the Los Alamos scientists, including Oppenheimer himself, were former colleagues of Heisenberg, Pauli, and others still in Germany. They knew full well the capabilities of these scientists. They also knew Germany had been actively working on development of fissile nuclear materials for some time. Heavy water, deuterium oxide, had potential use in a reactor to produce weapons-grade plutonium. The Germans appeared to be actively pursuing a parallel research.

The first lectures to present the Project's overview were to begin at nine o'clock in the library reading room of one of the first constructed buildings in the designated 'Technical Area'. About fifty scientists filed into the library of the building where the theoretical physicists had offices. The building was still under construction. Hammering could be heard from the second floor. Even the library was yet to have any books. There were maybe twenty senior scientists and an equal number of other younger scientists and engineers. These were some of the most talented younger generation recruited from doctorial programs, or just starting their post-graduate research work. Additionally there were a handful of VIP's. Besides me, there was only one other military officer, a Navy captain who I later learned was actually an accomplished engineer. We were seated in folding chairs facing a large blackboard.

Robert Oppenheimer made a brief introduction. "I believe you all know Dr. Robert Serber. I have worked with Dr. Serber for many years and felt he would be the best qualified to present an overview of the project. Contrary to General Groves wish to conduct our work along compartmentalized areas, the General has ceded that the objective can only be accomplished with shared knowledge of other areas of the work. That process will start with this series of lectures by Dr. Serber.

"We are embarking upon an unprecedented challenge. We not only need to develop the science, but we then need to translate that into practical engineering. While there are substantial efforts going on around the country, those are for the express purpose of supporting the efforts that will go on here. I appreciate the personal sacrifice that everyone is making. There is no need to dwell on the urgency of our task. Whether Nazi Germany is actively pursuing the same result is not known. What can be assumed however is that someone, some country, will eventually develop a nuclear weapon. The advances in theoretical work, as well as experimental results in the last several years, make that a certainty. We all agree it must be the United States that gets there first. Dr. Serber."

"Thank you Dr. Oppenheimer. Let me first frame the objective. Our task is to produce a practical military weapon in the form of a bomb in which the binding energy of the atomic nucleus is released by a fast neutron chain reaction in one or more of the materials known to show nuclear fission.

"That will be a daunting task. We need to better understand fast-neutron fission. In particular, we need to develop our understanding of the various nuclear cross sections. That data can only be ascertained through experimentation. What are the critical masses of uranium and plutonium? How do we experimentally approach a fast-neutron chain reaction in the laboratory without blowing up this whole place? We know comparatively little about the metallurgy of uranium and even less about plutonium. Then we have the task of developing a weapons design. That will require employing conventional chemical explosives in entirely new ways."

Serber's defining of the challenges was sobering. I wasn't even a scientist and I felt the task perhaps impossible within an imposed deadline.

Serber launched into the substance of his lecture.

"Let's begin with the foundation of what this is about. That is specifically the release of energy on a large scale due to a fast neutron chain reaction of a fissile material. That fission process results from the absorption of a single neutron resulting in a splitting of the fissile material nucleus into fast-moving lighter elements, and the resulting releasing of free neutrons. The process continues exponentially increasing the rate of neutron release. The potential of a kilogram of uranium-235 would theoretically release energy equivalent to 20,000 tons of TNT."

Those not privy to the underlying work were stunned. Such destructive force was difficult to envision. It put the scope of the project into perspective.

"While that provides a sense of magnitude, in practice that would not happen. First of all, some neutrons will be lost through the surface. But the real problem is containing the chain reaction long enough for the multiple generations of fissions to take place without this great ball of gas expanding too quickly and simply fizzling with the whole thing just flying apart.

"The direct energy release in a fission process is on the order of 170 Mev per atom. That is considerably more than 10^7 times the heat of reaction per atom in ordinary combustion processes. Therefore an atomic bomb would yield an energy release on the order of tens of millions of times that of a chemical explosion of an equivalent amount of material.

"It will take considerably more than one kilogram of uranium-235 of course to create a critical mass. How much? That has yet to be determined. How are the freed neutrons to be utilized, reflected back into the core as it were? That also has not been determined. So you can see, gentlemen, these are just some of the basic design challenges to constructing a bomb."

Another scientist approached Serber and whispered something in his ear.

"Yes, I understand," Serber said. Turning back to his audience, "Oppie would like me to cease using the term 'bomb' for security reasons. That goes for everyone else as well from here on out. As you can hear, there are many workmen about. I'm told the word 'gadget' will be the operative substitute."

To punctuate that security concern, a short time later a workman's leg broke through the thin beaverboard overhead between the room's ceiling joists.

Serber continued. "In a fast neutron chain reaction, it would take 80 generations of fissions to consume a whole kilogram of hypothetically pure fissile material. That propagation of reactions would occur in less than a millionth of a second. However, in an actual setup, some neutrons are lost by diffusion out through the surface. Therefore, there will be a certain size of say a sphere for which the surface losses of neutrons are just sufficient to stop the chain reaction. The radius depends upon the density. As the reaction proceeds, the material tends to expand because of the extraordinary temperatures generated, billions of degrees Celsius, increasing the required minimum size faster than the actual size increases.

"The whole question of whether an effective explosion is made depends upon on whether the reaction is stopped by this tendency before an appreciable fraction of the material is transformed into energy by fission."

Serber launched into the fundamental challenges. His points were annotated by formulas scrawled in chalk on the blackboard. I vaguely understood the basic concepts until Serber got into the much deeper aspects of nuclear science. Even with my abilities in higher mathematics, his equations soon left me in the dark. I would clearly need tutoring to sufficiently explain project progress in my reports to General Groves. I wondered if even he understood the science. Regardless, he would expect me to understand.

"The materials of interest are uranium-238, uranium-235, and the manmade element plutonium isotope 239. Central to our needs is the commonly occurring U-238. U-238 contains less than one percent of the lighter isotope U-235. U-235 is required to create a weapon. And therein lays the real challenge. Methods of enriching, or increasing the concentration of U-235, are not much developed beyond the theoretical stage. The task is to enrich uranium from a 0.7% natural concentration to over 80%. Only laboratory level experimentation exists. We will need processes capable of industrial scale production.

"Two such methods hold the best promise. Separation by gaseous diffusion is one such method whereby U-238 is converted to a gas. The process relies on the different rates of diffusion across a porous barrier to separate U-235. Unfortunately, the difference is very slight requiring a successive cascade of thousands of barriers to achieve sufficient concentration through repetitive cycling. Work has started on such a plant in Tennessee. The scale of the plant will be staggeringly large.

"An alternative process is electromagnetic separation that relies on the fact that an electrically charged atom traveling through a magnetic field moves in a circle at a radius determined my its mass. Ions of a vaporous uranium compound projected through a magnetic field inside a curved vacuum tank separate into two beams with the lighter U-235 following a narrower arc than the heavier U-238. The concept is derived from Dr. Ernest Lawrence's cyclotron at the University of California. It is a laborious, inefficient process as well. Magnetics of the size required have never been created.

"The third element is the artificially created plutonium-239. It must be produced in a reactor. In a reactor, fission neutrons are slowed in graphite and some are captured in the U-238 producing the isotope U-239. Since a neutron is added, the atomic weight increases by one. Later I will discuss the complexities of transformation in greater detail, but here are the basic equations."

Serber chalked a string of equations on the blackboard as he identified the mathematical basis of each. I was again quickly out of my element. Pointing to various parts of the math on the board, he continued, "In simplest terms the U-239 beta decays to neptunium-239, which in turn decays to plutonium-239 needed for a weapon. The resulting quantity of plutonium is however very small. A chemical separation process on a production scale will be pursued on a site being constructed in the State of Washington. Bear in mind that the knowhow to construct reactors is still in its infancy. Dr. Fermi is of course spearheading that work.

"One can see that while we have the daunting task here of developing a weapons design, monumental challenges exist to creating the means to produce sufficient fissile material."

Even with my education as a civil engineer, the complexity of the project was bewildering. Not only did scientific challenges remain, but the engineering required to produce sufficient fissile material was on a scale never before attempted. Actually achieving success in creating an atomic bomb seemed a nearly impossible undertaking. That of course would not be the conclusion I stated in my reports to Groves.

Elena Obolensky

CHAPTER 11

WASHINGTON D.C. – 1943

I RETURNED TO Washington D.C. in June. I had spent six weeks at Los Alamos and another two at Oak Ridge, Tennessee. I presented my reports on a range of subjects to General Groves. I was the first one to deliver transcripts of Robert Serber's five lectures, puckishly titled *The Los Alamos Primer.* I had spent considerable time studying them, seeking out various scientists to explain the meaning in layman language. Serber himself was a great help in this regard. I expected the General would probe my knowledge of the science. He also expected my assessment.

"You know I was against this sort of thing for obvious security reasons," Groves said holding up the mimeographed sheaf of *Los Alamos Primer* papers. "Oppenheimer was insistent to the point of rebellion. What's your opinion as to the value of collaboration across functional lines?"

"I spent considerable time with the scientists for over a month, Sir. Oppenheimer has organized his lab into specialized areas. Theoretical, experimental, ordinance, and chemistry," I said.

"I'm aware of that, Major. My question was about the effectivity of everyone knowing the whole scope of the Project."

"Yes, Sir. I observed how they interacted. I can't comment on the value of the technical exchanges between the different groups, but it was clear the approach created an energy, an excitement. Everyone could better see the contribution of their individual work. It definitely promoted the concept of a team. I believe this is how the scientific academic world works. It seems particularly necessary in this new science of theoretical physics."

Groves looked at me as if he was about to take my head off. It probably wasn't the answer he was looking for. Without comment he veered onto another subject.

"Your thoughts on Dr. Serber?"

"He's a first-rate physicist. Not only does Oppenheimer think highly of him, but he has the respect of the other senior scientists. He is able to explain the challenges to any level of depth required. His lectures were well received. The audience was always very attentive."

"You know that Colonel Pash thinks he's a closet Communist. The wife is perhaps even more left-leaning. They lobbied against allowing them on the Project. I overruled them based upon Oppenheimer's insistence."

That was perhaps a small victory for me by validating the boss' decision.

"Your comments on the base commander are critical. You believe he's a problem?"

I learned to not equivocate in my reports. Groves did not tolerate bureaucratically cloudy language or ass-covering.

"Yes, Sir. There is continual friction between the military command and the civilians. There is continued friction between Dr. Oppenheimer and Captain de Silva the head security. That probably is to be expected at this early stage. But Col. Harman is not able to find common ground and manage the situation effectively. It's only going to get worse as more scientists arrive. The addition of more families will make it an even more difficult command."

"And you recommend?" Groves asked although I know he read my recommendations stated in the report.

"Concentrate on isolating Los Alamos. Limit outside contacts and trips off the Hill. As to what goes on in the scientific work inside the Technical Area, let Oppenheimer operate as he sees fit. There is little choice if they are to be successful. To accomplish that, you need a different military commander to keep the peace. The guy has to be a real diplomat. More than that, he has to be highly adaptable. He'll have to define how to manage this entirely unique situation."

"Effective yesterday, Col. Harman has been replaced. The new base commander is Lt. Col. Whitney Ashbridge. We'll see if he has the necessary skills."

That was Groves way of saying he was way ahead of the situation. That was pretty much my meeting with Groves after two months of work. Obviously he read my entire report. Agreeing with my recommendations without acknowledgement was typical Groves. The fact that he didn't criticize some part of my work was an astounding feat. Groves usually criticized everything.

I was told I would be in Washington for a week before going to the Radiation Laboratory in California, then on to Oak Ridge, Tennessee before returning to Los Alamos. Would seem I should go to Tennessee first than to California, but that wasn't Groves' way. I had two days leave before attacking a stack of procurement bottlenecks and construction schedules. The University of California had been awarded the managerial contract for Los Alamos. While they had no direct involvement over the scientific work, procurement flowed through them. Groves pointedly told me they needed help. I was to fix it.

Jean O'Leary walked out of Groves' office along with me.

"I would say that went very well, Major Voronin," she said smiling at me. I'm sure she pitied the staff that frequently got their ass chewed by the General. "It's raining cats and dogs outside, Major. Take this umbrella."

I thanked Jean. It was a Friday and I had the whole weekend to relax. Even the rain didn't dampen my euphoria. I took the elevator down to the first floor. Looking outside through the large glass doors I saw that it was raining very hard. The wind seemed to be driving it at an angle.

I opened the umbrella and stepped outside. This was a real downpour. I started down the steps of the front of the War Department Building toward 21st Street. Once outside the protection of the portico under the tall columns, the rain hit full force.

Ahead of me the wind had apparently taken a poor woman's umbrella collapsing it the wrong way. She struggled to repair the failed mechanism as the rain drenched her hair. I rushed down the steps to help.

"Oh, shit!" she said then turned to look at me as I shielded her with my umbrella. "Oh, thank you so much. This is something awful."

She on the other hand was something extraordinary. Even with her hair plastered to her head I thought her terrifically beautiful. Conspicuously ample breasts with her coat belted tightly. Large blue eyes. Full lips with red lipstick.

"Glad to help. Where are you headed?" I asked.

"Home. By bus. Oh no! My bus is leaving!"

She started to run from under the umbrella.

I followed quickly behind her and yelled, "Wait, you can't catch it."

"Damn. It'll be another hour before the next bus. I'll wait inside. Thank you so much for helping, Major ....."

"Voronin. Mikhail Voronin. Mike to my friends."

"Ah, a good Russian name. And I'm Elena Obolensky," she said offering her hand. "My God I must look like a drowned rat."

"Hardly that. If I'm not being too forward, could I offer you a ride? I have a staff car at my disposal."

She looked at me as if measuring whether she should accept the offer. "That would be wonderful but I don't want to trouble you."

"It's certainly no trouble. It's a little bit of a walk to the parking area though."

She took my arm and bent close to me to share the protection from the rain. I could smell her perfume. It had been some time since I was this close to a pretty woman.

I arranged for an allocated staff car from the motor pool. While I signed for the olive drab Chevrolet, the sergeant could not take his eyes off Elena Obolensky. Actually it was her well endowed chest that riveted the soldier's attention. As for me, I was feeling pretty important. Here I had the use of an army car in war-rationed Washington, accompanying a very pretty girl for a perhaps a night on the town if I were lucky. She was not wearing a wedding ring.

Elena told me she worked as a secretary for the Office of War Mobilization. They had begun moving into the War Department Building since the newly completed Pentagon would accommodate the growing requirement for military headquarters space currently occupying the building. She said she roomed with another government secretary. They had a second floor apartment in a neighborhood of row houses on 19th Street, north of DuPont Circle.

"Some weather. My roommate Alice and I were thinking about going out tonight but not in this weather."

I couldn't resist the obvious hint. "Would you and your friend consider going to dinner with me?"

"Gosh, I don't know. I don't even know you."

"You'd certainly be doing me a favor. I've been on assignment out of Washington non-stop for at least three months. I've now got a hard-earned leave for the weekend before I'm off again. No fun spending it alone before I get back to the War. Besides, you'll have your friend along if she agrees. What do'ya say?"

"Oh, Alice will surely agree once I offer drinks and dinner with a good looking soldier, with a car to boot. So ok, you've talked me into it. You seem like a nice guy. You've got to give us girls a bit of time to get fixed up though. Especially to dry my hair and repair my makeup."

I pulled up at her address. "Can you give us an hour, Major?"

"No problem. And call me Mike."

I returned to my assigned bachelor officer quarters at Fort Myer across the Potomac River adjacent to the Arlington National Cemetery. After a quick shower and shave, I put on a clean starched tunic. This was the first time I had been on a date while on my brief stints in the Capital. It was also my first real date in a considerably long time.

An hour to the minute I returned to Elena's apartment. The rain had reduced to a light drizzle and the sun had just set. Inside the entryway I looked for Elena's name on the mailbox.

After just one knock the apartment door was opened. It was the roommate, Alice.

"Oh my! It's your handsome soldier, Elena. Come on in. Mike, right?" Alice said extending her hand and pulling me into the room. She was brasher than Elena. Not quite as pretty but I suspected she was a real partier. "You're right, Elena, he's a real hunk."

I blushed. Elena came out from the bedroom. "Alice, behave yourself. You act like he's the first man you've seen in a long time when it's been only two days since your last date."

"Huh. That guy was just a kid, a mere lieutenant. Now Mike here is something closer to a general, or a colonel, or something high up. I can't keep these ranks straight."

Elena piped in, "Especially when you add the Navy to the mix with its whole different set of ranks. Alice is a popular girl. She gets around."

"Now don't be giving Mike the wrong impression. I like a good time but I'm certainly not some sort of loose woman," Alice said. "I just like good looking men, good food, good booze, and a good time."

"See what you got yourself into, Mike," Elena said with a smile.

"We'll have a swell time. And Alice doesn't scare me," I said, also with a smile.

"Then off we go boys and girls," Alice said. "Where to?" She grabbed both Elena and I by an arm.

Elena looked at me. I said, "You girls choose. You know Washington. I don't. Pick a nice place. Both of you are dressed for it. It's my treat."

"What about Harvey's, next to the Mayflower? I've never been. I'd love some oysters," Alice said.

"We can't take advantage of Mike. That's a real swanky place," Elena said.

"Is it a good place?" I asked.

"I guess," Elena said. "It's been there forever I'm told. A place where the movers and shakers like to go."

"Then Harvey's it is." I said.

Harvey's was indeed a nice place. We entered and looked over the finely set tables and crystal chandeliers. White-coated waiters moved about. The maître d' wore a tuxedo. I wondered how much this was going to cost me.

Most of the diners were couples. Many of the men were in uniform, most outranking me. Some tables just had two or more men. Wartime Washington was always doing business. From those male groupings I caught discreet stares because of my two pretty ladies. Whatever the bill, it would be worth it.

We ordered cocktails. Manhattan's for the ladies which I thought appropriate. A martini for me. Dr. Oppenheimer had introduced me to his specialty cocktail in Los Alamos.

"What does that insignia mean, Mike? The little castle on your lapel?" Elena asked.

"I'm in the Army Corps of Engineers. I'm attached to the Manhattan Engineering District, but it's now headquartered here in Washington."

"You build things then?" Elena said.

"In a way. I'm a civil engineer. You know buildings, bridges, roads, dams. Lots of building going on with the war mobilization. But I guess you'd know all about that with your job. My job's to see that things are going according to schedule, so I travel around a lot."

The ladies and I had a couple of drinks. Alice had a few more than Elena and I. She could put the booze away. Dinner was superb. Even after wincing upon receiving the bill, I gauged it a fine experience. The girls were good company. More than that, Elena kept smiling warmly at me.

Alice was from Ohio and worked as a secretary in the office of the senior senator from that state. Elena surprised me when she said she was Canadian, from Montreal. She even impressed me with a few phrases in French. I too knew a little French since both my parents were fluent in the language, with French being important in Russian classical studies. She said her father was a chemist and worked for DuPont outside of Wilmington, Delaware, a couple of hours drive north of Washington. He was transferred from Montreal a little over a year ago.

From Harvey's we went to a nightclub close to where the girls lived. Alice knew the place well. It was loud, smoky, with beer rather than cocktails the preferred drink. Everyone was young. Almost all the men were in uniform. Not too many were officers.

We lost Alice right away as she planted a kiss on the bartender's cheek. Elena and I found a vacant table. The music was fast tempo swing. The dance floor was full.

"This is Alice's favorite place," Elena said. "I've only been here once before. I think it's gotten even nosier."

Alice took a soldier at the bar by the hand and dragged him onto the dance floor.

"Do you dance, Mike?"

A feeling of dread passed through me. "Not this energetic swing stuff. Maybe a waltz, but I'm not much of dancer."

"Me either. I like music though. And you?" Elena said.

"Oh yes."

"Who do you like?"

"Ah ..... The Andrew Sisters. Judy Garland. Jo Stafford."

"And I like the male singers. Frank Sinatra's my favorite. But I like the bands too. Duke Ellington most of all."

"That's what I listen to mostly; Tommy Dorsey, Artie Shaw, Glenn Miller."

Elena looked at me and smiled. "How about we leave this racket and go somewhere quieter with music we both like?"

"What about Alice?" I asked. Having Elena to myself was a pleasing prospect.

"Alice? Look at her. She won't miss us. She'll have guys fighting to escort her home. Besides, the apartment's close by and the rain looks like it has stopped. I'll just go tell her she's on her own."

Elena corralled Alice on the dance floor and said something close to Alice's ear. I settled the bill for the drinks. In a few minutes we were back into my car. Ten minutes later, Elena had me park close to a bar called Sugar's.

Sugar's was a homey place full of couples on this Friday night. An older clientele, less uniforms. An all black jazz quartet was playing at the end of the room.

"This is very nice," I said. "We can talk and hear each other too."

We both had plenty to drink over the course of the evening. I suggested brandies and coffee.

"So what did you do in Canada, Elena?"

"Went to school. McGill University. Got my degree in history. Taught high school for a couple of years."

"Is that what you want to do, be a teacher?"

"Goodness no. At least not teaching high school. Found that out. I was preparing to go back to school to get a graduate degree to pursue some other career when the war broke out. Last year Dad was offered a transfer to the DuPont plant at Carneys Point, New Jersey. So I chose to come to the States with them. I wasn't keen on Wilmington, Delaware though. After Montreal, it was something of a backwater. High time I was getting out on my own anyway. Washington was an obvious choice. I came here only six months ago. Lots of jobs, lots of excitement. With the War, it's the center of everything."

"Where are you from, Mike?"

"California. Southern California. Went to college in Los Angeles."

"Oh my. How exciting. Is California like in the pictures?"

"You mean photographs or the movies?"

We both laughed. "It's actually not either stereotype. Sure it's warmer, but you get a lot of haze that makes the sky gray. They've given it a new name; smog. It's caused by smoke pollutants and the natural fog from being close to the ocean. Rain in the winter. Brush fires. The occasional earthquake."

"The earthquakes would scare me to death."

"They're infrequent. Most are uneventful. If you're in a house you're pretty safe. Any wood frame structure won't fail even with a strong quake. They usually last just a few seconds anyway."

"What about that big quake years ago? Did you experience that one?"

"Oh ya. The 1933 Long Beach earthquake. That was definitely an exception. I was in college. My first year. I was having dinner at the cafeteria about six o'clock on a Friday when it hit. That did scare everyone, me included. The building shook something awful for a long time. Made a mess of the cafeteria but there was no structural damage. It was only about fifteen miles north of Long Beach."

"See what I mean," Elena said. "You'll probably think me forward for asking, but there's no special girl back home?"

"No. And there's no real 'back home'. Once I left college I got a job in the State of Washington. Worked on the Grand Coulee Dam for almost two years before joining the Army. Before I graduated from college, my parents returned to Russia. So California held no attachment other than good weather."

"Your parents returned to Russia? That's pretty unusual. Why return? Aren't things even tougher there?"

"Certainly appears that way now. I used to get regular letters. None for a long time now. The War is closer at hand than here. My father was a professor in classical studies. He lost his college teaching job during the Depression. Couldn't find work. Through contacts in the old country, he was able to secure a position at Moscow State University where he worked before coming to America. He and mother were still very much part of Russia so returning held emotional appeal. Of course there wasn't a war going on in 1935."

"My parents also emigrated from Russia," Elena said. "In 1925. Things apparently went better for my parents in Canada. My father's been with DuPont since he came there. The Company has always done well. Now with the War, DuPont is even busier. My father was just lucky for finding the opportunity."

"And you were born in Russia?"

"No. I was born in Canada. I'm twenty-four so you don't have to wonder. My birth parents died when I was four. They were also Russian immigrants. Boris and Vanya adopted me from an orphanage. I kept my birth parents surname. So in my heart I'm Russian as well."

In Russian, I asked if she spoke Russian. She responded with a smile and, "Да, но не очень хорошо."

"Очень хорошо," I said complimenting her.

"I'm certainly better off with English. I only practice Russian with my parents. But back to you. There's no special girl waiting somewhere? I guess I'm a little obvious asking that again."

The memory of Joanne Cartwright returned briefly, but she wasn't waiting for him. "Definitely not. Never had the time. I've had to move about constantly these last couple of years. Not even many dates these last few years."

Elena laid her hand over mine. "There's no one special in my life either. Just so you know."

Her touch sent a current through me. I suddenly realized how aroused she made me. I wondered if I was blushing.

Elena looked in my eyes intently. "I don't want any more to drink. I really like being with you, Mike. Could just the two of us be together?"

I had no idea where this was leading. Other than returning to her apartment, where could we be alone? I did not dare to ask as I settled the bar tab and took her arm. Outside, as I opened the car door, she turned and took my face in both of her hands and kissed me full on the lips. She said nothing and climbed into the seat.

I swallowed hard. My passion rising. Quickly I got in behind the wheel and engaged the engine. I looked over at Elena who was looking back at me. Her expression was intent.

"Where to?" I asked, probably sounding a little foolish with my feigned innocence.

She bent toward me and kissed me again. Without averting her stare, she said in a soft voice into my ear, "Let's go to my apartment."

I was glad it was only a short distance, still worried she might change her mind.

Elena did not change her mind. First she kissed me passionately then pushed me toward her bedroom, shutting the door behind us.

"What about Alice?" I asked.

"Alice won't be home for hours."

With that, she undressed me starting with my upper half. She continued to kiss me as she ran her hands over my bare chest. Pushing me back on the bed, she quickly pulled off my shoes and socks. By now, my erection was quite evident through my trousers. She brushed her hand over it lightly.

Standing, she then started to remove her own clothes. I was to watch. She unzipped her skirt and let it fall around her ankles. In garter belt and nylons, she unbuttoned then removed her blouse. Hooking her thumbs under the shoulder straps to her slip, she let it drop to the floor. Now in only undergarments, she stepped out of her heels. Unfastening the garter belt, she put her foot on my knee as she rolled down the stocking. After repeating the other leg, she looked at me and smiled as she reached behind and unfastened her bra.

She held the bra in place for a moment. Elena knew she had magnificent breasts. I watched entranced, anticipating. Pulling off the bra, she stood there with her hands on her hips for full effect.

Lastly, she removed her panties revealing dark pubic hair. Still insisting on controlling things, she unzipped my trousers. Pushing me back on the bed, she pulled them off along with my underwear.

What she did next, I had never experienced with a woman before. She got on her knees then took my erect penis fully into her mouth. The sensation was exquisite. Her hair fell over my thighs. As she worked me with her mouth, I feared I would not last very long.

Perhaps sensing I could not contain myself much longer, she climbed on top of me, guiding my erection into her with her hand. She was already moist as I entered her. Now I was looking up at those magnificent breasts. I grabbed her breasts in both hands. Her eyes closed as she began working back and forth. I could see her abdominal muscles tensing as she grasped me tightly inside of her.

I was not able to last as long as I feared she wanted when I climaxed with a great convulsion. The intensity was enhanced as her vagina gripped me harder, pulling every drop out of me. She shuddered and groaned with her own orgasm.

After almost falling asleep with Elena still on top of me, we agreed we should shower. Why not together? Washing me in the shower, Elena was able to get me hard again. Turning her back toward me, she bent over spreading her legs then guided me into her. I knew about this sexual position but it too was my first time. A whole new sensation with the seemingly deepened penetration. To my surprise, I was able to perform again to Elena's apparent delight as she let out a sound of approval and urged me deeper into her.

It was quite a night. After the shower, Elena would not let me leave. I was to spend the night. She would explain to Alice in the morning.

Morning came. It was a wonderful morning to wake to a naked Elena in bed. I dressed and Elena put on a robe. Alice's bedroom door was closed. We never heard her return the previous night, but after our lovemaking, that was understandable. We quietly made toast and coffee. Whispering, we made plans for the weekend. I would go back to my barracks for a change of clothes then return to the apartment at noon. Lunch and perhaps a drive to the countryside for the rest of Saturday? We left evening plans open but with the anticipation of renewed lovemaking. There also remained the prospects of spending Sunday together before I had to leave town again on Monday. That would now be terribly difficult.

I chastised myself for the self-pity. After all, the entire country was at war. Most soldiers were shipping out overseas for God knows how long. Cold food, no bed, no showers, no lovers. They were to confront an enemy trying to kill them. Here I was with a cushy stateside job. I could still go to restaurants, drink cocktails, and sleep with a pretty girl.

K-25 Gaseous Diffusion Plant, Oak Ridge, TN

CHAPTER 12

LOS ALAMOS, NEW MEXICO – 1943

I ARRIVED AT Oak Ridge, Tennessee after a week at the University of California Radiation Laboratory in Berkley. Ernest Lawrence won the Nobel Prize in 1939 for his work in high-energy particle physics using his invention of the cyclotron. Construction of the massive Y-12 electromagnetic separation process at Oak Ridge was based upon Lawrence's laboratory-sized cyclotron at Berkley. This technology was the first to be translated into an industrial-sized project on a gargantuan scale.

Fortunately I was able to catch military flights both to San Francisco and then from there to Knoxville, Tennessee. I was part of a group of radiation laboratory scientists and engineers from Stone & Webster the contractor for the Y-12 plant. Military flights were no frills but much easier than the endless hours spent on a cross-country train.

I was staying in a fleabag hotel in the small town of Clinton, Tennessee close to the area previously the site of the community of Oak Ridge. The Corps of Engineers had confiscated 56,000 acres including what had been the town. By March, 1943, all of the 3,000 inhabitants had been evicted and the area fenced in with checkpoints. The project was officially called the Clinton

Engineering Works, or just Oak Ridge. I was able to put a telephone call through to Elena using the one telephone in the hotel lobby.

"Elena, it's Mike. How are you?"

"Mike! Oh, my. It's swell to hear from you. Sounds like you're far away. Where are you?"

It was a poor connection with some static. Both had to raise their voices. "Afraid I can't say. Security you know. How've you been?"

"Fine. Same boring work at the office. You know how it is."

We kept up the small talk for several minutes. But I had to tell her why I really called. "Listen, Elena. We had a wonderful weekend a couple of weeks ago. Least I hope you thought so too."

"Oh I did, Mike. It was ..... Well, it was a really swell time."

"Well that's what I was calling about. I mean, I'd like to see you again."

"Me too. But are you going to be back in Washington soon?"

I hesitated. Even discussing my travel schedule was out of bounds as part of the Manhattan Engineering District. But it certainly couldn't reveal anything with my cover as an army engineer working on stateside construction projects.

"Maybe in a few weeks," I said. The thought of such a long time made me ache with desire.

At least I hoped so. My stint in Los Alamos was not well defined. Site Y was coming together as new scientists arrived. Newly constructed buildings would allow real work to commence soon.

Oppenheimer was creating the organizational structure of a weapons lab. Multiple areas of technical development were going on simultaneously. As advances were made, new sets of challenges became evident. As setbacks occurred, resources shifted. I was to help Groves make sense out of this complex mix. The success of the Project relied as much upon Groves management of resources as it did with Oppenheimer's development of the science.

For the moment, I was stuck in eastern Tennessee trying to understand the incredibly huge construction project of the Clinton Engineering Works. It would be the largest industrial project in the world. Equipment was being built before final designs were completed. Continual changes made for chaos. I was supposed to report on critical details that would affect the time to production. Since the processes were unproven at industrial scales, how I was supposed to evaluate things was unclear. General Groves just expected his staff to do whatever was necessary. The equipment under construction was grossly outsized industrial versions of laboratory processes. And because this was a race to beat the Nazis, there were to be two colossal-sized competing processes to produce concentrations of uranium-235 from the naturally occurring uranium-238.

"I do so want to see you, Mike. You'll think me brazen, but our lovemaking that weekend was so special."

The thought of that lovemaking caused me to become erect. "For me too, Elena. That's what I wanted to say to you. That's why I needed to call you."

"Think about how lucky we are that I'm not being shipped overseas. At least we can talk about seeing each other in a few weeks."

"I know. So come home to me when you can soldier-boy. I'll be waiting, Mike."

Knowing that Elena felt that way buoyed my spirits.

The next week was spent with endless meetings. I found the construction discussions fascinating. I poured over the blue prints with the Stone & Webster engineers and Tennessee Eastman scientists, marveling at the sheer size of the Y-12 plant. It was on a scale like the Grand Coulee Dam but infinitely more complex. It would eventually comprise two hundred buildings spread over 825 acres.

Oak Ridge was a secret government controlled city. Within two years it would grow to 75,000 people, all working to make fissile material to make atomic bombs. It was so vital to the program that the MED District Engineer was stationed here. Colonel Kenneth Nichols was a highly competent engineering officer. Nichols job was to develop the industrial processes to produce the fissile material for the weapons. Ernest Lawrence and Enrico Fermi headed the laboratories at Berkley and Chicago that supplied the science necessary to create the processes to produce fissile material. Talented private sector corporations had the daunting engineering tasks of constructing these industrial processes. Robert Oppenheimer's group of scientists at Los Alamos was to design and build the bomb.

I liked Colonel Nichols immediately. From what I knew of his reputation, he was a talented project manager. If he wasn't, he wouldn't be working for Groves. Nichols seemed to posses many of Groves' abilities without being a sonofabitch.

"Major, good to meet you," Nichols said as I entered his office in a newly constructed building. He offered me coffee from a pot on a hotplate behind his desk. "So how do you like working for the General?"

I was not sure how candid I should be so I gave a waffling answer, "The General can certainly be tough. Smart guy though."

"Sorry, Major, that wasn't a very fair question. Couldn't expect you to criticize our superior," Nichols said. "I had more hair before I began working for the General." He ran his hand over his deeply receding hair. "Just wanted you to know that I know what a tough job you've got. Being a surrogate eyes and ears for the General sounds like an impossible assignment. I'm sure if you were to be truthful, you'd have said Groves was the nastiest, the most arrogant sonofabitch you've ever met. That's because he is. He's also the most brilliant guy I've ever known. That's how he can get away with being a total asshole."

"Yes, Sir. I do know what you mean about the General's style," I said and smiled. "However, I can say that it's clear that General Groves values you highly."

"Oh? Did he say that?"

"No, Sir. That wouldn't be like the General. I can just tell by his manner when he makes reference to you."

"Thanks for that feedback, Major. So what are you supposed to accomplish on this visit?"

"I need to get a first-hand feel for the construction project. I've of course read the endless project documentation and seen the Gantt charts. I just came from Berkley. The Tennessee Eastman scientists said you actually procured silver from the U.S. Treasury for the magnetics?"

Nichols smiled. "That's right. There's a shortage of copper with other wartime demands, especially in the quantity we need for these giants magnetics.

"So this is coinage silver? How much will you need?"

"Well over 10,000 tons they estimate."

I almost choked on my coffee. "My God. Isn't that going to be a security headache?"

"Of course. But then, everything about this project is a headache. When I say project, I mean the whole range of projects. The Y-12 electromagnetic calutrons process, the K-25 gaseous diffusion process, a breeder reactor designated X-10 here at Oak Ridge, and then of course the reactors planned for the Hanford Engineering Works in Washington. Construction on the K-25 plant is to start next month. Work has already started on the X-10 reactor. You know the status on the science of these processes, Major. Our biggest challenge is to produce enough fissile material for a bomb, or realistically for multiple bombs. None of the competing processes have ever been attempted on an industrial scale. So the General has ordered we try everything to hedge the bet. Money apparently is not a limiting factor."

I was generally familiar with the various processes from the mass of classified information I had consumed. It was a long road for all involved. For insiders like Nichols and me, it seemed an almost impossible, desperate undertaking.

"I'm somewhat familiar with these projects, Colonel. I understand the Y-12 electromagnetic project is the principle focus right now. What's your biggest challenge with the Y-12 project?"

"Where to start? The first problem is the sheer complexity of the organizational pieces. We're simultaneously attempting to integrate basic research, industrial design of equipment, and construction, all on the fly. Modifications are the order of the day, many times by marked over blue prints before formal design changes can be documented.

"Stone & Webster is the contractor and Tennessee Eastman will be the operator. Then you have General Electric, Westinghouse, and Allis Chalmers all building the equipment. It was simply too large a project given the deadlines for any one company. Groves hand again. Makes sense but you can see that it breeds its own set of difficulties. For example, we're actually constructing buildings to warehouse expected equipment arrivals because the main building structures will not be ready at the time."

"Obviously my job is to report my opinions and recommendations to the General. I'd rather do that out in the open, Colonel. It's clear you are running this impossible task superbly. If I will be reporting anything critical to the General, I'll discuss the details with you first. I'm not the General's spy. I expect to contribute constructively."

"I appreciate that, Major. Given the complexity, I welcome a fresh set of eyes on things. I'm not hung up on pride of authorship. If it's a better idea, we'll implement it immediately. Obviously you understand project management or you wouldn't be on the General's staff."

Nichols was a first-rate guy. His job truly did look impossible. If I could help I would.

"So tell me more about the K-25 gaseous diffusion process project," I said.

"You've seen the designs," Nichols said. "The K-25 building will be 2,000,000 square feet. Bigger than the Y-12 facility and just as complicated. The process represents all sorts of difficulties with the equipment materials."

"I've read the technical papers on the process. It sounds straightforward but it seems laborious."

"You're right. It will be the largest industrial process in the world to produce relatively small amounts of enriched uranium. The scientists are not even sure of the production rate. But more than that, the equipment specifications, no leaks, internal pipe surfaces, temperature controls, and a list of other challenges are clearly going to be problems. The specifications are well beyond normal industrial requirements. Personally, I'm not optimistic. I'll put you with the chief project engineer from Kellex, the contractor. He's on site. The guy is already having reservations and the construction is barely started. If he's concerned, so am I."

"Do I say that in my report to the General?" I asked Nichols.

"Absolutely. But talk to the contractor and probe him on the specifics. We'll compare notes before you leave, Major. You know the General. He'll want to understand the underlying engineering in great detail which means you need to understand it just as well."

I spent two weeks at Oak Ridge. It was just as insular as Los Alamos but with a different ambiance. Both locations were under intense construction chaos, although Oak Ridge was on a much larger scale. The differences departed from there. Apart from the thousands of construction workers, most of the technical people at Oak Ridge were engineers. They were building things. They wrestled with problems of machinery design such as tolerances and material properties. How were these giant machines even to be produced in a factory? The Los Alamos scientists contended with the abstractions and unknowns of evolving nuclear science. Oak Ridge was a construction site, Los Alamos a university research laboratory.

Even as an engineer, working in the Los Alamos environment was more stimulating for me. I was using new found skills. I was interacting with some of the greatest scientific minds. It was heady stuff to be an integral part of those elite.

My stint at Oak Ridge was productive for providing a thorough grounding in the processes to produce the fissile material. There was little I could recommend differently. My report lauded Colonel Nichols command of the project. My recommendations paralleled his own.

After ten days, I was off to Los Alamos. Unfortunately I could not reach Elena by phone on my last night in Clinton. Equally unfortunate was the fact I had to take an overnight train to New Mexico. At least I'd be leaving Clinton, Tennessee.

Los Alamos had changed markedly in the few weeks I was gone. There were more buildings already erected in the technical area. More scientists had arrived. Spring was literally in full flower. The backwater industrial construction site of the Oak Ridge project was reminiscent of my time at the Grand Coulee Dam. In contrast, Los Alamos was a university campus. I realized I liked being a part of the intellectual atmosphere.

Oppenheimer had defined the organizational structure of the lab into functional divisions. I would certainly spend time with each division head, but their time would always be limited. Briefing an Army liaison officer would be a low priority. To grasp the underlying project details, I would also need more interaction with scientists than just briefings. I determined to cultivate personal relationships with key scientists from each section.

I therefore set about developing a core group of scientists that I could call on to explain the science. More than that, I needed a range of opinions on any given area of this collection of scientific problems. While I knew the organizational structure, it was more than just picking selected scientists. It would work best with those where I could establish a real working relationship. I would need to take up their valued time. They needed to appreciate my value to their work. I was a conduit to Groves so I had a certain amount of clout. They had to respect that for me to be productive. Better if they liked me as well. It was a different role for an engineer, an Army officer, but I realized I enjoyed the challenge.

The best way to make those relationships was at one of Oppie's famous cocktail parties. I could feel out the people that might be willing to give me the necessary time from a willingness rather than obligation. My first hurdle was to become one of their group. As an Army officer, the initial view of me was that of nuisance at best, an enemy at worst. The civilian staff experienced the Army mostly from a security standpoint. The Army was their warden, restricting their movements, censoring their mail, and generally intruding in every aspect of their life.

Beyond my role as Groves' direct liaison, Oppie seemed to take a general liking to me. But then again, Oppie made everyone feel special. I knew Hans Bethe a little. Robert Serber, Oppie's right hand man, had spent considerable time with me to elevate my knowledge level of the underlying science. He was a natural teacher. I met his wife Charlotte, taking an instant liking to this independent woman. So I had a good start. On my second day back at Los Alamos, Oppie's secretary, Priscilla Greene, invited me to the get-together that night.

Hans Bethe welcomed me warmly. He headed the theoretical division. These were the guys debating equations on the blackboards and doing complex calculations. My first acquaintances of Richard Feynman and Victor Weisskopf belonged to this section as group leaders for different subsets within the division. They were filling their plates with some sort of Mexican hors d'oeuvres.

Feynman saw me and came over to shake my hand. "A fellow pioneer returns to the wilderness. How are you, Mike? Robert, come over here. Meet Mike Voronin."

Robert Wilson introduced himself. He was almost as young as Feynman.

"Experimental Division. You head up the cyclotron group I believe," I said.

"That's right, Major," Wilson said with a wary expression. You're security I presume?"

"Mike's not security, Robert. He's General Groves' spy," Feynman said. Feynman's reputation for a joker was already becoming well known.

"What's the difference, Richard?" Wilson said.

This was not going well.

"I'm just joking, Robert. Mike's ok," Feynman said. "He's a project guy like Groves, just not an asshole like the General. If you use him adroitly, you can wangle all sorts of toys so you guys in Experimental can have more play things."

Victor Weisskopf stepped up to shake my hand. "Hello again, Mike. You will have to excuse Feynman here. As for you Robert, you should know better than to let Richard bait you."

"You want to know about electromagnetics and cyclotrons, Robert's your man," Feynman said. "Lawrence fired him from the Berkley Lab for being clumsy, but we won't hold that against him. Just be careful working around him. That's probably why they located Building X way away from the other buildings in case he blew it up. But since Oppie hired him to work with cyclotrons here, we assume he's rather good at what he does."

They all laughed and I could see that Robert Wilson could be an ally with Feynman's and Weisskopf's endorsements. All three were apparently friends. Wilson could be helpful with some technical questions I had about the Y-12 plant at Oak Ridge.

There were two other divisions that comprised Oppenheimer's lab. The Ordinance & Engineering Division was headed by a Navy captain, William Parsons. Nice enough guy, but it would be easier to work more closely with one of his deputies. That choice was easy. The leader of the implosion program, one of the two competing bomb designs, was George Kistiakowsky, a Ukrainian by birth. He actually joined the anti-Communist White Army after the 1917 Revolution in Russia. He spoke Russian. That could make for some common ground. Since he had to flee the Soviet Union in 1920 as the Bolsheviks prevailed, he must harbor strong anti-Communist sentiments. I would have to make sure I did not leave the impression my parents were in any way pro-Communism with their return to the motherland. Neither Parsons nor Kistiakowsky were at the party so that was for another time.

The remaining division consisted of scientists with narrowly defined specialties in chemistry and metallurgy. I'd have to see where I needed the most technical help as questions arose before determining whom best to seek out in these fields.

Kitty Oppenheimer remembered me and shook my hand. Eventually I made my way over to Robert Oppenheimer who greeted me warmly. He had been talking to Robert Serber and his wife, Charlotte when I approached. Others in the room would notice the attention that both Oppenheimer and Serber paid me. I was also the only uniform at the party. It was a very good start.

Robert Serber said, "You may want to attend another round of my lectures tomorrow, Major. I'm going to be covering ..... well let's just say it's some technical areas you missed out on when you were here last time." He obviously was groping for how to explain without breaching security since wives were present. Hard to believe that the scientists' wives didn't know details of their work, but those were the rules.

The next day I was nursing a slight hangover. Too many martinis at this altitude with too little sleep. Not the best basis for following what Serber was explaining. Except for me, the rest of the group was all physicists.

"For the purpose of brevity and security I guess, we should develop the habit of referring to the heavy element isotopes of interest as 28, 25, and 49. These are simply a combination of the last digit of the element number and the last digit of the atomic weight for that isotope. Since uranium is element number 92, the abundant naturally occurring isotope U-238, or 92^{238} becomes 28. The trace occurring lighter U-235, or 92^{235} that is fissile becomes 25. Plutonium is element number 94, with the isotope of interest having an atomic weight of 239, therefore 94^{239} becomes 49.

"Plutonium, material 49, is not naturally occurring. It is created from the neutron capture of 28. So far, only microgram quantities have been created. We need to learn a lot more about its properties, especially in larger quantities. It exhibits certain characteristics of interest distinct from 25 that presents design options for use in a *gadget*. We'll discuss what we know about 49 later. In simplest terms, plutonium is created when uranium is bombarded with slow neutrons converting it to neptunium, element 93 which then decays with a half-life of 2.3 days creating plutonium, element 94. Uranium was named from the planet Uranus, neptunium for Neptune the next further planet, hence the next element plutonium for the next outward planet Pluto."

Serber then launched into explanations of other parts of what appeared to be necessary parts of a bomb design. The first subject was the simplest estimate of the minimum size of the fissile material to produce an uncontrolled chain reaction, and explosion. This was referred to as the critical mass. His explanations were accompanied by a string of equations.

"As you can see, there are a number of variables that need to be experimentally determined to refine these calculations. What it does tell us is that a bomb of a realistic size is feasible. In fact, comparatively small manageable quantities of fissile material will be sufficient to create the several critical masses required for a bomb. That assumes of course that the engineering problems of producing fissile materials in industrial process quantities can be overcome. That is not yet clear."

"Where is that work being done?" one of the scientists asked.

Serber looked a little surprised. "That is highly classified just like us. Not within our need to know. We are post office box 1663. There are other post office boxes elsewhere."

Everyone at Los Alamos had the same address of post office box 1663, Santa Fe. Serber was implying that the Manhattan Project consisted of other secret installations.

"There are four essential elements of the gadget design. This applies even with different design approaches. First we have the fissile material core. The design is really about how to construct the fissile material in such a manner as to be able to take the material from a non-criticality state to forcing a critical mass, therefore triggering an explosion.

"The next component is called the 'tamper'. If the active core material is surrounded by a shell of inactive material of the right properties, that shell will reflect back some of the neutrons which would otherwise escape. The tamper will allow for a smaller quantity of active fissile material to achieve the same energy release. It is also essential for preventing the fissile material from blowing apart prematurely upon reaching criticality."

"What types of materials are suggested for the tamper?" someone asked.

"The densest materials appear the best suited," Serber said. "The initial focus is on tungsten, rhenium, uranium, and even gold."

"Gold?" someone said. "Is that even practical considering how much would be required?"

"Think of it this way. We will be spending money on producing fissile material at a cost exponentially that of the cost of gold."

Many of the scientists looked at each other. The strategic scope of the project was starting to settle in.

My head was spinning as Serber concluded that day's lecture. He told everyone that mimeographed copies of the lecture briefs would be available in a couple of days. That was helpful since I needed clarification on many subjects. It was difficult to take adequate notes and listen to Serber at the same time. The subject material was totally foreign. The foundation in nuclear physics to the equations was beyond me. My own notes would not be that helpful. I decided that I needed to set my sights on broader concepts and not attempt to understand the mathematical underpinnings of the science.

I remained at Los Alamos until the end of June. During that time I spoke to Elena a couple of times a week. When possible I placed calls from Santa Fe. Outgoing calls from the Hill were closely monitored.

Calling from the La Fonda Hotel bar in downtown Santa Fe a couple of days before I was scheduled to return to Washington D.C., Elena picked up on the second ring.

"Hello. It's Mike."

"Oh I was hoping it was you, Mike. Any news when you'll be back in Washington?"

"That's the good news. Two or three days. Depending if I can get a flight out of Albuquerque, or if I get stuck taking the train."

"So you're in Albuquerque?" she asked.

It just slipped out. "You know I'm not supposed to say. Security rules."

In the background, the bartender said, *"si señor"*, loud enough for Elena to hear.

"I know. You're at a bar in Mexico. No. Guess you wouldn't be in Mexico working for the Corp of Engineers. So you must be in the Southwest, and near Albuquerque?"

The bell struck the hour from St. Francis Cathedral Basilica just down the street.

"Are you in church or a bar?" Elena said laughing.

"In a bar. At a nice hotel. Just had dinner here."

"Alone I hope."

"Of course. Been working my tail off. I just came to town so I could call you. Don't like using the phones on the Hill. I can't wait to see you, Elena."

"Hill? You're in the mountains? I know. You're in Santa Fe."

I was silent for a moment. What the hell. No one knew what was going on here anyway.

"Elena, I'd tell if I could."

"I know. I'm just teasing. I've missed you so much. Thinking about where you are gives me the feeling you're closer. Not knowing where you are means I can't even imagine what you might be doing. I've had dreams about you. You'd like the dreams by the way."

I was becoming aroused and turned toward the wall afraid someone would notice the effect Elena was having on me.

"Will you call me from Albuquerque to tell me when you'll get into Washington? I really want to see you, Mike. You can stay at my place too. Alice won't mind. She knows I'm sweet on you."

"That'd be great. I'd like that too, Elena. If you're at work, I'll leave a message for you."

CHAPTER 13

Earle Theater, Washington D.C., 1943

WASHINGTON D.C. – 1943

I WAS ABLE to catch a military flight from Albuquerque into Washington National Airport. I had left a telephone message for Elena at her office giving my approximate arrival time. The message said I would meet her at her apartment by early evening.

Exiting the army C-47 along with other military officers, I heard my name being called out. It was Elena waving at me behind the tarmac security fence. Dropping my duffle bag we embraced. After a long breathless kiss I said, "What a surprise. I didn't expect for you to meet me."

She looked stunning even with her simple working clothes of white blouse and grey pants.

"I just couldn't wait to see you, Mike. It's been weeks. I've missed you so much."

She kissed me again and hung onto my arm with both her hands as I hoisted my duffle bag.

"Let's get home right away. I do so want to be alone with you."

It was hard to believe this was happening. Elena was smart, educated, and beautiful. Sexually she was uninhibited. We were good together in all sorts of ways. She seemed to feel as strongly about me as I did for her. I hailed a taxi.

Once we were inside her apartment, she kissed me again and said, "Let's shower. I'm sticky in this heat and I want to make love."

"And Alice?" I asked.

"Visiting her mother. She'll be away for a week."

"Sounds convenient."

Elena just smiled and winked.

We showered together. Both of us could not keep our hands off the other. Before climbing on the bed, Elena stripped off the blanket. After opening the window, she turned on a fan sitting on a chest of draws to blow air over us and exhaust out the window.

"It'll give some relief from the heat. But we'll have to be quiet or the neighborhood will hear us." She was doing all this totally naked. "You like my body don't you."

"Come here," I said pulling her down on the bed.

I had just pulled out of her after climaxing. I rolled off her and lay on my back. We were both bathed in sweat. The breeze from the fan felt wonderful. She in turn wrapped her arm around me, her breasts pressing against me. She began kissing first my chest then slid down brushing her lips over my stomach as she moved lower. To my surprise she took my still engorged penis into her mouth.

"I can taste both of us," she said making noises as if she were tasting a dessert. "Do you like this?"

"Oh yeah." It came out in as a guttural response. My erection stiffened further. It was covered with both our juices which she proceeding to lick clean. I wondered where she learned to pleasure a man like she did. Or was this just my inexperience? Whatever the case, it didn't matter.

Elena worked my erection vigorously with her lips and tongue.

"I'm going to come!" I said in a low guttural exclamation.

Pausing only for a brief moment, "I know," she said, then resumed.

Within moments I released again in a great convulsion. She kept me in her mouth gripping my erection firmly with her lips while stroking the base of my cock tightly with her hand. My ejaculate dribbled out the corner of her mouth. Eventually she released me with a slight gasp to catch her breath. She wiped her mouth with the sheet.

We showered again. She suggested a small Italian restaurant she heard about. Quiet and intimate. She said she just wanted to be with me and ask all sorts of questions about my life. I did too. I already felt this was more than a casual romance.

Into a second bottle of Chianti, we were smiling at each other like two teenagers. The waiter cleared away the dishes.

"I wish I knew what you did in the Army, Darling. God, it's so good you're not going overseas. Oh my God, you're not are you?"

"No."

"How can you be sure?"

"Well let's just say that I'm involved with something important here stateside."

"And you must be important too. You travel so much but always come back here to Washington. So you're an important officer. Aren't you?"

"I'm only a major. The work though is important. I have an unusual job."

"But you can't tell me about it. Would you tell me if I were your wife?"

That certainly flustered me. "Not suppose to. Even to a wife. That's the rules."

She reached over to hold my hand. "What you're doing is important to me because it's you, Mike. You're important to me. You can see that don't you?"

I gripped her hand firmly. "You're important to me too, Elena. I'm not sure where this is headed but I'm ….. very fond of you."

She looked into my eyes. I could see her eyes tearing. "Mike. I'm more than fond of you. I'm in love with you. Can't you see that?"

The declaration caught me off guard. I too was perhaps in love with her. At least I thought so. I hope I wasn't clouded by her feelings, and of course the sex. But isn't that how it works? If she is in love with me shouldn't that foster the same feelings for her? If I equivocated in my own expression of affection, wouldn't that surely hurt her? And why would I not think that I wasn't in love with her? Does it take a prescribed amount of time? Everything about her was right for me.

I gulped. I felt as if I was making a life decision. I probably was. "I love too, Elena."

"Oh my, Mike. That's what I had hoped. I know we've known each other for only a short time. But I know you're for me, Darling."

We kissed across the table and looked at each other without saying anything for several moments.

Elena broke the silence. "Would you like to meet my parents, Darling? They're up in Wilmington, north of here. Two hours by train."

"Sure. Perhaps next weekend. I think I'll be here in Washington for the next two weeks."

Things appeared to be getting serious. That thought didn't seem to scare me. In fact, everything felt right. It felt like a future. How much better could things be than falling in love with someone like Elena Obolensky?

"I just had a terrible thought. You're not doing something dangerous are you, Darling? You're not flying airplanes or something like that?"

"No, no. I'm an engineer, Elena. A civil engineer. I build things; buildings, bridges that sort of work."

"You're not building something like that now though. Why would that be so super secret?"

I wanted to tell Elena what I did. Brag a bit even. I was doing something exceedingly important. I was an important part of the *Project*. If we pulled it off, it could win the War. It was a once in a lifetime opportunity and I was at the very center. Yes, I wanted to puff myself up to Elena. In fact I wasn't all that sure the Manhattan Project could be that much of secret with so many people involved.

Even with all of General Groves elaborate security arrangements, thousands of people were involved. While only a comparatively small number knew the true scope of the project, all of the others had to speculate to each other, and to their wives, mothers, and fathers. As for the scientists, it was easy enough to see that virtually the majority of the world's leading physicists had been removed from academia. To the German Abwehr or Japanese military intelligence, we could only be working on some sort of secret weapon. Aircraft? Rockets? Why so many physicists? Obviously it had to be a weapon. The sheer scope of the unique equipment for the Clinton Engineering Works in Tennessee would suggest that some great development project was underway. The opportunities for information to leak, much less outright infiltration by spies, would seem impossible to control. The project spanned work all over the country. At Oak Ridge and Los Alamos it stuck out like a neon sign that something special was going on. Hanford in Washington would be the same.

"My God! The thought just occurred to me. We're at war. You're an engineer. It's some sort of terrible weapon. That means explosives. Tell me it's not dangerous work, Darling."

I nearly choked on my wine. I was right. It was not much of guess for anybody. What else could it be other than some secret weapon?

I looked around to see if anyone was close enough to our table to overhear. "Jesus, Elena, don't even speculate about such a thing. I could get into real trouble. And no, I'm not working where I'm in any personal danger."

"But you're making some special weapon, right?"

"Elena, cut it out. You know I can't say." I was feeling decidedly uncomfortable. Why were women so damn curious?

"I'm sorry, Darling. I wouldn't say anything. I'm so proud you're working on something important. Let's have some gelato and coffee."

We returned to her apartment. To my pleasant surprise, Elena slept in the nude. She said she loved the feel of the sheets on her body, even in the wintertime. Pajamas weren't comfortable. Nightgowns were just plain silly. Besides, it was too warm to wear anything.

Sometime during the night, Elena wrapped her arm over me. Minutes later her hand wandered down to my cock. It took little coxing to bring me erect. She climbed on top, guiding me into her with her hand. She rode me without saying anything except for the groan as we both came together. Rolling off me, she just resumed her position with her arm wrapped around me and went back to sleep.

During the week it was difficult to concentrate during the day thinking about Elena. She was working only a couple floors below in the same building. We were able to have lunch only two days during that week, the other days the General had his staff tied up all day with sandwiches brought in. But each night, we rendezvoused in the lobby. I again had the use of an Army car. Alice the roommate was gone for the week so we came back to the apartment each night. Elena cooked dinner a couple of times. We went to a movie, a new musical, *Coney Island* starring

Betty Grable. It felt like being married. It felt like a home. It felt good not to be lonely.

The plan was to take an early train to Wilmington, Delaware on Saturday. Although I had a car, I did not have enough ration coupons for the roundtrip gasoline. Elena had phoned her father. He would pick us up at the station.

On the trip north, Elena expanded on the background of her parents. Up to now, I only knew they were all Canadian citizens. Her father, Boris Ramazanov was a chemical engineer. He and his wife Vanya had emigrated from Moscow to Montreal in 1925. Vanya was a school teacher. Elena was also of Russian heritage, an orphan, adopted by the Ramazanovs. The Ramazanovs were ethnically Russian Jews by heritage. Although non-practicing, they still suffered from anti-Semitic persecution. For my part, I had only briefly sketched my parents' background, relating of course their unusual move back to Russia in 1935 because of the Depression.

To my surprise, I learned that Boris Ramazanov held a doctorate in chemical engineering. He was working on explosives for E. I. du Pont having transferred from their Montreal plant to the Carneys Point Works plant, located along the eastern shore of the Delaware River in New Jersey. That explained her concerns over working with explosives. She said she knew something of wartime security since her father also held a security clearance because he was doing government related work.

After graduating from Moscow State University in 1913, Boris was conscripted into the Russian Army after war broke with Germany the following year. Elena said her father rarely spoke about World War One. She knew of the terrible deprivations of the Eastern Front. He survived two years of the Tsar's generals squandering the lives of its young men. Severely wounded, he met her mother while recuperating in a hospital. Vanya left her university studies to volunteer as an aide to nurse the great waves of wounded returning from the front.

It was a difficult time for Boris Ramazanov. His father, a mid-level officer in the Tsar's army was killed, as was his only brother. His mother died of influenza soon after in the great pandemic of 1918. Vanya was now his life.

Civil war broke out in Russia immediately following Russia's armistice with Germany in 1917. The Communist Bolsheviks prevailed creating the Union of Soviet Socialist Republics in 1922. But Lenin, the leader of the 1917 Revolution, died in 1924. Joseph Stalin began consolidating his power with the attendant political convulsions throughout Russia. Although the Bolsheviks officially outlawed anti-Semitism, economic opportunities were still limited for those with a Jewish heritage. Their country had now been in turmoil all of their lives. Educated, Boris and Vanya decided to immigrate to the West. Both spoke English. He was armed with a degree in chemical engineering. The opportunity at E. I. du Pont in Montreal made the selection for Canada rather than the United States. DuPont even funded his graduate studies at McGill University in Montreal.

"But with all of my parents' success in Canada and now the United States, they are both still attached to Russia. To them it's still Russia. The Soviet Union is just a political label. Russia carries the meaning of their heritage. They follow events of the war on the Eastern Front closely."

"So do I. I'm worried about my own parents. Since the Germans invaded two years ago I haven't received any letters. If there are food shortages in Great Britain, it must be far worse in Russia."

"Do you think the United States is doing everything it should to help Russia?"

It was a subject that had troubled me for some time. The United States gave the Russians obsolete aircraft and only basic military goods. But there was to be no sharing of nuclear development research. While the British were an active part of the Manhattan Project, the Soviets were totally excluded. They are treated as a security threat no different than the Germans. Several of the Los Alamos scientists felt this was unfair. Beyond that, they felt it would have negative repercussions after the war.

"No. America is afraid of Communist ideology. Ever since the German defeat at Stalingrad a few months ago, that fear has increased. The Soviets proved themselves a powerful military force. The Germans will be defeated. The Soviet Union will have a big stake in whatever a post-war Europe will look like. That scares the American government."

"But you don't agree do you, Mike?" Elena said.

"No I don't. My parents live there. Like your parents, they feel themselves Russian. There's still a lot of Russian in me I guess. But there are other things that upset me in America too. Nothing unique about intolerance everywhere."

"Well you and Dad will have a lot in common. Mother too. She has strong political views herself."

I had a terrifying thought. "They're not Communists are they, Elena?" I was fortunate enough to conceal my own parents' involvement with the early Bolsheviks. If I was seeing a woman whose parents were Communists, I would immediately lose my security clearance. I'd be quickly shipped overseas to excavate forward airfields on some godforsaken Pacific island.

"Oh no. They're not Communists. Father would never have been granted a security clearance if he was. Father and Mother just feel strongly about Russia. It's cultural, not political."

That was a relief. At some point I had to assume there would be a further security check on the Ramazanovs. Especially if my relationship continued where it seemed to be leading. My security clearance went beyond top secret with a special access designation. Any of my associations would come under scrutiny.

Arriving in Wilmington, Elena spotted her parents on the station platform a short distance away. She pulled me along then hugged her mother first, followed by a kiss on her father's cheek. Boris Ramazanov looked to be about fifty. His appearance was professorial, balding with glasses. Vanya was close to the same age. Matronly. Probably a beauty in her youth, now a little on the heavy side. Both greeted me with genuine warmth. Vanya hugged me. Boris took my hand and placed his left hand on my shoulder.

Vanya remarked, "You were certainly right about your Major being handsome, Elena."

"And smart too. He's an engineer like you, Father. Some important job that he can't tell anyone about, so don't ask him. And like you Mother, his father was a professor of classical studies. So Mike is well read too. He even discusses Shakespeare with me."

Not sure we had ever discussed Shakespeare, but I reveled in Elena's compliments. She wanted to show me off to her parents.

"Mikhail, is that right?" Boris said.

"Yes, Sir. Being in the Army that became just Mike. Elena calls me Mike. But my parents always called me Mikhail."

"I will call you Mikhail as well if that is alright. It's a good Russian name. And you should call us Boris and Vanya."

We left the train station in Boris' 1936 Chevrolet sedan for the short ride to a small white clapboard house outside of Wilmington in a neat neighborhood. The front yard was well-groomed with several large trees. Vanya seated us at the dining table.

"Do you like traditional Russian food, Mikhail?" she asked.

"Very much," I said.

"Borscht?"

"Oh yes. My mother made excellent borscht. It's been a long time since I tasted good home-cooked Russian food."

"And vodka?" Boris asked.

I smiled. "That too."

"Excellent. Then we shall sample a very good Russian vodka before our lunch."

"Mikhail, beware of this old man. He may look like a book-worm but he can drink more vodka than is good for him," Vanya said jokingly. "Do not spoil our lunch, Boris."

Boris took a bottle of vodka from the sideboard and four shot glasses. Elena gave me a wink. Boris poured each glass to the brim. "To Mikhail Stefanovich. Elena told me your patronymic. To Mikhail Stefanovich who makes our daughter happy."

"Father! You're embarrassing both of us," Elena said.

"Well it is true is it not? You have said so," Boris said. Unlike his wife, he still had an accent.

Elena looked at me. "Yes he does, Father."

"See. Then one more vodka before lunch," Boris said.

"Only one. You see what I mean, Mikhail. My husband now has a drinking companion. And it's one only, Boris. I'm sure Elena and Mikhail are starved," Vanya said.

Lunch started off with marinated herring. Vanya had pre-pared a garnish of sour cream, chopped onions, and cucumbers. She set down a loaf of course black rye bread.

"The vegetables are from our own victory garden in the back. We are lucky to have space and good soil. With the ration-ing, we wouldn't have much of any vegetables beyond potatoes if we didn't grow our own. Good borscht would be impossible," Vanya said.

Vanya's borscht was excellent. She was right about the vege-tables. Borscht consisted of beets, cabbage, carrots, onions, toma-toes, and some potatoes. The meal alone would wipe out a month's ration book for vegetables even if you could find them at a market.

After lunch, Elena helped her mother clean up the lunch dishes. Boris and I retired to the living room. At one end of the room was a Philco console radio. On the opposite side was a ta-ble with a shortwave radio receiver.

"A shortwave receiver?" I asked.

"Yes it is. I can tune into amateur European transmissions. It brings the war closer. That of course can be very disturbing. I listened to broadcasts coming from Stalingrad for months. It was terribly upsetting. I believe Elena said you spoke Russian?"

I answered in Russian, "Yes. My parents always spoke Russian even though both spoke English very well. It was their way of preserving their connection with Russia. Language is the foundation of any culture my father said."

"It is that. I'm glad that you have retained that attachment to the Motherland," Boris said in Russian. "Vanya and I also speak Russian here in the house. Elena probably told you we immigrated to Canada in 1925. We're originally from Moscow."

"Yes she did. I believe she also said you were educated at Moscow State University. Both my parents also studied there before the First World War. My father returned to Moscow to accept a professorship there in 1935. He lost his position here in the United States two years earlier. It was an economic decision, but at least he could return to his career and the place of his birth. That proved fateful in light of the German invasion. My parents have had a difficult time of it. Life in Russia is desperately difficult now."

"That it is. Do you hear from them?"

"Not since war broke out with Germany."

"That must be difficult for you. All of us attached to Mother Russia wish we could help."

"It's too bad the United States does not embrace Russia as an ally in the same way as Britain," I said. "I believe the United States could do more to help."

"It's the fear of Communism," Boris said. "The ideology strikes fear for those in power in the West. Democracy here is founded on capitalism. Those in power control the wealth. After all, that's why they have the power."

"That's what I said to Elena. But do you believe Communism is a viable political structure?" I said.

"Certainly. But that's complicated. Our institutions and political cultures here in the West are more developed. The Soviet brand of Communism would be too crude. Remember, before the Revolution, Russia lived under what amounted to feudal role. It was politically a hundred years behind the West. You couldn't establish democratic institutions in such a leap. So I see the Soviet state as an evolutionary step. I believe Russia is better off today than if it were still ruled by a Tsar. Look at your own parents. They fled Tsarist repression only to return twenty years later to what they thought was an improvement."

"My parents told me stories of their early years before they immigrated here. Even then, most Russians just subsisted. People routinely starved. Surviving was a constant struggle. My parents had it better than most. They were academics, but their lives were uncertain too. After the failed revolution in 1905, they knew it was only a matter of time before Tsarist rule would have to end. Yet you lived through those times as well, Boris. If Communism was so much an improvement what made you leave?"

"Because at the heart of Communism is the sacrifice of self for a greater good. I simply wasn't that selfless. I thought of myself as an intellectual, like your parents. The idea of the State determining my future was not acceptable. The Soviet state was nothing more than a collection of bureaucrats, probably less educated than me."

"Yet you still say it was progress for Russia," I said.

"It has been. As rigid and flawed as the Soviet state is, the lives of the peasant class improved dramatically under Communism. Now here in the United States it wouldn't work. Just like it didn't work for me. But on the other hand, you would have to admit that there are many social injustices here that could benefit by major change."

Any right thinking person of conscience could see that.

I said. "Personally I'm most troubled with the racial segregation in America. It's an abomination. Negroes are no longer slaves but they're not equal citizens to whites either. I travel in my work. Many places have separate restrooms and drinking fountains for Negroes. Some restaurants have signs reading *whites only*. Even Washington D.C. is segregated. I work for a general who supervised construction of the new Pentagon War Department building. He said it has twice the restrooms necessary because there had to be separate facilities for Negroes because of segregation laws in the State of Virginia."

"That's what I mean. American capitalism has a long way to go. Eventually there must be a further evolutionary political advancement," Boris said.

Elena and her mother entered the living room.

"I see Father has already engaged you in politics. I have never figured out exactly what his politics are. I believe it's the debate he loves. You could probably argue persuasively for either side of an issue, couldn't you, Father?" Elena said.

"I'm not quite that objective. But that is my point. As an intellectual, I understand that most issues are complex. Most people want to reduce things to black and white. Most everything is some shade of gray."

Vanya interrupted. "I shall now rescue Mikhail from your father, Elena. It is such a nice day, let's go into the backyard. I had enough ration coupons to buy lemons and sugar to make lemonade. So all of you adjourn to the outside."

"Are your parents managing? Vanya said. "We know it's difficult, especially with the food shortages in Russia."

We were all seated in wooden lawn furniture under a large maple tree that afforded shade. The lemonade was a real treat.

"Their last letter was a long time ago. A few months after the Germans invaded. My father wrote that he had been conscripted to write military hardware instruction manuals, particularly those from the United States because of his proficiency with Eng-

lish. Mother volunteers at a hospital. Food shortages were becoming a problem even then. They did not complain. I suspect
they are not getting enough to eat since that letter was written.
My father wrote of the spirit of those defending Stalingrad. Even
though the Germans were defeated at Stalingrad, their armies
are still fighting the Russians. Western newspapers report severe
food shortages for the civilians. By the tone of their last letters, I
doubt my parents know of the terrible losses the Red Army have
been taking on the Eastern Front. I suspect Stalin keeps those
numbers secret."

"Do you think Roosevelt does the same?" Vanya asked.

"I don't know. It would make sense though, I guess."

"We have also received few letters from the Motherland,"
Vanya said. "Boris of course hears the broadcasts on his
shortwave radio. So many have been killed. So much destroyed.
I wonder how Russia will recover when the war finally ends. A
whole generation of so many young men dead."

"I worry about my parents. They're lives have been such a
struggle. Now they've gone into this terrible dark hole."

"We must all help. We must not forsake our families in Russia. The Nazis must be defeated." Vanya said. "It is depressing to
talk constantly of war. We here behind the front lines must also
survive. We must maintain our humanity in the face of this terrible catastrophe. I am educated in literature as your father is.
Elena says you discuss Shakespeare. Are the classics important
to you?"

I welcomed the change of subject from the political mine-
field. The influence of my father, and my mother, were deeply
ingrained. High school forced the obligatory reading of classical
Western literature. As a professor of classical studies, my father
could not accept the superficial treatment of American high
school teaching of the subject. But my father possessed the great
skill of being able to engage his audience. It was no different for

me as his son. He made literature come alive. The classics became a part of how I viewed life.

"Very much so. My father pushed me in that direction. I came to appreciate the richness of what great literature offered."

"Yet you became an engineer. That seems to be an entirely different direction," Vanya said.

"While I loved literature, I had no interest in teaching. It became clear to me that I must take up a different path. I loved mathematics. I love the exactitude contrasted to the ambiguities of philosophical thought."

"And your mother? How did she influence you?"

"Mother was a musician. A violinist. A classical violinist. Her Vivaldi renditions would bring tears to my father's eyes. He knew she should be performing at Carnegie Hall. Intellectually, she engaged my father as an equal. She would never back down if she disagreed with father. Imperious he would tease her. Yet she was warm to everyone."

"Ah. You accurately describe my Vanya too," Boris said. "As you see, she is a force to be reckoned with. Do you play chess, Mikhail?"

I smiled. How to acknowledge that I was *very* good at chess without sounding boastful?

"My father taught me. He was very good. So I know my way around the board."

"Excellent. We shall play then."

That seemed to be settled. The women said they would start preparations for dinner. Boris retrieved a chess board and brought it outside.

"You'll play white?" Boris asked.

"No, you. I insist," I said.

Boris moved P-K4.

I countered with P-K3.

The sequence progressed with Boris P-Q4, followed by my P-Q4, Boris P-K5, with my counter P-QB4, attacking Boris' pawn chain base.

Boris Ramazanov knew his way around a chess board also. This was a classic French Defense opening that would signal a duel for control of the center. Boris was certainly in a different class of chess proficiency than Happy Parker back in my days at Grand Coulee Dam. As the match continued, it was evident that Boris was an accomplished chess player, but I was still much better.

Boris attempted a subtle yet risky maneuver in mid-match. I countered with what appeared to be a sacrifice but was actually a well disguised trap. Boris fell into the trap by taking my knight. But in return, I was two pawns up, had the initiative, and board position with an array of attacking prospects which I exploited decisively.

After a further exchange of moves, Boris looked up and smiled, acknowledging my skills. The match progressed to move twenty-eight with my decisive B-R3. Boris grunted good naturedly and knocked over his King signaling his resignation of the match with inevitable checkmate.

"You are more than just a good chess player, Mikhail. I believe I am very good. You are way beyond that."

"My father taught me well," I said.

"No. Your skills are beyond being taught. You have a real a gift. Did you beat your father?"

"Eventually. Once I was older he could no longer beat me regularly," I said. I smiled with the memory of my father's pride as he frequently lost or played to a draw no matter how hard he concentrated.

In the short time that I was with Boris and Vanya, I felt relaxed. Although I held back not ready to confess my parents Communist beginnings, Boris had articulated a political perspective close to my own. Vanya's feeling that the United States was not doing enough for Russia also mirrored my own. All the Allied blood being spent in Europe was Russian. Hitler's ambitions had been thwarted by Russia. Even though the Allied forces had prevailed in North Africa, the terrible loses sustained on the Eastern Front had devastated the German Wehrmacht.

It was an extraordinary weekend. On a personal level, Boris and Vanya were wonderful. Intellectually stimulating. Very much like my own parents. They understood the more complex political undertones of what was going on. They were Russian. Elena loved me. All this was right. It was an opening into a life I never imagined. The departure at the train station was emotional. I already felt like part of a family.

We arrived back at Elena's apartment late on Sunday afternoon. Alice was home, but she informed us she was going out. The woman certainly had an active social life. Elena and I spent a long hour chatting with Alice. The talk was trivial nonsense about Hollywood gossip. I wondered how Elena put up with her shallow roommate. More immediately, I wondered when Alice's date would arrive so Elena and I could jump into bed. Two nights sleeping separately at her parents' house had left me hungry for her body. Elena's glances suggested she was equally aroused.

After lovemaking we laid quietly on the bed. The weather had cooled with nightfall. A breeze wafted in through the open window.

"I know I'd feel lucky to be stateside if I were in the military. But I'm a woman. We look at things differently than men. Do you wish you were on the front lines somewhere, Darling? Would you want to be leading men into combat?"

Of course I didn't. Not because I was a coward. You didn't have to risk death to be doing your duty. But there was a lingering sense of something like guilt that was difficult to describe. Much like a survivor in an accident where others died, there was a sense of unwarranted privilege. Why me? It was a feeling that surfaced periodically, usually triggered by some circumstance. Like now. Did Elena harbor some negative impression? Did she think I was serving some mundane support role safely positioned stateside? Worse yet, did she suspicion that I had inflated the importance of my work? I certainly had no question about the importance of what I was doing. It was frustrating not to be able to share that pride with someone you loved.

"Certainly not. I hope you don't feel that I've got this cushy job just to keep myself out of harm's way."

"Oh, Darling, no. I'd never think that. Besides, you're in the Army and don't get a choice where they send you. Don't be cross with me. I love you. I'm very proud of you."

"How can you be proud? You don't know what I do. Maybe I don't do anything all that important. Maybe I just made up that I work on a secret project."

I wasn't angry with her but it came out that way. I was angry at the constraints that didn't allow me to share what I did with the person I loved. And trusted? Of course.

Elena snuggled close and kissed me. Tears were flowing down her cheeks. I had wounded her.

"It's against the rules to talk about what I do. Believe me, those rules are uncompromising. If it were found out that I divulged what I'm going to tell you, I'd be placed under arrest. It's that tight. So you can't tell anyone anything, not even your parents. Not even any hints. Do you promise?"

Elena pulled back and sat up on her knees. She was naked. Looking at her breasts was disconcerting. But she was intently looking at me with an expression like an expectant child.

"Of course I promise, Darling."

This was wrong, very wrong what I was about to tell her, but I had to share something with her. The project might go on for a couple of years. Keeping literally everything a secret from Elena would eventually strain our relationship. Violating security in some small way would just enhance it. I hated my weakness, but the compulsion was too great. In the end it would be ok.

"I'm involved in a project personally authorized by the President. It has the highest priority in the war effort. It involves the best scientific minds in the country. Money is no object. If we're successful, it could end the War. I'm a personal liaison between the project's Army commanding general and the civilian scientists. I'm expected to understand everything. My job is to assess progress and make recommendations to the General. That's why I'm running all over the country."

Elena stared at me dumbfounded. Then came a look of concern. "It's some sort of bomb you're working on just like I guessed. But you promised me there was no danger. How can that be?"

"It's not at all dangerous for me. Nor for anyone else. It's not that sort of bomb."

"I don't understand, Mike. How can development of a bomb that could end the War not involve dangerous work?"

"Elena, that's why this is different. It involves a new science called nuclear physics. It's about releasing energy that binds the nucleus of atoms together."

"I don't even know what that means. From high school all I know is that atoms make up everything, including us. Father would probably understand."

"Jesus, Elena! Don't even think that. You can't ever use the word atom, especially not to your father."

"Of course I won't. I promised you, Darling. I didn't mean it that way. I meant it sounded so technical. But this could really end the War? Is that realistic?"

"Certainly. We're creating a weapon with the explosive force of 20,000 tons of TNT."

Elena's mouth gaped open. "I can't imagine what that kind of a huge number means."

"It means it will destroy everything within a radius of a couple of miles."

"My God. Whole cities! Such a bomb is possible?"

"Yes. Now you know. You shouldn't know, but you do. I violated security, Elena because I love you. I wanted you to know how important my work is. I wanted you to be proud of me."

"Oh, Mike, I am. I had no idea." She hugged me and kissed me repeatedly. "Thank you. Thank you for trusting me. I love you so much."

She started to stroke my cock. To my surprise I was able to become fully hard again. Elena was sexually voracious but I wasn't complaining. Rolling to the side, she pulled me down on top of her. Within only moments she gripped me tightly with her vagina as she came, her abdominal muscles tautly arching. I watched the expression of ecstasy on her face. Once she came down from her high, I resumed my rhythm until I released my own orgasm.

We lay back down, both spent. My stomach growled with hunger. We needed to eat but neither of us wanted to break the mood.

"Mike?"

"Yes?"

We both turned to look at each other.

"Let's get married," she said.

"Married?"

"Yes. Do you want to marry me?"

I did not hesitate. "Yes. Are you sure though?"

"Of course. Why do you think I took you to meet my parents?"

I wasn't all that sure I wanted to get married so soon, but I was in love with Elena Obolensky. There was no reason not to get married. Why wait?

I explained that I would need to inform the General. Because of my work, security personnel would have to check into her background and her parents. Did she mind? Elena said there was nothing in her background to embarrass me. She reminded me her father already held a security clearance so they understood the process.

What about the wedding? None of us were religious, including her parents. I suggested an Army chaplain could perform the ceremony. Elena said the ceremony was not important, only being my wife. We settled on an approximate time in September. That would allow sufficient time for the Army red tape. We couldn't set a precise date because my absences from Washington could not be anticipated that far into the future. This was wartime.

Joseph Stalin, 1943

CHAPTER 14

LIEUTENANT COLONEL FELIKS Antonovich Kirilov sat at his desk in the Red Army's headquarters building in the Arbat district of central Moscow. It was ten o'clock on a cold December night, two days before Christmas, but that held little meaning to Kirilov. The view from the window of his modest office looked out onto a typical stark utilitarian Soviet government building. Kirilov smoked a cigarette. The ashtray was overflowing. He knew he should cut back on the three packs a day, but it seemed his only pleasure lately. In the absence of exercise it at least kept him physically trim by diminishing his appetite.

Red Army headquarters occupied several blocks of buildings. Lights shown from most of the windows. War raged on. Moscow was no longer under threat, but German forces still held vast areas of former Soviet territory. Soviet counter offensives at Stalingrad had relieved the stalemate with the beleaguered city. Winter had arrived to become the Germans' worse enemy. The balance of power on the Eastern Front was tipping in favor of the Soviets.

Kirilov was a middle-level officer in the Glavnoye Razvedyvatel'noye Upravleniye, known simply by the acronym GRU, the foreign military intelligence directorate of the General Staff of the Soviet Armed Forces. It was a depressing night, but then again every day and night had become depressing for Kirilov. He had been at work since ten o'clock that morning and would not leave until well into the morning hours. Joseph Vissariono-vich Stalin was nocturnal therefore all senior officials throughout the government keep the same graveyard-shift hours. Since Kirilov's boss and boss' boss up the chain of command kept these hours, he was forced to do the same. Everyone worked under unrelenting stress. The purges of only a couple of years ago had set a tone of constant fear for anyone in a position of authority. Death or prison could come at any time for any manufactured reason.

He was disrupted by his aid informing him that his superior, Major General Golovchenko, required him immediately in his office. Although routine, such a summons always carried some level of fear. The purges of 1937-38 had decimated 50-75% of all senior government officials, including the military leadership. To be purged meant something far worse than losing one's position. It meant exile to a forced labor camp in Siberia for ten years or more. If you were a senior official, it meant you were executed, hopefully before you were tortured. Anyone could be removed for the vaguest of reasons, or for no reason. Stalin, clearly a psy-chopath, had descended into an unrestrained destructive mega-lomania. As his instrument, Stalin elevated a fellow psychopath, Nikolai Yezhov, to implement this culling of the Soviet leader-ship.

The last couple of years had seen Stalin retreat from at least the volume of excesses. The reasons were simply pragmatic. The War could not be sustained without a qualified general staff. The entire economic fabric of agriculture and industry was at risk of collapse with a decimated leadership. Fear at all levels of society had paralyzed the Soviet state.

Kirilov was shown into his boss' office. "Good evening Comrade General."

Major-General Golovchenko was only a couple of years older than Kirilov. Unlike the slender, handsome Kirilov, Golovchenko was shorter, barrel-chested, with thinning hair. He looked the part of a Soviet general. Golovchenko had been recalled from his post in London. Promoted two ranks, he was placed in charge of the GRU activities involving English speaking Great Britain and the United States. Like Kirilov, he was fluent in English. Kirilov liked Golovchenko, but he had also liked Golovchenko's two predecessors. Kirilov assumed Golovchenko had survived the great purge because he had been remote from the intrigues of Moscow.

As for himself, Kirilov assumed he had survived because of his mid-level rank of major at the time. He had also been cautious to avoid identification associated with any particular superior. Like his current superior, Kirilov was promoted to lieutenant colonel because of vacancies left by purged officers. There was no way to predict the capricious swings of power that could topple anyone at any time. For reasons unknown to him, the current GRU chief, Colonel General Fedor Kuznetsov, had seemingly taken a liking to him. Perhaps it was only because of Kirilov's area of operation. Regardless, it was certainly of no comfort because of the increased visibility. Kuznetsov himself was a blunt instrument in purging the GRU leadership. With that background, he could easily suffer the same fate. Kirilov attempted to stay as anonymous as possible. He actually hoped for no further promotion, at least while Stalin was in power. The higher you rose in rank, the more at risk you became.

General Golovchenko motioned Kirilov to take a seat. "Beria wants to see us. In one hour."

The color drained from Kirilov's face. Golovchenko appeared none too comfortable with that prospect either.

"Any idea what this is about, Sir?"

"No idea. I was just instructed to bring you. At least that's better than being summoned alone," Golovchenko said with a pained laugh.

Kirilov decided not to ask the obvious question. Why was Beria as the head of the rival intelligence organ, the NKVD, requesting a meeting with two Red Army GRU officers, bypassing the chief of the GRU?

For the last couple of years, being the GRU chief was life-limiting. Up until 1938, the same GRU chief appointed by Vladimir Lenin and sponsored by Leon Trotsky had served in that capacity for fifteen years. Nikolai Yezhov had him executed in 1938. Yezhov, who had engineered the purge at the NKVD, then purged the entire leadership of the GRU and effectively took over control of both intelligence directorates. Stalin feared Yezhov's growing power with this monopoly. After only six months, Yezhov too was liquidated. In the last three years there had been three different chiefs of the GRU. All were shot.

The current chief, newly promoted Colonel-General Fedor Kuznetsov was rumored to be in favor with Stalin and Beria. He had been the former deputy chief of the GRU and responsible for carrying out the purges under Yezhov. Who's to say what his longevity might be. Kirilov was glad that it would be his superior that would have to decide if he would tell General Kuznetsov what Beria wanted. Was this a Beria intrigue? If so, that meant it was a Stalin intrigue. This was an Alice in Wonderland-like nightmare where logic meant nothing and the slightest misstep meant death.

While their boss General Kuznetsov was to be feared for his ruthlessness, Lavrentiy Pavlovich Beria was higher up in the chain of power. Beria was at the center of this den of snakes. In 1938, as a trusted Stalin subordinate, Beria was directed by Stalin to end Stalin's own instigated purges by getting rid of Stalin's own hand-picked instrument to conduct the purges, Nikolai Yezhov. It was illustrative of the demented duplicity of Stalin.

Nikolai Yezhov was a malignant dwarf standing only five feet tall. He was a sadist, brutally liquidating the heads of the GRU as well as the NKVD, the state security directorate. The intelligence organs were jealous rivals prior to the ascension of Yezhov. Eventually viewing Yezhov as a potential threat, Stalin commissioned Beria to engineer Yezhov's removal. Yezhov had ordered the torture of the NKVD and GRU intelligence chiefs before their executions. Beria offered up the same treatment to Yezhov in 1940. He was tried in Beria's office, sentenced to death then taken immediately to the Lubyanka's basement. Beria ordered him to undress and then brutally beaten. Weeping uncontrollably, he was then shot in the head. Beria was the Stalin henchman my boss and I were being summoned to see in the middle of the night.

We arrived at the Lubyanka in a staff car with driver. It was notorious as a prison for political prisoners. It was here in the basements that high ranking officials were tortured and executed. The NKVD was also headquartered here. Even at this late hour, the place was a warren of activity. Lavrentiy Beria, arguably the second most powerful person in the government, made his office on the top floor.

Golovchenko and I waited almost an hour before being ushered in. My mind played all sorts of scenarios as to why Beria had summoned two senior officers from the GRU.

As we entered Beria's office, we saw our boss, Colonel-General Kuznetsov sitting in a chair with Beria seated behind his desk. My heart sank. Was this some prelude to Golovchenko and me being purged?

Beria wasted no time getting down to business.

"Comrade General, what do you know of atomic energy?" Beria said to Golovchenko.

Golovchenko looked quickly at me. "Ah ..... Very little ..... Comrade ....." Golovchenko faltered at how to properly address

Beria. He held various titles. "Comrade Commissar. A possible new source of energy I believe."

"And you?" Beria said looking at me.

"A potential source of energy as the General said. Some intelligence we have read speculates that it could theoretically be a means of constructing a powerful bomb. The Germans and British have been doing research. Theoretical at this stage."

Beria looked down at some papers. "The British are more than speculating. They have designated a secret program they call Tube Alloys to conduct research. They have now interested the Americans in the possibilities of this science. Roosevelt has taken a personal interest. The Americans have the resources to pursue this work. Their army has been given control over the project. That means it is about a bomb, not an energy source. Colonel, you have assets in America?"

"Yes, Comrade Commissar," Kirilov answered.

"The Boss wants to know what the Americans are doing on this atomic thing." The *Boss* was Stalin. "If it is progressing beyond the theoretical we need to know. The British and the Americans have chosen not to share this with us. Therefore, we must take action to protect our national interests. You will find out, Colonel. I want you to penetrate their program. You will report progress to General Kuznetsov. Is that understood?"

Both Golovchenko and I answered," Yes, sir."

"Your work has the highest priority. It has been assigned the code name ENORMOZ. All ENORMOZ intelligence is to now come directly to this office," Beria said, then dismissed us with the way of his hand. Although General Kuznetsov said nothing in the brief meeting, both Golovchenko and I came to attention and saluted.

Waiting for our car in the front of the Lubyanka, Golovchenko asked me in a whisper, "What the fuck do you make of this?"

"You mean why did Beria call us to his office rather than General Kuznetsov's?" Kirilov answered after first looking around. Kuznetsov was the head of the GRU and Beria of the rival NKVD.

"Of course, Kirilov. Yet General Kuznetsov was there. It may be Beria's way of signaling to Kuznetsov who has more power. But it does mean that both the GRU and NKVD are to target this American program. Beria made it clear that Stalin has set this as a priority."

"You know what this means, Kirilov?" Golovchenko said.

"Yes, Sir. If we fail, we will be removed."

"That's right. Both of us. So don't fail, Kirilov. I'd like to live a while longer."

The meeting was more than unsettling. Kirilov had been thrust into the spotlight. The place he had adroitly avoided during these dangerous last few years. The professional challenge to penetrate the American nuclear bomb project was however stimulating. But in the lunatic asylum that was the Soviet Union under Joseph Stalin, failure meant death. If he as the GRU were successful, that might mean resentment from powerful elements in Beria's rival NKVD. Being successful and therefore knowing too much might also mean death.

Up to now, Kirilov had taken great pains to avoid pitfalls in the hyper-police state that the Soviet Union had become under Stalin. Risk came in the form of friends and even family. An incautious comment could land you in a Siberian labor camp. If a parent was accused of anti-Soviet behavior, it could mean prison for a son or daughter. A friend meant an implied association with whatever politics the State might ascribe to that friend. Guilt by association was taken to absurd lengths.

By circumstances, Feliks Kirilov had limited personal associations for much of his life. His father died in combat in the First World War. His mother died of pneumonia in 1919. He was only thirteen years old. There were no siblings, no other family. Sent to an orphanage, he learned self reliance as a means of surviving that difficult environment.

By the winter of 1922, the Russian civil war had been settled. Russian society under Communism was beginning to form. Devoting his time to academics, Kirilov was recognized as a brilliant student. With state-funded education now based upon meritocracy, he was able to enroll in Moscow State University. After receiving his degree in mathematics in 1927, he joined the Red Army. Accepted into the Army's command school, the RKKA Military Academy, he achieved an advanced degree in political science. Along the way he discovered a natural ability with language. Upon graduating in 1933 with the rank of captain, he could speak English, French, and German. With these skills, he was an obvious candidate for the intelligence directorate.

By inclination, Kirilov limited personal associations. With such an intense pursuit of his ambitions, he had little need for romantic connections other than for occasional sex. Since he enjoyed the performing arts, woman served as temporary companions exchanging the night out for sex. By discipline, no relationship was allowed to progress further than the superficial. Whether he was created that way or formed by his life, Kirilov was an intensely private person. He was not a narcissist, but simply could find no capacity for sharing himself with others. In the paranoid environment that the Soviet state had become, this was an invaluable trait. Not only was romance unnecessary, so were friendships. Yet he still interacted effectively with others. Most of his associates found him interesting, although remote. It wasn't an act. It was always just professional, never personal.

None of that mattered now. The only way to survive was to fulfill this new assignment.

CHAPTER 15

Los Alamos, 1944

LOS ALAMOS, NEW MEXICO – 1944

NOW THAT WE were engaged, leaving Washington was even harder. Our brief courtship was something special. I was in love. Elena was beautiful. Our love making was decadent. I would never have imagined a woman being so assertive, so attentive, so bold, so creative. I had a great job. Out of harms' way. A career after the War. No one my age had it this good.

I typically spent several weeks at the various Manhattan Project sites, returning to Washington D.C. for a week. After briefings at headquarters, General Groves would give me a new agenda and off I went again.

Even with my uncertain schedule, Elena and I were married by an Army chaplain at Fort Meyers in September. General Groves graciously consented to be my best man, taking away from his limited precious personal time he reserved for Sundays.

By the end of 1943, the Manhattan Project had grown into an undertaking of monumental scope. The Hanford, Washington site for the production of plutonium selected early in the year was well advanced in construction by year-end. Hanford fit the criteria for ample water with the Columbia River, sufficient electrical power with hydroelectric sources, and sparsely populated.

Like Oak Ridge in Tennessee, it was a vast industrial installation. By War's end, it would occupy an area half the size of the State of Rhode Island and employ tens of thousands. It was now part of my regular assignment sites along with Oak Ridge, Chicago, Berkley, and Los Alamos.

But it was Los Alamos where I spent most of my time. That suited me. The intellectual atmosphere was stimulating. I felt at the heart of the Project, which it was. But the most difficult challenges were associated with engineering the processes to produce quantities of fissile material. Not as glamorous as the Los Alamos work. Oak Ridge and Hanford were just gigantic factories. Although the achievements of the brilliant, dedicated people associated with that side of the Project made the atomic bomb a reality, they were still industrial processes. Los Alamos was a university; a university with the most brilliant research faculty in the world.

I was feeling fairly cocky. As a civil engineer by training, nuclear physics was beyond my educational background. While General Groves had scientific advisors to tutor him in the science, I was expected to fend for myself. By any account, Groves was also brilliant with the ability to immediately grasp the most complex issues. Yet I was not only able to keep up with him, but often able to sufficiently explain scientific details unfamiliar to him. There was never a word of praise from the General, but continued acceptance of my reports received with more questions than criticisms suggested he trusted my work.

Elena's roommate Alice moved out just before we married. According to Alice, she was moving in with her latest boyfriend, a lawyer with the Justice Department. Alice was always convenient with her absences. Now we had a home to ourselves, although I was there very little.

I had a few days back in Washington D.C. for Christmas in 1943 before returning to the various sites. Under Leslie Groves' hard-driving project management the Manhattan Project had swelled in scope. New milestones related to producing fissile material in sufficient weapons quantities started to materialize. With progress came more demanding deadlines.

The first phase of the Y-12 electromagnetic separation plant at Oak Ridge became operational in November, 1943. The Oak Ridge X-10 reactor, intended to produce test quantities of plutonium, went critical that same month. Construction of the massive production reactors to extract large quantities of plutonium began at Hanford, Washington in October.

Project W-47, code named *Project Alberta,* was created at Wendover Army Air Field in Utah. *Alberta* was the parallel program to develop the means of delivering an atomic bomb. A bomb that was not yet created, its physical size unknown, nor the parameters for aerial delivery known. *Alberta* was not an expression of confidence, only of Groves' pursuit of all Project elements simultaneously. Everything subordinated to urgency.

All of these gigantic industrial projects were being started without the entirely new processes being fully designed. The equipment was being designed then continually modified, often after delivery to the site. It was organized chaos. These design concepts to extract uranium-235 from uranium-238 had never been tested beyond the laboratory. Same for the concept of a reactor to sustain a constant nuclear fission process which could produce the man-made fissile element plutonium as a byproduct. Engineering techniques were being invented. Much remained to be understood about the behavior of uranium-235 and plutonium-239. Nothing that was being attempted had ever been done on this scale. The Project had an artificially imposed deadline dictated by the War. Cost was not a constraint. Pragmatism had no place. Science did not proceed like this. Problems were inevitable. Even problems that could derail the project. Success within the imposed timeframe of less than two years was by no means a certainty. Early 1944 proved a dark period for the Manhattan Project.

The first problem occurred at the Y-12 electromagnetic separation plant. Operational for less than a month, the first Alpha racetrack failed.

The electromagnetic separation process grew out of Ernest Lawrence's work at Berkley. It consisted of a process whereby a material in gaseous form was bombarded with high energy electrons and then accelerated through a strong magnetic field. The magnetic field would bend the arc of elements with different atomic weights. These were then collected at different places at the end of the process. The purpose was to increase the concentration of the trace U-235 found in the naturally occurring U-238.

To do this required magnets a hundred times more powerful than anything ever made. These 15-foot electromagnets would be arrayed in an oval, hence the label *racetracks*. The Alpha tracks were the first to be installed. Problems materialized immediately. The first two tracks failed because of contaminated cooling oil and a fundamental design flaw. By January, only one track was limping along producing far from the expected output, at less than expected enrichment.

The racetracks proved a constant maintenance headache. Controlling the process was as much a black art as engineering. Rows of women sat at stations continually monitoring gauges and making slight adjustments. It was soon determined that the Alpha tracks would never achieve the enrichment goals.

Colonel Nichols took me into the Y-12 plant. There were few workers inside. The plant was effectively shutdown. For weeks, they struggled with trying to maintain operation by controlling the fluctuating magnetic fields through adjustments. In desperation, a decision was finally made to take apart several of the magnet assemblies in the first Alpha track. Regardless what they found, the huge magnet assemblies would then require return to the manufacturer. We were now looking at the disassembled Alpha-3 being prepared for return to the factory for rebuilding.

"Two problems. First, the cooling oil is contaminated," Nichols said pointing into the guts of the magnet. "Appears to be contaminants from the welding of the piping joints. Rust as well. We thought that was the cause of the magnetic field fluctuations. But it was eventually concluded that the conductors were spaced too closely together. That's a more difficult fix."

"I've read the reports," I said. "What's the status on the rebuilds?" I asked.

"The Alpha-1 magnets have just returned. The Alpha-2's are due back from Allis Chalmers in two weeks."

"Is Allis Chalmers confident about the rebuild fixes?"

"Yes. General Groves himself was involved in the discussions. But that's only part of the problem," Nichols said.

"What do you mean?'

"Well to start with, there're problems with the K-25 gaseous diffusion process as well."

The K-25 plant was eleven miles away on the Clinch River. In simplest terms, this process forced uranium hexafluoride gas through a porous barrier that progressively separated higher concentrations of the lighter U-235 isotope from the heavier U-238. This was repeated through successive cascades of diffusers, or barriers, to enrich the uranium to higher concentrations of the fissile U-235. The process was simple, the engineering challenging, and the size colossal. The building covered forty-two acres, four stories high.

Uranium hexafluoride was highly corrosive. It was also highly reactive to any organic materials. Therefore it posed problems with most metals, gaskets, and lubricants. I had read the reports about the contentious problem of finding a suitable barrier material.

"Nothing except nickel has been found to resist the uranium hexafluoride," Nichols said. "The problem is creating the millions of submicroscopic openings per square inch. Compressed powered nickel simply proved insufficiently fine enough for the openings. Alternative techniques are undergoing lab trials right now."

"What about this electro-deposited nickel material the reports sight?"

"Kellex is working in that direction. Prospects are encouraging. It might be months away though."

"And the problems with the sealing?" Gas-tight pump seals had always required grease which could not be used with the uranium hexafluoride.

"Without the ability to use a grease-based design, they've been a source of continuing problems. Seems to have been solved with the new seals using a new DuPont polymer called polytetrafluoroethylene. But that's not certain yet."

"What do you think about the Boss altering the enrichment approach?" I asked Nichols.

Because of the continuing problems with the K-25 diffusion barriers and the delays and low projected output of the Y-12 electromagnetic process, Groves made a tactical decision. The diffusion process would be used to only enrich the uranium to 50% U-235. This enriched stock would then be fed to the electromagnetic process for enrichment to greater than 80% as required for a bomb. As part of that thinking, Groves had ordered the construction of the Y-12 Beta racetracks to augment the Alpha racetracks to provide the electromagnetic processing with a secondary enrichment process. But this also seemed reactionary since questions were already arising about the viability of the electromagnetic process to yield large enough quantities of fissile U-235. The hope had always been on the gaseous diffusion approach. Groves was jerry-rigging making the bomb material.

"You mean are we going to make it?" Nichols said, obviously referring to the timeline. "Frankly I'm not at all optimistic, Major."

"It does seem like a spit and bailing-wire fix," I added. "The bright spot appears to be the X-10 reactor. At least that's working."

"True. But that's a slow process. It will still be a couple of months before we produce enough 49 to send to Los Alamos. And that'll still be just test quantities."

"But that's still amazing progress," I said. "Fermi's Chicago Pile, the first ever nuclear reactor, only went critical a year ago. X-10 is functioning as expected. The physicists at Los Alamos have high expectations for 49. It appears to have properties that might make it more suitable than 25. But the problem is there's still a lot about 49 that's still unknown. The theoretical work suggests the critical mass of plutonium might be only a third of 25. So it's important stuff. Especially if we can produce greater quantities than we can of 25."

Nichols and I were of course using the prescribed code designations of 49 for plutonium-239 and 25 for uranium-235. Plutonium was produced in trace quantities as a byproduct of naturally-occurring uranium-238 undergoing controlled fission in a reactor. Extracting the plutonium from the uranium-238 was a complex chemical process that was also undergoing development for large scale application.

"But the reactors are already under construction at Hanford. Even with everything we *don't* know. The chemical extraction process hasn't even been fully developed yet, much less the equipment designed. Are you comfortable with that?" Nichols said.

"No, especially after witnessed the scientific arguments about the reactor cooling system. But I've talked to Dr. Seaborg at some length about the chemical extraction process. There's been good progress using his oxidation-reduction cycling method. Seaborg is confident they'll be ready once the Hanford production reactors are operational."

Glenn Seaborg had been the first to produce plutonium in the laboratory. He had also developed an ingenious method for extracting the trace quantities of plutonium from the U-238 within the reactor that had undergone a sustained chain reaction. At best, the new element plutonium was found in a concentration of only about 250 parts per million. That was the quantity of a dime comingled in two tons of highly radioactive material.

I continued. "But I know what you mean. I was at the meetings with the General and the scientists about the debates over the reactor cooling method. There are a lot of assumptions. Problem was that all of the ideas appeared technically sound."

"What was the outcome?"

"The Boss forced them to reach a consensus. The risk has to be taken. But it didn't instill confidence."

"I understand the General's need to take risks. But we must expect problems if we force the science. No reason to believe the reactors at Hanford will be any different from the problems experienced here at Oak Ridge. I hope I'm wrong," Nichols said.

It was a train this time to Los Alamos. Given the time to write my assessment report, I was thoroughly depressed about the prospects of the Project. Without sufficient fissile material, the atomic bomb was just theoretical. For that matter, the design for the bomb had not yet been determined. More experimental work was required to understand the behavior of the fissile materials. So again, everything rested upon producing U-235 and P-239.

I was picked up at the Lamy rail station mid-morning. It was the first of February. The sky was clear with a few wispy clouds. The temperature was expected to reach 50 degrees. My first stop was to check in with Dr. Oppenheimer but I was informed that he was in Chicago. It was close to the lunch hour so I went to the library assuming Charlotte Serber would be there.

The outspoken Charlotte Serber was not only the wife of my friend Robert Serber, she was also the scientific librarian. She and her husband had been close friends to Robert Oppenheimer for many years. Project security had objected to the Serbers' extreme left-leaning political backgrounds to the extent they wanted them removed from the Project. Oppenheimer brushed aside the objections. In a slap in the face to the Army's security people, he made Robert Serber a group leader in the Theoretical Division, and Charlotte the librarian in charge of all of the documentation for all of the weapons laboratory work.

"Mike!" Charlotte said, and then came from behind her desk to give me a hug and a kiss on the cheek. "How's Elena?"

"Great."

"I hope to meet her when this is all over. Must be difficult being newlyweds and being apart so much."

"Can't complain. At least I get to see her every few weeks. You and Robert are very fortunate to be here together."

"Yes we are. And speaking of Robert, I was to meet him in the cafeteria for lunch. Join us?"

The original Fuller Lodge from the Boy's School was now the cafeteria. I shook hands all around with several of the scientists. Robert Serber greeted me warmly. He wanted to hear about how things were going with the production of fissile material but those discussions would have to wait until we were in a secure environment.

"Elena is fine I trust?" Serber said.

"Yes. It's tough with me being gone so much but she understands. Things have changed here in just the few weeks I've been away. Does the construction ever stop?"

Serber said. "It's a real city now. Schools, a hospital, municipal services. Colonel Ashbridge does an adequate job administering this place. Can't be easy."

"It's not all that good, Robert," Charlotte said. "It's still a prison. Shortages of various food items. Water restrictions. Then the security. That just gets worse. Particularly that asshole de Silva."

"Watch your language, Dear," Robert said.

"I don't care. De Silva's a Nazi. He's never liked Robert or me. Thinks we're not loyal. Doesn't trust Oppie either. All that washes over into petty restrictions. The Army has no regard how tough it is for civilians to be locked up like this. I don't mean to include you in my pique about the Army, Mike."

"No offense taken, Charlotte. I'm familiar with Major de Silva. He's a zealot. Sees things narrowly. Obviously General Groves has confidence in Oppie and by extension his team." Even so, I suggest you avoid any serious security breaches to stay out of the sights of Army intelligence."

I had already had my own run-in with Major Peer de Silva. Like Colonel Pash, he wanted me to keep alert for any security breaches in my unique role interacting with the scientists. I told him flat out that wasn't my mission. After a heated argument, I told him that I was not in the business of passing along what amounted to gossip so he could go on a witch hunt. I invoked the overarching priority of achieving project success, not satisfying security protocols. If he didn't like that, he could take it up with the General. I challenged him to see which of us had more clout. That was the last time we spoke which was months ago.

But I also knew Groves true feelings about the civilians locked up at Los Alamos. To his staff, he openly regarded them as 'children'. The base Army staff was tasked with not allowing living conditions or anything else to interfere with the Project's work. They were to see after the creature needs of the 'children'. Security on the other hand was a balancing act. No one was more paranoid about security than Groves himself so there was always friction.

"Did I hear a discussion about security?" Richard Feynman said as he walked over to our table and shook my hand. "Good to see you, Mike."

"Richard is our singular counter measure to the over-reaching security people here," Charlotte Serber said smiling broadly as Feynman joined us. "Tell Mike about your most recent adventure, Richard."

"Just a diversion to relieve the boredom, Charlotte. Nothing more than a little practical joke."

"Oh no. Richard is being too modest. This was an experiment to test the intelligence of the security guards. You see Richard found a hole in the fence. So he walked out the main gate, returned through the hole, and then walked out the gate again. He repeated this several times before the retards at the gate caught on that something wasn't right. De Silva wanted to arrest you didn't he, Richard?"

"All bluff and bluster," Feynman said. His mischievous grin identified his delight in harmlessly challenging the rigid security environment at Los Alamos.

Richard Feynman was the youngest of the senior scientists. He was recruited from Princeton through Robert Oppenheimer's personal efforts. Feynman was reluctant to come to Los Alamos because his new wife had tuberculosis. Oppenheimer personally arranged for her to go to a sanitarium in Albuquerque where Feynman could visit every couple of weeks. Oppenheimer recognized the young Feynman's brilliance and assigned him to Hans Bethe's theoretical division. Bethe took to him immediately. The renowned Danish physicist Niels Bohr, frequently consulting at Los Alamos, would seek out Feynman to discuss physics. Although Feynman was the youngest scientist at Los Alamos, he was the only scientist to speak his mind to the great Bohr. Their loud arguments became legend. Both Bethe and Bohr found Feynman's pure approach to arguing science useful in debating without consideration for exalted reputations.

Feynman was also a consummate prankster. That had a salutary effect on the stressed civilian population. Army security accused him of corresponding with his wife in code, demanding the cipher key. Feynman explained he didn't have the key since it was a game he played with his wife to practice code breaking.

Throughout his time at Los Alamos, Feynman's most auda-
cious prank was repeated safecracking. All the division heads
had personal safes. Technical papers were to be locked up when
not in use. Feynman was already an accomplished lock-pick so
doors and file cabinets were easy game. To this he developed
ingenious methods of discovering the combinations for safes.
His escapades were legendary. He drove security to distraction,
never owning up as the culprit. Only years later did he reveal his
secrets.

Everyone liked Richard Feynman, except of course Army security.

"It's Friday night. Robert and I will be over at Oppie's and
Kitty's for cocktails. Richard will be there too. Will you join us?"
Charlotte said.

"Shouldn't you ok that with Oppie or Kitty, Charlotte?" I
asked.

"It'll be fine. You're one of us."

Cocktails were well underway when I arrived. Kitty Oppenheimer gave me a kiss. I greeted all of the scientists and their
wives. All asked about Elena. They did in fact treat me as one of
their social group. I was again the only uniform at the gathering.

Oppenheimer arrived around seven. After making the
rounds with his famous martini in hand, he pulled me off to the
side. "Mike. Good to see you. You just came from Oak Ridge?"

"Yes, Sir."

"Your assessment? Are things really that bad there?"

"Bad enough, Sir. Everyone there is quite down, including
Colonel Nichols and the civilian contractors. They're working
like mad to resolve the problems. Eventually they will. The issue
is when? Frankly the problems seem so difficult I would not
even venture a timetable."

Oppenheimer lit another cigarette and signaled Kitty to refill
his martini. "Well things are not much better here on the Hill.

Without fissile material in larger quantities, the experimental work is delayed. Without the experimental work, the theoretical work cannot advance. We're at a point where we need to move beyond the approximations to tighter calculations. But I guess we shouldn't discuss that here. I can block out at least an hour tomorrow morning to bring you up to speed. Nine o'clock in my office?"

With that, Oppie left to find his martini.

Robert Serber joined me. We were both getting a little tipsy. Gin at this altitude had a more pronounced effect.

"Oh, there's someone you must meet," Robert said. "Come with me."

I followed Serber across the room. We joined a group of three men.

"George, I want you meet Major Mike Voronin. Mike, this is George Kistiakowsky. George just joined the team. He's been working at Harvard."

I was hoping to meet Kistiakowsky. We shook hands. He was tall and slender with thinning hair. He appeared to be in his forties. There was a trace of an East European accent.

"George is a fellow Russian, Mike."

"Not quite, Robert. I'm Ukrainian."

"But you fought in the Russian Civil War. Am I correct?" Serber said.

"That I did. I was studying in Moscow when the Bolshevik Revolution broke out in 1917."

"You fought in the Russian civil war? For which side?" I asked.

"For the Whites of course. I wasn't a tsarist, but the Bolsheviks were a bunch of fanatics with an ideology to simply give themselves power. Another dictatorship only with a different name. Joseph Stalin is the result."

"George is heading up the implosion program under Deke Parson's division. We'll talk more about that tomorrow. I'll be joining your meeting with Oppie." Serber said. "By the way, George, Mike may be Army but we don't hold that against him. He's more like one of us. A civil engineer by training so he understands the work. Works directly for Groves but we don't hold that against him either. Since the Army runs the lab, we have to expect their involvement. Believe me, dealing with Mike is a lot more pleasant than dealing with Groves."

"Your name, it's Russian, Major?" Kistiakowsky asked.

"Yes, Sir. First generation American. My parents came here from Moscow in 1913. They're academics. Too much political turmoil. It was fortuitous. They missed World War One, the Revolution, and the Civil War," I said. I omitted the fact they had returned to Russia.

Serber took my arm and moved us to a quiet corner of the Oppenheimer's large living room.

"Tomorrow when we meet with Oppie. Don't be surprised about his manner. He might seem a little depressed, at least not his usual self. It's about more than these recent difficulties with the Project. Have you ever heard the name Jean Tatlock?"

"No."

"Oppie was in love with Jean before Kitty. They almost married. Unfortunately, she was a troubled person. Suffered from severe depression. Even as a psychiatrist with a medical degree herself, she couldn't cope. About six weeks ago she committed suicide. The coroner's report said she died of drowning in her bathtub. They found the sedative chloral hydrate in her system."

Serber was right. Oppenheimer seemed subdued, maybe even a little remote when Serber and I joined him in his office. Not his usual ebullient engagement. His eyes, renowned for their piercing quality, appeared sad.

"Los Alamos has grown in just the few weeks I've been gone. Do you see the effects of the added staff yet, Doctor," I said.

"Too early, Mike. Ultimately it will make a difference. We have the best minds in the world right here. This directed scientific effort is unprecedented. The Army has even augmented the technical resources by setting up their so-called Special Engineering Detachment. These are people with scientific skills that provide us with talented technicians. Many of them were drafted from graduate studies. But all that breeds a whole new set of practical problems. We've grown to thousands. I believe the logistics involved with managing the care of so many is just as difficult as the scientific work."

"My opinion is you're doing an outstanding job. That's what my reports read," I said.

"What does the General think, Mike?"

"I believe he feels the same, Sir."

"Does he ever say so?"

"No, Sir. You know that's not the General's style. But there are never any negative comments I have heard from him about your leadership. He's not sensitive about criticizing others though."

"Thanks, Mike. Now, any good news from Oak Ridge?" Oppenheimer said.

"You've read the reports, Sir, so I won't rehash the technical details. As much as the setbacks with Y-12 and K-25 are serious, I believe there is an overall confidence that they will *eventually* be overcome. All the contractors are working non-stop on resolving the problems. Colonel Nichols is doing an outstanding job in managing this bewildering agenda. But no one appears confident about achieving the necessary production goals within the allotted year's time."

"That is of course the issue; *time*," Oppenheimer said. "All of us understand we are pushing the science. I'm proud how our team of scientists has adapted to the wartime demands to approach their work in a manner counter to all their training. But that still does not resolve the kinds of problems we are facing. For every two steps forward, there is a step backwards. Every new discovery we make changes something we had already built upon; the theoretical basis, a design, even the equipment under construction."

"Can you give me an overview of how work is progressing here at Los Alamos, Sir?" I asked.

"I'm not sure we're fairing any better than Oak Ridge. The gun design work is progressing. We're confident that the concept will work with 25 as the fissile material. Most of the work is now concentrated on the tamper and the initiator. But we are still a ways off from anything approaching a finalized design," Oppenheimer said.

"We're pretty confident about the performance of 25," Serber said. "Not so sure about how 49 will perform. What we do know is suggesting we would need to achieve a much higher velocity compared to 25 to drive the slug into the rings to achieve a super critical mass. Too slow a velocity of the slug would result in a fizzle. The problem is we need more 49 to do the necessary experimental work."

"Well you asked about the good news," I said. "Everyone is confident about the X-10 reactor at Oak Ridge. Things are on schedule. Fermi, Szilard, Seaborg are hovering over the work. That means you should receive working quantities of 49 for experimental work sometime in April. But I know what you mean about the potential for setbacks. Colonel Nichols said something along those lines about the reactors under construction at Hanford, when the prototype X-10 reactor is still not operational."

"What we don't know about 49 is part of the reason we are looking more closely into the implosion method," Oppenheimer said. "It's elegant in its concept compared to the rather crude mechanics of the gun design. Implosion represents a host of design possibilities not afforded by the gun method. But, and that is a big caveat, the thing is infinitely more complex. The theoretical work remains incomplete. But even with what we know, the engineering of a practical working design still remains well beyond our reach."

Serber said, "Richard Tolman originated the concept of implosion two years ago. Nobody was high on the approach at the time because of the obvious practical engineering hurdles. However, Oppie liked the possibilities it offered and set Seth Neddermeyer to work on the project. Neddermeyer's been doing experimental work for some time, but he still hasn't solved the problem of uniform shock wave propagation. That's why Oppie brought in George Kistiakowsky from Harvard. He's the best chemical explosives guy around. After the start of the War, he headed the National Defense Research Committee's Explosives Division."

"It's not only a chemical problem, but a mathematical problem of the highest order," Oppenheimer said. "Do you know John von Neumann?"

"I know the name from various reports. Mathematician isn't he?"

"Yes. Among other expertise. I believe he's the smartest mathematician of the century. He was one of the original four people selected for Princeton's Institute for Advanced Studies along with Albert Einstein. He's been consulting on the implosion problem. The problem is how to achieve the necessary symmetry of the shock wave to uniformly compress the plutonium core. The mathematics of the interacting physics is daunting."

"Speaking of the mathematics of implosion," Serber said, "Talk to your friend Feynman. He has taken on the task of marshalling the number crunching using IBM's new punch-card machines. Up to a short time ago, the calculations were done by manual computing with a cadre of scientists' wives using mechanical calculators."

Oppenheimer revealed a grin and the characteristic sparkle returned to his eyes. "That's because Feynman got bored with repairing the mechanical calculators. You see they were always breaking down requiring replacement. Feynman learned how to repair them. Drove Bethe nuts. Bethe thought it was a waste of time until they started to run out of working machines. But now Feynman has these new IBM toys."

"And true to his ingenuity, Feynman's already finding ways of getting faster results by an order of magnitude," Serber said.

"Is the implosion method going to be viable, Dr. Oppenheimer?" I asked.

Oppenheimer lit another cigarette before answering.

"Yes. I believe so. When the problem is solved it will most likely prove to be rather simple. But like everything else, when that will be accomplished is by no means certain."

I spent the next three weeks digging into the various areas of the project. If this were a normal research project one would have a feeling of confidence. We had the best minds in the world working on the problem. Resources were unlimited. But this was wartime. An enemy still remained that might well be engaged in the same work. Science did not operate along deadlines.

It was less than eighteen months from the target deadline to produce atomic bombs. There was currently no viable process for producing fissile materials in quantities sufficient for even one bomb, much less multiple weapons. Oppenheimer was discouraged. Groves must be also although he would never show it.

At least I was returning to Washington D.C. and Elena. It was spring. The cherry blossoms were in full bloom. Ironically the cheery trees were a gift from the Japanese over forty years ago.

CHAPTER 16

U.S. Capital Building, Washington D.C.

WASHINGTON D.C. – 1944

TRUE TO OUR routine, we made love as soon as I arrived back at the apartment. It was summer again. Even with the fan sending a breeze over us, we were both damp from our exertions.

"Good trip, Dear?" Elena said. She was propped up on her elbows, still naked. I hoped she would not try arousing me again as she sometimes did. I was thoroughly spent.

"Tough trip," I said. "Things are not going well."

"Not going well for you?"

"No, no. Things are fine with me. It's the Project. All sorts of technical problems."

"But this thing, this special bomb, can still be achieved?"

The guilt of violating security gave me pause. Here we were in bed casually talking about the United States' most secret war project as if it was about a day at the office.

"I believe so. I mean the scientists think so. It's more a question of when."

"Will they use this weapon against the Germans?"

"I suspect so. This whole race is to beat the Germans to develop the bomb first. The Germans are still a long way from defeat even with the Normandy landings two weeks ago."

The massive Allied amphibious landings of D-Day on the northern shore of France on June 6th had now opened a third front against Germany. The Germans were now defending Europe from all directions; from the east by the Russians, Italy in the south, now with the breach in Hitler's Atlantic Wall defense, from northern France. Round the clock bombing of their industrial base continued. The end of the Third Reich seemed only a matter of time. Unless of course they were to produce a game-changing weapon. German rocket development was well advanced. If they were to create an atomic bomb, they had the means of delivery on Great Britain.

"What happens if the Germans are defeated before we develop this atomic bomb? Would it be used against the Japanese?" Elena asked.

"I don't know. Probably. Hard to believe if this war is still going on that we would not use what could be a decisive weapon."

"What happens if the war is concluded with both Germany and Japan before we develop the bomb?"

"That I truly don't know."

"I know it will make the United States the most powerful nation in the world," Elena said. "Is that fair?"

"Fair? What do you mean?"

"If we win the war it will be because of the Soviet Union just as much as the United States. My God the losses they have taken. Continue to take. For two years, it's been mostly Russian soldiers dying. And the destruction. What will Russia be like after the war? And if the United States is the only one possessing this atomic bomb, then it will rule the entire world."

"I admit the United States would be the most powerful nation. But that doesn't mean it would *rule* the world."

"Well, I find it troubling. So do my parents. We talk about it all the time. Shouldn't we share the technology?"

"Nobody shares this kind of technology, Elena. It has potential commercial implications."

I was aware of similar sentiments among certain Manhattan Project scientists. Making the bomb had given rise to fundamental ethical concerns.

"Still, it seems unfair. So tell me about the people you work with."

I had already broken security by telling Elena about the Manhattan Project. That didn't mitigate the feelings of guilt, but it made further transgressions easier. Once I had crossed that line, further disclosures did not seem to worsen what I had already done. Besides, Elena was my wife. We were bound by trust. I did admonish her continually that nothing about what I did could be conveyed to her parents. I made that point strongly enough to frequently make her angry. But discussing personalities seemed less of breach of security than what I had already revealed.

"The scientists at Los Alamos are a swell bunch of guys. Brilliant, but friendly. Most of them have doctorates. Several have won the Nobel Prize."

"And you work with these people? Do you understand what their work is about?"

"I understand enough about their work to write my reports. You see that's what I do. My background is managing projects. Nothing like this of course, but I'm good at analysis. So that's my job, to analyze progress."

"And who reads your reports?"

"My boss. The head of the Manhattan Project, Major General Groves. I work for him directly. He told me that if he wasn't at one of our locations, then I will be there. I was to be his second set of eyes."

"Wow. So that's why you work with these scientists. I guess the Army runs the project so it needs to understand how things are going."

"Exactly. The civilians don't much like the Army, but they've accepted me. I've actually made many friends. There's one woman, her name is Charlotte. Always asks how you are."

"A woman? There are women at Los Alamos? I thought you said it was a bunch of scientists, men. And just who is Charlotte?"

I smiled at Elena's jealous tone. "Charlotte Serber. Married to my friend Robert. He's a theoretical physicist. Gives lectures to other physicists. Took a lot of his time to educate me in the science. Charlotte and Robert Serber are good friends of Robert Oppenheimer."

"Wait a minute. Go back. Are lots of women there? Mike, you'd better explain."

"Don't be jealous, Elena. All the women are married. Many of the senior scientists live there with their wives. It was necessary to entice them to work in this remote place. Everyone has very limited freedom to leave the Hill as we call it."

I chose not to be totally candid because of Elena's obvious concern about me being isolated where there were other women. I had just learned from Groves that a contingent of the Women's Army Corps was scheduled to join the growing Los Alamos community.

"The scientists with wives have their own small houses. The top guys have larger houses on what is called Bathtub Row because they are equipped with bathtubs rather than just showers. The Oppenheimer's have the largest home. They often throw cocktail parties. I'm one of the few people in uniform invited."

"Good for you mister bigshot," Elena said and playfully punched be in the ribs. "This sounds like some sort of country club."

"Not at all. Everybody works their butts off. Even the wives work doing computations. Charlotte is the librarian for the technical library. Everyone works long hours. Water is always in short supply. Too many people. The commissary has frequent shortages. Remember, this can feel like a prison to these people. They can't leave freely."

"And this Robert Oppenheimer – who is he?"

"Everyone calls him Oppie. He's the Scientific Director. An absolutely brilliant guy. But one heck of a nice guy too. Has this ability when you're talking to him to make you feel he is hanging on your every word. Has the most penetrating eyes you've ever seen."

I chose not to add the caveat that women adored him, probably because of those eyes. Best to avoid further mention of women.

"Anyway, all the scientists respect him. General Groves respects him, which is a pretty big deal."

"And this General Groves – what kind of boss is he?"

I smiled. "He's also brilliant. Blunt, arrogant, but he's got the stuff to back it up. Best project guy I've ever seen. Probably the best in the Army. But he's a real asshole to most everybody. Not too tough on me. Not sure why. Let's just say that I make sure my work is first rate. None of the staff wants to get crosswise with the General."

Here I was lying in bed with my naked wife violating security. I rationalized that the wives of the scientists probably knew what their husbands were doing. I'd be willing to bet that my officer colleagues at MED had at least told their wives something about what they did. Thousands knew about the Manhattan Project. I could trust Elena.

Two days later I arrived home late after a long meeting. Without waiting for my key to open the door, Elena pulled it open and kissed me quickly. "Mike, look what came!" All smiles, she held up an envelope. "A letter from Moscow. From your parents!"

I took the letter. It had been folded many times. One corner of the thin envelope had a large water stain. The Soviet Union postmark was dated three months ago. Not knowing where to address the letter, my parents simply forwarded it to the Army Corps of Engineers, Washington D.C. The apartment address was hand written on the envelope. Some War Department staffer had apparently taken the trouble to research my location in the personnel files.

Inside I extracted two pages. I smiled as I looked at each. One was typewritten. My father of course. He always preferred to type his correspondence, even to me. He would say that even he could not read his own scrawl so no one else would be able to either. The other was obviously from my mother.

My beloved Misha,

Oh how we miss you. It has been so long since we have received a letter from you. Know that we are keeping well. Your father constantly apologizes for our return to Mother Russia. I assure him that I do not. Our heritage is here. We are part of Russia. Part of you is Russian, Misha. The very foundation of one's soul gets its strength from the culture of their forbearers. As difficult as it is, we belong here.

My only regret is not being able to see you. This terrible war now makes that impossible until Germany is defeated. That seems so far in the future.

I worry that you may have to face danger. Your last letter before the war said little about what you do in the Army. I hope being in the Corps of Engineers has been good for you. I hope that you are able to build things rather than fight. I too work in the government as a translator, but cannot say anything about my duties. Your father teaches and translates English documents for the Red Army. The War has only

forced him deeper into his literary world. He has started
work on a new project of his own. That is encouraging be-
cause he sometimes appears so lost in the terrible real world
we are living in.

Do not worry about us. The food is meager. The worse is
the cold during winter with little fuel for heating. But we
survive. Russia will survive. We have each other which is
really everything.

Be safe my son. Write us. I know you must have written
often but your letters have yet to reach us. It has been so
long. I so cherish hearing from you, my dearest.

All my love my darling son,
Mother

Misha,

I am not sure when or even if you will receive this
letter, my son. Your mother and I have written for over
two years without receiving any letters from you. That
is understandable considering the War.

Things are difficult here but Russia is holding firm.
Comrade Stalin has marshaled our forces and stopped
the German advance. There is still terrible fighting but
our brave soldiers will prevail. We are thankful to them
for saving Moscow. The shortages of food and fuel are
severe, but we are fortunate to not have been living
further to the west of Moscow. Tens of thousands of
Russian civilians have been killed by the Nazi butchers
before they were stopped by the Red Army. So do not
worry about your mother and me. We are surviving.

I hope your career in the Army continues to advance.
We worry that you may end up fighting. The end of this
War is not yet in sight. At least you are an engineer.
Hopefully you can contribute in defeating our enemies.
Russia is now joined alongside America and the British.

America must continue to confront the Japanese in the Pacific, but I hope it will also assist Russia against Germany. Russia has single handedly held the Germans for over two years. The Germans are just as much a threat to America as the Japanese. Russia has sacrificed tens of thousands of young men. Those losses continue. It is difficult to envision Russia's future with a whole generation of young men decimated by the time this conflict is over. We look to America to help Russia after the War. Having lived in America for over twenty years, I know the American people have great compassion. Let us hope that political differences will not get in the way of humanity.

Life goes on for us. I continue to teach my students, but I contribute to the war effort in translating English documents for the Army. Your mother is working as a translator in the Foreign Ministry. She is enclosing her own letter. The post is still uncertain although we are told that there has been improvement. So we hope the chances improve to receive our communications. Please continue to write us in the hope that we might hear from you.

Do not worry for our safety. We are well.

Love,

Father

"Elena. Here read these!" I said excitedly.

"Darling, I can speak Russian but not read it."

"Oh, right. Then let me read them to you. This is wonderful news. They're alive. Things are difficult but they're coping. Here's what they say."

I immediately wrote a letter back, encouraged that communications may have improved. The letter's return address confirmed that my parents were still at the same Moscow address I had been using. That was a great comfort.

Two days later I was headed back out to Oak Ridge to monitor progress on the Y-12 and K-25 plants. From there I would go to Hanford to follow progress on the plutonium reactors construction. Then back to Los Alamos to determine if a bomb design will be ready for the following year. The nagging worry about my parents was much relieved. I had a feeling that things might now be changing for the better.

CHAPTER 17

NKVD Headquarters, Lubyanka, Moscow

MOSCOW, USSR – 1943

IT HAD BEEN almost a year since the meeting in Lavrentiy Beria's office. Lieutenant Colonel Kirilov had taken charge of the Soviet military's intelligence effort to penetrate the American-British atomic bomb development program. Although above his pay grade, Kirilov was also aware that the Soviet Union had established its own research into nuclear weapons two years previously. For some unknown Stalinistic logic, the program was placed under the Soviet Ministry of Foreign Affairs. The program was only of secondary interest in early 1943. It would not yield a decisive weapon before the end of the war. With the all-consuming industrial effort to counter the German invasion with men and materiel, funding for atomic weapons research was meager.

The Red Army's GRU had been aware of early German efforts directed at nuclear fission research. The discovery of nuclear fission was first reported by German chemists Otto Hahn and Fritz Strassmann in 1939. Austrian physicists Lise Meitner and Otto Frisch provided the first theoretical explanation of the fission process.

The brilliant theoretical physicist, Werner Heisenberg, winner of the Nobel Prize in Physics in 1932, along with Professor Kurt Diebner, began pursuing research in earnest shortly thereafter. At that time, the Third Reich was doing the most advanced research work into nuclear fission. With the occupation of Norway, Germany had a source for heavy water produced as a byproduct of a fertilizer plant at Telemark, Norway. Known as deuterium oxide, heavy water, ^2H_2O, acts as a neutron moderating source in a nuclear chain reaction fission process. Heavy water could be used as the moderating component in the construction of a nuclear reactor. A neutron moderator reduces the speed of fast neutrons, thereby turning them into thermal neutrons capable of sustaining a controlled nuclear chain reaction. In simplest form, a nuclear reactor consisted of fissile fuel surrounded by a moderator.

Soviet agents had reported that funding for the principle work being conducted by Heisenberg had been cut off in 1942 by Albert Speer the Reich's armament minister. By Heisenberg's own assessment, an atomic bomb could not be achieved earlier than 1945. Herman Goering then funded an alternate project. A third program was begun to explore nuclear propulsion for submarines. German nuclear research was now fragmented into separate programs. Clearly, nuclear weapons research was without support from the highest levels of the Third Reich. Furthermore, the German scientific community had been decimated by Hitler's virulent anti-Semitic policies, driving the leading physicists to Great Britain or the United States.

The Soviets knew all this. Soviet intelligence had made deeper penetrations into the German scientific programs than the British or Americans. They had simply been engaged in espionage longer. The Soviets knew that the Germans were not aggressively pursuing atomic bomb research. The British and Americans however appeared to be giving the research top priority. They had the physical resources and now the intellectual resources. Obviously the work was not being shared with their Soviet ally. From the Soviet perspective, the American effort was less about creating a weapon to win the War than about strategic world hegemony.

This unified program secretly called the Manhattan Project was the center of atomic bomb development. Because of the threat of German bombing and potentially even invasion, Britain had relocated its nuclear weapons development program, code named Tube Alloys, to Montreal, Canada in early 1943. That intelligence related to Allied atomic bomb research efforts had originally made its way to the Soviets by the spy code named LISZT. The spy that Kirilov knew only by the code name was run by the rival NKVD. He was a highly placed source within the British Secret Intelligence Service, MI6, providing the Soviets with the most sensitive strategic information.

Kirilov assessed GRU assets already established in Canada and the United States. In 1941, a German physicist, and former member of the German Communist Party was recruited by a major in Soviet military intelligence, Ruth Werner, code named SONIA. The scientist, code named REST had received his PhD in physics from the University of Bristol. As a GRU-run asset, Kirilov knew his real name – Klaus Emil Julius Fuchs. Fuchs was now working with the British Tube Alloys program and passing regular intelligence to the Soviets. The Tube Alloys program was being merged into the larger American Manhattan Project. Many of the British scientists joined that effort, including Fuchs.

There was another British physicist within the Tube Alloys program recruited by the GRU while at Cambridge. His name was Alan Nunn May, code named ALEK. He was now part of the British scientific group transferred to the Montreal Laboratory which was building a nuclear reactor at Chalk River near Ottawa, Canada.

Soviet GRU intelligence in Canada was run by Colonel Nicolai Zabotin, code named GRANT. Ostensibly he was the Soviet

Military Attaché in Ottawa. Zabotin's network had cultivated other sources within the atomic research program in Canada beyond REST and ALEK. Zabotin's coded transmissions related to atomic weapons now went to Kirilov's desk in Moscow. Unfortunately, those transmissions went through Soviet embassy cipher clerks also handling Soviet NKVD transmissions. While in different codes, Kirilov thought the system was an unnecessary security risk. For any new penetrations, Kirilov would employ a much more secure connection to Moscow than embassy cipher personnel.

With the British effort now integrated into the American program, Canada became peripheral to atomic bomb development. Zabotin's network would be of diminished value. Although REST had been assigned to the weapons development laboratory in New Mexico, the other Canadian spies were no longer central to the work. More than that, Kirilov was forced to hand over control of REST to the NKVD out of New York when REST was reassigned to the American laboratory. Espionage in the United States was principally controlled by the NKVD. Kirilov's security concerns about Soviet embassy-controlled espionage would eventually be well founded.

So Kirilov found himself with few assets in place in the United States. Scientific information related to nuclear physics had gone underground by 1942. It was apparent that a wartime program had covered the science with a security blanket. The only information finding its way to Moscow was third-hand material passed through sympathetic persons not thinking that anything they were doing constituted espionage.

While REST may become important inside the Manhattan Project, Kirilov knew he would need more. Besides, REST would now be run by the NKVD. The NKVD had a string of assets recruited primarily from the Communist Party of America. Kirilov thought these types of recruits added a further potential security risk because of their backgrounds. The NKVD was a bunch of stupid police-types. Their tactics were crude. Moscow allowed too much lower-level control. Their communications methods involved too many individuals. They relied on quantity rather than quality intelligence. Even if the NKVD willingly shared their intelligence with the GRU, Kirilov could not rely on them being successful. It was his neck if he did not deliver what Beria expected, and what ultimately Stalin expected.

Kirilov would pursue other avenues to gain access into the Manhattan Project secrets. The first source was an agent code named DELMAR. The agent was an American born to Russian-Jewish parents. His name was George Abramovich Koval. He was a brilliant student, graduating from high school at age fifteen. He then studied electrical engineering at the University of Iowa. Koval's carpenter father having immigrated to the United States in 1910, now chose to take his family back to Russia in 1932. The Organization for Jewish Colonization of the Soviet Union organized a bizarre venture in the eastern reaches of Russia near the border with Manchuria. This was the Communist answer to the Zionist movement in Palestine.

Already sympathetic to Communist ideology, Koval was recruited and trained by the GRU. After having earned an advance degree in chemical technology, Koval was returned to the United States in 1940.

But in 1943, Koval was drafted into the U.S. Army. Seemingly this put him out of reach for the GRU to direct his activities. However, recognizing his abilities and past education, the Army sent him to the City College of New York to study electrical engineering. He might be eventually useful, but not at this time.

With Koval unavailable, Kirilov reviewed the GRU's list of other sleeper agents settled in North America, some for many years now. This had been the vision of the first head of the Soviet Intelligence Service, Yan Karlovich Berzin. He personally recruited and ran the most outstanding intelligence officers of the GRU. It was Berzin himself that recruited Kirilov into the Service. Kirilov learned his trade from the old master. He hoped he learned better survival skills. Berzin was arrested and executed in 1938 along with most high ranking military officers during the Great Purge.

The list of sleeper agents was short. Only twelve individuals; seven in the United States, the others in Canada. Kirilov spent the next two days delving into the backgrounds of these agents to understand the limited tools at his disposal. Except for REST, there were no physicists among the Soviet sleeper agents. The question was therefore one of targets not weapons. How to recruit a high-level physicist? Recruiting meant for reasons of ideology, money, or blackmail.

There was a husband and wife team of sleeper agents in Montreal that was highly regarded by the Canadian GRU head, Colonel Zabotin. They had been activated when the British moved their Tube Alloys project to Canada. They were code named PUPPETEER and TRAVELER. PUPPETEER was a senior chemist. Working for DuPont in explosives research, Kirilov had communicated instructions through Zabotin for PUPPETEER to seek a transfer to a DuPont plant in the United States. Kirilov had no specific plan but was simply moving his chess pieces into a potentially useable position. Although not a physicist, PUPPETEER was still a scientist with a PhD. This might afford some future opportunity.

The resourceful PUPPETEER was successful in obtaining a transfer. The Chambers Works DuPont plant in New Jersey provided a perfect fit. The facility engaged in high-grade explosives research for the U.S. military. It was only two hours north of Washington D.C. DuPont was an important military contractor. The company immediately seized upon PUPPETEER's transfer request to bolster their war-effort research staff in the United States.

For the next two months, Kirilov focused on creating a list of potential targets. That alone was an intelligence gathering task.

The American Manhattan Project was cloaked in top secret security. Its weakness lay in the sheer number of people involved, particularly the number of civilian scientists. Kirilov had a small staff of three junior officers, hand-picked, bright, and dedicated to Kirilov.

The list of possible targets was centered on the scientific community, particularly physicists. Kirilov's staff worked through low-level intelligence reports by operatives probing U.S. research universities. The absences of the top names in physics from among the faculty signaled they were probably now part of this secret project.

The list produced was lengthy. It included not only biographies of the scientists, but a specific grading of factors that might suggest how each might be co-opted to spy for the Soviet Union. The prevailing thread among this group was a significant number of the top scientists were known to hold left-leaning sympathies. Some had openly Communist ties. Many rated high on the potential for recruitment based upon these ideological grounds. For that reason alone that would make them difficult targets since they would be regarded with suspicion by the Americans.

Beyond the list of targets, the staff had constructed a map of the key locations representing the Manhattan Project. The scientists would be sequestered under tight security. Correspondence and communications would be censored. If they had leftist backgrounds, they might be singled out for added surveillance.

It was one o'clock in the morning as Kirilov and his staff sat around a conference table. The room was stale with cigarette smoke. The table littered with files and coffee cups. They were reviewing the list in detail attempting to pare it down to a manageable short list. After twelve hours, all looked exhausted.

Kirilov's aide, Captain Dubrovsky summarized the list. "Comrade Colonel. This list of twenty scientists represents the best possibilities for recruitment. Some may actually be politically motivated if approached with the right overtures. I believe we must now shift to the means of how to approach them. Given the security we will need to find creative means. Beyond that, we will need to understand what assets are available."

"We have assets that can be deployed," Kirilov said. He alone knew the identity of these special assets. "But this list represents targets to be recruited solely based upon political inclination. Do we rule out money? What about blackmail?" Kirilov was playing the devil's advocate.

"Money is an unlikely inducement, Comrade Colonel. These are all successful academics. Money is not a strong motivator. As for blackmail, we have not uncovered anything compelling except for the Communist sympathies. But of course, that will already be known to American security. Their politics have not excluded them from this work. Perhaps there are sexual improprieties, but our intelligence has not revealed anything obvious we could use."

"Perhaps that is the way though. Use sex as a means of creating our own basis for blackmail," one of the other officers said.

"Explain, Oleg Sergeyvich," Kirilov said to the young lieutenant.

"These men not only have families, they have careers. Their prestige within the academic community is all important. The threat of loss of family and career would be very powerful."

Everyone paused to consider that idea. Kirilov chastised himself silently for having not thought this as an obvious avenue of attack.

Kirilov said, "Oleg Sergeyvich has made an excellent suggestion. We will take this list and do another assessment starting with the best possibilities among the candidates. Situations, age, looks, previous relationships with women. Homosexuality? But that will be for tomorrow. We are all too tired right now."

"Comrade Colonel. There is something else I would like to suggest," the same lieutenant said. "What about military personnel working on the American project? You have told us it is their Army's engineering corps that is in charge. There must be certain officers that have access to the scientific work."

"That would be even more difficult, Lieutenant," Captain Dubrovsky said.

Kirilov looked up from the list of names he had been staring at. "Perhaps. However we have only identified the senior army officers involved. Beyond this General Groves, we have not assembled much of list. If we take the Lieutenant's approach of a honey-trap, that could just as easily apply to an army officer. Captain, begin assembling a list of military staff down to junior officers within this Corps of Engineers. This is an engineering project. If it is headed by an engineering officer, then his staff will largely be from that background. Look at personnel records from even before the start of the War. Officers that may have worked for Groves. Those involved with this project would be officers with some experience."

Three days later, Kirilov's staff assembled again.

"Comrade Colonel. Lieutenant Alexeyev's idea has produced results," Captain Dubrovsky said. "We have three possible candidates among the American Army's staff running their bomb project. You were correct also, Comrade Colonel, they're all experienced Army engineers. But of the three, one individual clearly stands out. We've assembled his dossier, Sir. You'll see what we mean."

Dubrovsky handed a red folder to Kirilov.

"His name is Mikhail Stefanovich Voronin," Dubrovsky said.

Kirilov looked up. "Russian?"

"Yes, Sir. Born in the United States. Parents emigrated from Russia in 1913. But it gets better, Sir. Voronin's father was teaching at Moscow State University. Classical Studies. His mother taught music there. She was an accomplished violinist. The parents were early Bolsheviks. Committed activists. They were on the Okhrana's watch list. They immigrated to the United States to escape Tsarist prison."

"You've examined the original files?"

"Yes, Sir. I personally looked at the old Cheka files. The NKVD was unusually cooperative when I dropped your name, Sir."

The Cheka was the earliest Soviet secret police organization set up in 1917 immediately after the Bolshevik Revolution. Its name was an abbreviation of Vecheka, itself an acronym. It transformed in later years to the lengthy organizational names known under the acronyms GPU, OGPU, NKVD, MVD, and eventually to the KGB in 1954.

"No record of them ever joining the Communist Party of America. Appears they kept a low profile about their political views."

"Or they're not committed Communists. Maybe they just hated the Tsar," Kirilov offered.

"No, Sir. They were committed before they emigrated. The Cheka files documented their participation in a number of violent events. It equally makes sense that they fled because they were forced to. But even at that time, there was much anti-Communist feeling in America. They apparently never engaged in any political activity or their son would never have been given a sensitive security clearance."

"Very well. And the parents now? Are they a potential source of leverage?"

"Unfortunately no, Sir. The parents returned to Moscow in 1935. Voronin's father lost his academic position in California because of the economic Depression. He was offered a position at the Moscow State University."

"They're here in Russia?"

"In a manner of speaking. The father died last year. He was arrested for criticizing Comrade Stalin's conduct of the war. Sentenced to ten years hard labor, he didn't survive even one year in the Gulag."

"And the wife?"

"Also sentenced to ten years at the same time. She's now in a camp on the Upper Yenisei River in Siberia. On that matter our colleagues at the NKVD were not helpful. It will take someone with higher rank to know exactly what camp and her current situation."

Kirilov consulted the dossier and commented out loud. "Rank of major. Educated in the United States. Civil engineer. Unmarried. Believed to work on Brigadier General Groves personal staff? Doing what?"

Dubrovsky was stopped short. There was no way Soviet intelligence would know that. But he knew to answer concisely. Kirilov did not tolerate vague responses.

"That we do not know, Sir. We are not even completely sure he works on the commanding general's staff. Their bomb project is cloaked within their Army's engineering command structure. General Groves heads the Manhattan Engineering District which is the cover unit managing the bomb project. But it may have other unconnected functions. Our conclusion comes from Voronin's prior associations working directly for Groves monitoring Army construction projects. He's an engineer so he's not in intelligence. It appears General Groves' staff is very small. There's a good chance that Voronin works on General Groves' personal staff. All of that gives a high probability to his broad access within the program."

"Personal habits?"

"Not much is known since this comes from a low level source with only access to U.S. Army personnel files. No negative comments appeared in his record. Superiors consistently give him praise for his work, General Groves included. High intellect. That he plays chess at a very high level was noted for some reason within his file."

"Women?"

"Unmarried. Nothing from these records gives any indication beyond that. We have no photograph yet, but the source looking at his personnel photo said he was good looking. Average build by his physical description."

"Obviously we must rule out homosexual tendencies if we're to use a woman," Kirilov said. "Make the appropriate arrangements to find out more about all three of your candidate targets. We need to understand their personal habits. What do they do for fun? Circle of friends? And of course their sexual interests, including even the one target that is married. Use only GRU assets, no NKVD involvement."

Kirilov paused to light a cigarette. "You have all done excellent work. And I have also been working. You have found the target. I believe I have found the weapon. Assuming of course this Major Voronin is attracted to pretty women."

That weapon lay with the recently relocated agents, PUPPETEER and TRAVELER. The key was their adopted daughter. Now twenty-four, she was a university graduate. Her birth parents were Russian. Her adoptive parents had indoctrinated her politically. Intelligence reports from PUPPETEER revealed he had already recruited her, but she had not yet actively done any work. The three agents, now positioned in the United States close to Washington D.C., opened up promising possibilities. The target now was the American atomic bomb project. The photograph of the daughter clearly suggested she would be the ideal instrument for the sexual entrapment of a highly placed person within this Manhattan Project. He would code name her DANCER. With her figure and long legs, she looked like a dancer.

While the GRU handled atomic espionage in Canada, the NKVD was in charge in the United States. Since Kirilov was handed the task of penetrating the American atomic bomb program, he knew he was in a competitive race with Beria's own NKVD. For that matter, Kirilov was in competition with other

GRU operations. Once relocated to the United States, PUPPET-EER, TRAVELER, and DANCER were to be solely his assets. The long time resident GRU agent in the United States, Arthur Adams, code name ACHILLES, was in nominal control of all GRU agents in the United States, but his intelligence was shared too readily with the NKVD. PUPPETEER, TRAVELER, and DANCER would not work through ACHILLES.

Kirilov knew the value of PUPPETEER, TRAVELER, and DANCER. Already having reservations about security, he made sure that the relocated agents communicated directly to him rather than using joint cipher resources with the NKVD at embassies and consulates. His method of communications was more cumbersome but more secure. Kirilov would directly control PUPPETEER, TRAVELER, and DANCER. He would keep this deep and dark. Better for operational security, better to insure his personal survival.

CHAPTER 18

VICTORIA PRESCOTT WALKED out of the terminal at JFK International into a hot New York summer day. That was fine by her. Better than the cold of winter. That part of New York she always disliked. San Francisco was more her climate, but there was still something about New York. You felt like you were at the center of everything here.

She had declined her mother's offer to pick her up. She told her mother and father she would be in New York for a few days, but did not imply anything more than just an overdue family visit. First she would visit her grandfather at an assisted living facility just north of the airport. She wanted to ask him some questions without having to explain to her mother.

The taxi pulled up to a pretty two-story brick building. The lobby inside could have been an upscale hotel. But one look around the corner into the dayroom told you otherwise. Old people at the end of their lives. Prescott had been here several times since her mother had persuaded her grandfather to move closer after the death of his wife four years ago. The surroundings made her uncomfortable.

She purchased her grandfather's townhouse in San Francisco when he relocated to Long Island closer to his daughter. Aron Zielinski hated the idea of living around other old people, but his physical condition had deteriorated to a point where he could not adequately get along by himself. A legacy of a lifetime of smoking, he suffered from emphysema to the extent he now required an oxygen bottle as a constant companion.

Zielinski had a pleasant room with large windows. It was well decorated with some interesting artwork. To Victoria, it still had the decay smell of old people, of approaching death. After the hugs and pleasantries, Victoria got down to the reason for her visit.

"Grandfather, do you remember an army officer at Los Alamos by the name of Voronin?"

Zielinski thought for a moment. "Let me see. Voronin you say? Yes, of course. Groves' man. On and off the Hill. He wasn't stationed there."

"What exactly did Voronin do?"

"Do? He reported on our work. Reported to Groves on how we were doing. Groves needed his own source of information. Probably didn't trust Oppenheimer's reports. Groves was a real SOB. He was out at the Hill quite often too. I remember one time when ....."

Prescott had to cut her grandfather short to stay on track. "Back to this Voronin, Grandfather. Did you ever talk to him?"

"A few times I remember. He would of course talk more to my boss George Kistiakowsky, the guy heading the implosion group where I worked. You see we worked ....."

It hurt Victoria to see her grandfather with his brilliant mind and sharp wit starting to slip continually back into the past. Was this what the early stages of dementia looked like? The tendency to drift off into some remote place in his mind had been evident the last time she saw him.

"Oh I know what you did, Grandfather. Remember I wrote my thesis on the Manhattan Project. I know it like I was there. But I wasn't there like you were. So you are that window into things that are not part of the written history. Tell me what you can remember about Major Voronin."

Her grandfather's eyes took on some of the old fire of before.

"You're up to something aren't you young lady? Voronin seems like such a peripheral player. So I'll tell you what I can remember. But you'll tell your old grandfather what this is about won't you, Dear?"

"I promise, Grandfather. Now tell me what you remember."

"Not all that much since Voronin spent most of his time with the head scientists. Pleasant guy as I recall. He was always making notes. Wanted to understand things. Always asking us to clarify something or explain something further. Smart guy was my impression. I think he was some sort of engineer. Asked good questions. Used analogies to help himself understand the theoretical stuff. I could see why Groves choose him to report on progress."

"Did he socialize with the scientists?"

"Oh yes. But it was mostly with the bigshots, the department heads, the group leaders. The same guys that went to Oppie's cocktail parties on Bathtub Row. That was unusual. The Army officers were not well liked. We thought they were all a pain in the ass. Certainly the security guys were. The SED technicians were a good bunch, but then again they were drafted enlisted ranks. So Major Voronin was something of an exception."

"Did he have access to pretty much everything?"

Zielinski seemed to come alive. "Yes, of course. Probably most everything. And he came and went from the Hill. I know where this is going, Victoria. Are you suggesting he might have been a Soviet spy?"

Victoria smiled. This was the grandfather she chose to remember. The keen mind that always thought the Soviets must have had deeper access than Klaus Fuchs and the other known spies.

"Yes I do, Grandfather. I need to corroborate some things though. Still a lot of work to do, but it's him. I know it."

"And what makes you so sure, Dear?"

"Because of a link that can't be refuted, once of course I prove it. He married into a family of Soviet agents."

"Sonofabitch!" Aron Zielinski said, slapping his knee.

Victoria Prescott tearfully left her grandfather. She felt buoyed up by the visit. There was always a special relationship between the two. Even as a young girl, he treated her as an adult. And in his world that meant stretching her intellectually. Victoria's grandmother was every bit her husband's intellectual equal. They were never dotting. Victoria always felt like an adult around her maternal grandparents. The visit left the old man with a sense of excitement. He was rooting for his granddaughter.

She took a taxi to the train station for the ride into Manhattan. Her parents had an apartment on the upper Westside. It was only two miles south from the Columbia University campus where her father was a professor of political science. While Victoria Prescott's father had a distinguished career in government and academia, it would normally not provide sufficient wealth to afford the exorbitant real estate values of apartments with views of Central Park. That was satisfied with the high-salary income of her mother as a senior partner in an international law firm.

The trip was not entirely social. She had told her father only that she needed his help. To his question, "Are you in trouble, Victoria?" She laughed at his parental concern and told him no. It was about her book. That relieved the concern but provoked the comment, "Oh. Does that mean you're still obsessed with that undiscovered spy theory?" She avoided arguing on the phone, leaving it only that she needed his professional help. Besides she wanted to see him and Mom.

She arrived late in the afternoon. Her family got on well for a family of gifted overachievers. Her parents had well established professional careers. Her oldest brother was a surgeon. Another brother, three years older was successfully following his mother into international law, while she was following more closely in the academic path of her father. When the family interacted, the conversation more often turned to impersonal topics. You learned to debate in the Prescott household.

So the usual family social amenities were disposed of quickly after settling in the living room. Her book was nearing completion. Yes her live-in boyfriend, Phillip was doing well. In fact it was his expertise that made for the breakthrough in her research. She did not mention their domestic difficulties.

She and her mother were drinking champagne, her father a single malt Scotch.

"We have dinner reservations for eight-thirty, so we can get to what your visit is all about then have a relaxing evening," her father said. "So tell me what it is you want me to do, Vicky. It's about this spy thing isn't it?"

Victoria scowled at him. "Dad, it's not this obsession you think it is. I know what I'm doing. I admit it's been a pet project for years. But this thing now has legs."

"Ever since Aron regaled you with his Los Alamos stories, you've been absorbed with the Soviet espionage of the Manhattan Project. It was his theory that there must have been some high-level Soviet spy never discovered. That's just conspiracy nonsense with no foundation in fact."

"Maybe it was Grandpa Zielinski's theory. But it's more than that now, Dad. Let me lay out the case before you rush to judgment."

For the next thirty minutes, she went over the facts she had assembled. He father interrupted with a few comments related to the chronology. From a perspective of evidentiary construction, her mother asked questions about alternative possibilities.

When Victoria was done she said, "Well. What do you think?"

"You first, Ham. Does this rise to more than mere speculation?" her mother said to her father.

"I'll admit it bears further investigation. But these circumstances could certainly have other explanations. You know that don't you, Vicky?" her father said.

"Of course. I'm a scholar, no matter where my imagination takes me. But you do agree I should pursue this? You couldn't expect me to shelve it?"

"No. I wouldn't either. But look, you said yourself that the Venona transcripts that were made public last year make no references to these agents PUPPETEER and TRAVELER. Those names came only from the Gouzenko defection materials. And you say nothing appears after 1942."

"That's right. I believe they came to the United States. Voronin married Obolensky in 1943," Victoria said.

"But the FBI apparently never followed up on PUPPETEER and TRAVELER," her father said.

"Appears they didn't, but I'm not sure. That's what I want to find out. Since Gouzenko defected in late 1945, the War was already over. If the FBI pursued any connection with a Canadian chemist probably working for DuPont, then the trail would end with the Ramazanovs' deaths in September of that year. Could be there just wasn't any motivation to dig deeper. That's why I want to see their investigative files. It should also include the RCMP and the British MI5 investigations too. I'm looking for details beyond what was made public."

Victoria turned to her mother. "Mother, what's your verdict?"

"No verdict, Dear. You haven't got enough to take to a jury. But you already understand that. What you have is a very compelling set of circumstances that could, and I emphasize could, prove what you suspect. That's the basis of all legal work. You've got a strong argument I'll admit. I'm even curious to find out the truth. But you do know that your hypothesis rests solely on proving that this army officer's in-laws were Soviet spies. Even at that, it would not directly prove that he was a spy himself. He could have been a just a poor dupe."

"And that would be newly discovered history, but I'm not sure it would be earthshaking," her father said. "What's one more spy from that era?"

Christ, her own father sounded like Phil Baxter but she restrained herself.

"The difference, Dad, is this Mikhail Voronin had access to *everything*. Literally everything. Anything Groves saw, Voronin knew intimately, and in real time. All the other spies just had pieces. Even Fuchs. But more than that, if Voronin was a spy, he may have continued well beyond 1945 into the thermonuclear weapons era. He remained with the nuclear weapons program until 1959. If he continued after the War, he could have been the singular factor that gave the Soviets not only the atomic bomb earlier, but the hydrogen bomb much sooner as well. All the other known spies were arrested or left nuclear weapons development after 1945.

"Dad, you've written yourself that the Cold War came about not because of nuclear weapons, but the speed with which the Soviet Union gained nuclear parity with the United States. Right?"

"Yes. Timing made the difference. But tell me this is academically sound work, Vicky. This is not just some competitive thing with your colleague Dr. Holloway. You're working in the same field, in the same era after all," her father said.

Dr. David Holloway was a professor of political science and history at Stanford. He was Victoria Prescott's doctorial advisor and mentor in her chosen field of the Cold War and nuclear weapons. It was both her grandfather and Holloway that focused her interest on the origins of atomic weapons and the Cold War. Dr. Holloway had published *Stalin and the Bomb* just two years ago.

"Come on, Dad. That's not fair. It's as much your field too. You don't think I'm competing with you, do you? I'm just pursuing my own original work."

Her father was a highly respected political science academic, specializing in the Soviet Union. He lived the Cold War at the front lines serving as Undersecretary for Political Affairs in the State Department during the two Reagan administrations and the Bush administration. He was the ranking Soviet specialist. During that period of high U.S.-Soviet tensions, it put him close to Secretaries of State Shultz and Baker as well as Presidents Reagan and Bush as an influential Soviet expert. He returned to Columbia University in 1992. Dr. Hamilton Prescott was published and still consulted for the State Department and the Department of Defense.

"Ok. Let's hear it. What do you want me to do," her father said with a sign of resignation. He still wasn't completely taken with her premise, but he admired her talent.

"I need your influence. Nothing inappropriate. But you're still a big shot in all things political involving Russia. I know there's an old boy network. That's how things get done. I heard enough of your conversations growing up. So I need your influence, Dad. I need to see things, things in archives. Things to confirm or refute with certainty that this guy was a Soviet spy."

"And whose arm do you want me to twist, my Dear?" He smiled at the guile of his daughter.

"More than one actually, Dad. One is the FBI. The other maybe more difficult. That would be the Russian SVR."

"And obviously you have not been successful or you wouldn't be drafting me into this work."

"Only Partly. At least with the FBI. I've submitted a Freedom of Information request. Problem is that takes forever. Voronin is 83. He's still alive, but I don't know what his health is like. I need to complete the research and confront him to bring this thing full circle."

She explained that she wanted to review everything in the FBI files associated with the defection of the Canadian based Soviet GRU cipher clerk, Igor Gouzenko in 1945. She also wanted to see the background details related to the security clearance background check for a Boris Ramazanov. All that material should be declassified by now. Most was public knowledge. Ramazanov died in 1945. She sought her father's influence only to push things along, not circumvent any legal restrictions.

"Ok. I know someone that can help. Now what is it you want from the SVR? That'll be quite a different situation. They've really only existed for a couple of years under their new name. They're not my specialty, but I can tell you they are still in a state of some disorganization. They're mostly former KGB. That's of course the ones that survived the modern day purge after the KGB was dissolved in 1991 in the wake of the attempted coup against Yeltsin."

The Soviet Union ceased to exist in 1989 in its police-state centralized form with the election of a legislative body and a president, Mikhail Gorbachev. The various republics constituting the federation gained autonomy. It held at least the trappings of a democratic government. Too much for some old-line factions. In 1991, there was an attempted coup d'état to topple Gorbachev and the first elected president of the newly declared sovereign Russian Republic, Boris Yeltsin. Some units of the KGB participated, along with its head, Vladimir Kryuchkov.

The KGB was disbanded immediately afterwards. Dissident KGB personnel were purged, not by execution as in the old Stalinist days, but at least by job elimination. The process nevertheless was organizationally painful to the insular security service.

The successor SVR and FSB were formed, separating the former KGB's dual role of foreign intelligence organ and the internal enforcement instrument of a police state. The SVR became responsible for foreign intelligence, with the FSB responsible for internal security similar to the distinction of the United States' CIA and FBI.

"I don't know how cooperative they might be. That's why I need you to navigate. I'd have no stature over there. But I don't think I'm looking at things that should be all that sensitive. After all, just a couple of years ago, the Russians released volumes of material about their atomic espionage activities during the Second World War."

"That's what you want to look at? I thought you said your spies were foreign military intelligence, the GRU, not NKVD?"

"Well I would like to look at the GRU's files too. I assumed since that is military, it would be much more difficult. Since Beria was in charge of the Soviet atomic bomb program, I assumed that all GRU intelligence eventually flowed to him at the NKVD. It was that old NKVD archive material on atomic espionage that was released in 1992 after the KGB was broken up. The GRU was not that forthcoming. But if you're suggesting you could wangle that too, Dad, that would be terrific."

"You're right on all of that. And no I don't have any direct inroads into the Russian Army's military intelligence directorate. So what do I tell this someone from the old boy's club that my daughter wants to see?"

"Scholar, historian, Dad, not daughter," Victoria said rolling her eyes. "What I want to see is original material behind the things they already made public. Material related to the documents stolen by Gouzenko in 1945. That information came from Canada. That's the link. All of this is around Boris and Vanya Ramazanov. Where did they come from? Were they Soviet spies? I want to see what they might have on the earlier Canadian activities that were exposed with the Gouzenko defection. Mostly,

I'd like to see the investigation reports that followed the Gouzenko defection. What happened to pursuing this chemical engineer code named PUPPETEER? Were agents PUPPETEER and TRAVELER the Ramazanovs?

"I'm hoping if you can get me entry into the old NKVD and KGB archives, I might be able to negotiate my way into something from the GRU. Things work over there just like here. I know whoever you contact is some senior member of government. They'll know someone who knows someone in the GRU that might get me a look at their World War Two stuff too. You're my foot in the door, Dad. Once I'm there, I know I'll have to use my own ingenuity. Does your network from the State Department days extend to anyone that might help, Dad?"

"I think so. Can't promise you'll get to see everything you want to though, but I'll see what I can do."

"Could you maybe make that call tomorrow?" Victoria asks.

Her father shook his head but smiled. "Sure."

"And if you conclude your theory is not proven, at least with this Voronin, then what?" her mother said.

"Then I don't have a historical bombshell. I'm still pursuing this new book. It takes my doctoral thesis arguments further. It's some good scholarly work even if I can't establish this newly discovered Soviet espionage penetration of the Manhattan Project. It'll still be important toward my pursuit of tenure."

"And if you get the kind of proof that's academically sound, then what's next?" her mother said.

"Then I'm back here. I want you and Dad to agree that I should move forward. Not a family thing. It's your professional opinions I'm looking for."

"Ok. So if we concur that what you have is sufficient proof, what happens after that?"

"Then I confront Mikhail Voronin. Whatever he says is important to the story, even if it's just denials. Either he knew nothing of his in-laws and most probably his wife's espionage activities or he participated. If he really didn't know they were spies, then he still had to be the source of their information. What's that make him? If he trusted them and revealed secret information, then he was still a spy."

CHAPTER 19

Y-12 Alpha Track, Electromagnetic Enrichment
Oak Ridge, TN

LOS ALAMOS, NEW MEXICO – 1944

I RETURNED TO Los Alamos on the fourth of July. Not only did the array of technical problems confronting the project weigh on the scientists, but new developments in Europe resurrected renewed philosophical debate.

Four week earlier, the Allies had successfully mounted the great amphibious landing on the Normandy beaches of France. The maneuver was a success with the Allied armies now moving south from the beachheads. Although the fighting was intense, the Germans were falling back. On the Eastern Front, the Soviets continued to attack the German armies. Overwhelmingly outnumbering German forces, the Red Army was engaging the retreating German armies along a front extending from the Baltic States to the Balkans. Two days before the Normandy landings, Allied forces entered Rome. The end for Nazi Germany appeared in sight.

Knowledgeable senior scientists knew that with the remaining technical problems of creating an atomic bomb, it was very unlikely that a weapon would be developed before an end to the conflict in Europe. Only the unknown threat of a potential German nuclear weapon appearing as Hitler's secret weapon to stave off defeat remained.

But General Groves knew there was almost no chance that the Germans had, or would have an atomic weapon. I knew that too as did all of Grove's senior staff. Probably Robert Oppenheimer knew it as well.

In September, 1943, General Marshal had asked Groves if the Manhattan Project could take over responsibility for coordination of foreign intelligence activities related to nuclear energy. Groves put Colonel Boris Pash in command of the code named Alsos Mission. After the D-Day landings, Pash was now with the advancing allied armies pushing into France. Intelligence gathered to date pointed to a fragmented German nuclear energy program. There was no credible evidence that anything approaching a bomb development program was ever underway. Secret German weapons programs were clearly directed at creating jet aircraft and long-range rockets. Pash was there to assess just what Werner Heisenberg had been up to. His mission was as much to protect against any nuclear materials and scientists falling into Soviet hands as the Red Army advanced from the east.

The Manhattan Project was established out of the chilling fear that Nazi Germany was probably working toward developing an atomic bomb. That logic stemmed from the fact that the earliest work into nuclear science originated in Germany. Many of the leading theoretical physicists came from Germany, or studied the burgeoning field in its universities. With that fear, the Manhattan Project was granted virtually unlimited funding.

The threat that had provided the origin of the Manhattan Project seemed now to be nonexistent. No longer driven by that original fear, the scientists were simply making a new military weapon. Because it was possible. Because it was already well underway. But this was no ordinary weapon. Its extraordinary power would change mankind's concept of warfare. It was the ultimate weapon of mass destruction, by definition to be used against civilian populations. Would the United States alone possess this ultimate weapon? Would it be used on the Japanese, assuming it would even be ready before the conflict in the Pacific was concluded by conventional warfare? What about after the war? Would the United States take the moral high-ground to not leverage its unique power? Most of the scientists wrestled with the myriad philosophical implications. Many were morally conflicted. These questions increasingly became as much a part of the debate as was the challenge of their work. The strategic mission had become clearly something different.

And there was more bad news on the technical work. The day I arrived back at Los Alamos I attended a meeting of the senior scientists in the library reading room. Many already knew what Robert Oppenheimer was going to announce.

"As most of you know, we received the first quantities of 49 from the X-10 reactor at Oak Ridge back in April. It took Emilio only ten days to firmly establish the spontaneous fission rate of the 49. In short, that fission rate is far too high to consider a gun-type design. We've been working on the problem for the last three months. Without question, the required velocity to combine the two fissile masses in a gun-assembly is simply prohibitive. The *Thin Man* design will therefore be abandoned."

Emilio was Emilio Segrè an Italian physicist, a protégé of Enrico Fermi. He was stranded in the United States because of his Jewish background when Mussolini's fascist government passed anti-Semitic laws barring Jews from university positions.

49 was of course shorthand for plutonium-239, the alternative fissile material to uranium-235. Plutonium offered certain potential advantages over U-235 for producing a bomb. It also had the advantage of being produced within a natural uranium-graphite reactor. Uranium-235 in its small naturally occurring concentrations within uranium-238 was proving to be a frustrating processing challenge to achieve the necessary enrichment from 0.7% to over 80%. But that advantage of producing pluto-

nium-239 over uranium-235 was now complicated by the ability to incorporate it into a workable bomb design.

"But we've had lab samples from Berkley for some time. What happened?" someone asked.

"Firstly, the *Thin Man* gun design using 49 was always tenuous. The velocity of the 'bullet' to marry with the target core to achieve critical mass was originally calculated at around 3000 feet per second. The length of the gun barrel was calculated at something around eighteen feet in length to achieve that velocity. That would have been a challenge in itself," Oppenheimer said. "But that's a mute point now. The actual required velocity is now entirely prohibitive.

"As to what happened, it could be put down to just bad luck. Many of you know Glenn Seaborg the scientist that produced the first plutonium samples. He heads the plutonium section in Chicago. By the way I'll dispense with the 49 shorthand for a moment to better explain.

"Some time ago Seaborg suggested that the isotope plutonium-240 might form along with the desired plutonium-239 within a reactor process. The plutonium-240 unfortunately has a much higher spontaneous fission rate than plutonium-239. This of course is the product we will derive from the Oak Ridge reactor and the new production reactors in Washington. The original test samples from Berkley were much purer plutonium-239 concentrations produced in the laboratory cyclotrons. Unfortunately, Dr. Seaborg was right.

"With the plutonium-240 contamination, a gun-type plutonium device would end in a fizzle. The *Thin Man* design won't work," Oppenheimer said.

There was a collective murmur in the room.

"That means a plutonium weapon must therefore involve an implosion design," someone said.

"That's not going particularly well either," someone else commented.

"That's right. It must involve implosion," Oppenheimer said. "Nonetheless, it does make our task clearer. We will continue to develop the gun-type uranium weapon. *Little Boy* is a much more practical length than *Thin Man*. It will work. All we need is enough fissile U-235. But we will always be limited by the ability to enrich enough U-235 for multiple weapons. Therefore, we must develop a workable plutonium design to think in terms of an arsenal of bombs."

Oppenheimer was attempting to put a positive spin on the state of that work. Implosion was proving to be an intractable problem. The work had seemingly progressed very little the last several months. Now it was the only design solution.

"That means we will need to realign most everything here on the Hill to develop *Fat Man*. Because that is where we have to solve numerous problems, the implosion design will become the focal priority," Oppenheimer said referring to the assigned nickname of the spherical weapon contrasted with the torpedo-shaped gun design of *Little Boy* and the abandoned *Thin Man*."

Everything now centered on the ability to create a workable implosion device. In simplest terms, if a shell of plutonium-239 could be uniformly compressed, critical mass could be achieved quickly enough to allow for a plutonium weapon even with its high spontaneous fission rate. The problem lay with achieving the necessary uniformity with conventional chemical explosives. This required developing the explosives into a precision instrument to achieve a concentric, simultaneous compression of the plutonium shell. Military ordinance had never been used in this manner. Different chemical explosives would be required to generate the required shockwave geometry. The problem involved daunting mathematics derived from meager experimentation. The ability to precisely initiate the detonations of the multiple explosive charges simultaneously added further complexity.

John von Neumann, the imminent Hungarian mathematician consulting on the project, determined that the concept was feasible by calculating the allowable tolerance from optimum synchronicity. That alone was a breakthrough. He then went further to calculate the complex shape of the implosion lenses. While his work deemed it theoretically feasible, a complex problem of engineering still remained.

Some time ago, George Kistiakowsky, the brilliant explosives expert had replaced Seth Neddermeyer to head up the Implosion Program under the Ordinance & Engineering Division. Neddermeyer had made little progress after months of work. His experiments continued to result in severe asymmetries of the explosives shock waves. Neddermeyer was a plodder. He resisted adding additional talent to his team. Both Oppenheimer and Groves recognized the need for different leadership. Kistiakowsky was already consulting. Kistiakowsky was everything Neddermeyer was not.

Kistiakowsky was confident, outspoken, and pushy. He was perhaps the leading expert on explosives. His thinking was original and unorthodox. Kistiakowsky understood that chemical explosives could be constructed into precision devices.

Kistiakowsky had already struggled with the organization of the Ordinance & Engineering Division. The division was headed by Navy Captain Deke Parsons. Parsons was military and ran things with that brand of conservatism. Neddermeyer wanted to work in a vacuum. They never got along. Neither appreciated Kistiakowsky's interference. That now changed under Oppenheimer's reorganization.

Captain Parsons' original Ordinance & Engineering Division was dismantled. Parsons was furious, accusing Oppenheimer of circumventing him. Groves backed Oppenheimer. It was a master stroke of organizational management. Parsons was placed in charge of the *Little Boy* uranium-235 gun design bomb. The implosion problem to develop the *Fat Man* plutonium-239 bomb now was organized into the Weapons Physics Division headed by Robert Bacher, and the Explosives Division headed by George Kistiakowsky. The Theoretical Physics Division under Hans Bethe remained intact, but now became wholly directed toward developing the implosion solution.

Later that same day, I met with Robert Oppenheimer. He was clearly depressed.

"General Groves is pushing me on a target date for having a bomb ready. Is he being serious, Major?" Oppenheimer said.

I took the question as rhetorical. "Well you know how the General is, Doctor. He pushes everyone and everything to the limit."

"We're not even to first base," Oppenheimer said. "Everything at Oak Ridge is still questionable. No suitable barriers have been developed for the gaseous diffusion process. Electromagnetic separation is operating at less than one percent efficiency. This new project for using thermal diffusion seems an act of desperation."

The Naval Research Laboratory had been working on nuclear fission as a potential motive source to power submarines. Philip Abelson, a Berkley physicist had been working on a process of thermal diffusion to enrich uranium-238 to uranium-235. Lighter isotopes tended to diffuse toward a hotter region, heavier isotopes toward a colder region. The Army had previously discounted the approach since they already had two other more promising alternative methods to pursue. While the Navy was excluded from the nuclear bomb development work, Abelson went around the bureaucracy directly to Robert Oppenheimer. Oppenheimer convinced Groves that they should consider the approach in view of the significant problems plaguing the other uranium enrichment methods. True to Groves' style, he had contracted a month earlier for yet another massive enrichment process to begin construction at Oak Ridge, designated as S-50.

"What do you mean desperation, Doctor? It's my understanding you recommended we pursue this method."

"I did. But not enthusiastically. We need to cover our bets. Gaseous diffusion and electromagnetic separation still hold more promise. The problems we're facing at Oak Ridge are engineering problems. The real problem is time. Eventually, those engineering problems will be overcome. But everything cannot be forced by applying more resources. Thermal diffusion is simpler engineering, but the probable enrichment rate is still very low. We must try it though. Frankly, I can't be confident that it will change things unless the other processes can be made viable."

"What do you mean, Doctor?"

"Even if, or probably I should say when, the problems of gaseous diffusion and electromagnetic separation are resolved, the efficiency is still painfully low. If they do not live up to the anticipated yield expectations, then it will simply take too long to produce sufficient quantities of weapons-grade enriched uranium."

"So how is this new enrichment process even expected to contribute?" I asked.

"Easy. Well, not easy really. Nothing in this problem is easy. We are now theorizing that if we link the various processes sequentially, there might be a faster approach to achieving the necessary quantities of enriched uranium. Right now that's just another theory. Academic if we can't get all the processes operational.

"So now you see the new urgency with the implosion design. The uranium bomb design is comparatively straightforward, but plagued with the inability to produce enough uranium-235. That will always be limiting factor. The plutonium bomb design has a better chance of producing enough fissile material within the reactor process, but the ability to create a viable implosion design is fraught with a host of challenges.

"Join a meeting for eight o'clock tomorrow morning in the technical library. All the senior people working on implosion will attend. It's a working meeting. You can report to Groves if you think we know what we're doing."

"I have no question on that account, Sir. Neither does the General," I said and smiled. "There's something else I'd like to ask you, Dr. Oppenheimer. Off the record I guess."

"Off the record? Is there such a thing in your job, Major?" Oppenheimer said.

"In this case, it's just me asking. There's lots of talk among all the scientists about whether we should pursue the bomb. The Germans are on the run. Just a matter of time before they throw in the towel. What's your take on things, Sir?"

"What if the Germans were to have an atomic bomb?" Oppenheimer said. He paused to light a cigarette. "But we both know that is now very unlikely don't we?"

"Yes, Sir."

"If you're asking how I feel about proceeding, my answer is we must. Even though we haven't achieved success, it's only a matter of time. The genie isn't out of the bottle yet, but the cork has been removed. The science will move forward. There is no truncating the pursuit of knowledge. We simply must get there first."

"Will we use this against Japan if the war is still going on?"

"Best to ask General Groves or General Marshall that question. Logic suggests that given a decisive weapon, the military will be compelled to use it. And you, Major, would you use it?"

"I believe so, Sir. If it might end the war."

Oppenheimer stubbed out his cigarette. "But regardless of the outcome of the atomic bomb, or the ethical questions it raises, nuclear power holds the potential of a new source of energy. That economic incentive will continue to push the technology as much as the military implications of atomic weapons. But above all else, it's a function of bureaucratic inertia. The project now has a life of its own. With the enormous investment, it could never be abandoned."

The next day the principle scientists involved in the implosion design gathered in the library. Some sipped on their second coffee of the morning. Many smoked. Collectively they seemed to have adopted the informal uniform of white shirt and light weight summer slacks. No jackets or ties this warm summer morning.

Oppenheimer stood at the front of the assembled group. He too was dressed in an open neck white shirt, sleeves rolled to the elbows, and no jacket. He paused to light his pipe as a couple of stragglers took their seats.

"I have spoken with all of you about the reorganization. Some of you are understandably not pleased with the changes. Those decisions were largely mine so do not cast blame to any of your colleagues. I know that each of you will continue to do his best to achieve our objective.

"Perhaps to be redundant, I would like to summarize the reasons for the elevated focus on implosion before we get to the work of the day.

"First of all, the uranium gun-type weapon will have a limited yield in comparison to the plutonium implosion design. Secondly, producing sufficient quantities of highly enriched uranium for a great many bombs remains problematic and probably strategically unrealistic. Plutonium can be produced more reliably using reactors. Thirdly, implosion offers the prospects of higher explosive yields using comparatively less fissile material than the simpler uranium gun-type design.

"There is another further advantage. For the prospects of Dr. Teller's second generation 'super bomb' to be realized, implosion represents the only workable approach."

Edward Teller had been a vocal and even disruptive advocate of a fusion-based 'super bomb' from the day he joined the Manhattan Project. Disappointed that he did not get the leadership role of the Theoretical Division which Oppenheimer gave to Hans Bethe, Teller was allowed to work on his pet project. From the onset, Teller was in charge of the hydrodynamics of implosion as the necessary fission triggering approach to his fusion bomb concept.

"The mathematics of using explosive lenses has been worked out by Dr. Neumann. Most importantly, Dr. Neumann has calculated that implosion will be successful if within five percent from spherical symmetry. This gives us a practical tolerance within which to work. Dr. Ulam and Dr. Teller concur with Dr. Neumann's calculations. It's an extraordinary piece of work."

Sitting in the back of the room, von Neumann nodded in acknowledgement of Oppenheimer's praise. Ulam and Teller nodded their agreement emphatically.

"Most importantly, Dr. Kistiakowsky feels that the required precision of the chemical explosive devices is possible. Difficult, but possible.

"However, many of you correctly point out that there is a severe lack of empirical data in several critical areas. We cannot move toward a workable implosion design until we learn more. Therefore, Gentlemen, the next phase of our work is a crash program of testing. Dr. Bacher's division will work on the mechanics of compression of the tamper and the core, detonation method, initiators, and various other problems. Dr. Kistiakowsky will work on developing the chemical explosives themselves. Dr. Bethe's theoretical division will attempt to translate the empirical data into a useable design. Dr. Feynman will have a lot of numbers to crunch on his new IBM computing machines. I fear we're also in for a long period of continually being startled by explosions.

"We'll continue to pursue the uranium gun design bomb of course. It will work. The design is more straightforward and therefore more reliable. But much work still remains. If the uranium enrichment process problems can be overcome soon, it could be our first weapon. Captain Parsons will head that effort.

"In keeping with abbreviations for security, the implosion design will be now be designated as the *gadget*, distinct from the gun-design *Little Boy*. Since the *gadget* will be an infinitely more complex design, it will need to be tested before we can declare it can work."

Someone asked, "Do you mean a full blown actual test, Oppie?"

Several people snickered at the unintended pun.

"That's right. That future test will be code named *Trinity*," Oppenheimer said.

Someone else asked, "Where will that be? Is there any place remote enough to be safe?"

"We think so. There are a couple of sites under considera-tion." Oppenheimer hoped they were sufficiently remote.

I spent the next four weeks at Los Alamos. Each day was spent with a specific group of the implosion team. Groves want-ed me focused on monitoring the plutonium bomb design. He would concentrate on oversight of progress on resolving the uranium enrichment problems at Oak Ridge and reactor con-struction at Hanford. Where I was an observer, Groves would act as the autocratic, pushy project manager. What he did better than anyone. I believe Groves recognized that I had developed a particularly workable relationship with the scientists at Los Alamos. His visits to the Hill were frequently abrasive. His style was better suited to riding roughshod over the private sector contractors. Groves always assigned the appropriate resource to the task.

I attended another of Oppie's cocktail parties just before leaving to return to Washington. I had become an accepted regu-lar. Many of the scientists and their wives had become real friends. They openly made derogatory remarks about the military staff in my presence, not regarding me as part of that demographic. *'Of course you're different, Mike.'*

"Have you heard the latest, Mike? About our safecracker?" Charlotte Serber asked.

"Your what?" I said with some alarm.

"Tell him about it, Robert," she said as her husband approached.

"You know all of the group leaders have safes," Robert Serber said. "Every night all papers and notes are supposed to be locked up. Combination locks. Only that one person is to know the combination. Well there has been a rash of shall we say intrusions into those secure safes."

"You mean documents have gone missing" I asked. This was serious. Why didn't I know about this?

"No, no. Nothing missing. Just notes left in the safes. You know who it is of course?"

I shook my head and shrugged my shoulders.

"It's Feynman of course. He won't admit to it, but it has to be him," Robert Serber said.

"How can you be so sure?"

"Because he's an accomplished prankster. Great with figuring things out. Look at what he was doing to repair those mechanical calculators. Now he's working on how to optimize process routines with IBM punch cards to speed up the calculations. Feynman has to be at the center of this."

"I agree. It's Richard alright," Charlotte Serber said. "The only person with a real sense of humor. But the real delight is de Silva. He's beside himself. Treats it as a real security breach. The guy's a real Neanderthal. Hope he has a coronary over it."

"Don't get off on de Silva, Charlotte," her husband said. "But she's right. He's also in charge of the SED guys and that's a problem. They're a great bunch of technicians. De Silva still runs them as if they're regular army troops. Reveille at dawn. Falling

out in formation. Drills. Stupid army stuff. Makes them feel inferior to the civilians they work with."

Major de Silva was the head of security at Los Alamos. He
also commanded the Special Engineering Detachment consisting
of drafted army personnel with special technical skills. But the
Serbers' antagonism toward de Silva's came as a response to his
decided bias against them personally as well as Oppenheimer
and several other scientists. If not outright Communists, de Silva
thought Oppenheimer and the Serbers were at least fellow trav-
elers. Like other Army security officers, de Silva saw Communists behind every tree. To him these left-leaning academics
were clearly security risks. Groves ignored his concerns leaving
de Silva without authority in the matter. The acerbic Charlotte
Serber had more than one run-in with de Silva, further aggravat-
ing the relationship.

"Ok. So how's Elena, Mike? You guys still playing newlyweds?" Charlotte said.

"See what I mean, Mike. She's incorrigible."

I smiled enjoying myself. "Elena is well. I'll be seeing her in a
few days. And yes, the honeymoon hasn't yet worn off."

I arrived back in Washington in mid-August. I reported there
was a sense of renewed excitement at Los Alamos. Although still
contending with seemingly intractable problems, there was a
narrowing of focus. From the beginning with only theory, there
was now an array of options both at the production process level
for fissile material and for the actual design of a bomb. Much
had been learned in the year and a half since the project got underway. Setbacks still yielded new knowledge. The problems
were becoming more clearly focused. This was the way science
advanced.

Oppenheimer had reacted in dramatic fashion. Recognizing
not only the clarity of the problem, he understood the unique
capabilities of each of the scientists. Within two weeks, Los Ala-

mos was reorganized to focus on implosion design. Others would have to solve the engineering problems of producing the necessary quantities of fissile material. Oppenheimer would build the bomb. The contractors, America's foremost technology corporations building and operating Oak Ridge and Hanford, would eventually solve the process problems of providing nuclear fuels for the bomb.

The following day, General Groves surprised his staff by announcing that he was estimating the availability of the first atomic bomb by spring of 1945. All of us looked at each other with surprise. I knew the most so I was the most surprised. That was less than a year from now. There was no reason for optimism that any of the problems would be solved within that time, much less all of them. Had I made too much of the renewed enthusiasm of the scientific team? Did Groves know something I didn't? Was this some political necessity? Was it a political ploy? Was it even possible?

Groves did not elaborate to his subordinates the basis for such a deadline. Pushing the project further as if there was little doubt that all of the problems would be resolved, he said, "A full scale test of an atomic bomb will be conducted in a remote desert area of New Mexico, about 200 miles south of Los Alamos."

In typical Groves' style, he cemented that pronouncement with another announcement.

"We've now reached the point where we need to develop the means of delivering an atomic bomb to a target. It has been decided that the only capable platform is the B-29. Work has been ordered to begin modifications for an initial compliment of fourteen aircraft. The first three are due to be delivered next month. A special unit of the Army Air Corps is being organized."

With Groves, everything was about achieving the objective. Modifying an aircraft to deliver a bomb design that did not yet exist was simply another form of parallel project management. The organizational abilities of Robert Oppenheimer and Leslie

Groves were markedly different, as were their management styles. Deeply involved with their respective spheres of management, I was in awe of the genius of both.

X-10 graphite reactor, Oak Ridge, TN

CHAPTER 20

WASHINGTON, D.C – 1944

ELENA KNEW SHE looked good naked, and she knew I liked to look. In retrospect, I believe she planned the scene when she told me. This was high risk for her. Maintaining her hold over me was essential. What better way than capitalizing on my unabashed lust for her.

It was my first night back in Washington. As soon as we got home to the apartment, we were in bed. After the lovemaking, she was kneeling on the bed looking down on me in her typical fashion meant to entice me. I was propped up on the pillows. Looking at her firm breasts and pubic region was causing me to grow hard again.

"Mike, there's something I must tell you. Please remember how much, I love you. But there are other things in one's life, compelling things. Things that I cannot deny."

I sat up straight. Fear raced through me. What was she getting at? Another man? Something terrible in her past?

"What are you talking about?" The concern evident in my voice.

Elena averted her eyes. Looking back to me, she said, "It's about the Motherland."

"What? Canada?"

"No, Darling, Russia. I may have been born in Canada, but I'm Russian. Just like Mom and Dad. Just like my birth parents. Their fidelity to Mother Russia has remained strong. Through them, I feel that too. It's my heritage. It's your heritage too. I know that when we talk. Your parents are once again part of their roots. We are both part of Russia."

"Elena, what the hell are you trying to say?"

"We must help Russia in this terrible war. You've said America should do more. Russia has been bled with the war in Europe for the last two years. Her armies continue to battle the Germans. Russia will be crippled with her terrible losses after the war."

"Elena, tell me what's going on."

She took a deep breath then sighed. "I decided to help. I've been helping for some time. Mom and Dad were reluctant, but eventually agreed. Dad has been actively helping."

Now I was genuinely scared. "Helping? To do what?"

"I've been passing information to Moscow."

I felt as if I'd been kicked in the stomach. The instant stab of fear made me nauseous.

"My god, you've done what?"

"I've given Moscow information. After the war is over, the United States cannot dominate the world. It's already hostile to Russia even though Russia is doing more to win in Europe than the United States. If they alone have the atomic bomb, they can dictate everything."

"You've passed on what kind of information?" I asked, already fairly sure of the answer.

"Your stuff. Stuff about making the atomic bomb."

I groaned audibly. Now I was truly sickened.

"Jesus Christ. You've been passing on the things I've told you? You've been spying for the Soviets? Why have you betrayed me, Elena?"

"No, Darling, I haven't betrayed you. Don't say that. It's something I had to do. You know the United States should be sharing this new weapon with Russia. The British are part of it. Why not Russia? Because the United States fears Communism. So they let Russia bleed on the Eastern Front but won't share this military secret."

"Bullshit! You've betrayed me. That's what this is about. I trusted you. So much so I violated my own oath to keep everything about my work secret. I trusted you. You betrayed that, Elena."

"No, Darling ...."

She reached her hands to touch my face. I deflected her with my hand.

"Don't. You can't just cajole this away, Elena. You've destroyed me. You've destroyed us."

"Don't say that, Darling. We're not destroyed. No one will know. I love you. You still love me don't you?"

She was still kneeling on the bed. Her hands were gripped together tightly in front her. Tears flowed down her cheeks. She looked vulnerable. Much to my own shame, looking at her was arousing me in spite of what she had just confessed.

She reached out again with her hands and cupped my cheeks. Drawing her mouth down on mine, she kissed me. I could taste her tears.

Reaching down, she maneuvered her hand under the sheet and grabbed my cock. It was already fully erect. She quickly straddled me. Guiding my cock into her, she let out a groan of pleasure. Taking charge, she pulled my face between her breasts. Rocking back and forth, she brought herself to orgasm loudly. As I came, she clutched me even closer to her. Now she was crying openly, tears running down her breasts, onto my face.

Damn my weakness.

She eventually climbed off me and put on her rob. I did the same.

"Do you understand, Darling? I must do this," she said.

I looked at her. The implication being she intended to go on spying.

"You can't, Elena. Don't even think that. Tell me how far this has gone. Who's involved?"

She looked at me. "Father has helped me."

"Was this his idea?"

"No. Mine alone. I talked Father into it. Mother too. They agree with my reasons but did not want me to run the risk. They were both concerned about you. I wasn't supposed to tell you. They said that would put you in danger."

"No shit. If it were found out, I might be put in front of a firing squad. I took an oath. I've betrayed that trust. You've betrayed that trust, Elena. But back to my question. Who else is involved?"

"Father knew someone that knew someone at the embassy. I give Father the information and he transforms it into a coded message. He handles sending it."

"God, what have you done, Elena?" I was physically sick. This involved too many others. "We can't escape this. We'll eventually be found out. How could you have done this to me? To us?"

"Because there's more to life than just us, Darling. People are fighting and dying all over the world for what they believe. Russians are dying. I'm Russian. You're Russian too. Even if we were born elsewhere, it's our blood. We have a duty to help our Motherland. The United States cannot rule the post-war world. Any country with the sole power of this atomic bomb will use that power for its own self interest."

"And Stalin wouldn't?"

"Probably. But Stalin isn't Russia. Anyway that's the point. If Russia also has the atomic bomb, it will balance any threat from the United States. Neither side could use it. Russia isn't an enemy. Your own parents are making their life there, Mikhail Stefanovich."

I looked at my wife in a new light. We intellectually connected beyond our obvious sexual attraction, but this was entirely something else. She talked like spying for the Soviets was a natural thing. To Elena of course, it was Russia, not the Soviet Union.

"I understand your position, Elena. I share your feelings about helping Russia, but not this way. We can't do this. It will eventually destroy us."

Elena came over to stand in front of me. "It won't destroy us. I have been careful. Father assures me he has been careful. He uses a coded method of sending the information. He has no physical contact with anyone."

"All spies are careful and they still get caught."

"Who's been caught?" Elena asked. "There have been no reports of any Soviet spies discovered in the newspapers. Only clumsy German spies."

The debate went on for an hour. I exhausted my arguments to no effect. She did not relent to cease what she was doing, but steadfastly insisted she must continue. She had never pushed back against me with such resolve. Never had I seen her so determined.

Elena fixed us something to eat. A cabbage soup had been simmering on the stove. She had saved her ration coupons to add a small pork roast to the soup. We had vodka with the meal. Genuine Russian fare Elena pronounced.

I ate in silence. I wasn't going to be able to stop her. Did I stop confiding secrets to her? How would that affect us?

After finishing the meal and half the bottle of vodka, I said "You expect me to continue to tell you the details of my work after this?"

She looked at me intently. "Yes. You know it's for the right reasons. And you love me."

"What does loving you have to do with it?"

"Because you would not want to risk anything bad happening to me."

What the hell was she implying? If she stopped, how would that put her in further danger? From the Soviets?

"What do you mean? Where's the danger in stopping?"

"Because the people that get the information will be bound to pursue discovering what has happened. That means there will be some sort of physical contact. That means risk for me and Father."

And for me as well I thought. If my wife was caught spying, then I would immediately be at the center. It was atomic bomb secret information being leaked. At the least I was an accomplice. At worst, I was a full-fledged spy myself. No telling what the Soviets might do to continue access to my sensitive information. Might they not threaten us in some manner? I had to find some way of managing this nightmare.

"Saturday we're going to see your parents. I want to understand how far this thing has gone. Who your father passes information to and how? What are the mechanisms? It's now my neck too."

We argued further. I knew I was getting nowhere. My world had just turned dark. I drank the remainder of the vodka. Slightly drunk, Elena helped me to bed.

For the next few days, we both went about our work. It was difficult harboring such a secret. With everything I said I felt like a betrayer. But the old adage about adapting no matter how bad the circumstances was true. I was anxious to confront Boris and Vanya Ramazanov. What possessed them to condone and assist their daughter in this dangerous game? Who the hell did Boris know that was connected with Soviet intelligence? Was this Boris' doing?

We took the train to Wilmington Saturday morning. Boris and Vanya were expecting us. I hadn't yet decided how to handle this. No matter their politics, how could they let their daughter get involved in this? It was a chilly reception at the train station. Once settled back at the Ramazanovs' house, I was the first to speak.

"Do you know the danger you've put us all in," I said to Boris and Vanya. "Your own daughter. What the hell were you thinking?"

"That's not fair, Darling. It was my idea. I made Father help me."

"Nonsense. You could have stopped this, Boris. Why didn't you?"

Boris took off his glasses and began cleaning them with a handkerchief. "Two reasons. First of all, I was afraid Elena might try something foolish by going elsewhere. She was determined. Second, I guess I agreed with her view that we should help Russia."

I shook my head in despair. "Tell me how you transfer this information, Boris."

He told me he knew someone in Montreal, a former colleague at DuPont that had a relative working in the Soviet Embassy in Ottawa. Boris implied he had access to information that might be useful to Russia. Through this path, he eventually received a reply in the form of a letter from his friend in Montreal. In innocuous language, the letter suggested his friend would be visiting the Carney's Point, New Jersey plant on business. He would have some time to visit his old friend Boris.

Details for future communications were discussed when his Canadian colleague visited. The colleague said he had been given detailed instructions from his friend in the embassy. He gave Ramazanov assurances that his information would be handled differently from the normal channels of intelligence gathering.

There would be no further physical contact. Ramazanov would receive an encryption key via shortwave radio transmission. Ramazanov was a shortwave enthusiast, receiving transmissions from the war in Europe, particularly from Russia. Ramazanov would encode the information using the encryption

key which Moscow changed each time by predetermined broadcasts using the last encryption key as the means to identify the
new key. He said the method was called a one-time-pad. The
cipher was based upon applying the new key using modular
arithmetic to rearrange the letters.

"Vanya, some paper please," Boris said.

He then began to illustrate the cipher method. He first wrote
each letter of the alphabet then assigned each letter a numerical
value starting with zero for A and 25 for Z.

A	B	C	D	E	F	G	H	I	J	K	L	M
0	1	2	3	4	5	6	7	8	9	10	11	12

N	O	P	Q	R	S	T	U	V	W	X	Y	Z
13	14	15	16	17	18	19	20	21	22	23	24	25

"Let's assume the key is Dickens' *A Tale of Two Cities*. The
first line reads '*It was the best of times, it was the worst of times*'.
Now we'll note the numerical value of each of these letters. Let's
assume we want to translate the word *fountain*. The encryption
starts by combining the key and the message using modular addition. Decryption simply reverses the process. Let me show
you."

Message		F	O	U	N	T	A	I	N			
Key text		I	T	W	A	S	T	H	E	B	E	S	T
Key value		8	19	22	0	18	19	7	4	1	4	18	19

ENCRYPTION

Message		F	O	U	N	T	A	I	N
Message value		5	14	20	13	19	0	8	13
Key value		8	19	22	0	18	19	7	4
Message + Key		13	33	42	13	37	19	15	17
Message + Key (Mod 26)		13	7	16	13	11	19	15	17
Ciphertext		N	H	Q	N	L	T	P	R

DECRYPTION

Ciphertext	N	H	Q	N	L	T	P	R
Ciphertext value	13	7	16	13	11	19	15	17
Key value	8	19	22	0	18	19	7	4
Ciphertext - Key	5	-12	-6	13	-7	0	8	13
Ciphertext -Key (Mod 26)	5	14	20	13	19	0	8	13
Message	F	O	U	N	T	A	I	N

The concept was instantly clear to me. Simple, yet a completely secure method if the same key was never used again. Hence the name one-time-pad if a code book were used.

"By the way, FOUNTAIN is the code name for the source of our information," Ramazanov said.

"My code name you mean." I glared at Elena. She simply pursed her lips and nodded slightly. "Wonderful. And I suppose all of you have code names too?"

"Yes. Obviously. Our real names are never used, even in encrypted communications."

"So what are your code names?"

Ramazanov sighed with reluctance. "Elena is DANCER, Vanya is TRAVELER. I'm PUPPETEER."

"PUPPETEER? That's appropriate. Shouldn't I then be *MARIONETTE*? After all, you're pulling the strings and I'm just performing."

"Darling, please don't be cruel. This was my doing, not Father's."

I ignored her. "So once you have encoded the information, then what?"

"I take micro-photographs of the typed pages after encoding. A special camera. It reduces the image to a very small negative."

"Show me the camera," I said.

Ramazanov got up and returned moments later. He handed me an unusually small camera. Rectangular in shape, it was less than four inches in length and little more than an inch in width. The logo read *Minox Riga*.

"It takes film about nine millimeters in width. This small chain establishes the correct distance from the subject material being photographed. I then place the undeveloped negative in the binding of a book. I seal both ends with glue to prevent any light entering. Another added precaution. If someone were to probe further, they would undoubtedly remove the film and ruin it with exposure to light."

"Clever. And you were taught all this?"

Ramazanov shrugged his shoulders. "Once committed, I was determined to manage things as carefully as possible. I was instructed in the procedures. Moscow suggested the means for transmission and provided the camera."

"And where do you send these books?"

"To different post office boxes. One to a fictitious relative in Brighton Beach, Brooklyn. The other is in Montreal to a fictitious old friend. Both are actual people, but not involved. Nor did they rent the postal boxes."

"You're no amateur anymore apparently, Boris. Vanya, what do you say to all this? Did Elena bend you as easily as her father?"

Vanya answered, "Misha. You mustn't be angry with us. It's been done. It can't be undone. We can only go forward. To answer your question, in my heart I know we are doing something for Russia. Something important. I argued against this, but Elena threatened to seek help elsewhere. Boris and I could not let her take that risk. Who better to manage this than her own parents?"

"This is an unbelievable nightmare," I said and got up from my chair and began pacing the living room. "Tell me, what happens, Boris if I just stop giving you information? Will your friends in Moscow do something unpleasant?"

"Unpleasant? What do you mean, Mikhail?"

"I mean something to coerce us, or I guess more accurately, to coerce me to continue?"

Ramazanov pondered the question. "The truth, Mikhail, I don't know. I'm new to this as well. Before this thing about an atomic bomb there would have been nothing we could do to help Russia. This changed things however."

"You mean I changed everything."

"Yes. And perhaps that is how it's seen in Moscow. This information could equalize the post-war status for Russia. It's that important. I can imagine those that are receiving this information will do anything for it to continue. There is too much at stake, Mikhail. You must realize that the information you are providing is of incalculable value. Its impact will transcend the War. I really don't know to what lengths the intelligence people might resort to insure that it continues. Ugly things can happen in war."

The thought occurred to me that my parents could be in jeopardy if I were to refuse to continue to provide intelligence from the Manhattan Project. Did the Soviets know they were in Russia? Had Boris told them?

"Wonderful. I'm in league with a bunch of amateurs. If we don't continue we have Moscow to fear. If we go on, we'll probably end up in prison."

Dinner was a tense affair. Afterwards, I drank my fill of vodka. Once in the bedroom, I rebuffed Elena's overtures to make love. She cried herself to sleep. I lay awake for hours reviewing the impossibility of my position. I knew I could not give up Elena. Even had I emotionally been able to leave her that was not a practical option now. By confiding the details of my work I had cast the seeds of my own destruction. I had trusted her. Foolishly stupid. It was unnecessary. It was nothing more than self-interest to impress her. It was arrogance. Circumstances now were the equivalent of blackmail. Self-inflicted. I could continue or suffer destruction. There was no alternative option.

On the train station platform the next day, I considered the thought of throwing myself in front of a train. Feigning a slip while stepping backwards, and all this would end. The thought passed as quickly as it had intruded. I didn't have that sort of courage. I knew I would revile myself, but I would continue to spy for the Soviets. It seemed the only option to contain this other than death or prison.

CHAPTER 21

VICTORIA PRESCOTT'S EARLIER research had gathered the pertinent background information on the principle players in her theorized story of Soviet World War Two espionage. The Ramazanovs were the key. If they were Soviet agents than Mikhail Voronin was either their unwitting source or participant. Either way, he would represent the most highly placed Soviet penetration of the United States' atomic bomb development project. Far broader information than material Klaus Fuchs had access to. If nothing else, he would have provided corroboration of the Fuchs material and the other lesser Soviet spies. He would fill in additional detail. More importantly, Voronin's information would be invaluable for overcoming the problems in the enrichment processes that proved to be the most difficult technical challenges. Producing sufficient quantities of fissile material was the source of most delays toward completing the bomb. The majority of the staggering cost of the Manhattan Project was devoted to making the critical bomb core material. Benefiting from avoiding the American mistakes would be the real basis by which the Soviets advanced their own atomic bomb development by years.

Canadian Immigration records confirmed the arrival of a Boris Aleksandrovich Ramazanov, age 33, and his wife Vanya Ivanovna Durchenko Ramazanov, age 30, in 1925. Their statements indicated their former residence as Moscow. They listed themselves as Jewish, fleeing persecution. Both were educated with university degrees. Boris held a degree in chemical engineering. He had secured a position with E.I. du Pont in Montreal. Immediately, Boris enrolled in a doctorial program at McGill University in Montreal, financed by his employer.

Subsequently, after the outbreak of World War Two, Boris transferred to a DuPont plant in the United States engaged in military explosives production. U.S. Immigration records supported that Boris and Vanya Ramazanov, Canadian citizens, immigrated to the United States in 1942. They were accompanied by an adopted daughter, Elena Maximovna Obolensky, age 23.

In the course of Boris Ramazanov's work in a sensitive war related industry, his background was vetted for a secret level security clearance. Nothing of concern showed up, but it was impossible to obtain verifications from Russia. In 1942, the Soviet Union was in a desperate struggle to hold off the German eastward military invasion.

As to Mikhail Voronin's parents, U.S. Immigration records revealed nothing to arouse suspicions in 1913. His father's background as a professor at Pomona College, then the loss of his position during the Great Depression suggested nothing subversive. Except for their unusual return to Russia in the 1930's. That angle could only be explored from Soviet era archives.

The only area that needed to be more thoroughly researched here in the United States was the subsequent investigations by the Canadian RCMP and the U.S. FBI following the Gouzenko defection in 1945. She was not interested in the volumes of investigative material related to the discovery of Klaus Fuchs as a Soviet spy that originated with the Gouzenko documents. Nor was she interested in the trail that assisted in the investigation of David Greenglass leading then to Julius and Ethical Rosenberg. She was very familiar with that documented history and the common thread of the same courier, Harry Gold. The Ramazanovs and Voronin would not be part of that spy network. What she was looking for was the more obscure investigative record that did not lead to these headline-grabbing revelations of Soviet espionage.

Hamilton Prescott had arranged for Victoria to access the old FBI files. The files had been declassified some time ago, but the FBI was always guarded with their information. Nonetheless, it was fairly easy to grant Victoria Prescott access since she was an accredited historian. What her father was able to do was get the assistance of someone from that era. Someone that had participated in the investigations following the Gouzenko defection. Someone intimate with Soviet espionage of that era.

Arman Turov was now 77. In 1945, he was a young FBI special agent. A third generation Russian, he was fluent in the language. Starting with that first evidence of the scope of Soviet espionage directed to the West, he spent the remainder of his FBI career on the Soviet counterintelligence desk. Hamilton Prescott interacted with Turov on a regular basis during his tenure at the State Department during Reagan's first term. Now retired, Turov still consulted for the FBI. More than access, Turov would be able to cut through much of the research time examining these files. She harbored little expectation that anything important would be discovered in the FBI files, but it was a base that had to be covered. The real data mining would happen in Moscow if her father could get her similar access into Stalin-era intelligence archives.

Victoria Prescott took an early train from New York to meet Turov at FBI headquarters on Pennsylvania Avenue in Washington D.C. A slender, distinguished looking old man with thinning white hair and glasses approached her after she checked in at the reception desk.

"Ms. Prescott, very good to meet you," he said extending his hand.

"Thank you Mr. Turov. I appreciate you assisting me in my research. I know you're retired. Father speaks highly of you. Says you know more about Soviet espionage in the United States than anyone."

"Well I don't know about that. Your father and I worked together for several years when he was at State. The eighties was a rough time in U.S.-Soviet relations. But of course you know that better than anyone. I'm aware of your academic credentials, Ms. Prescott. So let's get down to the basement where the stuff you're interested in is stored."

After getting her clearance badge, they descended to a basement area. She and Turov signed the security log. A young man said he was assigned to assist in pulling files for them.

"What is it you are interested in, Ms. Prescott?" Turov asked.

"The investigation files related to Igor Gouzenko's defection in 1945. But I'm not interested in the material that led to Fuchs and the Rosenbergs. I'm interested in a name that surfaced in those documents. Actually a code name, PUPPETEER. Would that ring any bells?"

Turov thought for a moment. "PUPPETEER? I vaguely recall the name but I can't place any significance to it."

"It was among the names of Soviet assets operating in Canada. PUPPETEER was identified as a chemical engineer with a major chemicals company."

"Very well. Let's start with that document where PUPPETEER first appears."

Turov sat at a desk with a computer monitor and typed something into the search engine. Scrolling down, he clicked on what he was looking for. He scribbled down a sequence of numbers. Back at the screen, he executed another search eventually writing down another set of numbers. The note was handed to the archive assistant.

While they waited for the files to be retrieved, Prescott explained her interest in PUPPETEER to Turov.

"So you're investigating whether this PUPPETEER was this engineer named Ramazanov? You'll forgive me for saying that's a pretty thin thread to follow, Ms. Prescott."

The file boxes arrived. The archivist placed them on a long table.

Turov located the file he was looking for. "These are the original 109 documents Gouzenko took out of the Ottawa Soviet Embassy. GRU and NKVD documents. Certainly brings back old memories. As FBI liaison, I spent a lot of time participating in the RCMP's debriefing of Mr. Gouzenko because of my fluency in Russian."

Turov thumbed through the file until he found the document he was looking for. "Here it is. Do you read Russian, Ms. Prescott?"

She answered yes in Russian. Turov handed her the single page.

The page consisted of a number of messages transmitted on March 21, 1942. Its importance was the mention in each cable of a code-named agent. Among these was the reference to PUPPETEER: *Agent PUPPETEER has been instructed to attempt to gain access to research being conducted by British and French physicists at the University of Montreal. As a chemical engineer, PUPPETEER is best qualified to evaluate technical information on heavy water research. Confirm reassignment.* That was it.

While she read the document, Turov was looking into the second file box.

"And here is the subsequent investigation reports related to PUPPETEER. Both the RCMP's and the FBI's," Turov said handing her two folders. "Besides this PUPPETEER, there were others never identified either."

The RCMP investigation had identified a long list of chemical engineers employed at various chemical firms and universities. The RCMP could not find evidence to cast suspicion upon anyone on the list. Their investigations led to many other arrests so they were pretty thorough. The hunt for PUPPETEER discovered several marital infidelities, one homosexual, and one falsifying of academic credentials. They dug deeply but found no basis for suspecting espionage among those people. This was now 1946. Several individuals on the list immigrated to the United States. Those made up the FBI's shorter list of possible PUPPETEER candidates.

Boris Ramazanov was one of those that had come to the U.S. Nothing in his background suggested any reason to suspect espionage. The investigation found little momentum since Boris Ramazanov, his wife, and their daughter had all died in an accident that same year. A review of Ramazanov's security clearance background check found no reason to raise any questions.

"Didn't the fact that the Ramazanov's son-in-law was associated with the Manhattan Project raise suspicions?" Prescott said.

"Not necessarily. You can see here that the association with one Major Mikhail Voronin of the Army Corps of Engineers is noted. On the staff of General Groves. Held the highest security clearance possible. Somebody must have vetted him many times over. A note here says that Groves squelched any further investigation. That sounds in character, but I wasn't directly involved. The War however was over. The Ramazanovs were deceased. Nothing further was done."

"Why not? By then we'd dropped the bombs on Hiroshima and Nagasaki. So you knew what Voronin was involved with."

"You'll forgive me for saying this, but what you have is nothing more than a conspiracy theory, Ms. Prescott. This Ramazanov could be this Soviet agent PUPPETEER, but nothing points to that. Certainly nothing points to this Army officer, Voronin. As to this PUPPETEER person, the most probable scenario is recall to Russia, or he could have been assigned a new code name. The document brought over by Gouzenko mentioning PUPPETEER was dated March of 1942. Your Boris Ramazanov came to the United States in May of that year. Seems in contradiction to the message about his assignment to penetrate British efforts at the Montreal Laboratory.

"There is no further mention of PUPPETEER throughout the body of material on Soviet espionage. I worked with Gouzenko on the Venona transcripts. The name has never cropped up again in any signals intelligence. It might have been a duplicate code name, perhaps abandoned for some reason."

Prescott was not disappointed. Nothing here ruled out Ramazanov as being PUPPETEER. She did not really expect to find anything new in the FBI archives. It was simply a necessary box to check off. It was enlightening to understand from a first-hand participant why PUPPETEER had ceased to be of interest. The name would join the many other code names never identified with the actual individuals.

Her hopes for unearthing new material evidence would only come from old Soviet archives.

CHAPTER 22

VICTORIA PRESCOTT TOOK a flight from New York's JFK Airport to Paris' Charles de Gaulle. Connecting to the four-hour flight to Moscow put her into Sheremetyevo Airport early afternoon local time. Her father gave her instructions to go to SVR headquarters. She was to ask for Colonel Anton Grigoryev. He would be expecting her. She planned an early dinner and a good night's sleep before getting down to business the following day.

The SVR was the Russian Federation's foreign intelligence service, successor to the former KGB First Chief Directorate. The KGB was the Cold War era successor to Stalin's NKVD. The SVR was the next incarnation. It was responsible for intelligence and espionage activities outside the Russian Federation. While working with improved cooperation compared with the old days, the rival military foreign intelligence GRU still overlapped foreign intelligence gathering activities.

Her father had indeed reached high into his network of Russian contacts. It seemed Hamilton Prescott was on close terms with the newly appointed foreign minister, Yevgeny Primakov. After the failed 1991 attempt to overthrow the government of

Boris Yeltsin, Primakov became the first director of the newly formed SVR. The KGB was promptly reorganized after playing a role in the failed coup. Primakov headed the SVR until 1996 and his promotion to foreign minister. Hamilton Prescott described Primakov as a tough negotiator, pragmatically pursuing Russian interests, yet someone you could ultimately do business with.

The two diplomats developed a personal relationship that Victoria had not been aware of. Her father told her that Primakov agreed to arrange access to at least the old NKVD files. A gifted scholar was welcome but he commented that she would find little that had not already been made available by the Russians in 1992. There was nothing to hide from that era fifty years ago. The fact that the Soviets had engaged in espionage of the United States atomic bomb project was already well documented.

Victoria Prescott was jetlagged when the plane landed at Sheremetyevo Airport. An indeterminate hassle of queuing up for immigration entry then repeating the same at customs, still lay ahead. She had been to Moscow several times. Sheremetyevo was not a pleasant experience. Even with the dissolution of the Soviet Union, some things never change. Because of her fluency in Russia she was at least better able to navigate the surly staff and security personnel. A shower, room service dinner, and a good night's rest still seemed hours away.

"Victoria Prescott?" someone asked in Russian-accented English from behind.

She stopped and turned. A handsome man, maybe early forties, well dressed in a blazer and turtleneck had apparently addressed her.

"Yes. And you are?"

"Colonel Anton Vladimirovich Grigoryev. I'm with the Sluzhba Vneshney Razvedki. The acronym, SVR. I am Deputy Director in charge of the Political Intelligence Directorate. Welcome to Moscow."

Prescott extended her hand. In Russian, she responded by thanking him for meeting her at the airport personally. She was expecting to see him at his office tomorrow morning.

He smiled broadly and said in Russian. "Your Russian is excellent. I am very much impressed. Now, we must get you out of this dreary place."

Grigoryev guided her by the arm toward the front of the immigration lines. Prescott tried to avoid the angry looks of the long lines of arrivals awaiting entry. As a security officer made to intercept them, Grigoryev showed his credentials. The officer studied Grigoryev's ID, saluted, and then led the way to one of the passport examiners. Prescott's passport was quickly stamped with barely a glance. She had to smile at the thought that the security personnel must be wondering what kind of trouble she was in being escorted by a colonel from the foreign intelligence service.

After getting her luggage, Grigoryev repeated the same move on the customs officers to pass through without any of the usual bureaucratic tactics. Like a scene from a movie, at the curb was a young man in a leather jacket, leaning against a black car, illegally parked, smoking a cigarette. Seeing Grigoryev, the cigarette was quickly discarded and the rear door opened. Even jetlagged, Prescott was impressed with the theatrics.

In the car, Grigoryev said, "I shall take you to your hotel. It is still early. You can rest from your long flight. May I suggest dinner? We can discuss your project. It will allow me to better assist your search. Minister Primakov requested I personally see to your needs. Shall we say eight o'clock?"

So much for a good night's rest. But it would make sense to explain what she was looking for. She was anxious to see just how helpful the Russians would be. The social interaction would be a good start. Besides, Grigoryev was an attractive man.

That thought made her think of Phillip. They had spoken only once since she had left San Francisco over a week ago. The conversation had been a bit strained. The relationship had been strained for some time. Only inertia kept them together. So why not enjoy the company of a new man for at least an evening?

A two-hour nap followed by a shower did wonders. What to wear? The one classy blouse she brought of course and the black skirt, a tight black skirt. Black heels. A simple gold chain necklace with gold hoop earrings. Putting on her makeup, she realized she was looking forward to what felt like a date. Why not? Research didn't typically offer such diversions.

She entered the hotel lobby promptly at eight. Grigoryev was already waiting. He was dressed in a medium grey suit, black shirt with a striped tie. Elegant would describe the impression. He smiled broadly taking in an equally elegant Victoria Prescott.

The same driver chauffeured them to the Café Pushkin. The restaurant was located in the very center of Moscow on Tverskaya Street. The maître d' acknowledged Grigoryev, "Good evening, Colonel," then escorted them to the second floor. The *Library Room* was decorated in a décor of telescopes, globes, and old books. The style was intended to be Russian nineteenth century aristocratic with high ceilings and rich wood paneling.

"Apart from well prepared Russian cuisine, the Pushkin has an excellent wine list. You do enjoy good wine I hope?" Grigoryev said.

"Certainly."

"French wines?"

"Especially French. How did you guess? Burgundy is my favorite."

"Ah, very good. What appellation do you prefer?"

"My favorites are mostly Côte de Nuits," Prescott said.

"You do know your wines, Ms. Prescott. I am impressed. I can assure you they will have a good selection here," Grigoryev said and motioned for the waiter.

Suave and charming this handsome intelligence officer. Probably a former KGB spy? Now there was something to think about.

Wine was served. Prescott and Grigoryev made small talk and filled in abbreviated backgrounds. Prescott assumed he already knew much about her, including what wine she liked. He would at least have prepared a basic dossier. So she wouldn't lie about Phillip if the subject came up indirectly. It didn't. However Grigoryev found it convenient to point out that he was divorced. There was a teenage daughter, proudly showing her a photograph.

After dinner, Grigoryev brought the conversation back to business. "I've been instructed by Director Trubnikov to provide you whatever assistance possible. Foreign Minister Primakov spoke to me as well. Until last year, he was our director so he is familiar with intelligence affairs. Please tell me briefly what you are looking for, Ms. Prescott. Obviously, Minister Primakov gave me a general idea. World War Two Soviet espionage directed at the American atomic bomb project. He implied you were researching still unidentified spies from that time."

The feeling of a date vanished. Back to work. "That's generally correct. But I have some specific names I would like to explore. I believe I have found a connection that may lead to identifying a previously unknown, highly placed Soviet spy."

"I see. These are old speculations I understand. I did my own research into that time when I was advised of your visit. The Americans suspected even the scientific director of the project after the War, Dr. Oppenheimer. Other scientists too. By the 1960's those spies from the 40's and 50's had all been identified. All the Soviet spy networks had been eliminated. None since have been discovered from that time. And you think you have found something, someone new? Would it even be important now?"

"I think so. That's what history is about. Trying to discover more facts. The more we know, the clearer our understanding of the events of the past. The more we know of the past, the better we understand the present."

"That is good to use as an explanation for your students, Professor," Grigoryev smiled.

Prescott realized how pompous her statement sounded. "Well, let's just say that it's the historian's function to explore all avenues of information, no matter how obscure. It's detective work. You sift through evidence and search for more. Sometimes leads go nowhere; sometimes they give a whole new understanding of events."

"Very well. We will see if your detective instincts lead anywhere. Tell me where you would like to start."

Prescott took out several typed sheets of paper from her purse. She told Grigoryev of her interest in identifying a GRU spy, code named PUPPETEER. Included were the backgrounds as she knew them from immigration records for Boris and Vanya Ramazanov. She told Grigoryev that she believed Boris Ramazanov was PUPPETEER. If that proved to be the case, it led directly to a highly placed figure in the Manhattan Project.

After reading the material, Grigoryev said, "Much of what you are looking for would be in GRU files, not NKVD files. I can get you access to the old NKVD archives from that period, and even material from before the Revolution, but not the GRU files. Cooperation with our sister foreign intelligence organ is much better than from those times, but we're still competitors. The military always guards its independence. The Foreign Minister himself could not gain direct access for you. He requested I do whatever possible with my counterparts at the GRU."

"Even if from GRU sources, I hoped there might still be information in the NKVD archives since they were responsible for atomic bomb related espionage in the United States. Everything related to atomic research eventually came to Beria. The GRU connection started in Canada. The GRU operated the earliest espionage operations directed at the British Tube Alloys Project relocated to there. That's where this PUPPETEER started operating. But I suspect he came to the United States. That was NKVD turf."

"I underestimated the depth of your knowledge about things from that time. Perhaps you are correct. If not, perhaps I can still help with my colleagues at the GRU. They might be inclined to respond to specific inquiries from me, particularly about events fifty years ago. Mentioning the Foreign Minister's interest in assisting you might also prove helpful."

They spent another leisurely hour over coffee and brandy. Grigoryev delivered her back to the hotel at midnight. She knew she would regret drinking so much alcohol come morning, but the evening could not have gone better.

Grigoryev's driver picked her up at nine o'clock the following morning. He assisted her through the entry process to SVR headquarters, and then escorted her to Grigoryev's office.

"Good morning, Ms. Prescott," Grigoryev said in Russian. "You slept well I trust?"

"Very good actually. Better than expected with all of the alcohol."

"Excellent. Please sit down. I have some preliminary information already. Before I retired for the evening, I telephoned staff on the night shift to commence a computer search for the code name PUPPETEER and this Boris Ramazanov."

Prescott sat forward in anticipation.

"Let's start with the name PUPPETEER. There is very little from NKVD files since he was a GRU asset. Two references in signals traffic from Ottawa, Canada in 1942. Not very helpful. Here, see for yourself."

Grigoryev handed copies of the transmissions to Prescott.

"As for this Boris Aleksandrovich Ramazanov, there is no record of that name that fits your profile. Several by this name appear in various records. None of these fit the age or place of birth. Military records from World War One record four men by this name. Three died in that war, the other a few years later. There is no record of a Boris Ramazanov and wife, Vanya, immigrating to Canada in the 1920's."

"What about Ramazanov's degree from Moscow State University?"

"There is a record of his being awarded a degree in chemical engineering in 1913."

Prescott deflated with that part of the news. The absence of immigration records from that chaotic time in Russia meant nothing, but it was still disappointing.

"However, there is something wrong with that university record," Grigoryev said.

"What do you mean?"

"I mean the record is apparently false. It's my guess that it was fabricated in case there was any background check. Standard tradecraft to build a false background. You see that is the only evidence of Ramazanov at the University. It doesn't go any deeper than the statement that he was awarded a degree. No student records, no evidence of attending any particular classes. Sloppy intelligence work. The record was obviously planted, probably in the 1920's."

"Then it was a fictitious name," Prescott said. "That could be just as important. But that will make it more difficult trying to determine his real name. I was hoping it might be a real name. A sleeper agent with no need to disguise his real background. Well, detective work is rarely easy."

"Perhaps you have been lucky. Even in the spy business, professionals often are careless. It appears that was the case back in those early days. Look at the history of this person. Does this fit the profile of your Boris Ramazanov?"

Prescott read the brief biography. The chronology fit perfectly. The basic background pieces fit. He was a World War One veteran, wounded. A chemical engineering degree from the Moscow State University, a wife named Vanya. But of more interest was this person's service in the intelligence arm of the Bolshevik Red Army during the civil war against the anti-Bolshevik White Army. Good credentials for a spy. His background was Eastern orthodox Catholic, not Jewish as Ramazanov claimed. Typical legend for a spy; build on as much real background as possible.

"But the name, Boris Pavelovich Dmytryk? How did that come up?" Prescott said.

"There was the mistake. Turning up nothing on the name Ramazanov, we tried the wife. Her maiden name was Vanya Ivanovna Durchenko. She was in the files. Several files. She was an early Bolshevik. Active in the Party. What led to Boris Dmytryk was the record of Vanya's marriage. Vanya Durchenko became Vanya Dmytryk."

"Thank you. That's very good news. Then we have a name to pursue. Can I look at these records myself?" Prescott said.

"Yes, certainly. I am having them brought to a conference room."

"Wonderful. But nothing on the code name PUPPETEER?"

"Nothing yet. I am having lunch with someone I know well at the GRU. PUPPETEER was their agent. They will have records. I cannot promise they will give me the information you seek, but I will do my best."

"I don't suppose I could join you?"

"I think not," Grigoryev said shaking his head. "Even though a beautiful woman might soften my colleague, he is all military. The GRU is an old bureaucracy. They have not gone through the same transformations as the NKVD did to the KGB, then now to the SVR. Being the military, they still cling to older ways. The United States is no longer an enemy, but still an adversary. Best to keep this a Russian security matter. Allows them to maintain control. Considering this information is sought by a western academic, I would not expect their cooperation without the pressure of the foreign minister. However, we're still not asking all that much. As I understand it, all you want is to identify this named Soviet agent, PUPPETEER, as this Boris Dmytryk, aka Ramazanov. Your important spy is someone else. Correct?"

"Precisely, Colonel. PUPPETEER's source. Obviously I'd like to see everything in their files. My spy must be in there somewhere. But I know that may not be realistic. Even though your agency made public much information a few years ago about Soviet espionage from that time, I'm sure you did not reveal everything either."

Grigoryev smiled and nodded slightly. "Such is the nature of the intelligence business. But we shall see what we can find for you."

"I can't tell you how much I appreciate your efforts on my behalf."

Grigoryev smiled. "I wonder if you would consider doing me a favor, Ms. Prescott."

"Certainly, Colonel. What might that be?"

"I have two tickets to the Moscow Philharmonic this evening. I was to take my daughter. She was to return from visiting her cousins outside the city today. She called earlier to say she would not be back for another day. You know how teenagers are. It's a Bach concert. His most famous violin concertos will be performed. I have a weakness for violin music. Would you be so kind as to join me?"

Two nights in a row. Victoria was not sure she believed the daughter excuse. Was she replacing another woman?" This was turning out to be quite a personal adventure. A date with a Russian spy?

"Why thank you. I'd be delighted."

"Excellent. Now, I will take you to the conference room to review the documents. You can make notes, but no copies. I must approve anything leaving this building. As for lunch, since

I am otherwise committed on my errand to probe the archives of the GRU, my secretary will escort you to our cafeteria. It is acceptable. This way you can work on the files the rest of the day. I will be occupied this afternoon with other duties, but I shall pick you up at seven o'clock this evening at your hotel. The concert starts at eight. We shall have a light dinner after the concert."

Grigoryev escorted her down the hall and handed her off to his secretary. "Good luck. Perhaps you will find other useful information."

"Thank you again, Colonel. Just one thing further. It would be most conclusive if I could get a fingerprint of this Boris Dmytryk. And his wife also."

Grigoryev smiled. "I'll see what I can do, Ms. Prescott."

Victoria was in her element pouring over original archival records going back before the October Revolution in 1917. She could feel the characters seep from the pages. With the name Ramazanov now known to be false, she knew she was close to the evidence she needed. It was almost too easy. Thanks to her father's high-level connections in the Russian government. And thanks to a cooperative intelligence officer. No question that he was going out of his way to assist her. Because he was attracted to her? After the recent rough spots with Phillip, it was nice to feel the attention.

She started with the oldest records first to build the chronology of Boris and Vanya. There was a brief reference to a student named Vanya Ivanovna Durchenko, born in 1895, appearing in a report from the Tsar's secret police, the Okhrana. The files had been confiscated after the fall of Tsar Nicholas II in 1917. Durchenko was suspected of subversive activities against the throne. She was clearly a committed Bolshevik.

The afternoon was spent immersed in the various bits of information on Boris Dmytryk. Prescott was totally absorbed as the facts paralleled the apparently fictitious Boris Ramazanov.

Chemical engineering degree from Moscow State University. In his case, supported by other university records. Junior officer in the Russian Army. World War One veteran, wounded January, 1915 at the Battle of Bolimov in Poland. Met Vanya Durchenko, a volunteer nurse, while recovering from wounds at a Moscow military hospital. Recruited by Durchenko into the Bolshevik Party. Married Durchenko in 1918. Active in the Red Army Intelligence Directive from 1918 to 1925. Then a brief entry with no detail, *Boris Dmytryk died of natural causes in a military hospital in 1925.*

Died? Her heart sank for a moment. 1925? Of course he didn't die. Dmytryk just became Ramazanov with a new life as a sleeper agent sent to the West. It didn't say that, but the evidence was clear. He was a chemical engineer with a degree from Moscow State University. A falsified diploma easily created by the GRU as Ramazanov. A false birth record indicating parents of Jewish background, conveniently deceased during the Spanish Flu pandemic in 1918. As for Vanya, her real background did not need alteration, just a new marriage certificate in the name of Ramazanov. Fortunately some low-level clerk seventy years ago screwed up by not destroying the Dmytryk marriage record.

There was a poor quality photograph of Dmytryk in uniform from 1914. Prescott compared it to Ramazanov's Canadian immigration photo from 1925. Inconclusive. There was no photograph of Vanya Durchenko. She made a note to request other places where photographs might exist. Hopefully the GRU would give up a photo from just prior to Dmytryk/Ramazanov's emigration to Canada. Fingerprints would be gold. She already had copies of the Ramazanovs' fingerprints from their 1942 U.S. immigration applications.

This was good material they assembled, but still not conclusively proving Ramazanov was a Soviet agent. It all fit, but she needed the direct evidence that Dmytryk was Ramazanov, and that Ramazanov was the Soviet agent code named PUPPETEER.

That information apparently resided only in the GRU files. For that, she would have to rely on the indirect approach of SVR Colonel Grigoryev.

At seven o'clock, Victoria Prescott entered her hotel lobby. Fortunately she had thought to bring along the ubiquitous black dress for just such an eventuality. Same black heels, same gold necklace as the night before, but a more formal looking package this night. The dress made her look good, especially the plunging neckline. Not bad for an academic she thought to herself.

The concert proved enjoyable. Prescott was intrigued by the intensity with which Grigoryev was consumed by the music. They did not talk about what went on with his visit to the GRU until after the concert.

They went to a small ethnic Georgian restaurant. It was an intimate place but not sufficiently private enough for them to talk specifics except in hushed tones.

"Forgive me for being anxious, but how did you make out today, Colonel?"

"I think the term would be guardedly optimistic. My colleague there was willing enough to help, but made it clear that several levels of approval would be required. That was to be expected. My colleague thought the letter from the Minister should help expedite things. But still, he said it might take some time."

"How long?"

"Possibly a week."

"Oh, that long?" Prescott said. That was probably to be expected but still a little disappointing. "Maybe I could make use of that time to explore some other materials within your archives."

"And that would be?"

"Lavrentiy Beria materials. Stalin put him in charge of the Soviet atomic bomb program. So most everything acquired through spying on the American atomic bomb program would have eventually flowed to him. Even GRU intelligence. Operation ENORMOZ was a joint operation. Even if Beria headed only the NKVD at the time, he had broader power. He had a hand in the Red Army purges so the GRU would have feared him. I might find something that will suggest intelligence from this unidentified spy."

"Excellent. I continue to forget that you probably know more about Soviet intelligence history than I do. I believe I can arrange that. I will give you the assistance of one of our best archivists. He's old enough to have lived those times. Comrade Beria covered a lot of ground. Files relating to him are voluminous. Old Igor will be invaluable. It may still occupy days of work for you."

On balance, it was a wholly productive day. She was still very much in the hunt for her spy. The evening was delightful. The night turned out even better.

A taxi instead of the chauffeured official car tonight. At the hotel, Colonel Grigoryev opened her door. "Please wait," he said to the driver.

A twinge of disappointment? What was she expecting or hoping?

Inside the lobby, Grigoryev said, "Thank you so much for joining me this evening, Ms. Prescott. I hope you enjoyed the music."

Victoria Prescott made a quick decision. She touched his arm. "Please don't leave."

They looked at each other for several seconds without saying anything.

"A moment please," Grigoryev said. He lightly touched her hand still resting on arm.

Walking the few steps over to the hotel desk, he said to the clerk, "Tell the taxi driver I won't need him."

Handing the clerk currency to cover the fare, he came back to Prescott. "Yes of course, let's go up."

B Reactor, Hanford, Washington, 1944

CHAPTER 23

LOS ALAMOS, NEW MEXICO – 1944

I LEFT WASHINGTON within days of that fateful week. Things had been difficult, but I found myself adapting to this new reality. Ever the pragmatic engineer. Elena did everything to please me. My resistance was only superficial. I played the martyr but responded with little reluctance. Elena was an addiction.

Upon leaving, Elena said, "I love you. Thank you for being with me in this."

I said nothing other than goodbye and gave her a kiss. For the first time, I hoped I would be gone for a long stretch and therefore unable to pass on new information. That would be a difficult decision when the time came. Up to now, I had been an unknowing accomplice. That next step would amount to a willful act of espionage against the United States. My parents now being part of Russia was poor reason. No matter that I shared some of the feelings of my wife and her parents about Russia. Several of the scientists on the Hill had voiced similar feelings. Everyone knew that the atomic bomb was something uniquely different than just another weapon. All of us knew it would fundamentally reshape the world's political dynamics. Yet I doubted anyone else had done what I did. Circumstances had fated that I give up my soul in this clash of ideologies.

I flew to Albuquerque. It was now early September. Groves told me I would remain focused on Los Alamos exclusively. Even though he received constant technical reports from Oppenheimer, he wanted me to give him a parallel assessment. What was my feeling about progress? Were the key scientists suited for their individual roles? Was Oppenheimer's reorganization proving effective? How was morale? Was reported progress getting us closer to a successful design? Were there obstacles that could be fixed?

The longer my current stint at Los Alamos the better. The longer I could delay knowingly participating as a traitor, the better. But I knew I was still trapped. There was no middle ground.

The Manhattan Project was at a crucial juncture. Nothing was working as planned. Worse yet, new problems continually surfaced. Things would have to change soon or the project would be considered a failure. Even if the situation turned around, it was becoming increasing unlikely that a bomb would become operational before the war in Europe ended. With the imminent defeat of Germany on the horizon, we now knew the Nazis never had a viable atomic bomb program.

The race to beat the Nazis to such a weapon, the original catalyst for the United States development of an atomic bomb, was no longer the issue. The urgency now shifted toward Japan. But it wasn't about Japan. It was about validating the very reason for the Manhattan Project. Validating the enormous expenditure without Congressional approval. Validation would best be accomplished through use against an enemy. Use against the Japanese would send a strong signal to the Soviet Union. The United States not only had the technology, but the will to use this weapon an enemy. Some believed the Soviet Union might become that enemy.

The Oak Ridge K-25 gaseous diffusion plant was still not producing enriched uranium. Useable diffusion barriers had yet to be developed. The Y-12 electromagnetic process was operating at less than one percent efficiency. The newest process, thermal diffusion, initiated under a crash construction project, began partial operation. Like the other enrichment process, the S-50 plant represented unprecedented engineering challenges. Start-up trials showed serious leaks. The remedial rebuilding would setback even proving the viability of that third uranium enrichment process. It was by no means certain when sufficient quantities of U-235 would be produced. Colonel Nichols, the MED Chief Engineer, had his hands full marshalling the civilian contractors' efforts to resolve the many engineering problems. I could imagine his stress with Groves breathing down his neck demanding unreasonable results.

The alternative fissile material, element 94, plutonium, was produced as a byproduct in a reactor using naturally occurring uranium-238. The Hanford Engineering Works in the State of Washington was devoted solely to the production of plutonium. Within a couple of weeks B Pile, the first full scale plutonium-producing reactor, was scheduled to start up. The reactor consisted of 200 tons of uranium and 1200 tons of graphite as a moderator, assembled into a cube measuring 46 feet by 38 feet, 41 feet high. Enrico Fermi was personally supervising. Output was projected at six kilograms of plutonium per month. The process had substantially been proven by the X-10 prototype reactor at Oak Ridge which was built on the design of Fermi's first nuclear reactor constructed in Chicago. Producing sufficient quantities of plutonium appeared to have a high probability for success. A lot of hopes were riding on Hanford.

However, a workable design for a plutonium core bomb using an implosion concept did not yet exist. Here again, engineering problems continued to be vexing. At the very least, a viable implosion design would be a complex, extraordinarily precision device.

Even though September, 1944 represented a low-point for the Manhattan Project, it was also the turning point. For the most part, all of the fundamental problems of both physics and engineering were now known. The tasks could now be more clearly defined. Testing could be directed toward resolving specific engineering design problems.

Oppenheimer's reorganized Los Alamos Lab became principally focused on an implosion-design bomb using plutonium as the fissile material. While not an absolute certainty, the gun-design uranium bomb would work. The engineering was fairly straightforward. The problem was producing comparatively large quantities of uranium-235. That was now in the hands of the contractors responsible for the Oak Ridge enrichment processes. Plutonium held the promise for the ability to produce in sufficient quantity to sustain a multi-bomb program. The problem remained the plutonium bomb design. That was the responsibility of Los Alamos.

The crux of the implosion design problem was to achieve symmetrical compression of a plutonium core. My friend Robert Serber proposed a test method using a radioactive material known as lanthanum as the test substitute for plutonium.

"We've named it the RaLa Experiment," Serber explained to me. "That's a contraction of radioactive lanthanum. Lanthanum-140 is a decay product of barium-140. We chose it because of its particular emitting rate of gamma ray energy. Good for taking test readings. It also has a short half-life of only 40 hours so the resulting contamination dissipates within a reasonable time."

"So how does this experiment work?" I said.

"Let me draw a diagram. We take an eighth-inch sphere of the lanthanum and insert it into the center of a small metal sphere. We replace the hole in the sphere with a plug. The metal sphere is surrounded by the spherical explosive lens configuration of explosives. We'll detonate the conventional explosives then measure the degree and symmetry of the compressive forces by measuring the changes in gamma radiation in the metal as it underwent compression."

"Where do you do this testing?"

"Haven't yet. First test will be tomorrow. A couple miles from here. Place called Bayo Canyon. Bruno Rossi is the group leader. Luis Alverez heads up the work on the electronic detonation circuits.

"We're simultaneously testing for a number of design problems. First is the whole compression idea to achieve the necessary rate for the core to go super-critical. Then there's the design of the explosive lens. Beyond the precision of the lens' shape, Kistiakowsky also has to achieve the required wave force by using both fast and slow explosives. The geometry is exceedingly complex. And then of course the array of explosive lenses must be detonated precisely at the same time."

"Can I witness this test tomorrow?" I asked Serber.

"Not closely. We're using two army tanks specially outfitted to monitor the test results. Limited room inside. You can come with me and look over the test site. It's called Technical Area 10. Then we have to pull back, a long way. We're not sure of the level of radioactivity that will be dispersed. This is still dangerous stuff. The lanthanum is a decay product from the spent fuel from the Oak Ridge reactor."

After looking over the test set-up with Serber the next day, I was glad to leave the area. The scientists and technicians wore special coveralls. Geiger counters were used in various locations. There had already been incidents of radiation exposure handling the radioactive lanthanum. I was glad there was not room in one of the tanks. I'm sure they provided adequate protection against the blast, but not necessarily against the radiation. Radiation could be lethal. Two scientists had been killed by radiation exposure only two weeks earlier at the Philadelphia Navy Shipyard working with a prototype thermal diffusion process enriching uranium.

That first RaLa test was inconclusive. As much as anything, it provided a basis to refine the test set-up instrumentation. Each week thereafter, at least one new explosion could be heard on the Hill from Area 10. Experiments were being conducted elsewhere, but the RaLa tests would ultimately be the proving ground for something approximating the implosion design on a small scale.

On Wednesday morning, September 27, I attended a meeting with several senior scientists in Oppenheimer's office. Oppenheimer was beaming while puffing away on his pipe.

"I spoke with Enrico late last night. At around midnight, B Pile went critical. By two o'clock in the morning it was operating at a higher power output than any previous chain reaction."

There was a collective exclamation of cheers from everyone.

"I spoke again with him this morning. B Pile has been powered up now for about eight hours. So that means we may have sufficient quantities of 49 maybe sooner than 25. Puts greater pressure on coming up with a workable implosion design. I telephoned General Groves a short time ago with the news."

In an adhoc celebration, I joined a small group at the Oppenheimers' for cocktails that evening. At seven o'clock, Oppenheimer's secretary Priscilla Greene knocked on the door. She whispered something to Oppie. His face went rigid. Uncharacteristically, we heard him say, "Shit".

Gathering us together he said, "Gentlemen, we have a problem. Let's go to my office."

On the way over, all he would say is there was a problem with B Pile. Priscilla Greene placed a call to Enrico Fermi at Hanford. For the next ten minutes all we heard was Oppenheimer's side of the conversation. *What happened? When? The rate of output decline? What's your best guess?*

Oppenheimer hung up. Letting out a sigh he said to everyone, "B Pile shutdown an hour ago. The chain reaction ceased without warning."

Several scientists fired off questions. Oppenheimer held up his hand. "To early to tell. But there's nobody better to have there than Fermi. Crawford Greenewalt from DuPont is there too. He's the guy that solved the canning problem of sealing the uranium slugs in the reactor's aluminum cylinders. Brilliant engineer. Nothing we can do but let them work on the problem. The minute I hear anything I'll let everyone know."

After everyone left I said, "What's this mean, Doctor?"

"It means we're up here in the mountains working to design a weapon that might as well be something out of a Buck Rogers comic strip. It's all premised on theoretical physics for isotopes that might not be able to be produced in any significant quantity."

"Perhaps that's premature, Doctor. After all, Fermi successfully produced the first reactor at Chicago. Then we have the X-10 reactor at Oak Ridge. They're successful. Maybe it's something with the scale of the B Pile. The basic concepts appear proven."

"Maybe you're right, Major. Eventually we'll overcome all of these obstacles. That's the nature of scientific advancement. The question always remains one of time."

"Are you going to call the General?" I asked.

Oppenheimer nodded with a grim look on his face as he picked up the telephone.

Groves was decidedly unhappy. He ordered that one of the small reactors in Chicago, CP-3, be run at full power continually in an attempt to duplicate the problem. He was irritated that this had not been done some time ago to look for any unforeseen problems such as those now being experienced by the first production-scale Hanford reactor.

The next couple of days were a roller coaster of emotions for the scientists at Los Alamos. First, early Thursday morning the pile came back to life and began running well above critical again. Twelve hours later it died again. A mood approaching despair prevailed over Los Alamos for the next several days. No parties that weekend. Probably an excess of alcohol consumption however.

On the following Tuesday, we convened again in Oppenheimer's office. It was the old ebullient Oppenheimer this time.

"Fermi's team found the problem. Actually John Wheeler did. Princeton theoretician. Worked with Greenewalt from DuPont on the Hanford reactor design. Seems he was concerned early on about fission product poisoning. The short answer as to why the reactor shutdown is xenon poisoning."

"Can you give me the layman's version, Doctor?" I asked.

"In simplest terms, a parent byproduct, iodine-135 is formed after a period of time with the pile operating under a sustained chain reaction. Iodine-135 has a half life of 6.6 hours. It then decays to xenon-135. Unfortunately, xenon-135 has an extraordinary neutron absorption rate. So when the concentration reaches a certain level, the chain reaction simply stops. It's like sticking a super control rod into the reactor."

"Why the uncontrolled restart?" someone asked.

"Xenon-135 has a half life of 9.2 hours. It then decays into a third non-absorbing neutron element. The process simply starts over again repeating the cycle."

"Then the reactors at Hanford are useless? D Pile is already under construction using the same design as B Pile. Where does that leave us?" I said.

"That's the good news. Theoretically at least. No pun intended. At least I hope it is. You see, Wheeler made enough of a case to the folks at DuPont, Greenewalt in particular, about the possibility of reactor byproduct poisoning. The B Pile is designed as a gigantic cube. Wigner's economical design called for 1500 uranium channels arranged in a cylindrical pattern. Wheeler persuaded DuPont to add another 504 channels for a margin of safety into the corners as it were of the square, That's what we now have available. Fermi is sure that using the added fuel channels will overpower the xenon poisoning effect. But it will take a couple of months to rig them and connected to the cooling water supply. D Pile under construction might actually be ready with the new arrangement before the retrofitting of B Pile."

Personally, I did not share the renewed optimism of most of the others. It seemed to be just another desperation fix to an untested design that could return yet another disappointment. I gathered more data on the mathematical basis of how the xenon poisoning effect would supposedly be overcome by the reactor redesign. Were the scientists just grasping? My report to Groves reflected those thoughts.

Maybe all these setbacks would relieve me of revealing anything but problems to my new masters. Maybe I could relate only problems going forward? Simply ignore any successes, if any were ever achieved? Not likely. If there were successes I would not be able to hide that indefinitely. That would amount to feeding the Soviets false information. With certainty, that would carry repercussions. At least I was stuck at Los Alamos for the time being.

October and November passed with little technical progress. The only encouraging news was a consistent output of 40 grams per day of 80 percent enriched uranium from the Y-12 electromagnetic process plant in Oak Ridge. It suggested progress, but a long way from success.

On a personal level, I called Elena once a week from Los Alamos. The calls were monitored so our conversations sounded polite but never intimate. Under the circumstances, that suited me fine.

Life on the Hill continued to have its challenges. More staff arrived each day. The ranks of the Army's Special Engineering

Detachment swelled to fill the ever increasing demand for technicians to man the experiments. The parallel demand for additional clerks, stenographers, telephone operators was filled by the growing number of the Women's Army Corps contingent. Los Alamos was a military base, the Manhattan Project a military operation. Only the scientists were civilians.

With the growing population, Los Alamos continued to suffered problems. Water shortages remained a chronic recurring issue. Housing was always in short supply even with continual new construction. The hospital was being overrun with infant births. Alcohol consumption was pronounced. Fraternization between the hundreds of male SED and female WAC staff was rampant, regardless of prohibitive regulations. Some WAC's had even been charging for sexual favors. There was little recreation other than sex and drinking.

Tensions between the civilian personnel and base security continued. The principle source of friction continued to be the base security officer, Major Peers de Silva. He was the only West Point graduate permanently stationed at Los Alamos. It was an undesirable wartime posting. He expected the place to operate with the semblance of a military base. De Silva was a humorless pain in the ass, universally disliked. Unfortunately, he was also the commander of the SED detachment.

The SED worked alongside the civilian scientists. Some even had graduate degrees. De Silva impressed military living conditions on these troops; bunks made up, spit-shined shoes, and inspections. They were expected to fall out for reveille each morning, followed by calisthenics.

George Kistiakowsky, the head of the implosion explosives group had a lot of the SED personnel on his team. He was particularly incensed by the treatment of *his* men. There were a number of heated exchanges with de Silva. The last of which ended by de Silva telling Kistiakowsky to take it up with Groves. He did.

On a brief visit to Los Alamos, Kistiakowsky prevailed on Oppenheimer to bring up the subject to Groves. Oppenheimer got nowhere. Kistiakowsky then confronted Groves. Short on time, Groves said he would discuss the matter if Kistiakowsky rode with him to catch his plane in Albuquerque.

It was over a two-hour ride and the two of them argued all of the way. Groves liked Kistiakowsky. Liked his White Russian anti-Communist background and former military service. Liked the fact he worked with explosives, something tangible contrasted to the academics engaged in theoretical physics. But on this point, Groves dug his heels in.

Getting nowhere, Kistiakowsky used his ultimate weapon. He simply threatened to resign from the project. Carrying the threat further, Kistiakowsky said that he was too old to be drafted therefore Groves could not prevent his departure.

Groves was furious. He told Kistiakowsky he would reconsider the matter. As with any other problem, Groves took immediate action. Within a week, Major de Silva was replaced as commander of the SED personnel with Major T. O. Palmer. Reveille and calisthenics were discontinued. Not liking de Silva myself, I told Kistiakowsky, "Good work. My reports about de Silva never got anywhere. Seems you've got more pull with the General."

With this long stint at Los Alamos I found myself with more free time for socializing. Instinctively, I shied away from fraternizing with the military officers. Not only to maintain my stature with the scientists, but by inclination. I was increasing troubled by the circumstances of what would happen after creating an atomic bomb. Although guarded, I shared many of the more expansive and the often left-leaning philosophical views of many of the scientists. Perhaps also because I was now a traitor to my uniform. I was accepted by the scientists as one of their group. That fit from all standpoints; my job, my social preference, and now my spying.

Up to now, I had little time for pursuing chess. One evening I was kibitzing with my friend Richard Feynman who was finishing a chess game with Oppenheimer at his house. Oppenheimer was sipping a martini and had young Feynman in difficult circumstances.

"Might as well resign, Richard. I have mate in three moves I believe," Oppenheimer said. He looked up at me. "Do you play, Major?"

"As a matter a fact I do," I said.

"Would you agree that I have Dr. Feynman in a death grip?"

I studied the board for a few moments. "I'm not so sure, Sir."

Feynman looked up at me. "You think there's a way out? Tell you what, you finish for me."

I did. Oppenheimer didn't win. After his third cigarette I had Feynman out of his positional hole and played the game to a draw.

"I'll be damned. That shouldn't have been possible to wriggle out of my trap. Just how good are you, Major?" Oppenheimer said.

"My father taught me. He was a master. My mother was pretty good herself. Took lessons when I was young. Couldn't beat my father until I was older. Haven't trained in lots of years though."

Feynman said, "I'll set you up with George. He thinks he's pretty good. At least he beats me. Maybe you can put him in his place."

Two days later I found myself across the table from George Kistiakowsky. Richard Feynman, Stanislaw Ulam, and John von Neumann hovered about as spectators. All of them fancied themselves pretty good chess players, but Kistiakowsky had roundly beaten them all.

Kistiakowsky said, "Chess is a matter of training. It can't be played well by dummies, but intellect alone does not insure a high degree of ability. If so, our esteemed audience watching us would always win with their towering intellectual capacities. Am I right, Mike?"

"Essentially yes. Training, but also study. Pretty good spatial visualization ability helps too."

"I agree. We shall see how well you were trained, Mike. Shall we begin?" Kistiakowsky said as he put out both his closed hands with a pawn of each color concealed.

Kistiakowsky would play white. We even had a timing clock so the game had a defined duration. We agreed upon ninety minutes, forty-five for each player.

Kistiakowsky opened with P-K4. I responded with P-QB4. Black followed with N-KB3. It was the normal course of the variation known as the Sicilian Defense. By not playing the almost automatic black first move of P-K4, the P-QB4 opening thwarted any preconceived ideas by white. It opened subsequent opportunities for both white and black.

Play progressed. My ability to visualize the board was very acute. Coupled with an understanding of the positional significance of typical formations drawn from good coaching, this gave me the equivalent of forward looking intelligence. Kistiakowsky was an accomplished player, but not equal to my level. Fifty minutes later, play had advanced twenty moves. I was clearly better positioned on the board forcing white to respond to my attack. Kistiakowsky's clock had only twenty remaining minutes whereas mine showed thirty-five. My opponent was under increasing pressure.

Before time ran out, I concluded the game with Kistiakowsky resigning his indefensible position. He stared at the board for a moment before declaring, "Goddamn. I don't think I had a chance after your N-N3 somewhere in the middle of the game." He reached over to shake my hand."

"I told you he was good, George. Guess I can't use you now as a ringer to lay wagers," Feynman said to me.

We retired to the canteen. Kistiakowsky was buying drinks. He personally brought his own bottle of favorite vodka. Kistiakowsky commented that for those of us who had East European backgrounds other than Feynman, vodka represented the equivalent to the national drink.

"Because of Prohibition, America's national liquor is moonshine," Feynman joked. "I think I prefer this vodka."

We sat around drinking Kistiakowsky's vodka and smoking. Eventually the conversation came around to the bomb, the ethics of what we were doing. All except Feynman were hawkish on the singular objective to develop an American atomic bomb. Should we use it against the Japanese? Germany would probably be defeated before a bomb was ready. It would be a weapon of mass destruction, killing civilians indiscriminately in vast numbers.

"We should clearly use it against the Japanese. Why not? Is it any different than firebombing their cities?" von Neumann said. "Besides, it'll be necessary to demonstrate the use of the atomic bomb for the Soviet Union. They're our next enemy."

"How's that?" Feynman said. "Because of them, Germany has been brought to her knees. What makes them our enemy?"

"Because Communism can't abide democracy," von Neumann said. "They're only allied with us because Hitler turned on them. They had no choice but to cooperate with us. After the war, it'll be them against us. I'd prefer we have the bomb and they don't. What do you say, George? You fought the Communists in your youth?"

Kistiakowsky replied, "The politics doesn't matter as far as our task to make the bomb is concerned. It must happen. The science is too far along. We simply need to be first. Then let the philosophical arguments decide. If we were to abandon the project, then someone else would possess the weapon. So we have no choices. If Stalin had the bomb he would use it as a hammer over our heads."

"So following your arguments, we must develop the bomb because someone else will," Feynman said. "I can accept that logic. But you, John, you suggest we need to use it as both a test and a political weapon."

"Yes I do. In fact, if we don't use it against the Japs we should maybe consider using it against the Soviets. Cut Stalin off at the knees before he can become a threat to America."

"Jesus, John, that's a helluva thing to say. Maybe too much vodka?" Feynman said.

"And what about you, Mike? What are your thoughts?" Feynman said to me.

I lit a cigarette to buy a few moments. "Look gentlemen, this is an Army project. Give the Army a new weapon and they will naturally want to use it against an enemy. An enemy which America is still fighting. An enemy still costing American lives. But using it will be a political decision. I don't have a political view on this. That'll be for the President. Since there must be a test, I'd make it a demonstration. I know I wouldn't want to be the one to drop this on a city."

We continued the discussion for some time, well into a second bottle of vodka. Regardless of any individual's position on the ethics associated with an atomic weapon, the work would go on. Everyone was trapped by the same reality. The science made clear that an atomic bomb was possible. Therefore, it would eventually happen. Even for those opposed to its actual use, it was better to be in command of the technology. Most took the view that America would act responsibly, whereas the Soviet Union would not. It was clear that the post-war world would be dominated by the United States and the Soviet Union, probably as competitors.

By the middle of December, the entire Manhattan Project took a positive turn. After months of setbacks, successes started to multiply.

The Y-12 electromagnetic enrichment plant increased the output rate to 90 grams per day. Still insufficient to meet the demands for a uranium bomb, but suggesting a continued improvement. The gaseous diffusion K-25 plant was still not operating. However, new diffusion barriers were scheduled for installation soon after Christmas. Tests showed real promise in the improved design.

Most importantly, the prospects for the implosion plutonium bomb improved significantly. Kistiakowsky's group had achieved the first successful explosive lens test. Much work remained, but the test empirically established the feasibility of the concept. And for the fuel, Hanford's D Pile went critical a week before Christmas. The additional uranium fuel proved sufficient to overcome the xenon poisoning effect. That also meant that the refitting of the B Pile would be successful. It was scheduled to become operational right after Christmas. F Pile was scheduled to go operational within a couple of months. Regardless of the uranium enrichment process difficulties at Oak Ridge, Hanford's reactors meant that sufficient plutonium could be created for a succession of bombs. The vision of that plutonium bomb design was now coming into focus.

Project Alberta, the delivering of atomic bombs to enemy targets, was moving forward. Lt. Col. Paul Tibbets was organizing the designated 509th Composite Group at Wendover Field in Utah. Once the bomb was ready, so would the means of deploying it against the enemy. That enemy was clearly going to be Japan.

As was my standard practice, I typed up my reports weekly for General Groves. The dispatches were sent in the weekly courier run to Washington via military aircraft from Albuquerque. For the last several weeks, I had typed carbon copies of my reports. It was a direct violation of security. Because of the sensitivity of the material, only a single copy of my eyes-only reports was supposed to reside in Washington. I still didn't know if I could hand over these carbon copies to Boris for transmission to Moscow. But I knew I would have to. I was in too far. Elena had seen to that.

I was scheduled to return to Washington two days before Christmas. I had a week's leave then due back at Los Alamos. As much as I dreaded what I was about to do, I was anticipating seeing Elena. I was still angry with her, but I still wanted to be with her. A character weakness distorting my judgment, but I needed her. I fantasized making love to her after being away for so long.

On my last night on the Hill, the Serbers invited me for dinner at their house. It was just the three of us. Before dinner, we enjoyed a few drinks. It had turned cold so there was a fire going in the pot-belly stove that served to heat the small four-room house.

The wives of the other scientists knew only vaguely what their husbands were doing. Technical discussions outside the various labs were prohibited. Since Charlotte directed the technical library, she was intimate with all that went on toward developing the atomic bomb. She and her husband could therefore talk candidly without breaching security protocol.

"The situation has brightened up considerably for the Project in the last couple of weeks," I said.

"Most certainly," Robert Serber said. "It's clear there will be a bomb. The implosion bomb might even be first. Just a question of time. I assume that's what you're reporting to Groves as well?"

"Yes. Things seem to be coming together. The timing seems to be the only uncertainty."

"Of course it's all about the timing. Groves expects to have a bomb by the middle of the year, not because it's possible, but because that fits for the Army's schedule," Charlotte said.

"What do you mean?" I asked.

"I mean they want it in time to use it against an enemy. That's Japan for now. But not for long if the news reports are accurate. I think the Army wants a practical demonstration for the Soviet Union."

"That's a little conspiratorial isn't it, Charlotte?" Her husband said.

"I don't think so. For some reason, the mood in the country has turned decidedly against our ally. There's no regard for what they've done to crush Hitler. It's all about Communism. Anything socialistic brings fear to Americans. They don't realize that everything Roosevelt did to bring us out of the Depression was socialistic."

"Charlotte's right about the mood being anti-Communist. That's clear from reading the newspapers. How do you feel about that, Mike? Your heritage is Russian. Your parents even came from Russia I think you said."

Although it was in my Army personnel file, I had told no one that my parents had returned to Russia. With the rhetoric that abounded, there was no reason to introduce unwanted attention to that fact.

"I understand yours and Charlotte's feelings about Russia. I think it's really about Stalin and less about Communism. I think the Soviet Union should have gotten more help from us."

"What about now? Should we share the bomb with them?" Charlotte asked.

Her husband was aghast that she would say such a thing. It was an element of her trust of me that she knew I would not relate such a subversive comment to Groves.

"I won't even venture a comment about that, Charlotte. That's for the President to decide. It's easier if I just follow orders and do my job. It doesn't ultimately matter what I think, or any of us involved with the Project. Even you senior scientists won't have any influence about whether to share any of this with the Soviets."

Robert steered the conversation to other topics. Charlotte was a handful. He had the same kind of issues with his wife that I now did. Elena was also a handful and decidedly more dangerous than Charlotte Serber.

I would be leaving Los Alamos the following morning. As usual, an army driver was assigned to drive me to Albuquerque to catch a plane to Washington. At the main gate, the guard stopped us and asked for my credentials. He asked if I had any classified documents in my possession. The usual question to which I acknowledged yes as usual. The guard asked that I wait a moment and went inside the gate building.

Out came Major de Silva. He leaned into the open window of the car, "I'm sorry to trouble you, Major. I must examine what documents are being removed from the base. It's a new security precaution. I'm sure you understand."

That had never happened before. Panic rose inside me. In the past, I just had my notes. Sensitive materials but not carbon copies of my eyes-only reports to General Groves in direct violation of security rules like this time. I could probably explain it away, but it could become ugly.

My first act of spying and I had already made a fundamental mistake.

"That's not possible, Major," I said. "The information I have is sensitive beyond your clearance level."

"I don't believe so. Not if you're leaving the Hill with them," de Silva said.

De Silva may have actually grinned. We didn't like each other. He resented my close association with the scientists. Worse yet, I was close to the Serbers which he particularly hated. This might be more than de Silva's usual overbearing tactics. He was probably still smarting from being relieved of command of the SED detachment.

"Then I must demand to see Colonel Ashbridge," I said, exiting the car.

Colonel Whiney Ashbridge was an able officer who managed the impossible command that was Los Alamos. It was a diplomatic job contending with a growing civilian contingent at what was the most secret U.S. military installation in the world.

Ashbridge tried to mediate some common ground between de Silva's demand to see the contents of my brief case and my refusal. After fifteen minutes of wrangling I played my trump card.

"I work directly for General Groves. These documents are classified for his eyes only. Please get him on the phone, Colonel."

De Silva did not look pleased. Perhaps he was regretting having taken this so far. As for me, I knew Groves would not be happy having to resolve a petty bureaucratic problem. I hoped Ashbridge would simply defuse the matter and allow an exception in my case. Unfortunately he did not. He put the call through to Washington.

Colonel Ashbridge explained the situation to Groves. After a few moments, Ashbridge handed me the phone.

"Major Voronin, Sir," I said.

"What the hell's going on, Major. Do you really have materials in your briefcase that are sensitive? What for?"

"Extensive notes, Sir. I've been here a long stretch. There's a huge amount of material to assimilate. I assumed I would need those notes to review my progress reports with you when I return to Washington. You're bound to have questions. Nothing I haven't done before. This is some new security precaution. In the past I was exempt from search. I didn't think I should reveal any of this material to the normal security personnel since it crosses so many operational compartments."

Groves was a fanatic about compartmentalization. Everything was about the need to know. I was hoping to play into his hyper-sense of security.

"I agree, Major. Put Ashbridge back on the line," Groves said.

The conversation was brief. Ashbridge repeatedly said, yes sir, concluding with I understand, General."

I was free to go. No one was to examine the contents of my briefcase.

I returned to my car. My hands shook as I lit a cigarette.

Los Alamos colloquium

CHAPTER 24

WASHINGTON D.C. – 1944

I HAD BEEN away from Elena for almost three months. Anger had transformed into resignation with the new reality of my existence. Amazing how people can adapt to even the most terrible of circumstances. Did murderers learn to live with themselves? I was a spy. Even before I handed over the contents of my briefcase to Boris, I was already guilty. I had violated basic security that resulted in classified information being passed to the enemy. Not yet perhaps a real enemy I rationalized. The Soviet Union was officially an ally fighting the avowed mutual enemy, Nazi Germany. Regardless of the tangled ethics, I was already a spy. Therefore, going forward was no worse a transgression. At some higher level there might even be some broader humanistic justification. At a lower level it was simply necessary self preservation. Adding to that emotional mix, my longing for Elena had not diminished.

The flight back home gave me time to organize my thoughts. There were only two other officers on the C-47 transport aircraft. They slept most of the way. I smoked and sipped on a pint of vodka. I was drinking more than ever, but that seemed the least of my concerns.

What was it to be like now with Elena? I had left in anger in September. Our last night, we didn't make love. Even though I castigated myself for being weak willed, I still lusted for Elena. I fantasized about touching her body. Stronger images about her touching me aroused me. My infatuation for her overwhelmed everything else. Being pragmatic, I decided to go with the flow. Elena would be anxious to please me. Why resist?

Somewhere flying over the Midwest I made up my mind. My life had changed but it wasn't over. I would simply have to compartmentalize the distasteful task of betraying my country, separating it from my personal life. In the end it all came back to no acceptable alternative. I would focus on turning that philosophical corner so as not to keep agonizing about circumstances beyond my control. In this realigned frame of mind, I disembarked the plane in Washington. Just like that first time, Elena was there to greet me.

She rushed toward me grabbing my face with both hands. Tears streamed down her face. I kissed her passionately.

"You're not angry with me anymore are you, Darling? I've been sick with worry since you left."

"Yes I'm still angry. But I love you too much," I said. We kissed again. She surreptitiously touched my obvious erection with her thigh as we embraced.

It was an expansive evening of lovemaking. Elena did everything she knew I liked. Repeatedly it seemed. I didn't resist. In the course of our passion, she guided me to pleasure her in ways she especially liked. I didn't hesitate. In for penny in for a pound. Just like a junkie, I abandoned to the drug.

My transformation to this new reality became complete a few days later. Christmas Eve. Our first together. We took the morning train to Wilmington arriving at noon. I was admittedly a little cool toward Boris and Vanya. They were wary as well. There were no questions during the short ride to their house.

I needed to get this unpleasantness over with as soon as possible, so once we entered their house I said, "Boris, I have some materials for you."

After retrieving an envelope from my luggage, Boris and I sat down at the dining table. Elena and Vanya excused themselves to the kitchen sighting the need to begin preparing for dinner later.

I extracted a thick stack of typed pages. Carbon copies of three months worth of classified reports to General Groves.

Boris scanned several of the pages. The level of surprise was evident in his expression.

"And this diagram?"

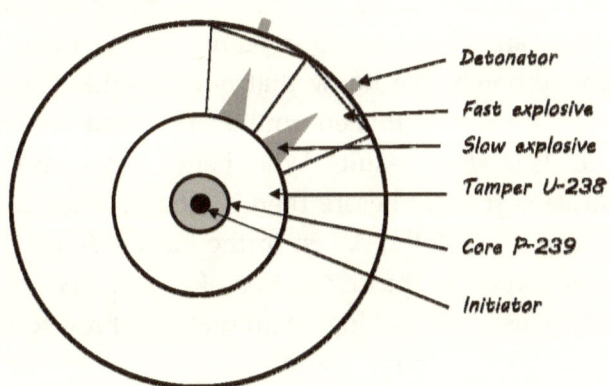

Detonator
Fast explosive
Slow explosive
Tamper U-238
Core P-239
Initiator

"The implosion design. What they call the *gadget*. At least the conceptual design. It's my own diagram. That's what all of the work is about now. The problems are in the details. When you read the text you can understand the complexity of the challenges. This is the plutonium bomb. The uranium bomb is simpler. But the *gadget* holds more promise."

After several more minutes Boris said, "This is extraordinary. It's all here. Your last report says they will achieve success. Do you believe that?"

"Yes. In one form or another. Either a uranium bomb or a plutonium bomb. Maybe both. I'm not as optimistic as General Groves about the timing though."

"What about the scientists? Do they think a bomb will be ready this coming year?" Boris said.

"Generally I think they do. No one will be pinned down to a date though."

"Why has General Groves gone out on a limb to fix the date as mid-year?"

"You'd have to know the General to understand. That's how he gets things done. But I think he's being pressed politically."

"What do you mean?" Boris said.

"I mean the war is coming to a close. Germany will probably collapse before an atomic bomb is ready. The German's don't have an atomic bomb. We know that now. So that leaves only the Japanese. To validate this enormous effort and expenditure, the Army needs to show results. What better way than to use it. If the Japanese surrender before there's a bomb, then it will be deemed an expensive folly. A test in the barren desert will not have the same impact as the destruction of a large city."

My God. I was freely talking about matters of top secret classified national security with my father-in-law. A Soviet intelligence agent. But then again, so was I now.

"I think you are mistaken, Mikhail. Maybe not about the motivations of General Groves, but about the impact of the atomic bomb. Even if it does not play a part in this war, it will determine the future of the world. I think that's what is driving the effort now. It's a contest now with Russia. If the United States is the only power with an atomic bomb, then they will dictate world affairs. That is what we seek to equalize. Any one country with unlimited power is a danger."

I didn't want to discuss the philosophical justifications of our actions any further. What was done was done. I just wanted to get on with it, to get the unpleasant part over with.

"So how is all this material to be encoded, Boris," I said signaling an end to the discussion.

Boris removed his glasses and rubbed the bridge of his nose. "Well. I'm not sure. There's so much here. It's overwhelming."

"You explained how it was done. You encrypt the information with an assigned numeric value derived from a key text. So what key text is to be used?"

"The key is a given Shakespearean sonnet, line number, and starting letter within that line. The text continues going on through subsequent sonnets as necessary to encrypt the message."

"So where's the problem?"

"This mass of information. It will be an enormous task to encrypt this much material."

"We'll see. I can help. Do you know what the key is for your next transmission?"

"Yes of course. It too is encoded as derived from a date. I receive a shortwave transmission providing some date in an innocent sounding message with a key identifying word. The algorithm takes the number of the month, multiplied by the day of the week with Monday as one, plus the day of the month to fix the sonnet number. The next date for the key is Wednesday, January 24, 1945. Therefore, 1 x 3 + 24 = sonnet 27. The line number of the sonnet is the month number and the starting letter of that line is the month plus the day of the week number. The start of the next encryption text begins with sonnet 27, the first line, and the fourth letter.

"This will take maybe more than a week to encrypt, Mikhail."

I shook my head. "It must be done while I'm here. I'm not leaving these copies, Boris. Once you've encoded them I want to see them burned. So we will all help with decoding. You, Vanya, and I will do the encryption. Elena will type the cipher as we feed her our work. It's a string of letters, right?"

"Yes. Arranged in six-character groupings," Boris said.

Thinking about how to expedite the task of encrypting this much material, I came up with a better organization for the work.

"I have another idea. It will take far too long to encode this much material sequentially. There are twelve sets of documents here. We need to break them up into twelve separate packets so we can encode them separately. That way three of us can do simultaneous encryptions. It will also prevent errors that way.

"You mean use different keys? How do we do that?" Boris asked.

"Reverse the process to selecting the key. Give Moscow twelve different keys in the form of dates. That's your next encoded message using the key Moscow just provided. You will tell them of the different keys for the encryption of this packet. We can than start on the encryption immediately. Is there a public library nearby?"

"I'm not sure. Why?"

"Have Elena get two more copies of Shakespeare's sonnets. It will speed things along."

Had I embraced this thing so fully? Not really. Just the way I functioned. If I had to do something, I attacked it with organization. It was all about getting the thing done. Especially an unpleasant task.

Elena and I spent the Christmas week at her parents. Some holiday. By day we worked at the encryption. Vanya was a good cook. We ate well with our pooled ration stamps. In the evening we drank vodka and listened to the radio. At night Elena and I made love.

Espionage as a cottage industry. A typical Russian family I joked to myself in black humor, devoted to eating, drinking, fucking, and spying.

We had become a strange family group, bound by a terrible secret. I grew up avoiding political conversations, afraid I would reveal the Communist origins of my parents. I now seemed freed to express those repressed social views with my new family.

I was sympathetic to the Left's view of how the working class suffered at the hands of the rich. In capitalist economies, the rich controlled the government. Wealth was created on the backs of the working class. The Great Depression was the singular example. The terrible discrimination of Negroes in the United States troubled me greatly. The ugly side of capitalism in the form of Wall Street clearly dictated social issues in the United States. The only redeeming factor was a middle class. But the larger majority was poor and would forever remain poor.

Yet I declared myself non-political. I was repelled by all brands of politics. No matter the rightness of the cause, political activity was narrow-viewed, self-interested, and given to extremes. The plight of American Negroes was a perfect example. How could the Constitution's Bill of Rights be perverted to deny those fundamental rights to a class of its own citizenry? The Communist experiment in Russia had mutated into a virulent dictatorship. The array of political parties in Western European countries created bloated corrupt bureaucracies impotent at governing. Those in Eastern Europe just killed each other.

The Russian working class suffered under a new form of oppression. I tried to convince my parents about the new reality in what they saw as the motherland. My father argued that while the United States had fallen into years of continuing decline because of the greed of Wall Street, Soviet Russia had improved since the Revolution. The Russian peasant no longer starved. In the end, it was simply the economics of survival that forced my parents to return. None of us knew at the time that the academic position at Moscow State University had become available only as a result of indiscriminate purges of the faculty. But in the face of the inability to find work in the United States, was there really any choice?

My parents never revealed their Bolshevik pasts. They never engaged in political activities during their years in the United States. I learned from a young age to keep our family secret. Apart from the Army knowing of their return to Russia, I never spoke about it. Now I had a considerably deeper secret to conceal.

Life went on. Not as before, but with a new kind of routine. There of course could be no true normalcy. Spying did not allow for that. I became more hedonistic. More sex, more liquor. I tried with some difficulty to separate what would otherwise be the ideal life that was now corrupted by this other thing. I wanted to find an alternate word than *spying*. That was a delusion. No matter the contrived philosophical grounds, no matter that I was conscripted into it, I was still spying, still betraying my country. Pragmatic in this as well, I would simply have to learn to live with it.

Once the laborious encryption task was completed, I watched Boris photograph the pages. He repeated the process a second time using additional roles of the miniature film.

"Just in case. This material is so important that if one copy should be lost, then we have a second set," Boris said. "It is easy enough to conceal somewhere."

"Lost? How would that happen?"

"Remember, I send this film concealed in the spine of a book. It's posted through many hands. I'm not even sure how it eventually gets to Moscow. So a precaution. I'll destroy it once I know the material has arrived."

I wasn't entirely sure a second set of microfilm should exist, but I could see Boris' point. But I was anxious to destroy the direct evidence of my complicity. I gathered the copies of my reports as well as the hand-written encryption copies, along with Elena's typed copies. It was quite a pile of paper.

"I want these burned. All of it. Can't very well light a blazing fire in your back yard. Don't want the neighbors wondering what we're doing in the middle of winter. How do we do that, Boris?"

"Let's see. How about I back the car out of the garage? We can burn the pages individually in front of the car to shield what is going on. We'll lift the hood. I'll use a pail to catch the ashes. If we do it one page at a time it will create limited smoke. Might just look like the radiator is overheating if anyone gets curious."

I left Washington D.C. again on New Year's Day, 1945, to return to Los Alamos. This sendoff was replete with smiles and kisses. While I would miss Elena's physical affections for another undetermined duration, it was a relief to be coming back to what felt like the normal world. The War could be understood. My work was understood. I was part of a great enterprise. We were about to create something extraordinary. In contrast, my private life had taken on a shameful skulking in darkness, not at all to be understood.

CHAPTER 25

VICTORIA PRESCOTT WOKE with a bright morning sun filtering through the sheer curtains of the hotel window. They had neglected to close the heavy opaque curtains. They? Where was he?

A moment later, Anton Grigoryev came out of the bathroom. He was wearing his pants but no shirt. He was toweling off his face.

"Good morning, Victoria."

Last night they had become Victoria and Anton.

"What time is it?" she asked sitting up in bed holding the sheet to cover her breasts.

"Early. Six o'clock. Did I wake you?"

"No. The sun woke me."

Yawning, Prescott worried about what she must look like. Hair a mess, makeup smeared. A little vulnerable being naked in bed and Grigoryev at least partly dressed. Awkward and sleepy. Mornings were not her best time.

Grigoryev came over and gave her a kiss. "I had a magnificent night, Victoria."

"So did I. The music was good too."

He laughed. "But I need to leave. I will get a taxi to return to my apartment. I'm sure I need a shower after last night." He said with a smile. "Yuri will be along to pick me up at eight-thirty. Then we shall drive back here to pick you up. You'll be ready?"

"Oh yes. That will give me plenty of time."

"Excellent. Maybe you will make good progress today with Igor."

Grigoryev came over and gave her a longer kiss. "I hope your work keeps you in Moscow for a while, Victoria."

She did also.

Grigoryev and his driver Yuri picked her up as planned. Once at SVR Headquarters, Grigoryev escorted her back to the conference room that was serving as a makeshift office. A short, stocky old man was standing stiffly. He had a full head of thick white hair. She gauged him to be in his seventies. Cheap suit, awful tie. He appeared ill at ease. She assumed he was the archivalist, Igor. Probably unaccustomed to interacting with the top brass, and certainly not with the rare western visitor.

"Ms. Prescott, this is Igor Vasilievich Nikulin. He is our senior archivalist," Grigoryev said in Russia.

Nikulin responded in Russian, extending his hand to Prescott. She greeted him in Russian. His eyes lit up. She went on to say that she appreciated his making time from his schedule to assist her. He smiled broadly and complimented her on her excellent Russian although she knew her accent identified her as a foreigner.

Grigoryev left her with Nikulin, promising to return to take her to lunch.

"The Colonel said you were interested in Lavrentiy Beria. Materials related to the Soviet Union's atomic bomb program."

"Actually, I'm interested in materials related to operation ENORMOZ. The espionage activities directed toward the American bomb program. I'm aware that Beria was responsible for the Soviet bomb program, but I'm interested in how the intelligence obtained from the American program assisted the Soviet program."

Nikulin's eyes lit up and he smiled again. "Yes. It was an extraordinary intelligence coup. Do you believe it speeded up our program?"

Prescott noted a measure of pride in Nikulin's tone. "Oh yes. Most historians do as well. I'm looking into the possibility that operation ENORMOZ was even more successful, more of a factor than previously assumed. I believe others were involved beyond those spies that were identified after the War."

Might as well play on the old fellow's sense of pride. Grigoryev said his whole career had been spent in the NKVD, then the KGB, now the SVR.

"I see. This should be most interesting. Now that I know what you are looking for, let me begin searching some different archives. Give me until this afternoon. In the mean time, you may wish to review these files I have already selected. They deal with Comrade Beria's involvement with the Soviet atomic program."

I spent the rest of the morning reviewing these peripheral materials. I knew a fair amount about the Soviet's own program. There were some interesting pieces of correspondence directly between Lavrentiy Beria and the scientific head of the Soviet's own atomic bomb program, Dr. Igor Kurchatov. She wondered how much of this material her Stanford colleague, Professor David Holloway, had seen in preparation for his book, *Stalin and the Bomb*.

At noon, Anton Grigoryev interrupted her immersion into the past by entering the conference room and suggesting lunch.

It was a two-hour lovers' lunch. No shop talk, just personal stuff. They laughed and drank too much wine. Both regretted leaving to return to work.

"Would it be too much to ask to see you again tonight, Victoria?"

That was something to look forward to. Prescott fortunately had the capacity to intensely focus on work to the exclusion of other distractions. This was a unique opportunity to look at extraordinary original historic materials. Grigoryev was certainly a distraction though.

By mid-afternoon, Nikulin wheeled in a cart with boxes of new archival materials. He explained that these materials were from Beria related archives, subcategorized under operation ENORMOZ. This would provide a starting point. As she discovered information of interest, he assumed she would redirect her search into other archival areas. Nikulin knew how research was conducted.

By the end of the day, she had found some interesting information.

Memo from Beria to Colonel-General Kuznetsov, chief of GRU, dated November, 1940: *'Comrade Stalin has given me the task of overseeing a Soviet program to develop the potential for weapons of massive force using atomic science. The British and Americans have already initiated scientific work toward that possibility. In support of the Soviet effort, all intelligence gathered by the Glavnoye Razvedyvatel'noye Upravleniye related to this work in the West is to be forwarded directly to my office. On this there must be a coordinated effort between all Soviet intelligence organs for the greater security of the Soviet Union.'*

Beria's internal meeting record from December, 1942: *'Met with General Kuznetsov, General Golovchenko, and Lt. Col. Kirilov. Golovchenko and Kirilov control GRU operations in North America. Both read and speak English. Informed them of British-American collaboration to develop an atomic bomb confirmed by NKVD asset code named LIST. Americans expected to take the lead with their superior resources and scientific talent. Soviet Union has been excluded. Directed Golovchenko and Kirilov to attempt high-level penetrations of the American project. Soviet assets within British government and scientific circles may become peripheral if Americans take charge. Joint*

NKVD and GRU operation to acquire atomic bomb intelligence will be code named ENORMOZ. All related intelligence is henceforth to be forwarded directly to this office.'

Before leaving SVR headquarters, Prescott met with Grigoryev in his office.

"Could you follow up with your colleagues at the GRU for materials on two officers, from the 1940's? A Major General Golovchenko and a Colonel Kirilov. They were GRU officers in charge of North American espionage operations. Dmytryk-Ramazanov-PUPPETEER must have reported through them."

"Very well. Tomorrow," he said smiling. "Now to personal affairs. Shall we leave?"

This time Grigoryev was driving himself. At the hotel he escorted Prescott to the lobby.

"Take your time. No need to dress up. We shall go to some place unpretentious, very ethnic."

Ever the gentleman Prescott thought. Why should he wait in the lobby after what happened last night?

"Come up with me, Anton."

Once in the room she brazenly said, "I don't want to wait until later. Let's make love right now."

For the next two days, this was their new schedule, sex before dinner. No alcohol to inhibit performance. No sexual tension through dinner knowing what would come later.

As for the research, there was not much more to glean from pursuing the trail through the Beria files after two days. Until in one last box dated 1945, Prescott discovered two back to back memos.

Beria to Igor Kurchatov, January, 1945: *'The accompanying documents provide detailed technical information and summaries of the American atomic bomb development project. The source is newly developed and believed to be reliable. Disinformation cannot however be ruled out. Please have your team review and advise your opinion. Be scrupulous since disinformation might be in the form of a subtle but critical misstating of some technical detail.'*

Kurchatov to Beria two weeks later: *'The recent intelligence information forwarded on the American program is most comprehensive. Further study is required however I feel the material is genuine. Most interesting are the analysis of the uranium enrichment process problems and the plutonium reactor design. This will expedite achieving effective processes within our own program by avoiding failed techniques. The information appears to be in the form of many summary reports over a period of time. It lacks technical detail and associated mathematics as other intelligence materials previously provided, but is of extremely high value. I have personally compared this material with other technical intelligence previously forwarded. This new information corroborates prior technical details. Further, it puts other technical information into the larger context. This new material provides a broad understanding of the construction of the American program and allows the technical intelligence to be better understood. I would agree with the conclusions stated in these reports. The Americans will probably be successful in developing an atomic bomb this year. Can further information of this kind be expected?'*

Here was the smoking gun. The reference to a new source of intelligence. Probably starting in latter 1944 by the dates of these correspondences. *It wasn't Klaus Fuchs.* His material had been flowing to Moscow earlier than 1944. The previous technical intelligence referenced by Kurchatov was probably from Fuchs. Beria specifically said, *'The source is newly developed and believed to be reliable.'*

Over the following several days she delved into the extensive NKVD files related more broadly to operation ENORMOZ. She scrupulously explored references to Soviet code names that came from the Venona transcripts just made public in the United States a year ago.

The Venona project was a joint intelligence effort by the United States and Britain to decrypt Soviet signals during World

War Two. The seemingly secure Soviet transmissions relied on the use of one-time pad encryption. The method was virtually secure against even modern computer decryption, provided the encryption key is used only *once*. Soviet cipher clerks had become sloppy, often reusing encryption keys with the flood of signals traffic. The code cracking was not perfect, leaving undecipherable gaps in some messages. Invaluable information related to Soviet agents was still culled from 2,200 deciphered messages.

Venona was an intelligence coup in its own right. From the decrypted messages, first hand evidence was revealed of extensive Soviet espionage. It exposed government officials and scientists. From these the identities of Klaus Fuchs, Alan Nunn May, Donald Maclean of the Cambridge Five, Alger Hiss, Julius and Ethel Rosenberg were discovered, along with a host of others. Prescott was interested in code names appearing in the Venona transcripts that had *not* been identified. At the least, she wanted to exclude these as possible references to her super spy.

Everything rested on the agent code named PUPPETEER. There was nothing from the NKVD files other than the two references in signals traffic from Ottawa, Canada from1942 that Grigoryev showed her earlier. That was ok. It just meant that PUPPETEER was run by the GRU and handled more securely outside of Soviet signals transmissions. If he was that highly placed, special precautions would make sense. The use of encrypted radio transmissions from Soviet embassies might have been avoided altogether. Hence no reference appears in the Verona transcripts.

After a week in Russia, Prescott had pretty much exhausted the search for relevant material from the old NKVD files. Everything now rested on what the GRU might provide. Grigoryev entered the conference room just before lunch time.

"I have received a package of materials from my friends at Glavnoye Razvedyvatel'noye Upravleniye, Victoria. Shall we see what they have provided?"

This was it. What she had had up until now was not yet conclusive evidence that Boris Dmytryk, aka Ramazanov, was the Soviet agent PUPPETEER.

Back in Grigoryev's office, he emptied the contents of the large envelop. Encouragingly, it was a substantial amount of material.

First was the background information on Major General Golovchenko mentioned in Beria's notes. "Probably not of interest," Grigoryev said, handing the single sheet of paper to Prescott. "He didn't make it. Must have fallen out of favor somehow. He was purged in 1944. Shot."

Grigoryev scanned the next page. "Now this Lt. Colonel Kirilov might be of interest. I would think that he would have been in direct charge of the Moscow desk controlling any GRU espionage in North America during the war years. He apparently escaped the fate of his immediate superior."

Prescott scanned the biographical information on Feliks Antonovich Kirilov. Born 1906. Degree in mathematics. Military Academy graduate. Assigned to the foreign intelligence directorate of the Soviet military in 1933. Headed the Moscow desk for GRU activities related to operation ENORMOZ. Promoted to lieutenant colonel in 1940. Fairly young for that rank. Probably because of the vacancies within the upper ranks caused by Stalin's paranoia-induced great purge of 1937-38. Promoted to major general after World War Two. Died of unspecified natural causes in 1955.

"Must have been successful to rise to that rank and not get purged. Bad luck to die so young after getting that far," Prescott said. "So he would have known all the Soviet spies, at least the GRU assets. That would include Fuchs. Fuchs was recruited by the GRU, only handed off to the NKVD when he went to the

United States. This Kirilov should have handled PUPPETEER then."

"Let's see what our GRU colleagues turned up on PUPPET-EER," Grigoryev said.

After several minutes, he said, "You'll like this, Victoria." He handed her the faded, yellowed copy of a signals form.

Signals traffic from Kirilov to Soviet Military Attaché, Col. Nicolai Zabotin code named GRANT: *'Advise PUPPETEER to seek transfer to a strategic U.S. location. Control to be direct from MOTHER. No other GRU or NKVD intermediaries to be involved. Remove PUPPETEER and TRAVELER from any current operations. Further instructions to follow by courier arrangement once PUPPET-EER and TRAVELER are relocated within U.S. PUPPETEER to communicate by prearranged method provided to GRANT.'*

"Oh my God! This is the proof. That's what happened to PUPPETEER," Prescott said.

"But you would also like confirmation that PUPPETEER was Boris Dmytryk. Let's see what else the GRU has provided."

Grigoryev thumbed through a couple of pages. "Look here. The original file on Boris Dmytryk when he joined the Red Army. The picture is better than what we retrieved from the NKVD archives. December, 1917. This is right after the Revolution. Take a look."

Prescott looked at the photocopy of the old record. The picture could be of Ramazanov, but more importantly there was a fingerprint. This was gold. If the fingerprint matched Boris Ramazanov's immigration application. If the photocopy of this eighty-year old record rendered a good enough reproduction of the fingerprint.

Grigoryev had lunch brought into the office so they could work through the remaining package of old documents. There were several of importance. One dated 1943 was a report by Kirilov to his boss General Golovchenko that a list of potential targets within the Manhattan Project had been created. Unfortunately, there was no accompanying list.

But another Kirilov report dated December, 1944, this time addressed to the head of the GRU, General Kuznetsov, provided additional evidence for Prescott's super spy. '*Successful penetration has been achieved at highest level as part of operation ERORMOZ. Asset is at least equal to CHARLES in the level of access to information. New source is code named FOUNTAIN. Recommend entirely independent control from CHARLES to maintain highest security. Control will be maintained direct from this office with dedicated secure communications.*'

"There it is! Confirmation of another high-level spy. Parallel to Klaus Fuchs, code name CHARLES. We even have a new code name, FOUNTAIN," Prescott said.

"Seems to coincide with the Beria material passed on to Kurchatov in early 1945. It also shows us something about this Colonel Kirilov," Grigoryev said.

"What do you mean?"

"Sounds like he was hedging his bets. It indirectly suggests that he should retain GRU control over this new asset to maintain a separate method of transmitting information back to Moscow. Kirilov would have run Fuchs before being forced to surrendering him to NKVD control in the United States. He didn't want that to happen in the case of FOUNTAIN. Kirilov also doesn't trust NKVD methods, or NKVD cipher clerks. For good reason as it turned out. Probably looking to help protect his own position. It emphasizes a parallel source to Fuchs their premiere spy. The report was also written directly to General Kuznetsov. No telling what may have been going on at the time at the GRU. His former immediate superior, Golovchenko had been removed and shot only a month before."

The balance of the materials was interesting but did not bear any further revelations.

"What's missing is the specific identification of Boris Dmytryk as PUPPETEER," Prescott said.

"But you do have proof that Dmytryk is Ramazanov. Provided of course the fingerprints match. Then you have Dmytryk being GRU. Now you have proof that agent PUPPETEER continued operating in the United States. That's fairly strong evidence that Ramazanov was a Soviet agent. And you have a new spy code named FOUNTAIN."

"As you point out, it rests with the fingerprints."

"Do you have the fingerprints from Ramazanov with you, Victoria?"

"Yes."

"We have a lab here. Experts in such technology. Shall we find out?"

Prescott fairly came out of her chair. "Of course. How long will it take?"

It took a little over an hour. A lab-coated technician entered Grigoryev's office. He acknowledged the attractive woman briefly then addressed Grigoryev formally.

"Are these fingerprints from the same person?" Grigoryev asked.

"Yes, Colonel."

"No doubts? Both are photocopies of copies of very old documents. Even I can see they're not of the clearest clarity."

"That is true, Colonel. However the fingerprints are both complete. We have software that enhances any missing fragments. Under magnification we can qualify the enhancement to see if it precisely supports the conclusion. In this case, these are definitely the same person."

The technician left and closed the door.

"There you have your proof, Victoria. Ramazanov and Dmytryk are the same person. Ramazanov is clearly a false name. PUPPETEER continued to operate in the United States after 1943. Most probably, TRAVELER is his wife Vanya. Husband and wife team. They appear to be the key players in a successful penetration of the Manhattan Project run by the GRU running a high-level source code named FOUNTAIN."

This evidence was better than she could have hoped for.

"Why wasn't this material released with all the other sensitive stuff release by Russia in 1992?"

"I can't answer that. But let me speculate. Remember, even today Russia and the United States are not close. Perhaps no longer on the brink of nuclear war, but still often antagonistic. This was probably not included because the United States didn't ask about this in specific. Everything that was released only confirmed U.S. suspicions. Little in the way of new information was released. That was glasnost in controlled measure."

"So why the cooperation now?"

"This is nothing more than an extension of that glasnost process. Cynically, I believe there is another motivation. It would suit our current leadership to have some new revelation of Soviet espionage success from that time be uncovered. It would be a black eye for the United States even though it happened fifty years ago. Better still that such a revelation would come from a discovery by a western academic."

"And how do you feel about this, Anton?"

"In the first place, it is old information. As a senior Russian intelligence officer, I see it only adds to the history of proficiency of our espionage organs. Your CIA has quite the opposite reputation. So that is productive for us. The United States is still a competitor in world affairs. You were fortunate that our interests coincided, Victoria."

"More than interests coincided, Anton."

Both Prescott and Grigoryev smiled knowingly at each other.

Unfortunately, this brought to an end her work in Moscow. That also meant an end to an affair that had moved further than just a sexual adventure.

Making love to Anton was a different experience than Phillip. Both were considerate and attentive in their lovemaking. But where Phillip was intense, Anton was relaxed. Phillip talked dirty in bed, Anton said little. Phillip had a competitive edginess in his manner. Anton was gracious. Both were smart. But even with a doctorate, Phillip didn't act the intellectual. Beyond his brilliance in computer science, he had typical guy-habits. Anton appeared the cultured intellectual preferring symphonies and fine wine to Phillip's sports and beer. The contrasting traits seemed reversed for the two men. Phillip was a professor in a geek profession, Anton a Russian spy master.

Leaving Moscow probably meant she would not see Anton again for at least some indefinite time. Neither had suggested the relationship was anything more than a romantic interlude. Unforgettable, but not something that would cause either to drastically alter their lives to pursue further. They both had careers on opposite sides of the world, in opposite worlds really. Prescott didn't have affairs so this was a new experience. Parting from Anton Grigoryev would be emotionally wrenching.

This affair with Anton would cause her to rethink her relationship with Phillip. But Anton was a fantasy. He was a Russian and would remain in Russia. Moscow was not a place she could live. Could she make things better with Phillip? Life was too short to be in a relationship that seemed to be a contest all the time. That would have to change. She could try harder. Did she feel guilty sleeping with Anton? Not really. Had Phillip ever been unfaithful?

"I hope you didn't go beyond what was allowed because I was sleeping with you?" Prescott said. She offered a smiled, but the thought was real. Was she trading sex for information? Was she herself being used? After all, Grigoryev was a career spy.

"Not at all. You have not received any information that might compromise Russian interests." Grigoryev said a little formally. He did not smile. "Did you sleep with me to gain special consideration?"

She reached out and touched his arm. "Oh no, Anton. Of course not. I didn't mean it that way. A dumb thing to say. The truth is I don't want to leave. But I must."

"Victoria, what has been between us is personal. I'm glad that I could assist you. But I will remember our intimate times with great fondness. We shared much more than what you Americans call a one-night stand."

She didn't want to part on a sour note. What a bitch she could be. Tears ran down her cheeks. Anton's eyes also reflected a real sadness. One long farewell kiss. Neither said anything about seeing each other in the future. That was uncertain at best. He wished her great success with her book. Anxious to learn the identity of this newly discovered Soviet spy. An autographed copy was promised.

Once on board the plane, Prescott composed herself by focusing on what she had accomplished. She had won. It was an astounding success. She had sufficiently strong evidence to go public. It was academically sound work. She would still peer-review the evidence starting first with her parents. She had the necessary documentary proof that Mikhail Voronin, personal aide to General Leslie Groves, was a Soviet spy. He was recruited by his in-laws, probably through his wife. She could conclusive prove the Ramazanovs/Dmytryks were Soviet agents. Most certainly Voronin's wife, their adopted daughter, was also a Soviet agent, probably the hook. It had all the elements of a classic honey-trap that the Soviet KGB would later refine during the Cold War era.

Mikhail Voronin might be judged a bigger spy than Klaus Fuchs because he had broader access across virtually every aspect of the Manhattan Project. His information would have greatly enhanced the material being provided by Fuchs. Voronin was also a military officer. Soviet code named FOUNTAIN. And he was never caught.

Unfortunately she did not discover any further direct evidence about FOUNTAIN other than the single mention in the one Kirilov report. Did Voronin continue spying after the death of his wife and in-laws? If so, perhaps much of the intelligence on the hydrogen bomb attributed to Klaus Fuchs actually may have come from Voronin. Ultimately it did not matter. The fact that there was a senior military officer on Groves' staff that was passing intelligence to the Soviet Union was sufficiently sensational. It wasn't a contest over which spy did the most damage.

The culmination of this original detective work could come in the form of an admission by Voronin himself. Does he still have his mental faculties? Why should he confess after fifty years? Under threat of taking the evidence to the FBI? Espionage had no statute of limitations.

Regardless the outcome, confronting Mikhail Stefanovich Voronin was the last piece of the puzzle.

Goldmine at Kolyma Gulag
Siberia, Soviet Union

CHAPTER 26

LOS ALAMOS, NEW MEXICO – 1945

THE FRUSTRATING DAYS of setback after setback in the latter months of 1944 were now replaced with successes moving the project forward at an accelerated pace. January saw the successful RaLa tests demonstrating successful symmetrical compression in an implosion design. These tests also validated the use of exploding bridgewire detonators. These devices used high electrical currents to detonate the conventional explosives with simultaneous timing precision to create uniform detonation of all thirty-two lenses.

The Y-12 plant at Oak Ridge had increased output to 204 grams per day of 80% enriched uranium-235. Still a long haul to create the 40 kilograms required for one uranium bomb, but it was improvement. Newly designed barrier tubes for the K-25 gaseous diffusion plant arrived at Oak Ridge. The first stage of the plant was charged with the corrosive hexafluoride and began to successfully operate. The brilliant engineering work among the civilian contractors breathed renewed life into the project.

In February the F-Pile reactor at Hanford went on line raising production of plutonium to 21 kilograms per month. It appeared that the intractable problems of producing both fissile fuels in sufficient quantity had finally been overcome. It was still an issue of time, but the underlying engineering problems appeared resolved.

Oppenheimer froze the gun design for the *Little Boy* uranium bomb. Much detail work remained to be done by Deke Parsons team, but it now amounted to final engineering of the components for the thing. The device could be assembled and it would work. It was now just a matter of waiting on enough highly-enriched uranium from the Oak Ridge processes.

I attended a high-level scientific meeting in Los Alamos along with General Groves on February 28. All the division leaders were present. The purpose was to fix the design for the key components of the plutonium implosion weapon *gadget*. While the fundamental design was agreed upon, substantial work still remained.

The most difficult construction task on the implosion design was molding the high explosive lens components of the bomb. These were shaped in a complex geometry consisting of 20 hexagon facets interleaved with 12 pentagon facets into something resembling a giant soccer ball. Adding to the complexity, both fast detonating and slow detonating explosives were required to achieve the uniformity of the resulting shaped compressive force. The task was to construct the lenses with sufficient precision to fit together uniformly within thousandths of an inch, creating a sphere 60 inches in diameter. George Kistiakowsky's team had the difficult task of making these uniquely precision high explosives. Molding the explosives into these shapes was itself a demanding task to avoid air bubbles through rigorously controlled cooling. Finished castings were x-rayed to examine for inclusions. Many were rejected. Those deemed of the required quality underwent a final machine finishing to achieve the required dimensional precision.

By the end of March, the intractable problem of designing barriers that could withstand the corrosive effects of uranium

hexafluoride for the gaseous diffusion process of enriching uranium had been solved. With the new diffusion barriers, the K-25
plant at Oak Ridge continued to successful operation.

The S-50 thermal diffusion plant came on line and began
producing enriched uranium. While encouraging, its output level of enrichment was only modest. There were now three separate enrichment processes operational at Oak Ridge. Unfortunately, the collective output rate was still far less than required.
Even with expected improvements in process efficiencies, there
would be only a sufficient quantity of 80%-plus enriched U-235
for a single bomb by the end of the year.

Robert Oppenheimer came up with solution to accelerate
production. He refined Groves' earlier approach to linking the
processes sequentially. Oppenheimer ordered all three processes
linked in series to optimize the collective capacity, yet incorpo-
rating the differences in the various process output rates and enrichment capabilities.

The thermal diffusion process became the first stage, providing feedstock of modestly enriched uranium of less than 2%.
This material was fed into the gaseous diffusion process which
elevated enrichment to about 23%. This product was in turn fed
into the electromagnetic calutrons which boosted the U-235 concentration to a weapons-grade level of 84%. Under this new process scheme, a sufficient quantity for at least one weapon would
be available by mid-1945. The uranium gun-design bomb, *Little
Boy*, was close to reality.

The implosion design plutonium weapon *gadget* was moving
closely to that same reality. Implosion testing continued to advance toward a workable design. Although other engineering
details remained to be refined, Oppenheimer froze the explosive
lens design. Von Neumann's mathematics was proven.
Kistiakowsky's team had successfully achieved the engineering
for constructing the precision explosive lenses. Empirical testing
confirmed the concept of creating the sufficiently symmetrical

explosive force to compress the fissile materials into a super-critical mass. As complex as the *gadget* was, it would work provided all of its components functioned unerringly.

Preparations began on the Island of Tinian in the Mariana Islands chain to support the relocation of 509th Composite Group's B-29's from Wendover Field in Utah. Tinian in the South Pacific was 1500 miles from the Japanese mainland. The atomic bomb was clearly going to happen. If the Japanese did not surrender first, then it would be used on their cities. There might be conflicting ethical views among the scientists at Los Alamos, but within the small group in Washington that would make that decision, there was no debate.

For a brief time, that certainty may have faltered. On April 12, 1945, Franklin Delano Roosevelt, 32nd President of the United States, died suddenly. He had been in office since 1933. Even though the nation knew he was in ill health, his death was still a collective shock. This was the leader that had led the way out of the Great Depression. This was the war-time President that managed the creation of the staggering U.S. war machine that had beaten back the Axis powers in Europe and the Pacific. In his place was the little known Vice President, Harry Truman.

I was in Washington D.C. when the news arrived. It was late in the afternoon on Thursday. General Groves was holding a meeting with senior staff. Jean O'Leary entered the office.

"General, Secretary Stimson is on the line. He said it was urgent. He's on line two."

Groves answered the telephone. Within seconds his face tightened. He said little other than, "Yes, Sir, I agree..... I understand..... I will be there within the hour."

"Gentlemen, I regret to inform you that President Roosevelt has just died," Groves said to us.

Everyone including Groves was shaken. However, after a few moments, in true Groves' fashion upon hearing bad news, he set to work on the problem.

"Gentlemen, you'll resume your duties. No one should assume that there is any change in our mission. Convey that message to everyone. I'm leaving to meet with Secretary Stimson and General Marshal within the hour."

Two days later, Groves convened another staff meeting.

"Gentlemen. I have good news. Secretary Stimson and I met with President Truman this morning. The President has ordered that the Project is to proceed with all haste. His tone suggested that he was in full agreement as to the objectives. He directly said that if this new weapon is ready in time, he would not hesitate to use it on the Japanese. As an aside, he stated that he did not trust Joseph Stalin's ambitions. He said the Soviets will be a problem after the imminent defeat of Germany. The Red Army will wind up in Berlin before us. The President suggested they might not give it up. He had the insight to understand the importance of possessing atomic weapons in the post-war world. I'll tell all of you, I was impressed with our new President."

I returned to Los Alamos immediately. Everyone on the Hill was working at a fevered pitch, but now with renewed motivation as things began to come together. I drank martinis with Oppenheimer, played chess with Kistiakowsky, socialized with the Serbers, and listened to the latest escapades of Richard Feynman.

Periodically the gnawing guilt resurfaced. I didn't exactly feel I was betraying these particular people that had become my friends. My betrayal was to something personal. I despised myself for what I had become. My center was gone, replaced with something venal. I always fell back on the underlying rationale that I had been tricked into this and now had no other reasonable choice. At least no choice I was willing to make. In the end, the guilt was always returned to storage.

So I pushed the spying into a segregated part of my mind. I dealt with it as I would any other disagreeable task. Simply get through it as expeditiously as possible. The mechanics of my spying were simple. I did not have to smuggle out papers. These were my own reports. No furtive photographing with a microfilm spy camera like Boris. No practical chance of getting caught unless Boris or his mode of transmitting the materials to Moscow was compromised. Even then, the encryption was sound. Once completed, I personally destroyed the original evidence. Theoretically, if the contents leaked from the Moscow end, it could be argued that others within the MED had access to my reports. All I did was make duplicate copies of my own assigned work. Even though possessing copies of my reports violated security, I could still explain them away as beneficial for doing my work. I was trusted and the documents were nothing more than my own work. There was little spy tradecraft involved in my espionage activities. Perhaps that made it easier. There was no lurking about looking over my shoulder. It only became real when I turned the materials over to Boris.

I had another week in Washington before I was to return to Los Alamos. A week after the President's death, Elena and I took the train north to Wilmington. Boris and Vanya were grieving over President Roosevelt's death like everyone else in the country. The thought struck me that even though they were spying for Russia, the United States was not their enemy. Competitors perhaps. They could love both. One can see the progression of my distorted rationalizations.

We first got the encryption of my new reports out of the way. A family effort again. This was the third time that I had passed my reports to the Soviets. The same feeling of guilt persisted. After dinner, talk turned to my work. We all talked openly about the Project no different than I did with the scientists at Los Alamos. But this was outside the absolute security cordon surrounding the Manhattan Project. Scientists told me that their wives did not know what they were really working on. But once you have sinned, successive transgressions become all that much easier.

"So there will be an atomic bomb. Equivalent to 20,000 tons of TNT. What kind of damage will that cause?" Boris asked.

"Depends on the target. But the target will be a large city. Most structures within two and a half miles from ground-zero will be destroyed or damaged. Most people will be destroyed. Within a mile and a half radius, everybody will be dead," I said.

"My God. Is that possible?" Vanya said.

"The best physicists in the world think so," I said. "The scientific basis for the amount of energy released is very well understood now. Developing the means to release that energy is the challenge."

"And you're sure it will be used on the Japanese?" Elena asked.

"Yes. Unless they surrender first. Groves has already advised that plans are underway to convene a target selection committee soon. Special B-29 aircrews have already been training. Preparations have begun on a forward base in the Mariana Islands. From there the B-29 bombers have the range to reach the Japanese mainland."

"You're sure the new President will use the bomb against Japan?' Boris said.

"According to General Groves, Truman has already said he will."

"Who might influence the President's decision?" Boris said.

"Is this for transmitting to Moscow too, Boris?" I asked.

Boris paused for a moment. "Mikhail, this information is just as valuable as the more technical materials contained in your reports."

Why should I balk at revealing this information after turning over my top secret reports?

"I'm not sure, but I think it's a small group. Secretary Stimson, General Marshall. General Groves of course. There are very few in the upper reaches of government that even know of the existence of the Manhattan Project. The funding has even been obscured. So the group must consist of only a very few."

"How many bombs will the United States have by next year?"

"No way to tell. I believe that will rest on plutonium production from the Hanford reactors. It doesn't appear that the uranium enrichment processes will produce at a rate to yield enough fissile material for very many weapons. Depends on how many might be used on the Japanese."

"Will there be a test first? A full scale test?"

I hesitated. That was the deepest secret of all.

"Yes. I believe so. It's a subject of discussion among the scientists. Oppenheimer firmly believes it is necessary. The *gadget* is just too complicated to commit its use without knowing if all the theory has produced a workable bomb. Some of the scientists feel strongly that the test should also serve as a demonstration. They think it perhaps might avoid having to use such a terrible weapon on civilian populations."

"So there are scientists that disagree with using the bomb against the Japanese?"

"Boris, I won't discuss any of the scientists' views. Those are secrets Moscow is not entitled to."

"I understand. But you can see where the end of the war will lead. The United States will be the only healthy nation standing. All of Europe, all of Asia has suffered widespread destruction. Cities are wrecked. Industry is wrecked. Economies are destroyed. Hundreds of thousands of young men of a whole generation have been killed. Only the United States will be economically stronger than before the War. If the United States uses the atomic bomb against the Japanese, it will demonstrate it also possesses a military capability greater than the Soviet Union. We hope there are those in the scientific community that see that so much power in the hands of one government will inevitably corrupt."

"I may hold some of those same views, Boris, but I won't involve others in any way."

Boris changed the subject. "Has it been established that the Germans never progressed very far in developing their own atomic bomb?"

"Yes. There is a mission pressing right behind the advancing Allied armies to determine just what the Germans were doing along those lines. But it's clear they never had a bomb program. Groves said he wants to capture any nuclear materials, along with the German scientists before the Red Army does."

"See what I mean. The United States is already treating the Soviet Union as a potential future enemy. What's this mission called?"

"Alsos. It's headed up by a Colonel Boris Pash. I know him. He's a fanatical anti-Communist."

We did not typically make love at the parents' house. Elena said we made too much noise. Once we entered back at our apartment from the mid-day Sunday train, Elena was particularly assertive. We made love most of the afternoon interrupted only by a break for a sandwich.

"I miss our lovemaking when you're gone, Darling. This afternoon should help for a while though," she said smiling at me. As was her habit, she was kneeling on the bed, naked, making sure I took in the sight of her breasts. "I love you, Darling."

The next morning I left for the office. I had a meeting with Groves then was scheduled to catch a plane for Albuquerque.

At the end of our brief meeting, Groves said, "This is the final push, Major. I'm expecting that we'll have bombs available by July. That's what I have committed to. Oppenheimer is guardedly optimistic. I want you to stay close to progress on implosion. I expect you to identify anything you see that might delay the timetable for the *gadget* test. I get the technical reports, but nothing replaces being right there with the scientists. You know them well by now. They accept you. That's why you have this job."

I stopped by my office before leaving for my plane to Albuquerque. Some mail had been placed in my in-box. Among mostly copies of internal memorandums was a filthy brown envelop.
My heart leapt as I saw the Russian postmark. The address appeared to be in my mother's handwriting. My heart leapt. I tore
open what apparently was a crudely fabricated envelop of glued
coarse brown paper, badly soiled and crumpled. The post mark
was in Cyrillic letters. Some place in Russia I did not recognize.
There were postal stamps from Finland and Great Britain. It was
addressed to me. Like the previous letter from my parents, the
address was only the U.S. Army Corps of Engineers, Washington, D.C. Somehow this letter made its way to my designated
posting rather than my home address.

Opening the envelope, I was taken aback by the makeshift
quality. The paper was a used typewritten sheet consisting of
some sort of list. On the reverse side was hand written script in
pencil. The signature was my mother's, but her fine hand was
not evident in the appearance of this erratic scrawl.

My Dear Misha,

*I have been promised that this letter will be smuggled
out. From there I can only hope it makes it to you so very far
away. Correspondence is forbidden. A guard has agreed to
send the letter on its way. I have my friend Olga to thank for
that. We have become close. She is young and pretty. She
trades her sex for small favors. Extra food, clothing. I am too
old for the guards to be interested. I am fortunately allowed
to play my violin.*

*I am rambling. I realize that you must not know what I
am talking about, where I am. I am in some terrible godforsaken place east of the Urals. Siberia we are told. It is a
camp, a prison camp. It is designated only by a number. Political prisoners. We are labeled enemies of the State as the
result of careless opinions. We live in wooden barracks. No*

insulation. It is so cold in the winter. In the summer, mosquitoes are a plague. We survive on potato soup. A piece of fish is a delicacy. Every day we work at sewing machines making military uniforms. I have been here over two years.

Misha, there is no way to avoid telling you the worst news. Your father is dead. He was sent to a worse place than this. Further north. I learned that it was a hard labor camp. Some sort of mining. He died after only a few months. I was officially informed. Died serving the greater Soviet cause the official letter said.

Why did this happen to us? Because we made comments about Comrade Stalin's leadership of the war. Someone betrayed us. The siege of Stalingrad was raging. Soldiers of the Red Army were dying in the thousands. Stalin had no regard for his soldiers. We did not understand that we lived in such a police-state. A knock came at our door in the middle of the night in November, 1942. That was the last time I saw your father.

It was a mistake returning to Russia. The ideals that drew your father and me to Communism are not part of the Soviet Union. Stalin has perverted the spirit of the October Revolution. Stalin is no better than Hitler. Your father got a job teaching at the university only because so many professors had been purged. We were blind to what was going on. Blind and careless. It cost us our lives.

I do not know if I will survive this place. Not sure I care to. I was given a ten year sentence. I'm told that often when one's original sentence is up, some new sentence is imposed. If I was stronger, I would take my own life.

Know the truth, but you must forget me, Misha. There is nothing you can do. I love you so much my son. Remember me always.

My love forever,
Mother

I was devastated. Father was dead? Worse perhaps, Mother was wasting away in a Siberian prison camp? I slumped in my chair. Fortunately, my office door was closed. I wept openly for some time. Then a compounding realization struck. The letters received last year from my parents must have been false. Forgeries? Soviet intelligence did this. Help Russia, help your own parents. Moscow destroyed my parents, now I was spying for them. Spying for the monster Stalin.

The implications of the deception unwound further with a worsening speculation. Did Elena know? Was she part of the deception? What about Boris and Vanya? Were they even her parents? Why did the forged letters come to the apartment? And the worse unknown; was Elena's professed love just a ploy to entrap me? Were the Ramazanovs nothing more than a family of Soviet agents with an assignment to infiltrate the Manhattan Project?

These black thoughts overwhelmed me for some time. Rage replaced tears. At least I was immediately returning to Los Alamos rather than having to face Elena. I needed time to think.

Trinity Test Site Base Camp, 1945

CHAPTER 27

I WAS EMOTIONALLY devastated during the trip back to New Mexico. Everything in my life was shattered. My father was dead. My mother was doomed to a terrible end. My wife and her parents were Soviets spies, maybe even complicit in this conspiracy. I probably had been literally seduced into spying against my country. Nothing was left. Upon first learning of Elena's spying, I thought nothing could be worse. I was wrong.

For the time being I would continue. But not for long. Even it meant my own life, I could not continue this. Helping the killers of my parents? I had to find a way to confirm my suspicions about Elena and her parents. Was this all just a set-up? Is Elena's affection just an act?

I arrived at Los Alamos on April 30th. I was able to sufficiently will myself to focus on the work. The reality of the atomic was in sight. One week later on May 8th, we received the news that Germany had surrendered. The war in Europe was over. As the bomb became closer to reality, the ethical debates increased in earnest. The original reason for racing to develop the bomb no longer existed. Japan was on its last legs. Should we use it to finish them off? It would clearly kill tens of thousands of civilians.

Nothing new about targeting civilians but the atomic bomb seemed a weapon of an entirely different category. Should we demonstrate its power before dropping it on a city? Should the United States be in sole possession of this weapon? Would there be an arms race with the Soviet Union? What would the world be like with two nuclear armed adversarial powers?

The key project tasks now had clear timelines. Oppenheimer had advised Groves that a sufficient quantity of enriched uranium-235 would be available by July 1. Sufficient for only one bomb, one *Little Boy* bomb. The mechanics of the design were relatively simple. The physics were certain. The gun castings and the subassemblies were all ready. All that remained was the uranium-235. The weapon could be planned for direct use on Japan.

Plutonium production had ultimately proved easier to achieve. Fermi's original experimental Chicago reactor produced one watt of power. The intermediate X-10 reactor at Oak Ridge produced one million watts. The three giant reactors at Hanford designated B, D, and F produced a staggering 250 million watts. There was no attempt at capturing the vast amount of heat generated at Hanford. Their single purpose was to produce plutonium as a reactor byproduct. Producing plutonium proved more efficient than the problem-plagued uranium enrichment processes at Oak Ridge. Chemical separation of the plutonium from the spent uranium was a straightforward process.

The complexity of the implosion *gadget* mandated that an actual test must be performed. The physics were complicated and the precision engineering systems involved were all newly invented. *Little Boy* was a blunt tool. *Fat Man* was an intricate machine. However, the major design hurdles had largely been resolved. Repeated experimental results indicated that a sufficiently symmetrical implosive shockwave was achievable. A plutonium shell could be compressed into a super-critical mass.

Oppenheimer now advised Groves that a plutonium bomb would be ready by August 1. Sufficient plutonium would be available for multiple bombs, multiple *Fat Man* bombs. At the theoretical output rate of all three Hanford reactors producing 21 kilograms of plutonium per month, there would be enough plutonium for eighteen bombs by the end of 1945.

"Interested in going with me down to Omega Canyon?" Richard Feynman asked me.

"That's where you're conducting criticality experiments, right?"

"Yep. Brings us theoretical guys into the real world. It's away from the Hill for good reason. If something were to go badly wrong, the place would be irradiated."

That was not a comforting thought. Even if death was my way out, not that way. I was well aware of the protracted, painful death that resulted from radiation exposure.

"So how do you perform tests for criticality? By definition aren't we talking about a runaway chain reaction?"

"Technically that's right. Otto Frisch thought up the first experimental configuration. He assembled dozens of three centimeter blocks of enriched uranium hydride into a stack with a hole through the center. Then another block of uranium hydride was dropped through the hole. The whole assembly goes critical for just an instant as the plug passes through. Enough time to get readings that can be useful."

"Jesus. What happens if the plug gets stuck?"

"Everybody dies. Massive radiation exposure. The place becomes heavily contaminated, essentially forever. Not something to be imagined. The experiments have now moved to plutonium. The configuration is different but even more dangerous. I said it was like tickling the tail of a sleeping dragon. The name stuck. Now they're called the Dragon Experiments. Personally, I'll stay with my equations."

This was far more dangerous than the RaLa experiments. I recalled that first visit to the Omega Canyon compound when a few months later a young physicist named Harry Daghlian irradiated himself. He was conducting a criticality experiment using plutonium. In his case, he accidentally dropped the core into the assembly. He died in agony 25 days later. I remember meeting him. A big young kid in his twenties. He explained the experiment to me that would soon cost him his life.

Less than a year later another physicist, Louis Slotin was conducting a similar experiment. He was using the same plutonium 6.2 kilogram plutonium core that Daghlian had used. This time a screw driver being used to remove shims separating the two hemispheres of plutonium and beryllium slipped. The core went promptly critical before Slotin knocked the beryllium half to the floor. His quick reaction saved others in the room, but Slotin died nine days later. The plutonium core gained the name, the *Demon Core*.

Oppenheimer invited me to accompany him to the Trinity test site. It was a four-hour drive south. A place on the map called the Jornada del Muerto desert. The Spanish name, translated as the 'journey of the dead', aptly applied to this desolate place. The Army controlled several hundred square miles designated as the Alamogordo Bombing and Gunnery Range. It was as remote as anywhere yet still comparatively reachable from Los Alamos. Oppenheimer had designated the location as *Trinity*. This is where the *gadget*, would be tested - the first detonation of an atomic bomb. I offered to drive which allowed for frank conversation during the trip.

"General Groves sent me a dispatch yesterday. It's about the German atomic bomb program. I assume you know as well?" Oppenheimer said.

"Know what, Sir?"

"Groves' Alsos people have secured the principle locations where the Germans were conducting atomic research. Rounded up most of the scientists, even Heisenberg. Turns out their nuclear research program was still in its infancy. They had yet to even construct a working reactor. The Germans were years away from being able to produce fissile material in any substantive quantity. Seems the whole premise for our great effort was built upon an unfounded fear."

"But our work continues," I said. "What's your feeling about that, Doctor?"

"Well of course it continues. The project is too far advanced. It must be completed. The science is too far advanced. Atomic weapons will therefore become a reality. It's imperative that the United States be at the forefront of the technology. The atomic bomb transcends being just a powerful military weapon. It means absolute superiority in every sense for the country that possesses the means to create these weapons."

"Unless another country also possesses the same technology," I said.

"Ah. And therein lays the moral dilemma, perhaps now more a political dilemma."

"What do you think we should do, share the technology," I said.

Oppenheimer looked at me before answering. "Groves hasn't co-opted you to probe my position on the subject has he, Major?" His tone was sharp.

"No, Sir. Of course not. I apologize. It was my own question. As the bomb gets closer to realization, it's on everyone's mind. All the scientists have opinions."

"I believe it would ultimately be better if the technology was widely understood. If the United States attempts to create an arsenal of atomic weapons, then there will be an arms race. That means unchecked development of great numbers of bombs. That will breed an unprecedented level of danger for mankind. As weapon yields increase, which they invariably will, then we could reach a point where there might be sufficient weapons to destroy all mankind."

"An arms race presumably with the Soviet Union?"

"Of course," Oppenheimer said. "They have the means, and there is a widening ideological antagonism between our countries. Wouldn't you agree?"

"Yes, Sir. Seems that way."

"The future of atomic weapons will be more engineering than physics, Major. Our whole program has been dominated by developing the processes to produce fissile material. According to Groves, over ninety percent of the project costs have been consumed by that effort. The theoretical physics are known. We know how to make a bomb. So will anyone else. That knowledge cannot be kept secret. So it will be a matter of the ability to produce enough fissile material. The British have no reason to expend capital to engage in an arms race with us. The Germans are out of the picture. The Japanese will soon capitulate. That leaves only the Soviets.

"However, there will be no grand gesture to share atomic technology. The course of world politics will simply evolve along predictable lines. We shall open this new chapter in mankind's evolution at *Trinity*. The *Trinity* test is necessary to see if the *gadget* works. After that, it is largely out of the hands of us scientists."

"And *Little Boy*? You're that confident that it will work without conducting a full-scale test?" I said.

"Yes. Confident enough that I have recommended it be used first against the Japanese. Even if the *Trinity* test of the *gadget* is successful, there is still a risk of failure for *Fat Man*. Beyond the complex precision of the various design elements of the implosion design, *Trinity* will be detonated from a static position, not dropped from an airplane."

I was aware of the high-level discussions concerning using the atomic bomb. Oppenheimer was an advisor to the Targeting Committee. Unlike certain scientists that were arguing forcefully that we should demonstrate the atomic bomb before actually using it against the Japanese, Oppenheimer sided with the Army against any such plan. President Truman agreed. There was no debate about the use of the atomic bomb against the Japanese. A group under Bethe's Theoretical Division had calculated the damage on an urban environment. A demonstration in the desert devoid of structures equivalent to that of a large city could not convey the necessary impact. Worse yet if *Trinity* proved a failure.

The Targeting Committee had already decided to reserve three potential targets: Kyoto, Niigata, and Hiroshima. Reserving in the sense they would not be subjected to mass-incendiary bombings by U.S. B-29's. After all, it would be necessary to properly assess the destructive effects on an intact city.

The following month, Oppenheimer was on the scientific panel of a committee set up to discuss post-war issues related to atomic weapons. He unsuccessfully lobbied for an approach for the Soviet Union to share in atomic power development, and thereby avoid an atomic weapons arms race. It was the same stance he discussed in 1943 with Boris Pash, Groves' security chief, that forever made Oppenheimer's political leanings suspect.

We rode in silence for the remainder of the trip as Oppenheimer worked on paperwork. I retreated into my own personal dark thoughts.

Whatever Robert Oppenheimer's political views, he had never carried them to espionage for the Soviets. I had, and for self-serving reasons. Beyond a tragedy if Elena was knowingly bait for the deception. If so, then everything was an elaborate charade. Was I just an assignment for her? Was she a Soviet whore? Who were Boris and Vanya? When I returned to Washington, I must find out.

Arriving at the *Trinity* site, I fell back into being a professional. The excitement of what was soon to take place, the making of history, was infectious to all of us within the Project. Even for me with my life shattered, being part of this was compelling.

Trinity was not like Los Alamos. The gate was simply a makeshift guard shack on a newly paved road stretching to a desolate horizon. No other buildings were visible from the small guard station. The vast ordinance testing range was not fenced. Security was maintained by patrols in jeeps or on horseback.

Base camp for the site was several miles further down the road. It consisted of hastily constructed buildings constructed only to provide essential shelter for living and working for this single test. Oppenheimer said the base camp was still ten miles from where the *gadget* would be detonated. Tomorrow we would tour the three observation bunkers and the acting field laboratory.

"Oppie, good to see you. What brings you to this incarnation of hell?" Norris Bradbury said. He and Oppenheimer were close. They shook hands effusively, both all smiles.

"I hope we do not create a real version of hell here, Norris," Oppenheimer said. "You know Mike Voronin here."

I saluted and shook Bradbury's hand. We had met several times since he arrived at Los Alamos less than a year ago but I did not know him well. He held both a doctorate in physics as well as the rank of commander in the Navy so he outranked me. Like most of the scientists, he was young, in his mid-thirties. Bradbury was in charge of assembly of the *gadget* for the first test of an atomic bomb.

"Things are going according to schedule, Norris?" Oppenheimer asked.

"Pretty much, Oppie. Can't say it's been easy though. Water's been the biggest headache. Potable water has to be trucked in from Socorro. The water from various wells around here is fouled with gypsum. Nasty stuff. Have to use Navy saltwater-soap. Discourages showers."

"Is Ken here?" Oppenheimer asked. Ken was Kenneth Bainbridge tasked with creating the *Trinity* site.

Bainbridge was a Harvard experimental physicist with a talent for managing projects. *Trinity* was not just a single site. It was a complex laboratory situated in a particularly inhospitable, remote place. The Jornada del Muerto Desert was an arid span of sand with mesquite and yucca, populated with scorpions and centipedes. *Trinity* was spread over a vast area. The various observation bunkers were each located miles from what would become ground-zero for the detonation. A temporary laboratory and growing base camp were connected by newly constructed paved roads. All of these locations spanned an area greater than 150 square miles. For scientists and military personnel alike, this was a most unpleasant place made even worse with the encroaching heat of summer. Duty at *Trinity* represented an entirely worse level of isolation and deprivations than Los Alamos.

"Ken's at the McDonald Ranch right now. He'll join us tonight."

The only ranch building in the area had been transformed into a laboratory ten miles from the base camp. The *gadget* core would be assembled in the ranch house before being hoisted into the detonation tower.

That night we had a minor celebration with the senior staff at the site. Oppie and I had brought down a good supply of whisky and gin. Oppie mixed more than one batch of his famous martinis. The drinking was followed by an excellent meal of local antelope shot by the MP's.

We left the dining hall and walked to another building being used for offices. About eight of the most senior staff at the site joined us in what served as a conference room. We brought along the liquor.

"Doctor Oppenheimer believes we can be ready for the Trinity test by mid-July. Do you agree?" I asked both Bainbridge and Bradbury.

"That's more General Groves' date, but I generally agree it is possible," Bradbury said. "Criticality tests are still ongoing at Los Alamos to validate precise aspects of the implosion design. But we're close to nailing down all the final design details."

"As far as site preparations, we're on schedule to support that timing," Bainbridge said. "The real work is now up to Norris' team."

Bradbury was in charge of assembling the *gadget*. It was a constantly evolving list of new challenges. New staff arrived almost daily. Coordination with Los Alamos understandably added difficulties. And all this complex new science needed to be accomplished in a most difficult environment.

"We'll be ready down here," Bradbury said. "As difficult as it is working here, everyone sees the end in sight. Everyone is committed. Besides, there are no distractions here. However, this new stock of alcohol is most welcome, Major. I'm sure it will serve to expedite the work."

Everyone laughed. It was a convivial meeting. I would report to Groves that I too thought that mid-July was possible. I was aware of the general aspects of *Operation Downfall*, the planned U.S. invasion of Japan starting in November, 1945. General Groves was under mounting pressure to produce his atomic bomb. If the United States had to resort to an invasion to defeat the Japanese, then the Manhattan Project would be viewed as a failure, and so would Groves. Groves had never failed.

The following day Bainbridge and Bradbury accompanied Oppenheimer and I on a tour of the various locations making up *Trinity*. I drove again which allowed for unrestricted exchange between the four of us.

Oppenheimer appeared almost reverential when we arrived at what would become ground-zero. We all gazed up at the 100-

foot steel-frame tower where the *gadget* would be hoisted into place. The years of work and hundreds of millions of dollars would soon come down to this single event. All the science, all the experimental work pointed to the implosion-design atomic bomb working. But would it really?

A half a mile away was a gigantic steel container, twenty-five feet long and twelve feet in diameter, resembling a gigantic thermos. It weighed 214 tons. It cost $142 million. It was now a white elephant, never to be used. Nicknamed *Jumbo*, it was a visible symbol of abandoned parts of the Manhattan Project in the rush to create an atomic bomb in the shortest possible time. Its intended use was for the first test detonation. If the detonation 'fizzled' the theory being that the disintegrated core of valuable plutonium could be recovered. Ample production output from the Hanford reactors now made such rationing precautions unnecessary.

After two days at *Trinity*, I was glad to leave. *Trinity* made Los Alamos seem like a resort. My next trip back to *Trinity* would be for the real thing. That time was not far away.

Detonation tower at Trinity test site, 1945

CHAPTER 28

WASHINGTON D.C. – JUNE, 1945

T HE EXCITEMENT OF seeing the development work finally materialize into a workable bomb made for a diversion from my personal conflict. Once I left Los Alamos to catch a plane back to Washington, the reality of my circumstances plunged me back into a dark depression.

The Soviets had betrayed me. They had killed my father. Imprisoned my mother in a place where she would eventually die. Yet here I was spying for the Soviets. The rage I felt when I left Washington a few weeks previous returned full force. I would now have to confront the situation. I must find out if Elena, Boris, and Vanya are part of this. How? I worked through all sorts of scenarios on the plane trip east. One thing was clear; this is the last time I would pass information onto the Soviets. No matter what they threatened, this would end.

Fortunately I was scheduled to be in Washington for only a couple of days. Groves had called together all his senior staff for final assignments as the birthing of the atomic bomb approached. Along with Groves and his newly appointed deputy for operations of the Manhattan Project, Brig. General Thomas

Farrell, I would be a witness to the *Trinity* test scheduled for July.

As the Army C-47 approached Washington, a plan came into focus. A plan to find out if my wife was a whore for Soviet intelligence. If she knew nothing of the fate of my parents, then perhaps we had a life. If she did? Well that was not yet clear what I would do.

My friend Richard Feynman, the brilliant young physicist and incorrigible practical joker, had shared a particular trick that might now prove useful. Feynman delighted in circumventing the security systems at Los Alamos. In addition to his safe-cracking stunts, confounding censors by encoding letters to his wife, was his telephone trick as he called it.

Feynman loved mechanisms. Over a bottle of Scotch one evening, he was showing Victor Weisskopf and me his latest prank.

"You remove the top of the phone to expose the inner workings by unscrewing these two screws on the bottom," Feynman said. This was the standard Western Electric Model 302.

"See this mechanical arm here. That's the tilting switch mechanism. When you lift the handset, a spring forces these contacts to complete the connection to the outside circuit. When you replace the handset back on the cradle, the weight overcomes the spring and cuts off the connection. So if I remove these two small pins, lifting the handset allows the spring to force the contacts to complete the circuit, but it no longer disconnects the circuit when you replace the handset."

"And the purpose of this?" I asked.

"I'll show you," Feynman said. "I'll go into the next office and call this extension. Answer when it rings then hang up the hand set."

I did as instructed. Feynman then told me to come into the next office. He had not disconnected the call by hanging up that phone.

"Victor, I'm going to close this door. Speak in a normal voice. Recite a poem or something."

From the handset in the next office I could hear Weisskopf speaking. Somewhat muffled but still intelligible.

"You can now eavesdrop on the unsuspecting party who answered the phone. Assuming they stay fairly close to the telephone," Feynman said with his characteristic mischievous grin.

So a plan quickly formed with Feynman's trick as the key. I would tell Elena to call Boris and Vanya to come to Washington immediately. I had important information to pass on but did not have the time to travel to Wilmington. I was here in Washington only for a couple of days, which was true. Once they were at the apartment, I would manufacture a controversy, create some sort of argument, and then leave. From a payphone I would call the apartment on some pretext. I would have pre-rigged our apartment phone to not disconnect when the handset was replaced. The contrived argument would have to do with my spying. Hopefully Elena and her parents would talk candidly with me gone.

I arrived home in the evening by taxi. Elena jumped into my arms. She wanted to make love right away but I claimed being starved. I watched as she prepared some leftovers, wondering if her smiles and touches were all an act.

"I need you to call your parents. I have information. But they need to come here. Actually tomorrow. I will be in town only a couple of days then leaving again. Can't get up to Wilmington."

"Why such a short time? Are things getting close?" Elena said.

She set the food in front of me. I was glad for the distraction.

"Yes. That's what I have for Boris. The test will be soon. I'll be there. Just back to coordinate things with Groves. I'll be tied up in meetings for the next two days then I'm back to New Mexico. This is it, Elena."

Elena called her father. In veiled language she wondered if he and mother could come down to Washington tomorrow. Mike was home. Boris Ramazanov understood.

That night we made love. I had become a consummate liar so in this too I played my role. With Elena's typical sexual attentions it was not difficult. I was perhaps slightly more aggressive than usual as I fucked her.

Early the next morning a staff car picked me up. I had not lied about the high level staff meeting. This was the final push. Twelve of us sat around a large conference table next to General Groves' office. We were about to test the first atomic bomb. Even with my conflicted circumstances I still felt the excitement, the sense of being a part of history.

"The first test of an atomic bomb is now firmly scheduled for Monday, July 16, subject to change only for reasons of weather," Groves announced. "That date was officially set this morning. Criticality tests have confirmed the integrity of the core design. As you all know, this will be a plutonium implosion device. The pacing factor has been the delivery of full-sized molds for the implosion explosive lens segments. Air cavities have proved problematic in the casting process. However, a sufficient number of successfully cast lenses have been produced within the last two weeks to allow us to move forward. According to Dr. Oppenheimer, the bomb components will be transported from Los Alamos to the *Trinity* site on the 12th of July. Assembly will be completed at the McDonald Ranch House field laboratory at *Trinity* on the following day. The *gadget* will then be transported the two miles to the detonation tower at ground zero."

I found Groves' optimistic assessment of the status of the lenses inconsistent with the facts. George Kistiakowsky's team was still working around the clock. More lens castings produced were defective than acceptable. To make matters worse, Oppenheimer was insisting on a full-scale test of a copy of the *gadget's* implosion lens. That would require twice as many suitable castings. Kistiakowsky resorted to personally drilling into defective lens to locate the air cavity inclusions revealed by x-ray. He then poured molten explosive into the voids. I had reported all this to Groves so he knew how tenuous the situation was with the lenses. But Groves was Groves. The deadline would be met.

"General Farrell and Major Voronin will be present along with me for the *Trinity* test," Groves said. "In concert with the *Trinity* test, plans are underway to ship bomb components to the Pacific. The 509th has positioned their specially adapted B-29's on the island of Tinian in the Marianas within striking distance of the Japanese homeland."

"How many bombs will be sent to the Pacific, Sir?" Someone asked.

"At this time, two," Groves said. "The *Little Boy* uranium gun-design and the duplicate implosion-design of the *Trinity* test device designated *Fat Man*."

And if *Trinity* works I thought to myself.

"Then it's a go to use this against Japan, Sir?" Someone asked.

"Yes. President Truman is committed. Targets have been selected," Groves said. "It will end the War."

It was an intense day to be followed by another long day tomorrow. The day after that I would return to Los Alamos. *Trinity* was little more than two weeks away. With a mix of dread and anger, I now must resolve my personal problem that night.

Late the previous night with Elena asleep, I had rigged the phone. As I drove the fifteen minutes to our apartment, I strategized my charade for the evening.

Boris and Vanya were there as I knew they would be. Elena was home for the day. She was preparing spaghetti for dinner using saved ration coupons for tomatoes and cheese. I could smell fresh baked bread in the oven.

After exchanging pleasantries, I got down to business. I gave Boris a copy of my last report to Groves. I then told him of the schedule date for *Trinity.*

"And if the bomb works, what's next?" Boris asked.

"I don't know. I don't know if the President has committed to using it against the Japanese. Probably depends on how many bombs we have. Right now there are only *Little Boy* and the test *gadget* for *Trinity,*" I said. "If the gadget works, then we can assemble a couple more."

For the next couple of hours we encrypted my latest reports. Boris photographed the encoded ciphers. This would be the last time. I burned the incriminating papers in the bathroom, flushing the ashes down the toilet.

"There's something else, Boris," I said. "I want something from our friends in Moscow."

"Oh? And what's that, Mikhail?" Boris asked with a look of concern.

"It's apparently easy enough to get classified information to Moscow so I want a letter delivered to my parents. And more than that, I want a return letter from them."

"Mikhail, I don't know. That's personal business. There's a war going on."

"I don't care. I want it done. Right now! Here's my letter. I want a reply from my parents. I want it within thirty days from now."

"I'll try, Mikhail, but I can't promise."

"You can tell them there will be no further information until I hear from my parents."

"Mikhail, you can't threaten these people."

"*These people*? Soviet intelligence you mean? The same type of arrogant bastards we have in U.S. intelligence? And yes I can threaten them. They'll do what I demand or the information ends."

"Why are you so angry, Misha?" Vanya asked.

"Because I've been risking my neck and should have thought sooner to get something in return."

"We all are doing this for Mother Russia," Boris said.

"Bullshit! The Soviet Union isn't Mother Russia. Stalin isn't Russia. He's even ethnically Georgian. I'm sick of all of this. So just get this letter to my parents. I want to hear that they're ok. Perhaps I should also stipulate that Moscow see to it that my parents are looked after. Why not?"

I stood up and paced the room with my fabricated sense of anger.

Elena came over and put her head on my shoulder. "Please, Darling, calm down."

"Sure, sure. I'm sorry. You must realize the stress of what I'm doing. I need a drink. And I forgot to buy vodka on my way home. I'm going out to get some."

"But Darling, dinner's almost ready," Elena said.

"I won't be long. It's just a couple of blocks to the liquor store," I said and left.

At the liquor store there was a payphone outside. I called the apartment. "Elena, the liquor store is out of vodka. I'm walking down to Clancy's bar. Won't be long though. Sorry I made a scene. Wait dinner for me. Love you."

I could hear Boris in the background if I pressed the handset tight to my ear. The connection remained open. I was now listening in on my in-law's conversation. Hopefully my outburst would provoke something revealing.

The sound level was barely audible but adequate by pressing the receiver to my ear and covering my other ear with my hand.

"….. we have little choice. You will just have to compose another set of letters from his parents. Once back home we'll see what he has written and respond accordingly," Boris said.

"I don't like it. Too much chance he'll get suspicious," Vanya said.

"Why should he? It worked before. He simply wants to hear that they're surviving."

"What happened to his parents anyhow?" Elena said.

"Sent to the camps in Siberia," Boris said. "The father died some time ago. Not sure about his mother. Regardless, no one returns from the Gulag. If she's alive it's a prolonged death."

"If he learned the truth, I'm not sure what he'd do," Elena said. "You heard him earlier. He's never been committed to this. It's only because of me he does this. Russia is only about his parents."

"...... you need to .... He's infatuated with ..... you're the ultimate leverage if he .... Is everything fine between you two?" Vanya said but was too far away from the telephone to catch every word.

"Of course. If you mean is our sex life satisfactory, he can have no complaints," Elena said. "I control him by sex. He would never give me up. But if he learns the truth about his parents, there's no telling how he will react."

I hung up, disconnecting the circuit. I had suspected the worst but hoped I was wrong. My guts twisted with the implications. Everything was gone. My mother, my father, my wife, my career, my honor. Worst yet, I was a willing accomplice in my own downfall. For sex, I had traded my soul. A true-life Faustian bargain.

I went into the liquor store and bought a bottle of vodka and a bottle of wine. Before returning home I smoked a cigarette. It was a full moon night. The air was still sticky from an unseasonably hot day. Summer had arrived early. I had no idea what I would do now. I lit another cigarette and walked back home. At least I would be away from here soon. Time to think.

I feigned contrition for my earlier outburst. It was the stress. The stress of my real job, the stress of spying. Although I had little appetite, I ate Elena's dinner. I made sure I drank heavily as well. Falling asleep in the chair made the excuse to avoid love-making.

The next day at the office, General Groves summoned me to his office.

"You're to return to Los Alamos tomorrow, Major. I want you at the *Trinity* site in advance of the *gadget* assembly once you are sure that all of the components are on schedule. From now on I want you hovering over the *gadget* like an expectant father. Anything and I mean if anything gets in the way of the schedule, I want to know immediately. Farrell and I will join you a couple of days before the test. Up to that time, you are my eyes. I want no surprises. Understood?"

"Yes, Sir." Sure that I couldn't prevent surprises and hoping not to be the messenger of any.

"One more thing, Major. After *Trinity*, you'll immediately fly to the Pacific. You'll continue nurse-maiding *Little Boy* right up to the moment of its release over Japan."

"Have the targets been selected, Sir?"

"Yes."

That afternoon I returned to the apartment. I packed clean uniforms and my toilet kit. I left a note for Elena. It explained that I was called away this very afternoon. Sorry that I could not spend a last night home before leaving.

I spent the night at Fort Meyers' transient officers' quarters before my flight to Los Alamos. Spending another night with Elena would be impossible knowing the truth. Eventually I would have to confront that truth, but that was for another day.

That day must bring an end to this twisted mess of deceit. At least I would have some time to contemplate a choice between terrible alternatives.

The gadget in the Trinity test site tower, 1945

CHAPTER 29

TRINITY TEST SITE, NEW MEXICO – JULY, 1945

I ARRIVED IN Albuquerque on July 3rd. For the next two weeks, I would observe every detail of the final preparations for the first test of an atomic bomb. The stakes in this great gamble were staggering. After a secret expenditure of two billion dollars hidden from Congress, everything came down to this moment. If it didn't work, or didn't achieve the spectacular projected theoretical scope of power, the careers of a good many military officers and renowned scientists would be destroyed. President Truman had postponed the Potsdam Conference with Winston Churchill and Joseph Stalin to buy more time for a successful test to be used as a political leverage. The success of the atomic bomb was now as much an issue related to the Soviet Union as one of bringing the Japanese to capitulation.

Japan was already defeated. It was only a matter of how and when the War would end. If Japan could be forced to surrender by using this unprecedented weapon of mass devastation, than a Soviet invasion into Manchuria to pressure the Japanese from the west would be unnecessary. The United States and Great Britain already expected difficulties with the Soviets over control of post-war Germany and Eastern Europe. An eleventh-hour Soviet intrusion against Japanese occupied territories would present the same potential problems in the Far East. That was the real reason for considering an invasion of Japan. Otherwise, Japan could be simply left to internally fall apart. They were totally isolated, without a navy or defense against air attacks. Bringing the war to a decisive conclusion would save American lives involved with an invasion of the Japanese homeland. More strategically, it would leverage American might to counter increasing Soviet belligerence. Popular history in the future would probably not see these interlocking complexities.

The pressure at both Los Alamos and the *Trinity* site was unrelenting. Two small plutonium hemispheres had been cast then nickel plated. This was both to guard against corrosion and for the nickel to increase alpha particle absorption to trigger the fission chain reaction. Beautiful in appearance, but a problem soon developed within a couple of days.

Plating solution trapped under the nickel started to blister. This would disturb the close tolerance fit of the core within the assembly. The problem threatened to postpone the test. Creative metallurgists salvaged the castings by partway grinding down the blisters and delicately smoothing the surface with gold foil.

With the numerous interconnected systems newly created from evolving science, all of which were complex and never fully tested, problems continued right up to the end. Success had to be credited to the brilliant ingenuity of the people working on this project. The repair of the plutonium core and George Kistiakowsky's dangerous repair of the explosive lenses were but a couple of examples.

The 100-foot tall steel detonation tower was complete upon my return. The feverish task was now the laying of miles of wiring for the test. Every element of control for the detonation had to be located miles away from ground zero. Not only the circuits to trigger the detonation, but the vast array of instruments for all manner of tests. *Trinity* was far more than just a test to see if the *gadget* worked. The *gadget* was the first of a new generation of weapon. Elegant in design, but yet still a crude prototype compared with what would follow. Every facet of its performance would be invaluable in the evolution of nuclear weapons.

On Thursday, July 12, Norris Bradbury's team and a crew of Special Engineering Detachment technicians began assembling the high explosive lenses in a remote canyon outside the Los Alamos mesa. The explosive castings charges, all x-rayed a final time and numbered, were assembled together. The fit required precision, snugness, and no air spaces. This was accomplished with adding facial tissue and scotch tape. Once the lower hemisphere of the lens assembly was complete, the heavy tamper sphere of natural uranium-238 was lowered by winch into the cavity. It looked like the pit resting in a halved avocado. The tamper had a cylindrical hole where it would receive the plutonium core during final assembly at the *Trinity* site. The hole was sealed with a precision machined uranium plug to maintain the continuity of the spherical uranium tamper. For transport to *Trinity*, one set of high explosive castings was left out with the open cavity sealed against dust or moisture. This cavity would allow for the pit assembly containing the plutonium core to be placed within the uranium tamper. The uranium plug would then be secured. The missing high explosive casting would complete the uniformly spherical assembly with the plutonium core nested in the very center.

The plutonium core left Los Alamos at three o'clock in the afternoon of July 12th. It rode in the backseat of an Army sedan. A carload of armed guards took up the front position, with another carload of pit-assembly specialists bringing up the rear. I rode next to the driver. That evening we arrived at the makeshift field laboratory of what was the McDonald Ranch house a couple of miles from the tower at ground zero.

To avoid traffic, the high explosive assembly would travel by night from Los Alamos south to the Jornada del Muerto desert.

While the plutonium core weighed only 13.5 pounds, the 5,000 pound high explosive assembly comprised half of the *gadget* weight. It was wrapped in plastic then secured within a crate. It would take eight hours to reach the Trinity tower travelling in the bed of a five-ton Army truck at only thirty miles per hour. George Kistiakowsky had personally inspected the *gadget* lenses the previous day. How well the high explosive lens assembly performed would determine the success of the *gadget*. Kistiakowsky now babysat what was arguably his baby for the slow ride leaving the Hill at midnight of the 12th.

I spent the night at *Trinity* base camp. My quarters consisted of a large field tent shared with several others. This was home for the next four nights. I made my way to the mess tent, delighted to find Robert Serber, Richard Feynman, and Victor Weisskopf there. I had come to think of them as friends. My seeming betrayal of them gnawed like an ulcer in my stomach.

"Mike, good to see you. Come have a drink," Serber said to me.

I shook hands with all three.

"Richard. I heard about Arline when I was down here a couple weeks ago. I'm so sorry for your loss," I said. Arline Feynman had finally succumbed to her long illness with tuberculosis.

"Thanks, Mike," Feynman said.

"Were you with her at the end?"

"Just barely. I was with her for her last few hours. Thanks to Fuchs. He loaned me his car so I could drive to Albuquerque. You know Klaus Fuchs don't you? The Brit, actually he's German. Came over from England. You met him a couple of times. Quiet guy. I almost didn't make it in time. Car's a real piece of junk. Had three flat tires on the way. But I was grateful all the same."

We all sipped on Scotch brought by Serber. "To Arline," we toasted.

I pondered the feeling of losing my own wife to her betrayal.

What's your schedule, Mike?" Serber asked.

"Tomorrow I'll be at the McDonald Ranch house for the pit assembly. On the big day, I'll be at S-10000," I said.

S-10000 was the earth-shielded reinforced concrete bunker, so-designated for being 10,000 yards, or six miles, south of the test tower. It would serve as the control center for the test on Monday before dawn. Two other bunkers designated N-10000 and W-10000 would house personnel manning instrumentation and cameras at the same six-mile distance from ground zero.

Base Camp was another four miles south of S-10000. Twenty miles to the northwest of ground zero was Campania Hill. This would be the viewing point for most of the scientists and other visitors.

"Ah, running with the big dogs," Feynman said referring to the few top scientists who would be huddled at S-10000 on test day. "We'll all be up on Campania Hill. But then again, maybe that's just as well. You'll be up close to this, perhaps too close my friend."

Feynman was joking but not entirely. While everyone worried about the test being a low-yield dud, the opposite might happen, contrary to theoretical calculations. Was six miles a sufficient distance? Might there be some unforeseen atmospheric reaction? The concerns were remote, but could not totally be discounted.

Before dawn the next morning, I drove out to the McDonald Ranch house with Brig. General Thomas Farrell. The night before, Army technicians had vacuumed the interior of the small house. The windows were sealed with electrical tape to create a crude clean room. Everyone donned white lab coats. General Farrell hefted one of the plutonium hemispheres. Since it was an alpha emitter, it felt warm in his hand. He quickly put it down.

The pit assembly consisted of the plutonium core split into two hemispheres. Within the plutonium core was the internal neutron initiator. As the uranium tamper contained the plutonium pit assembly, within the pit assembly was a pit within a pit, the neutron initiator.

Code named *Urchin*, the initiator was an interesting design in itself. It was a comparatively small component within the massive bomb. About the size of a marble, it consisted of a beryllium pellet only 0.8 cm in diameter. The pellet was coated with nickel over which was a layer of gold. The coated pellet was surrounded by a beryllium shell with a diameter of 2 cm. Inside the thin shell wall with a thickness of only 0.6 cm were 15 concentric wedge-shaped grooves. Like the pellet, the inside of the shell was coated with layers of nickel and gold. Within these grooves was a very small quantity of polonium.

Polonium was a strong alpha particle emitter. The nickel and gold insulated these emissions from the beryllium. When the explosive lenses detonated, the assembly would compress everything toward a center point. The polonium would mix with the beryllium. The polonium alpha emissions would cause a corresponding burst of neutrons to be released by the beryllium. This would trigger the neutron chain reaction within the plutonium-239 as it was compressed to critical mass. The tiny *Urchin* assembly was the spark plug for the *gadget*.

On Saturday, July 14, Norris Bradbury supervised the winching of the *gadget* to its high platform within the tower. The openings where the detonators would be installed where covered with plastic and tape. It looked unremarkable for all the effort expended in its creation.

Once in place, a white tent had been erected over the five-foot diameter *gadget*. This afforded protection when the covering over the trapdoor access plug to the center was removed for final arming.

The plutonium pit assembly was then delivered from the McDonald Ranch house and hoisted to the high platform. To maximize the density of the uranium tamper, the clearance between the plug and the mating hole within the tamper shell was only a few thousandths of an inch. After inserting the plutonium pit assembly, the tamper plug was lowered toward the center, deep within the high explosive shell. *It would not slip into position.* Already under terrible stress, the assembly team stared at the problem in disbelief. What could have gone wrong? Frayed nerves gave way to despair at this latest problem.

The physicist in charge of assembling the plutonium core, Robert Bacher, knew that the fit tolerances had been carefully checked. He quickly thought he saw the origin of the problem. The plug had been in the hot ranch house and had expanded slightly. The tamper was deep inside the insulating mass of the high explosives and at a lower temperature. Bacher suggested they take a break. A short time later, the temperatures of the two components had equalized. The plug slid into place.

The missing explosive lens casting was secured into place. Lastly, the firing circuits that would detonate the high explosive shell were connected. Redundant checks were made by different scientists. The first ever atomic bomb was now ready for detonation.

Bad news struck again that same day. The full scale detonation test of the duplicate high explosive assembly outside of Los Alamos had been conducted. The call came to Oppenheimer that the test results indicated the *Trinity* test was likely to fail.

I was with George Kistiakowsky when Oppenheimer telephoned him the news. Everyone was terribly upset and took it out on poor Kistiakowsky. Even Oppenheimer was uncharacteristically critical.

"If the test doesn't work, then everyone will have their scapegoat," Kistiakowsky said to me.

"Do you have any idea what could have gone wrong?" I said.

"Wrong? No. Nothing should be wrong. We've been over every aspect hundreds of times. All of the castings for *Trinity* are as perfect as realistically possible. Better than most used on the

many successful tests we've conducted. They're absolutely good
enough to do what is expected."

"Weren't the castings used in this last Los Alamos' test just
as good as those you selected for *Trinity*?" I asked.

"Yes, of course. Then again, why should the high explosives
be at fault? There could have been a problem with the detonation circuit timings. I'm very confident *Trinity* will work,"
Kistiakowsky pronounced, perhaps to himself as much as to me.

It was not necessary for me to report this calamitous news to
Groves. Groves already knew. He had chimed in with his own
blunt criticism toward Kistiakowsky.

Saturday was difficult. Everyone at Base camp was visibly
depressed. Kistiakowsky was shunned like a leper.

Sunday brought a ray of hope. The pragmatic Hans Bethe
had spent the entire Saturday night studying the electromagnetic
theory of the recent high explosive implosion test results. He
concluded that the instrumentation configuration would not
have recorded different oscilloscope results had the geometry of
the implosion forces been perfect. In short, the recording instrument design gave inconclusive results. Everything would have
to fall back on theory and rely on earlier empirical tests.

Early Sunday evening, Oppenheimer climbed the test tower
for the last time. This was his creation. The *gadget* looked ungainly, clearly a prototype. It was bandaged in tape. Wires protruded
from everywhere. Would this thing work? Would it be as spectacular as theory suggested?

Back on track, the concern was now about the weather. The
wind started to kick up dust as Oppenheimer left the tower. The
shot was scheduled for 0400hrs Monday morning. At 2000hrs
Sunday night, thunder and lightning began over the area. Wind
increased to thirty miles per hour. The Project meteorologist was
confused and rattled, clearly out of his element. The stress rendered his advice unreliable. At the eleventh hour, Groves called
in an Air force meteorologist, the same officer that had provided

the forecast for the weather window for the Normandy D-Day landing last year.

General Groves arrived at the S-10000 control bunker at 0100hrs Monday morning. General Farrell and I were already there along with Oppenheimer, Bainbridge, Kistiakowsky, Bradbury, and his arming team.

Oppenheimer was a nervous wreck. Groves kept close to him and frequently pulled him aside in private conversation. These two dramatically different personalities had a personal bond. Oppenheimer speculated that there was good reason to postpone. Groves stated emphatically the test would go forward as planned. There were added risks to postponement. Besides, the level of anxiety among everyone could not be sustained without causing further problems.

It was a miserable night. Thunderstorms moved into the area around 0200hrs. Wind gusts reached 30 miles per hour. Little rain fell on Ground Zero but a heavy downpour soaked the S-10000 control bunker. Concerns arose about possible shorts in the complex electrical control circuits. The other meteorological conditions of visibility, humidity, and inversion layers at varying altitudes were all less than optimal. Regardless, Groves ordered the test would still go forward.

Groves had ultimately set the test date based on political considerations not the weather. President Truman's conference with Churchill and Stalin at Potsdam in occupied Germany would commence the following day. Truman wanted this new weapon as a bargaining chip in the European post-war negotiations with Stalin.

Based upon the final weather forecast at 0245hrs, Groves reluctantly moved the detonation time from 0400hrs to 0530hrs. The chief meteorologist reported there would be a window of opportunity for several hours sometime after 0400hrs.

Groves bluntly told him, "You had better be right on this or I'll hang you."

By 0400hrs, the rain had stopped. As predicted, the winds began abating. The detonation time of 0530hrs was now fixed.

For security reasons, Groves left the more forward S-10000 bunker at 0510hrs to return the four miles to the Base Camp. There was still some element of risk related to the possible range of damage. To avoid a common disaster, the leadership of the Manhattan Project should not be in the same location when the bomb exploded. General Farrell and I remained at S-10000.

Bainbridge unlocked the master switches at 0508hrs. The twenty minute timing switch was started.

At 0525hrs a green flare arched into the nighttime sky. A siren sounded at Base Camp.

At two minutes to detonation, another warning flare shot into the sky. Another followed at minus one minute.

The automatic timing circuit was switched on at 45 seconds to detonation time.

The control bunker was crowded. I looked over at Robert Oppenheimer. He was pale and seemed to be hardly breathing. I stood next to George Kistiakowsky. He appeared no better.

At minus ten seconds a klaxon sounded within the bunker. Everyone donned welding goggles. We were still told not to look directly in the direction of the blast.

At 0529:45hrs the firing circuit closed. Electronic detonators positioned symmetrically about the *gadget* simultaneously triggered thirty-two separate explosions of the chemical high explosive charges. The shaped charges focused the expanding shockwaves uniformly toward the core. The uranium tamper collapsed followed by the plutonium core. Within the initiator at the very center, the beryllium and polonium mixed. The alpha emissions of the polonium triggered the beryllium to release a burst of neutrons into the now crushed and super-critical plutonium core. Fission multiplied exponentially through tens of generations of the plutonium-239. All this occurred within an infinitesimal fraction of a second.

Witnessed for the first time, the staggering magnitude of re-leased energy defied any description. For a few seconds the nighttime sky was brighter than any daylight. Kistiakowsky em-braced Oppenheimer. Theirs was a particular feeling of success. Among all the scientific contributors, their leadership was cru-cial to the successful outcome of the endeavor.

The blast was equivalent to 20,000 tons of TNT. The steel tower was vaporized. The massive Jumbo casting 800 yards from ground zero was ripped apart. Theoretically, the temperature at the blast center reached 60 million degrees centigrade, 10,000 times hotter than the sun. The physical blast wave reached the nearest observers within 40 seconds. The sound reverberated against the surrounding mountains. A mushroom-shaped debris cloud quickly rose to an altitude of 40,000 feet. It took on a pur-ple luminescence caused by the radioactivity within the cloud.

Robert Oppenheimer would later recall that the Hindu scrip-ture from the Bhagavad Gita came to mind at the moment: 'Now I am become Death, the destroyer of worlds.'

For myself, I had the uncomfortable thought that we would now use this against a large populated city. A city of tens of thousands of non-combatants. How was this any different than chemical warfare that the modern world had outlawed since World War One? Perhaps no different than the massive fire bombings of cities such as Tokyo, but it still felt different.

The Alamogordo Air Base issued a short press release to the effect that a remotely located ammunitions depot containing substantial supplies of high explosives and pyrotechnic muni-tions had exploded. There was no loss of life or injury to person-nel.

I returned to base Camp with Oppenheimer and General Farrell.

Farrell congratulated General Groves by saying, "The war is over."

Groves replied, "Yes, after we drop two bombs on Japan."

CHAPTER 30

Fat Man atomic bomb, Nagasaki, Japan
August 9, 1945

HIROSHIMA & NAGASAKI, JAPAN – AUGUST, 1945

AFTER THE SUCCESSFUL *Trinity* test there was a wide range of emotions among those closest to the Project. Noticeably absent were any celebratory expressions after the initial backslapping. The deeper implications now came to the forefront. Most everyone wrestled with their own moral position. Even for those fully supportive of using the atomic bomb on the Japanese, this was a terrifying weapon. A weapon to be used on civilians; women and children. All of us had some hand in creating this thing. It was now clear the science had moved solely into the military realm.

Bob Serber said to me, "How do you feel about what we created, Mike?"

"Probably like most everybody else, Bob. Troubled I'd say. It's one thing to hear you guys talk in terms about the power of this thing, but seeing it explode was something else. I was six miles away and it still scared the hell out of me."

Serber nodded. "I know the physics but can't still imagine what this will mean when exploded over a large city. *Trinity* was exploded from a 100-foot tower. Nowhere near optimum for destruction. When they use it for real it will detonate at a much higher altitude to increase its span of destruction. Can you imagine killing tens of thousands of people in an instant? I can't."

"You even named these bombs, Bob. How did you think they'd be used," I asked.

"I wonder about that often, Mike. Like everyone I was caught up in the heady rush of participating at the center of this great scientific project. Patriotism. Getting the bomb before Nazi Germany. The scientific challenge. Ego. Avoided thinking of the logical consequences of success. Somebody else's decision. Intellectual snobbery. Who can say? The atomic bomb is much simpler than the human character."

To seal the fate of thousands of Japanese, United States President Harry S. Truman, United Kingdom Prime Minister Winston Churchill, and Chairman of the Nationalist Government of China Chiang Kai-shek issued the Potsdam Declaration on July 26th demanding the surrender of Japan. Already outside the club, the Soviet Union was excluded. There was no serious expectation that the Japanese would accept the terms outlined. Like the Treaty of Versailles at the end of World War One, it was meant to be punitive. No threat of a super weapon was mentioned. As expected, the Japanese publically rejected the ultimatum two days later.

My personal thoughts were conflicted. I was as much part of this as anyone else within the project. How would history view this? View us? A lot of the scientists felt that way. But this thing would go forward. Too many inertial factors made it inevitable. Like me, Bob Serber was also headed to Tinian. For both of us, the bomb would become even more personal over the next couple of weeks.

Within two days, I was on a C-47 with General Farrell heading to the Pacific. We stopped first in San Diego then flew to Pearl Harbor. From there it was another thirty-seven hundred miles and twenty-five hours island-hopping to Tinian Island in the Marians chain. It was southeast of the Japanese mainland within striking distance by B-29 bombers.

Tinian had been taken from the Japanese only one year earlier. Hundreds of Japanese soldiers held out for months in the jungles after the U.S. Marines had gained control. In the middle of summer, it was no real improvement over the Jornada del Muerto desert in New Mexico. The dry oven of the desert was replaced with oppressive tropical humidity.

Two days before the *Trinity* shot, a small convoy left Los Alamos carrying the non-nuclear components and the uranium projectile for the *Little Boy* gun-design bomb. These were flown to San Francisco and loaded onto the heavy cruiser *USS Indianapolis* for transport to Tinian. The uranium target component would fly to Tinian for the simple reason it was not ready in time to leave on the *Indianapolis*.

Once the *Little Boy* pieces arrived, the center of activity became the assembly shed. Navy Captain Deke Parsons was in charge of preparations. It was miserably hot and humid in the shed. Everyone was soaked in perspiration.

I asked Serber the obvious question. "Why is everyone so sure *Little Boy* will work? You never tested it. And why did you give it the name *Little Boy*? I can see why *Fat Man*, but *Little Boy*?"

Serber had assigned the nicknames which stuck.

"Originally there was *Thin Man*, from the Dashiell Hammett detective novel. That was the long, slender plutonium gun-design that we later found wouldn't work. The rotund implosion design then became by contrast *Fat Man*. From the Sidney Greenstreet character in *The Maltese Falcon* movie. So to distinguish from the abandoned *Thin Man* design, *Little Boy* was coined for the uranium bomb.

"To your second question, it will work because the physics are well understood and the design is crudely simple. Unlike the implosion design, *Little Boy* is nothing more than an artillery piece. As long as the chemical explosive goes off, the uranium core will go super-critical. It's not viable for the long term as a weapons design because of the difficulties with producing sufficient quantities of U-235. Plutonium is much easier to produce and requires less for the same yield as uranium. So the implosion design is the future for nuclear weapons. That's why *Trinity* was necessary."

Little Boy looked like a conventional bomb only larger. It was 120 inches in length, 28 inches in diameter, and weighed 9,700 pounds. Functionally it consisted of an 85 pound uranium-235 projectile driven into a 56 pound four-inch diameter target cylinder of uranium-235 by the ignition of cordite explosive. Collectively, the uranium would amount to two critical masses when mated together. The projectile piece would travel 42 inches down the 6.5 inch smooth-bore gun barrel at 1000 feet per second to mate with the target piece.

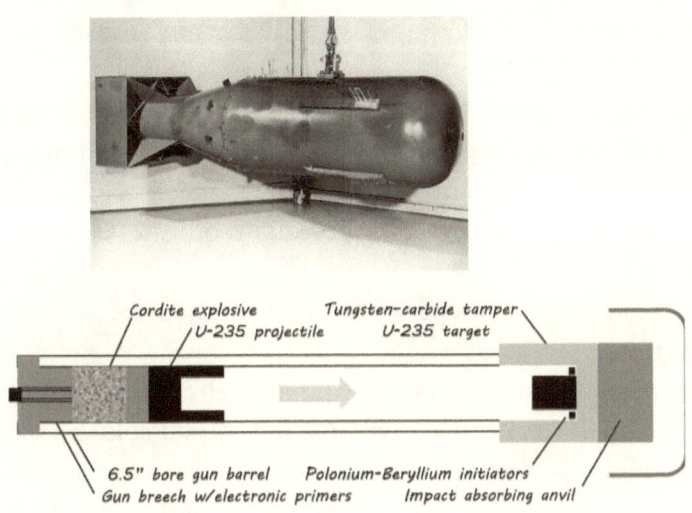

In order to maintain two critical masses of U-235 in two pieces, the solid piece must be less than one critical mass and the other piece shaped such that increased surface area was provided for fissioning neutrons to escape. Since reflecting back neutrons was necessary to containing the chain reaction longer to increase the energy release, a reflective tamper needed to encase the uranium when it went critical. Half the weight of Little Boy was the tungsten-carbide steel tamper in the form of a cylinder containing the uranium target. Seemingly counter-intuitively, the projectile was the larger mass of uranium with a hollow interior cylindrical hole to receive the target member. The interior cavity gave it greater surface area thereby preventing it from reaching critical mass until it mated with the target piece. For the same reason, it could not be retained within the reflecting tamper. The physics dictated it must therefore be the projectile.

Little Boy was ready on July 31st. The weather over Japan however was overcast with rain. One of the prerequisites decided on by the controlling Interim Committee was for the bombardier to have visual acquisition of the target. Accuracy was paramount. Radar was not to be used for final delivery targeting. On August 4th, the weather was reported improving. For the first time, the crews of the 509th B-29's were advised of their mission.

Parsons described the weapon they were about to deliver. "It is the most destructive weapon ever produced. We think it will knock out everything within a three-mile area. It will deliver the kind of devastation that would typically require 2,000 fully loaded B-29's."

After months of intensive training, he had the attention of the air crews.

The primary target was Hiroshima, a city with a population of 320,000 in 1945; 280,000 civilians and 40,000 soldiers. Several army headquarters were located there. The city was a minor logistics center for military supplies, along with some industry. Surrounding hills should considerably increase the blast effect.

The cities of Kokura and Nagasaki would be secondary targets.

On August 5th, weather was forecast to be clear over the primary target the next day. Air Force Commanding General

Curtis LeMay gave the order for the attack to take place on Sunday, August 6th.

On Saturday at 1400hrs, *Little Boy* was loaded onto a trailer and taken to the loading pit. Because of the size of the bomb, it required the B-29 to be positioned over the weapon in the pit and then hoisted up into the bomb bay. At 2300hrs, the crews of the three aircraft that would make the actual bombing run assembled in the briefing room. The *Enola Gay* would carry the weapon. Colonel Paul Tibbets, the commanding officer of the 509th would pilot the delivery aircraft. The B-29 named the *Great Artiste* would carry blast measurement instrumentation. The *Necessary Evil* would provide strike observation and photography. Three other B-29's would provide weather reconnaissance over each of the three targets.

I received orders that I was to be an observer onboard the *Necessary Evil* aircraft. Groves wanted his own eyes on the culmination of his creation.

As with every step of the Manhattan Project, there was one last-minute bit of drama. Parsons became concerned about the risk associated with taking off with the fully armed bomb. Many a B-29 had crashed during takeoff. For the same reason *Little Boy* was a simple design, it also represented a risk in a crash. If the bomb was fully armed at takeoff, a crash could ignite the explosive cordite charge and detonate the weapon. All of Tinian could be destroyed, including the *Fat Man* bomb being readied. Everything would be irradiated by the radioactive fallout. Parsons told General Farrell he would rather arm the bomb once in flight. I was there when he told Farrell.

"Captain, that's against instructions. General Groves would not approve," Farrell said.

"It's a technical question, General. It's clearly the safer way. It should have been considered earlier," Parsons argued. "It's an oversight I'm correcting. Trust me."

"I know you're the expert, Captain, but do you know how difficult it will be to do this in the cramped bomb bay of a B-29?" Farrell said.

"I know. So I've practiced for the last several hours since the bomb was loaded in the aircraft. I can do it with my eyes closed. It's really not that difficult a procedure."

Farrell looked at me. "Your opinion, Major?"

The question was way out of my league both technically and politically. Groves would have a shit-fit. He didn't like changes of plans. He would have little regard for the risk of a takeoff crash. After all, risk came with command.

"I don't know enough to have an opinion, General," I said. "But Captain Parsons knows this bomb intimately. I would trust his judgment."

Farrell thought for several moments. "Very well, Captain. Proceed with your plan to arm the bomb after takeoff. Unfortunately, or fortunately, there's not enough time to get this cleared with General Groves. Don't screw this up, Captain. It'll be all our heads."

The *Enola Gay* rolled down the runway at Tinian at 0245hrs on Monday, August 6, 1945. Parsons completed arming the bomb at 0730hrs. It took him only fifteen minutes. The safety devices were then removed. At the same time, the weather plane reported only light clouds over the primary target. Tibbets announced they were heading for Hiroshima. The *Enola Gay* climbed to 32,000 feet.

At 0709hrs, air raid sirens on the ground sounded as the lone weather plane flew over Hiroshima. The sirens ceased at 0731hrs as the single B-29 weather aircraft flew off. At 0810hrs three more B-29's came into view. The sirens again sounded. Hardly anyone went to the shelters.

Hiroshima came into clear view for the air crews. The *Enola Gay* bombardier found the aiming point in the Norton bomb sight. The distinctive T-shaped Aioi Bridge lay at the city center.

The bomb bay doors opened. At 0815hrs, *Little Boy* was released. Tibbets immediately pulled the B-29 into a hard turn to gain speed and distance while the bomb fell the prescribed 43 seconds before detonation at 1900 feet by redundant altimeter firing circuits.

At two minutes before release, the *Enola Gay* blipped a radio signal. Just prior to the bomb release, the radio operator announced to the other escort B-29's, "Fifteen seconds she goes." The radio tone then became constant until release. My aircraft was standing off fifteen miles from the drop point. After the radio tone ceased signaling release of the bomb, I put the welding goggles to my eyes and counted the seconds to detonation.

First came the blinding light as with *Trinity*. Seconds later the B-29 was hit with the shock wave. The energy released by *Little Boy* was equivalent to 16,000 tons of TNT. Minutes later, the distinctive mushroom cloud rose eventually higher than our aircraft altitude. At its base was a roiling black cloud obscuring any view of the effects of the blast. I was told that would be the debris from the destruction of the city. Hiroshima ceased to exist.

After some initially uttered exclamations, the crew remained silent. We tried to grasp the scope of what we had just witnessed, what we had done. There was no cross-talk on the radio. After some minutes, Col. Tibbets radioed the order to return to Tinian.

After returning from the Hiroshima mission, I avoided the celebration of the flight crews. I sought out my friend Bob Serber. We sheltered in the mess tent over coffee.

"Tell me about what it looked like, Mike," Serber said.

"Awful I guess. Looked like *Trinity* but from a different angle. Same mushroom cloud. A beautiful clear day. Couldn't see any detail on the ground, just billowing smoke. Some evidence of fires. That was just as well. I'd rather not think about all the death down there."

"I'm scheduled to go on the next mission. You too I understand," Serber said. "If there's to be another mission."

"There will be, Bob. Groves is determined to drop *Fat Man*. And soon. The prevailing wisdom is to deliver a right upper-cut following the Hiroshima left-jab to finish Japan. The President was delighted after *Trinity*. The power of this thing is seductive. Besides, it has to be used in order to pay for itself."

Along with preparations for *Little Boy*, the *Fat Man* components had arrived on Tinian on August 2nd. The *Fat Man* bomb was now ready. Actually three separate assemblies arrived. There was every expectation that *Fat Man* would be used on another Japanese city within days. One assembly was expended testing the components without a nuclear core one last time.

I was correct. The announcement quickly came that *Fat Man* was scheduled to be dropped on August 11th. But weather again intervened, causing the schedule to be accelerated to Thursday, August 9th rather than be delayed.

On August 8th, *Fat Man* was situated in its loading pit and winched up into the B-29 named *Bock's Car*. At 10,200 pounds, it was only slightly heavier than *Little Boy*, but with a rotund shape like an egg. It was similar in length but with a girth of 60 inches. Still, it looked like a bomb with its stabilizing fins compared with its ungainly prototype twin detonated at *Trinity*.

The primary target was the Kokura Arsenal on the north shore of Kyushu. The secondary target was the port city of Nagasaki. The mission plan was the same as for Hiroshima. In this case two weather reconnaissance B-29's, a blast measurement instrumentation B-29, a photography B-29, and the delivery aircraft.

I was onboard the blast measurement instrumentation aircraft named *The Great Artiste*. Bob Serber was scheduled to operate the high-speed camera on the photographic aircraft, *Big Stink*. Unfortunately he forgot his parachute. The aircraft commander ordered him off and he missed the takeoff.

Major Charles Sweeny was at the controls of *Bock's Car*, the bomb delivery aircraft, when it took off from Tinian at 0345hrs on August 9th. Weather at both targets was reported clear by the reconnaissance aircraft. *Bock's Car* and my own aircraft, *The Great Artiste*, reached the rendezvous point thirty minutes from Kokura. We circled thirty minutes longer than the allotted waiting time for the photography B-29, *Big Stink*. During the delay, cloud cover moved in over Kokura.

Out of time, Sweeny finally ordered us to proceed to Kokura without *Big Stink*. When we arrived over Kokura, the aiming point was now obscured by cloud cover. Sweeny was under orders to drop the bomb only with visual aiming, not by radar. Sweeny made three bomb runs over the next fifty minutes but the bombardier was unable to make visual acquisition of the target.

By now Sweeny was becoming anxious. Fuel consumption became a critical factor. During the pre-flight checklist Sweeny had made the fateful decision to continue the mission after discovering an inoperable fuel transfer pump. This would rob him of accessing the 600 gallons of fuel in a reserve tank. The extra time waiting for the *Big Stink* now threatened their ability to return to Tinian.

The mission was in jeopardy. I alone among the crews possessed the additional concern about *Fat Man* even exploding successfully. It was an entirely different device than *Little Boy* that destroyed Hiroshima. Now we were headed for the secondary target with the delivery aircraft short on fuel.

Sweeny reduced power to conserve fuel and turned toward the secondary target, Nagasaki. Twenty minutes later we arrived on station over Nagasaki to find it obscured by clouds as well. With fuel levels now critical, Sweeny decided to disobey orders and release the bomb by radar targeting. He was out of time. The thought of landing with the armed atomic bomb was unnerving. With the extra weight of *Fat Man* in the bomb bay, they also did not have sufficient fuel to return to Tinian. Toward the end of their one and only bomb run, the bombardier was momentarily able to visually identify the target aiming point through a small break in the clouds.

At 1101hrs on August 9th, *Bock's Car* released *Fat Man*. Like *Little Boy*, it dropped for 43 seconds, exploding at an altitude of 1650 feet. The blast was substantially larger than the Hiroshima bomb with the equivalent of 21,000 tons of TNT. However, it missed the aiming point by one and a half miles. As a result, a major part of Nagasaki was shielded from the direct effects of the blast by intervening hills. Nagasaki was still essentially destroyed.

Later we learned that 70,000 people were killed at Hiroshima and another 100,000 injured. Half of those injured would die within days. At Nagasaki, the death toll was 40,000 from the initial blast, rising to 70,000 by the end of 1945. In both cities, eventually 54% of the population present during the bombings would die as a result of the atomic bombs.

Six days after the bombing of Nagasaki, Emperor Hirohito announced Japan's surrender. World War Two came to an abrupt end. The Soviet Union was put on notice. The United States had a bigger hammer and was prepared to use it.

CHAPTER 31

" YOU'RE TELLING ME you went on both the Hiroshima and Nagasaki bombing missions?" Victoria Prescott said. "I know this history intimately. There's no record of you on either *Necessary Evil* or *The Great Artiste*. How's that?"

"I don't know about that. Military record keeping probably. There were no journalists on Tinian. Only one journalist was allowed at *Trinity* for that matter. And it was a last minute thing. Groves called Farrell and told him I was to go the day before Hiroshima. Groves wanted his own man as close as possible. He did not want his information filtered. Groves trusted me to be his eyes and ears. That had been my role for two years."

They were again in the living room of Voronin's home. It was late morning. It had been less than a week since the elderly Voronin had agreed to collaborate with Prescott on her book in exchange to be allowed to die in peace. It was becoming easier for him to recount his extraordinary history. The confessional aspects were easier as he unburdened his betrayal of the United States. To her credit, Prescott was non-judgmental, although her questions were often uncomfortable for Voronin. It was like talking to a therapist. For this old dying man, he would never tell his story to anyone else.

"Let's go back a bit. Back to Los Alamos," Prescott said. "You mentioned Klaus Fuchs. Did you know him?"

"Met him a couple of times. A quiet mousy guy. He was somewhat friendly with Feynman. Worked in the Theoretical Division. Of course I never knew he was also a spy for the Soviets. His being found out and put on trial a few years after the War gave me sleepless nights for some time fearing I too might be found out."

"Historians claim that because of Fuchs, the Soviets not only developed their own fission bomb sooner, but may have also accelerated their thermonuclear bomb development."

"Maybe. He was part of Hans Bethe's Theoretical Physics Division. He knew most everything about the atomic bomb design. He even did calculations for Teller, so he understood Teller's work on the super bomb, the fusion thermonuclear weapon. I don't know what he gave the Soviets. Must have been difficult for him to pass information. Apparently dangerous too since he was eventually caught."

"Do you think your information was more important to Soviet Union's nuclear weapons development?"

"I have no way of knowing, Ms. Prescott. That's what you'll have to explore in your book I assume. I'll tell you this, what the Soviets got from me was the same as General Groves got. So that was literally everything. And on a regular basis since I was free to leave Los Alamos."

Prescott nodded, then asked, "Would you agree with the theory that your high-level data would have greatly assisted the Soviets when it was augmented by Fuchs more technically detailed intelligence?"

"Is that going to be the premise you'll argue in your book?"

"Well, it clearly makes sense. Not only Fuchs, but Greenglass and this Theodore Hall also passed technical data on the atomic bomb work. Your comprehensive reports, with unlimited access to everything, would have tied everything together. Before I press that conclusion, I will review the theory with various notable scientists."

"Once I'm gone of course," Voronin said.

Prescott was momentarily taken back with Voronin's matter of fact treatment of his impending death.

"Of course, Mr. Voronin. By the way, did you know David Greenglass? Or Theodore Hall?"

"I do not recall Greenglass, except from the Rosenberg trial publicity. As you can expect, I was deeply concerned with all the details of that trial in 1951. It was the following year after Fuchs was tried. It made me more anxious that somehow the FBI might find me out. From the newspapers I learned that the atomic bomb secrets that convicted Julius and Ethel Rosenberg of espionage came from Ethel's brother David Greenglass, apparently a SED technician at Los Alamos. The execution of the Rosenbergs was understandably unnerving."

"And Hall?" Prescott asked.

"Only read about him after these old Venona decryptions became public a couple of years ago."

"Did this new information coming out a few years ago about Soviet espionage from fifty years ago raise new concerns about your involvement being discovered?"

"Some concern of course. But I assumed if there was something incriminating about me in this old information, it probably would have surfaced long before. If not, I was now too old to worry anymore."

They broke for lunch. As was their routine for the last couple of days, she drove into the quaint downtown of Claremont. The streets were tree-lined, almost a Midwest feel. The San Gabriel Mountains loomed just to the north, shrouded in smog a good deal of the time, but spectacular on clear days.

Prescott drew some glances. She was that attractive. Voronin assumed everyone thought it must be his daughter but realized it would probably be *granddaughter*. Nice to be out with a pretty woman though. When had he gotten so old?

Back at Voronin's home, Prescott resumed, "You say you were conflicted about the morality of using the bomb, or about the United States being the sole possessor of such a weapon?"

"Both. But that wasn't unusual as you know. A lot of the scientists felt the same."

"Yet all of you still worked hard to create the Bomb. How do you reconcile that?"

"I don't. I'm not a psychologist."

"Was it like the camp guard at a concentration camp? Following orders, no alternative, that sort of defense?"

"Defense? I don't feel the need to defend anything. But no, it wasn't like the concentration camp guard. More like the guy that made the bombs the Nazis used. It was just a weapon."

"Well not exactly. It was a weapon of mass destruction. By design it was intended to kill large numbers of civilians. Wasn't it more like the guy who made the poison gas in World War One?"

"For the record, Ms. Prescott, you can state that I was conflicted but did my duty. Both sides killed civilians in large numbers in World War Two. I was just a minor cog in a vast machine. Regardless of all the political and pragmatic reasons for developing the atomic bomb, it still brought an abrupt end to the War. Except for a few who relished the idea of the power of the atomic bomb, most of us wrestled with all of these moral issues. But that's all it was, just thinking about these broader questions. Questions with no clear answers. So we just got on with our work. Got on with our lives."

Prescott looked at Voronin with a quizzical look. "But in your case, that was not really possible."

"No, of course not. I was still a spy. That did make my circumstances different."

"Do you believe you harmed others by spying for the Soviets?"

"Others? You mean people in general, or the United States?"

"You see a difference?"

"Of course. The government of the United States isn't necessarily the people of the United States. Stalin certainly wasn't Russia," Voronin said but paused for a moment. "But that's just intellectual fencing. Admittedly a poor argument at that. So I should be more honest. Sure I harmed people. I owed the government and the Army for their trust. I owed real people that trust. I betrayed that trust. Fortunately, most everyone that granted that trust is now dead. They won't be hurt when this comes out. The most harm was what it did to me. I had always had to hide my parents past. But they never did anything wrong, so it was just a necessary secret to get along. However, by spying for the Soviets I had done something fundamentally wrong. Now I maintained the secret of a criminal. I was a criminal. From the time I begin spying, I was never the same person."

"The most harm wasn't to you, or any particular person, Mr. Voronin. It was to the whole world. In large part because of you, the Soviet Union may have developed the atomic bomb sooner. Followed by the inevitable arms race. By your high-level espionage, you contributed to the Cold War and all the harm it did for over forty years."

"Don't lay the blame for the Cold War at my feet, Ms. Prescott. Others contributed. And that even ignores the fact that the Soviet Union would have developed their own atomic bomb without ever accessing U.S. technology. Would a couple of years have made any real difference?"

"History suggests it probably would have," Prescott said.

"Perhaps with those extra years, the United States would have acted aggressively just like many feared. Not sure that would have been a desired outcome. But all that is now moot with the dissolution of the Soviet Union. Just an academic debate between you historians."

Prescott ignored Voronin's barb with a smile. For an old guy he was not only still sharp but combative. Here was a spy, the one her grandfather had speculated about, but she still found herself liking the old devil.

"Yet you say your leftist leanings did not play a part in your willingness to spy for the Soviets. So how do you explain, or maybe reconcile is the better word, spying for the Soviets? When this comes out, there will be all sorts of analysis as to your motivations. This is your chance to put your own voice into the historical record."

"Not sure I really care, Ms. Prescott. But let's look at it this way. Forget that my parents were Communists. Forget that I loved my parents and therefore their politics shaped a lot of my thinking. Ignore the fact they returned to their homeland, Russia, at the time an ally of the United States, carrying the burden of fighting our common enemy. Leave all that aside even though the critics will not. It comes down to basically this; my wife was caught up in something that would destroy both of us. I was in love with her. I chose to protect her, protect us. I was not willing to give up our life together. In so doing, I became equally guilty. It's as simple as that. Self interest, survival, nothing more. Once started, there was no turning back. Everything else is rationalization. Put that in the book."

Prescott scribbled notes for several moments. Looking up she said, "But it became more complicated for that same reason. Once you learned that your wife and her parents had recruited you, that the wife you loved had only seduced you for political ideology, everything must have changed. By your own admission, she bound you to her by sexual gratification. You betrayed your country because of her then you discovered that you were duped. The whole thing was a charade. Would you like to know the background of your in-laws?"

Voronin nodded. "Yes, of course."

"I suspect they were at the heart of your *recruitment*. Their adopted daughter was probably raised to be an instrument of the family business. Boris and Vanya Ramazanov were Soviet agents when they first came to Canada."

Prescott recounted her research. First the valid aspects of the Ramazanovs background; immigration to Canada in 1925, Boris' chemical engineering degree, employment with E. I. du Pont in Montreal, their adoption of a six year old orphan girl, Elena Maximovna Obolensky, their immigration to the United States in 1942. Then she told him of her findings from the Russian archives.

"Ramazanov was not Boris' name. His real name was Dmytryk. The Soviet Red Army's GRU fabricated the Ramazanov identity. Dmytryk was a real chemical engineer, but he also had a background working for Red Army intelligence from its inception in 1918."

"And you found this out from old Russian records? That's impressive. Go on," Voronin said.

"Dmytryk was recruited into the Bolshevik Party by Vanya. He was recuperating in Moscow from wounds incurred during World war One. It was Vanya that provided the link to Ramazanov's real identity. The record of her marriage was in the name of Dmytryk. There was a false record of Dmytryk's death, and a false record of a university degree in the name of Ramazanov. Ramazanov/Dmytryk was working for Red Army Intelligence when he came to Canada. He was a mole until activated as World War Two approached."

"Because Boris married Vanya that makes him this intelligence officer Dmytryk?"

"Yes. Vanya Ramazanov's immigration application identifies her maiden name and background. The original record of her marriage to Dmytryk makes that link."

"You are that sure?"

"Yes. Because of the final evidence. Fingerprints of Dmytryk and Ramazanov prove they're the same person."

"I wonder then if Elena's adoption was by design to raise her to participate in the family spying business? That's a pretty disturbing thought," Voronin said.

A fit of coughing interrupted the conversation. Once recovered, he motioned for Prescott to continue.

"Would that make a difference how you felt toward her?"

"Interesting question. If she was raised to be a whore for her parents ideology would I condemn her less? Don't know. Just makes the circumstances more complicated."

"The trail leading to you was through Ramazanov. If Ramazanov was the code-named agent PUPPETEER from the Gouzenko files from Ottawa, then you had to be the high-value source within the Manhattan Project. That connection was made through records of one Lieutenant Colonel Feliks Antonovich Kirilov of the GRU. He was the guy running PUPPETEER/ Ramazanov from Moscow."

"So that was where Boris sent my intelligence reports?"

"Yes. Smart guy. Didn't trust normal communications. You were too important so he devised his own means as you described. That's why you were never discovered. No transmissions, therefore never any record showing up in the Venona decryptions. No couriers, no dead drops. So no Harry Gold that led to Klaus Fuchs and David Greenglass. Here's an old photo from 1938 when he was promoted to lieutenant colonel."

Voronin took the photograph. He stared at it for a long time before handing it back to Prescott.

"Did you know him?"

"No. Never heard the name. Just wanted to reflect on who was behind this."

"Unfortunately I couldn't interview him. Did well for himself, maybe because of you. Eventually promoted to major general. But he died in 1955 of unspecified natural causes."

"Apparently didn't leave much of trail in his own archives, although you seemed to have pieced things together. I was somewhat concerned when the Russians released old records about Soviet era espionage after the Soviet Union collapsed. Guess I can thank this Colonel Kirilov for being especially secretive."

"So now World War Two is over. You're going home. But to what? Nothing can be the same. What happened when you returned from the Pacific?"

Oak Ridge, TN, August 14, 1945

CHAPTER 32

WASHINGTON D.C. – SEPTEMBER, 1945

I REMAINED ON Tinian until September 3rd, the day after the official signing of the Japanese surrender on the *USS Missouri* in Tokyo Bay. No more atomic bombs would be dropped on Japan.

On the long flight back to the United States mainland I contemplated what I was about to do. There would be no further exchange of intelligence to the Soviet Union. More than that, I would sever the link with Moscow. If the Soviets retaliated, then I was prepared to accept the consequences. That was the least of it. Dealing with Elena, Boris, and Vanya was far uglier. But in that too I knew what needed to be done.

My orders were to return to Los Alamos. I was to assess the situation regarding the prevailing sentiments of the scientists. It was assumed that most of the top scientists would return to their pre-war academic positions. But there was a cadre of young middle-level scientists that might be persuaded to continue with the program. How did they feel about continuing further weapons development work? Which ones were important to the work? While most of the civilian scientific team resented the military, I was singularly accepted. Groves understood this and wanted to leverage that rapport. There was concern that an exodus of experienced personnel would cripple the post-war nuclear weapons program.

I was promised leave back to Washington D.C. within two weeks. That was fine by me. No hurry. No anticipation, only dread. I knew what I must do upon my return. My personal circumstances had reached critical mass.

The stint back at Los Alamos went by in a blur. Everything was anti-climatic. We had achieved this great thing now it was unclear what the next step would be. Washington had no defined post-war nuclear strategy. Most of the civilian scientists wanted to resume interrupted careers from before the war. Continuing to work for the Army to develop nuclear weapons technology held little interest. More than a few wanted nothing to do with bomb development. Personally, I was preoccupied with a greater dilemma.

I arrived back in Washington by air on a Thursday afternoon. Groves wanted a briefing the following day. Then I had three days leave. The problem was Thursday night. Elena would understandably want to make love. I was not sure I could fake it anymore. Not feeling well? Not convincing enough if I was still able to report to work the following day. Besides being away from a young wife for weeks, I would have to be on my deathbed not to want sex. I needed Elena to feel all was normal. I would be suggesting we take the train to see her parents on Saturday. Much to talk about. Playing sick was a not an option.

Elena knew my arrival time. She was at the airport to greet me. All kisses and physically affectionate. We took a taxi to the apartment.

"You don't look happy, Misha? Is everything alright?" she asked.

"I'm fine. Happy to see you. Happy to be home. But this has been a difficult two months. Nothing like it in history. A lot to come to grips with. Just coming down from the stress."

"I can't imagine. I knew about this test in the desert. You didn't tell me about using the atomic bomb against the Japanese right away."

"I didn't know the timing. That was a very closely held secret," I lied. "But you don't know the half of it. I was in an observation aircraft on both missions over Japan."

Elena jerked back in surprise.

"Oh my god! No wonder you're a little preoccupied. I can't wait to hear what that was like."

Before going home, I insisted stopping for an early dinner. The condemned man ate a hearty dinner. A couple of drinks also helped.

As expected, Elena wanted to make love once we entered the apartment. No excuses about showering. To ensure my agreement, she removed all her clothing and then pushed me back onto the bed. With her breasts in full view, she removed my clothes. Regardless of my hatred at her betrayal, it did not diminish my physical arousal. I knew she was not doing this based upon affection. Just as well since it would make things easier. On her knees, she took my now erect cock in her mouth as I sat on the bed. It was not difficult to act my part in this tragedy.

After lovemaking, Elena telephoned her parents. We would be in Wilmington Saturday afternoon on the four o'clock train. Friday night, I suggested we celebrate. By design, I drank too much, although not as much as it appeared.

Saturday, I feigned a hangover that was still with me into the afternoon.

"I bought this very good vodka for your parents. Not sure I'm going to have any though. I feel like shit after last night."

"No wonder, Darling. You should know better. But I guess you deserved it after what you've just been through. Hopefully Mother's made something for dinner that'll be easy on your stomach. Stick with tea, Darling."

At Union Station, I gave Elena money to buy two round-trip tickets while I went for coffees.

Boris and Vanya met us at the Wilmington train station. I put on a convincing act. Once we arrived at their house, Boris thrust letters into my hand with a broad smile.

"Mikhail, from your parents. They arrived a week ago. Thought it best to have them sent here."

I opened my mother's letter first. The writing *could have been hers*. Whoever did the forging was very good. But of course it was not from her. She was a prisoner in a Siberian labor camp. This letter spoke of Moscow. Things had returned to pre-war conditions. Food was now in better supply. Life was resuming some normalcy. All lies of course. To add insult, the forger had inserted a plea that hopefully the United States would assist Russia in recovering from the war devastation.

It was difficult to contain my revulsion as I read the letter out loud.

My father's letter was typed as was his style. But of course he was dead. Several years dead. More as a taunt to these forgers, I had laid a false trail in the letter to my father that I gave to Boris. Father was a Shakespeare scholar. He bristled at the conspiracy theories that Shakespeare's work was actually penned by someone else.

Edward de Vere, the 17th Earl of Oxford, had been one of several people speculated to be the true author of the celebrated works of William Shakespeare. All such speculations were founded only upon the humble circumstances of the relatively uneducated William Shakespeare of Stratford-upon-Avon. I had inserted a ridiculous reference in my letter to the effect that I had reread *Hamlet* and did not see how he felt it made a strong case for de Vere being the author.

This forged letter had my father making reference to similarities between Polonius of *Hamlet* and the Earl's guardian, William Cecil. De Vere did not cease his literary pursuits at an early age, but rather continued writing under the pen name of William Shakespeare. It was one of many unsubstantiated theories promoted in the early decades of the twentieth century. Easily found with a little research. The forger fell into the trap. I commented to Boris that my father was a little irrational on this particular conspiracy theory having researched this de Vere's life extensively.

"So tell us of these spectacular events. The news reports tell little except that these atomic bombs destroyed two cities," Boris said.

We were all seated in the living room.

"There's much to tell. Much to celebrate. I brought along a very good vodka to celebrate the ending of the War," I said.

I rose to retrieve the bottle from my suitcase. "Just three glasses, Vanya. I'm going to pass. I'm afraid I celebrated too much last night. Suffering for it today. Some tea would be easier on my stomach if you wouldn't mind."

Vanya put some water to boil. Once ready, she served me. I poured everyone shots of the vodka.

"Real Russian vodka. Where did you get this, Mikhail?" Boris asked.

"A high-end liquor store in D.C. Asked the guy for something special. He had this from before the War. I'd join you, but with the way my stomach feels, I'll stay with the tea."

We toasted to the end of the War. As the three of them downed the vodka, I refilled their glasses. Two shots would probably be enough. After an hour, the bottle was mostly gone. Within another thirty minutes, all three were asleep.

I formulated my plan right after the *Trinity* test. It was clear what I would do. Only the method needed to be worked out. To start, I feigned difficulty sleeping to the doctor on Tinian. He prescribed sedative chloral hydrate. For the month I was there, I accumulated a significant quantity. Enough to heavily doctor the bottle of vodka.

Chloral hydrate dissolves in alcohol remaining tasteless, thus forming the classic 'knockout drops'. I had to assume it would remain in the tissue of the body, but hoped it might be overlooked if autopsies were performed since the cause of death should be obvious.

I retrieved Boris' microfilm camera and unexposed film rolls from the removable floorboard he showed me under the bed. Boris was careful. There would be no other evidence. For good measure, I took his volume of Shakespeare's complete works.

I washed and dried my tea cup, careful to not leave fingerprints. Same for the vodka glasses which I replaced next to each person. From the cupboard, I took a bottle of Boris' vodka. Emptying all but a half-inch down the sink, I poured a little into each glass.

Raising the top to the kitchen gas range, I found the burner adjustment screws that controlled the mix of air to natural gas. The ideal mixture gave a blue-tipped flame. An oxygen-starved flame was yellow. Carbon monoxide gas is formed from partially combusted carbon-based fuels. The gas is colorless, tasteless, and odorless.

Carbon monoxide is highly toxic, combining with blood hemoglobin to produce carboxyhemoglobin, which is ineffective for delivering oxygen to bodily tissues. Worse yet, the effects are cumulative so even lower concentration levels can prove lethal if exposure is long enough. I adjusted all four burners and the oven to the lowest possible oxygen mix to produce the maxi-mum amount of carbon dioxide. I prepared two pots, one with potatoes, one with a roast. These were props for later.

For the last time, I touched Elena's cheek. I watched her chest rise and fall as she breathed. As keen as I was on committing her murder, tears still formed in my eyes. Rage? Loss? How had it come to this? I had loved her once.

I gathered my suitcase and the empty drugged vodka bottle. Fortuitously, it was a cool evening. All the windows would understandably be closed. I left the house. The sky was overcast as dusk descended suggesting a dark moonless night. The next several hours were spent sitting in Boris' car.

With a handkerchief covering my mouth and nose, I entered the house. With some difficulty I forced myself to reenter the living room. I checked for a pulse in the carotid artery of the necks for all three victims. They were all dead. I lingered briefly looking down on Elena. No time to lament since I didn't know how lethal the atmosphere might be.

After ducking outside, I took several renewing breaths and went back inside. I adjusted two of the four burners to normal air flow mix then turned them off. The two back burners were left air restricted. On these I put the two pots of food. I turned off the oven. It was to appear as an accident with just two burners malfunctioning as a result of the adjusting screws not being tightly secured. Would the investigators see it that way?

I locked the back door with Elena's key. There were no lights on within the neighboring house. I walked the two miles to the railroad station. The last train south to Washington left in thirty minutes. I was never here.

Two hours later I was back at Union Station. Again I walked home. There would be no cab drivers to recall me. I changed into uniform and went to a late-night bar, making sure to strike up a conversation with the bartender. I planned this well although it was never to be the perfect crime. Autopsies might reveal the chloral hydrate. Why were the burners improperly adjusted? Was I seen leaving the house? There were few late-night passengers on the southbound train back to D.C., but might the conductor recall my face? Even though they could recall me being at the bar, it was not a solid alibi. I still could have been in Wilmington at the time of the deaths by car or train.

It didn't matter. If I was caught, what was one more capital crime? It was time to end this. End this charade of a life. End the spying. Both connections were now severed.

I still had scenes to play. They must be convincing. First were calls to the Ramazanov house. It was long distance from Washington so there would be records. I called three times that night. The first time I literally jumped as the operator came on to announce there was no answer. For a brief moment, I thought Elena had answered the phone.

Early the next morning I placed two more calls. I then asked the operator to connect me with the Wilmington police. I stated my concerns, requesting a patrol car check on the house.

An hour later, my phone rang.

"Yes, this is Major Voronin."

"I'm very sorry to have to inform you, Sir. I'm afraid your wife and your in-laws were found dead. After receiving no response knocking on the door of the residence, our officers looked in the windows. Your family was seated in the living room, all apparently unconscious. The officers forced their way in but it was too late to save them. According to the fire department, the deaths appear to be from carbon monoxide poisoning. They mentioned a faulty kitchen stove as the source. I'm very sorry to have to break this news to you by telephone, Sir. Can you get up to Wilmington today? Unfortunately, we need you to positively identify the victims," the officer said.

I gave a rehearsed grief-stricken response. It was easier without having to be face to face. I dressed in a clean uniform. My eyes were suitably red and puffy from lack of sleep and too much coffee. I should appear suitably stricken.

It was Sunday. The remainder of the day was scripted. I took the train, and then checked in with the police. Escorted to the morgue in the basement of Wilmington General Hospital, I first viewed Elena's body. She was still beautiful even with the stark white pallor of an oxygen-deprived death. It was not difficult to feign grief. There was genuine grief. Grief over the circumstances that led to this terrible ending.

"Will autopsies have to be performed?" I asked the morgue attendant.

"Probably not. Once we get back the toxicology results, the cause of death as carbon monoxide poisoning should clearly be indicated. In the absence of external injury, I would think the medical examiner will forego a full autopsy. If that happens, we should be able to release the bodies in a few days."

I reported to General Groves Monday morning. He was aghast to here of my loss, immediately placing me on bereavement leave. Jean O'Leary, his personal secretary was beside herself. She and I liked each other. We both cried.

I returned to the apartment to wait. Waited and drank myself to sleep. Autopsies were not the issue. Would the chloral hydrate show up in the toxicology? Would it be sufficiently subtle as to be overlooked with the pronounced effects of the carbon monoxide on the blood hemoglobin as I had read? Would the pathologist simply be looking for the expected forensic evidence to validate the obvious? I half suspected a knock on the door from police investigators. Not that I would have really cared. I was barely holding on. What exactly did I have to live for?

There were no autopsies, nor any knock on the door. The bodies were released that Thursday. Cause of death was listed as accidental carbon monoxide poisoning. I buried Elena and the Ramazanovs on Sunday.

On Monday, I reported to the office. I pleaded to Groves the need to immerse myself in work as the best way to deal with my loss. The atomic weapons program was at a critical juncture with the ending of the War. Ever the opportunist, Groves leaped at the chance to redeploy me. I was needed at Los Alamos. Organizationally, I had a broad understanding of the bomb making program. A demonstrated record of understanding the enormous complexity of the Manhattan Project made me invaluable. This was one area of the military that would not scale back in the post-war era.

Beyond needing something to focus on, it would take me out of harm's way. I would be going back to Los Alamos, still the most secure military installation anywhere. If the Soviets wanted to reestablish contact, they would have a difficult time getting close to me.

I gave away everything in the apartment to the Salvation Army. Nothing of Elena's remained except for a single photograph. A photograph I took from behind as she looked out our apartment window. It was subtly erotic with her body visible through a sheer nightgown. It did not show her face.

CHAPTER 33

CLAREMONT, CALIFORNIA – 1998

PRESCOTT WAS AGAIN sitting with Voronin in his living room. For the last two hours he had related the events upon his return from the Pacific. She asked few questions sensing the aguish of those memories. At the conclusion, the old man seemed exhausted. Prescott was stunned with his telling of the murders. Not only was Voronin a Soviet spy, but a murderer as well. That confession made this out to be something more than a literary pursuit to rewrite history. She did not feel equipped to confront the pathology of an old triple murder. This had more the makings of a novel.

"Jesus Christ. I didn't see that coming." Prescott said. "I knew they died in an accident in 1945. I was waiting for you to eventually get to that. But not this."

"What did you expect? A convenient circumstance? My problem solved by a chance accident? I couldn't just walk away. I chose this instead. Severe the connection. Make it difficult for the Soviets to reestablish a connection. Remove the only known witnesses. It seemed to resolve everything."

"Somewhere along this long path of ..... whatever this could be characterized as, you had other options."

"Sure. The option to play the hero? Fall on my sword? Sorry, I was only being human. Survival won out over self sacrifice."

"So murder was preferable to just ending the relationship? Leave Elena, simply stop spying?"

"And risk going to prison?" Voronin said. "I was too important to the Soviets. They would hold that threat over my head. They would not let me just stop. They'd find a way."

"Nonsense. Why would they turn you over to the FBI? They'd get nothing out of it. It would only add fuel to the antagonisms at the War's end. You murdered them for revenge, Mr. Voronin. The Soviets killed your parents. Elena and her parents were part of that apparatus. They betrayed you. Elena most of all because you loved her. So you killed them."

"Are you qualified as a psychologist, Ms. Prescott, or is this just your opinion?"

She looked at Voronin for a moment. He perked up as she pushed him. Feisty guy for someone his age dying of cancer.

"At the least, if I left Elena I would be under constant threat that she, or Boris, or Vanya might give me up in the future if they were ever caught. I would be the ultimate bargaining chip. I would live forever in constant fear. Murder was the only solution that offered the prospect of freedom."

"Isn't your real motive obvious? Wasn't it purely revenge born out of your rage? Even this ending left the risk of going to jail so it wasn't a sure resolution. Wouldn't the penalty for murdering three people be worse than espionage?"

"Sure it was revenge. I was deeply in love with Elena. We enjoyed each others' company. She couldn't have faked that all of the time. I've told you of our physical attraction. Her strong sexual appetite. Even now I can't imagine she faked our lovemaking."

"Why not? The best call girls apparently fake intimacy with their practiced sexual performance."

In Prescott's view, Voronin was nothing more than an unrealistic romantic. Elena simply fucked him to make him do something contrary to his nature. Sexual obsession can do that. History is replete with endless examples. Voronin's story reads like a Greek tragedy.

Voronin shook his head. "You can't know what it was like together with her. I don't believe it was faked, at least not a good deal of our intimacy."

"Now I don't understand," Prescott said. "So a part of her loved you and that was a motive?"

"Her betrayal was all that more terrible because of it. I believe she probably loved me in her own way. Yet she was still willing to risk sacrificing both of us for her ideology. It may have been because of Boris and Vanya. I'm aware how my own parents influenced my thinking."

Prescott did not buy Voronin's rationalization of his wife's affections. She saw nothing more than a well planned honey-trap with a consummate actor. Elena Obolensky had only carried on this romance for two years. Well within the durational boundary of an espionage *assignment* by a trained agent. Regardless, Voronin's solution was the most practical. Sever ties to Soviet intelligence while eliminating the witnesses. Revenge may have been the catalyst, but the solution came from clear-eyed pragmatism. She would include Voronin's pronouncements, but that's the way she would write the history.

Prescott was irritated with herself for losing objectivity. This was not helpful to getting Voronin's story.

"You're right. I'm being judgmental. That's unfair. I don't know what I would have done. I'm sorry, Mr. Voronin. It's just troubling to hear about murder. It seems out of character."

Voronin nodded. He detected that at some level Victoria Prescott had come to like him. They bonded through the thread of a common history; he having lived that history while she knew it as a scholar. He had damaged that. She was right about her feelings. Nothing about his story evokes sympathy. Faced with moral crisis, he repeatedly responded with survival rather than a moral solution. Yes, he was trapped, betrayed, manipulated, coerced, threatened. Justification? Obviously there were alternative actions. He had never come to terms with his past, why should anyone else.

"You mean my story has turned ugly? Not just the intellectual game of giving away state secrets? Not the soap opera of love and betrayal? Just the real world. Way too much of a past for apologies. I suppose there is a part of me that wants to set the record straight. But I have no illusions how history will view me though. I expect no special sanitizing when you write this, Ms. Prescott."

"I intend to chronicle your story as best I can. This is to be a fact-based work. As to judgments, I will only include your own comments, not mine. Again, I didn't mean to moralize. That wasn't professional."

"No harm. Nothing wrong with letting your hair down. There's no criticism you could hurl at me that I haven't done to myself a hundred times over. Remember, I'm not relating this for some catharsis to unburden my sins or seek forgiveness. I'm telling you all this because we have a bargain. You get your historical blockbuster. In return I get your silence until I'm dead."

Prescott thought about the ramifications of her professional conduct in this whole matter. Was it ethical to strike a deal to withhold publication until Voronin was safely dead? Now with this revelation of murdering three people, did she have a legal obligation even though it happened over fifty years ago? Still, what was the alternative? See justice done by incarcerating this old man for his final months? She had given her word. Since it troubled her, there was obviously a basis for concern. Then again, only she and Voronin knew of the bargain to await his death before going public. Who's to say that the research did not conclude just as Voronin's cancer claimed his life?

They spent the rest of the day bantering back and forth.

"Tell me this, Ms. Prescott. How will I fare in history once your book is published?"

"Come now, Mr. Voronin, you can well imagine. Certainly vilified. Traitor. Cold War Communist sympathizer. The great Soviet spy that was never discovered. Of course everything about you, your parents, the Ramazanovs will be probed beyond what I write. After all, my book is about Soviet espionage not your biography."

"But I will be the star character in your book. I will make it a popular best seller, more like a novel than a scholarly work.

Prescott smiled. "It's too bad you will not be around to appreciate your notoriety. You seem to enjoy that thought."

Voronin shook his head. "Not really. Just exercising vicarious speculation. In the end, I am a villain. A terrible villain. A betrayer of my country. A murderer. Everything I grew up to honor I threw away. Only fitting I should be reviled. But I still wish it were otherwise.

"I'm somewhat tired now, Ms. Prescott. Let's resume these reminiscences tomorrow morning shall we?"

Prescott agreed. She needed a break as much as Voronin. With the revelations of the murders, there was a pit in her stomach. Fortunately, Voronin's story appeared to be at its end. Just as well. Hearing about these murders left a feeling of decided unease. Naturally there was more to his life that would need to be covered but that was just necessary filler. She was wrong.

The next morning they resumed. Voronin was unusually cheerful. He was dressed in pressed gray slacks, white shirt, and a navy blue cardigan sweater. Perhaps unburdening this terrible secret of the murders lighten his conscience. He announced he was making omelets for breakfast. Coffee was brewing. Like two old friends just having a chat.

Once breakfast was out of the way, Prescott asked, "So what did you do with the War over and ….."

"And no wife?" Voronin said. "No need to be delicate. I'll give you an abbreviated history for the remainder of the decade following the War."

They settled into their typical spots in the living room. Voronin sipped on his third cup of coffee. A bright California sun streamed through the windows. An incongruous setting to be discussing this old man's dark tale.

"Whether I embraced making atomic bombs or not, I had found a special niche in the Army. At the end of the War, the Army retained control over nuclear weapons development. Nothing changed including the leadership. The Atomic Energy Commission took control of atomic energy from the Manhattan Engineering District in January, 1947. To manage nuclear weapons, the Armed Forces Special Weapons Project, acronym AFSWP, was formed under control of the Army. The AFSWP was commanded by General Groves. Bomb making would remain under direct control of the Army. The only change was the inability to conscript scientists to work on nuclear bomb making. Groves wanted me on his staff, recognizing my abilities to work well with the civilian scientists. They would now be independent of Army control."

Voronin recounted major events in the immediate years following the War. He was promoted to lieutenant colonel in December, 1945. No small accomplishment with the demobilization of the war-time army. As a further inducement, he was allowed time to attend the University of New Mexico in Albuquerque to complete a masters degree in civil engineering. His knowledge of the nuclear weapons program was invaluable to the Army, particularly with the uncertainty following the War and the hemorrhaging loss of experienced technical staff.

In 1948, Voronin meets Teresa Johnson, the daughter of an army officer. She had interrupted her education in 1943, postponing entering law school at the University of New Mexico to join the Army Air Corps. She flew Army C-47 domestic flights, ferrying personnel and cargo. Remembering the frequent flyer, Major Voronin, shuttling between Los Alamos and Washington D.C., she recognized him one day at the university cafeteria. They married after six months. There had been no attempted contact by Soviet intelligence. After three years, that chapter in his life appeared closed.

"In 1949, the Soviets detonate their first atomic bomb test. What did you think at the time? Did you feel in some way responsible for their success?"

"I didn't really know. For all I knew, they were proceeding independently with their own program all along. My information may have been just helpful. When Fuchs, Greenglass, and the Rosenbergs were convicted of espionage in 1950, I felt the importance of my contribution was probably limited. Fuchs and Greenglass would have passed real technical details, equations and such. Mine were just reports, more valuable politically than scientifically."

"So you remained in the Army making nuclear weapons. Why is that?"

"Like I said, I had a specialty. I was good at what I did. Effective. Recognized. I hadn't done civil engineering for a long time. Perhaps a little apprehensive of going back into civilian life. So out of habit, I took the easy route. At any rate, I stayed in the Army until my twenty years were up in 1959. The Army paid for my graduate degree. Why not enjoy military retirement benefits and embark on a second career at age forty-five?"

"And after your retirement from the Army? What then?" Prescott asked.

"You mean did I live a normal life? Happily ever after into my comfortable old age? No that didn't happen. The rest of my life did not advance gracefully. Just like it's not even ending gracefully this late in my life. There's still more to tell you, Ms.

Prescott. More you haven't even guessed. For you the historian, my story gets even richer. I fear however, you will find it troubling as well."

CHAPTER 34

Operations Crossroads "Baker" test
Bikini Atoll, Micronesia, 1946

LOS ALAMOS, NEW MEXICO – 1946-1948

M Y PERIOD OF sham mourning consisted of two weeks. I worked light duty at the Washington office, suitably sad and withdrawn. Three days after the funeral in Wilmington, I was on a plane headed for Los Alamos.

The nuclear weapons program entered a time of uncertainty by 1946. Groves himself addressed the Los Alamos staff soon after the bombings of Hiroshima and Nagasaki. He wanted to avoid the expected mass exodus of large numbers of the civilian staff from the MED. President Truman was sponsoring an atomic energy bill that would establish a new federal agency to administer the nation's nuclear program. Los Alamos could be expected to continue as the principle research center for nuclear weapons. Unlike other areas of the enlarged wartime military, nuclear weapons development must move forward for security of the country. It would continue to be a challenging field for scientists and engineers.

Move forward it must. Even in 1946, it was becoming clear that the Soviet Union would be a future threat to U.S. security, although Groves was not that blunt in his address. International accords to limit nuclear weapons would not happen. The Soviet

Union could not afford to leave the U.S. in sole possession of nuclear weapons. Any agreement to curtail development would not be in their interest. From the opposing perspective, the U.S. needed to preserve its primacy to counter Soviet territorial designs in Europe. Restrictions on nuclear weapons development ran counter to strategic interests of both sides.

Groves seized on the changes of senior staff at Los Alamos to move bomb assembly operations to a location adjacent to Kirkland Field outside of Albuquerque. Kirkland was being developed to serve as a facility to load atomic bombs into specially modified B-29's after the war. Groves feared that bureaucratic infighting gave the nuclear weapons program an uncertain future. He felt that weapons should firmly remain under military control. The scientific aspects of nuclear energy would almost certainly fall under this new federal agency. Los Alamos would probably transfer to civilian control. Bomb assembly was more of an engineering operation than a scientific research function. Groves promoted the logic that as a weapon it was best kept under military control.

Robert Oppenheimer was the most visible defection from the project. His work was completed. He had delivered the atomic bomb. His foreboding thoughts about that creation were now even more evident. Oppenheimer was opposed to the creation of the 'super' fusion bomb on the grounds that it had no legitimate place as a weapon of war. He returned to his former academic position at Berkeley.

Groves took the opportunity to meld scientific leadership with a military person at the head of the Los Alamos Laboratory. Navy Commander Norris Bradbury was the former number two man in the Explosives Division, and in charge of assembly of the *Trinity gadget*. As a physicist, he was well respected by the civilian scientists.

So nuclear weapons development proceeded. Kenneth Nichols was recruited by Groves to reorganize the production of nuclear weapons. Nichols had been the Chief Engineer of the MED and managed the vast uranium enrichment operations at Oak Ridge, Tennessee. Nichols was promoted to brigadier general and set to work immediately to re-organize weapons production.

Up to this time, nuclear bombs had been laboratory devices. Improvements came incrementally. Scientists worked on all aspects of each bomb. The explosive lenses were hand-cast. The process was slow. Nichols recommended that production of bomb components be undertaken by outside contractors. Bomb assembly should be moved to the special military unit located at Sandia Base outside Albuquerque. This would free the scientists at Los Alamos to concentrate on advancing weapons technology. Nuclear weapons were about to be transformed to a manufactured product.

I fit right in with the post-war reality of nuclear weapons. I now reported directly to General Nichols, splitting my time between Los Alamos and Sandia.

By June of 1946, the United States possessed nuclear cores sufficient to assemble only nine bombs. These were *Fat Man*-type bombs the same as tested at *Trinity* and dropped on Nagasaki. Two of these were exploded in tests in the South Pacific to test the effects on naval ships. *Able Test* was an airborne explosion, followed three weeks later by an underwater detonation called *Baker Test*. I was present at both tests from an observer ship. To the Army Air Force's chagrin, many of the derelict ships survived the *Able* blast. The subsequent underwater *Baker Test* effectively destroyed the target fleet but only as a result of widespread radiation. Hundreds of sailors were exposed to harmful post-blast radiation. The unsuccessful decontamination effort was aborted after sixteen days. It was the world's first nuclear disaster. Yet another indicator of the dangerous new world order we had created.

1947 was an eventful year for me. In January, President Truman signed the Atomic Energy Act to bring control over nuclear technology. As part of that realignment to bring overall civilian control, military weaponry remained in the hands of the military with the formation of the Armed Forces Special Weapons Project. The AFSWP took over from the Manhattan Engineering District. General Groves was placed in command. The 2761st Engineering Battalion was established to assemble and maintain the country's nuclear arsenal of atomic bombs at Sandia. Groves appointed Colonel Gilbert Dorland as commander. I became his executive officer.

My role became even more vital. So many scientists had left Los Alamos in the year following the war, that it was unclear how many weapons could be counted as available. Not only components were in limited inventory, but the means to assemble into viable weapons was questionable with the loss of experienced technical personnel. I was one of maybe only four individuals that actually knew how few nuclear bombs the United States possessed. I felt relieved that I would no longer have to agonize over divulging such sensitive intelligence to the Soviets.

A year and a half after murdering Elena, I was beginning to feel life once again. I was enrolled in graduate school at the University of New Mexico in Albuquerque, pursuing my masters' degree in civil engineering. It was close to both Sandia and Los Alamos. Keen to retain me in the weapons program, I was allowed whatever time necessary to pursue my studies. The Army probably would have preferred a course of study more closely associated with my work, but I had aspirations beyond my military career.

It was at lunch in the university's cafeteria one day that things turned even brighter.

An attractive woman with dark hair approached my table, tray in hand, looking directly at me and smiling.

"My word. Aren't you Major Voronin? But now a colonel it seems."

I couldn't place the face.

She set her tray down across from me.

"I'm sorry. You probably wouldn't remember me without my cap. I flew you to and from Washington a number of times. Always wondered who you were and what you did, sometimes as the only passenger. I'm Teresa Johnson, formerly Lieutenant Johnson of the Women's Air Corps. Now I'm a student again after the War's interruption."

We finished our lunches and talked for a while. I learned she was enrolled in the school of law. I told her I was involved with classified work during the War. That was the reason for my commuting across the country. Still involved, so I could not tell her what I was doing for the Army.

"Obviously I can guess. Not much of a secret about what Los Alamos does, nor Sandia Base outside of town for that matter. But I won't press you with uncomfortable questions. Got to make my one-thirty class. So good to see you again, Colonel Voronin."

With that, she shook my hand again and left. Admittedly I felt stirrings. There was no wedding or engagement ring. She was attractive but different from Elena's charms. Where Elena was voluptuous, overtly sexy, Teresa was taller, slender, her face more angular, with a distinct expression of intelligence. Elena's eyes were animated, Teresa's penetrating. She wore minimal makeup. Elena was a seductress. Teresa would make a good lawyer.

The fleeting thought occurred to me that she might be another Soviet seduction lure. But rationally that made no sense. If the Soviets wanted to re-establish contact they would just do it directly. They did not need to entrap. That had already been accomplished.

Over the next several weeks, I saw Teresa Johnson only a couple of times from a distance around the campus. I found myself thinking a lot about her. One day again in the cafeteria I decided to try my luck and ask her out for dinner.

"I would love to, Colonel," she said. "About time. I thought maybe you weren't interested."

Teresa knew my work was classified and never asked uncomfortable questions. Her father was a retired Army general. She understood the drill.

We were married the following spring. While joyous with the promise of a life, it was equally disturbing. Here I was bringing Teresa into the sphere of my terrible past. If that past ever caught up to me, she too would be destroyed. Fortunately, children were not part of her immediate agenda. She was an overachiever with her sights set on a career in law, possibly politics.

While my personal life looked bright, the plight of the world was anything but. The exhausted western European nations of Great Britain, France, Belgium, and the Netherlands started to give up their colonies. This lead to the onset of local clashes as competing interests vied for power in the vacuum. Foremost among these great colonies of the nineteenth century was India. Now given statehood but divided into the states of India and Pakistan along religious lines. The first of many wars broke out resulting in the deaths of 400,000 people during the mass relocation migrations of Hindis and Muslims.

While Western Europe lay in ruin, the United States and the Soviet Union emerged as super powers. As for the Soviets, defeating Nazi Germany left them in possession of Eastern Europe and most of Germany. While ostensibly an ally, it was an alliance of convenience only. They had no intentions of retreating back to pre-World War Two borders.

Communists seized power in Poland in January, 1947. In May, President Truman proclaimed the Truman Doctrine vowing economic and military support for Greece and Turkey to remain outside the Soviet sphere of control. In August, Communists seized power in Hungary. In China, Mao Zedong was leading his Communist People's Liberation Army in a civil war for control of China against the U.S. supported forces of Chiang Kai-shek. In France and Italy, their respective Communist parties, with links to Moscow, gained considerable strength in the chaos of post-war Western Europe. The world had clearly begun to align itself between the United States and the Soviet Union.

While the Soviet Union increased its hostility toward the West, U.S. nuclear weapons control was still a contest between the newly created civilian Atomic Energy Commission and the military's Armed Forces Special Weapons Project. Not helping matters was General Leslie Groves. He had commanded the wartime Manhattan Project with almost absolute dictatorial powers. His abrasive, confrontational style made for a host of enemies, and few supporters. Seeing the handwriting on the wall, Groves opted for retirement early in 1948. His former deputy and chief engineer of the MED, Kenneth Nichols, now promoted to major general, took command.

I liked Nichols. He had Groves' level of intelligence cloaked in a personality that invited respect rather than intimidation. We worked well together when he ran Oak Ridge during the War. He immediately transferred me directly to his staff. I was in charge of special projects. Nichols wanted me to do the same job I did for Groves. I joined General Nichols immediate staff as his chief troubleshooter. This kept me based in New Mexico.

In June, 1948, the Soviets tested United States resolve directly. Post-war Germany was divided under occupation with the Soviets in the east and the Western Allies in the west. The city of Berlin was itself divided among the four victorious powers, but geographically lay within the Soviet occupied zone now known as East Germany. In a move to wrest total control of Berlin, the Soviets closed all rail, road, and canal access to the city. The United States responded in a massive airlift to supply the city for almost a year. The Cold War was officially launched. Nuclear weapons would soon become the coinage of international power.

While the concept of a super bomb based upon energy released when nuclear fusion took place originated early on within the Manhattan Project, it gained little attention, or resources. The demand to develop the simpler fission-based bomb was daunting enough. A fusion bomb was a quantum leap in theory from the as yet undeveloped fission weapon. The *super* was cloaked in complex mathematics, based upon aspects of physics not yet well understood.

Once the fission bomb became a reality, the lure of a weapon with the destructive power hundreds if not thousands of times more powerful than the *Fat Man* class of fission bomb, was compelling. While work on the next generation of fission bombs continued, these would lead to weapons that would top out at explosive yields of 160 kilotons of TNT equivalent, whereas the fusion bomb was expected to yield in the area of 10 *megatons*. The predicted nuclear arms race truly began. The Soviets would sometime soon develop a fission bomb. The destructive potential of a fusion bomb represented the next generation of nuclear weapons.

Edward Teller had proposed the concept of a fusion bomb as far back as 1942. While a brilliant theoretical physicist, Teller was a social misfit. He was arrogant and blunt, often acting impetuously. In the close community of Los Alamos, he irritated his neighbors by often playing the piano late into the night. Passed over to head the Theoretical Division of the Manhattan Project, he refused to do calculation work associated with the implosion design. He was therefore shunted aside from the main fission bomb development effort, but left to continue his singular work on the *super*.

I found Teller personally objectionable as well. Fancying himself a first-rate chess player, he challenged me once he found out that I was a well regarded player. After beating him two straight games, Teller stalked off saying nothing to me. I could have told him, chess is more than intellectual prowess.

The super fusion weapon and the fission weapon are however symbiotically connected. Quite simply, the fusion bomb required a fission explosion to generate the conditions sufficient for the appropriate nuclear fuel to undergo fusion. Whereas an uncontrolled chain reaction released the binding energy of atomic nuclei, fusion was a forced-combining of nuclei. Fusion was known only to take place as the process fueling stars.

Thermonuclear generated fusion was the next logical evolutionary step in weapons development. The political climate of the post-war United States seemed to demand a wholesale arms race to counter Soviet imperialistic aspirations. It was a competition of product innovation.

While Teller was a gifted theoretical physicist, he had shortcomings working with the esoteric mathematics demanded for resolving the problems of creating a fusion bomb. Fortunately, several other brilliant scientists remained involved with the weapons development program after the war. Hans Bethe, although initially opposed to development of a fusion weapon, continued his contribution in the theoretical realm. John von Neumann, considered by many the foremost mathematician of the latter twentieth century continued as a contributing consultant. Stanislaw Ulam, a mathematician at Los Alamos since early 1944, would provide the key to solving the method by which a fusion bomb could become a workable device. The combined mathematical work by von Neumann and Ulam had solved the intractable problem associated with the explosive lenses design making the implosion fission bomb possible.

The secret to solving the fusion bomb problems lay in the application of a new realm of mathematics. Much of Edward Tellers' prior work on his 'classical Super' was flawed. Only the underlying physics was valid. Oppenheimer later remarked that had the Soviets pursued his design, it would have almost certainly retarded their progress. Later when the news of Klaus Fuchs wartime spying for the Soviets became public in 1950, I knew that he could not have imparted much worthwhile intelligence related to the fusion bomb to the Soviets. Since Fuchs worked within the Theoretical Division he had access to virtually all technical information. So the Soviets would surely have benefited from his fission-related intelligence. But Fuchs' work with Teller would have yielded nothing of real value associated with early work on a fusion bomb since it was nowhere near what became a workable design.

After the Soviets detonated their first fission bomb test in 1949, U.S. efforts to develop the more powerful thermonuclear fusion bomb took on new priority. Teller returned to Los Alamos in 1950 to join Ulam and others in the heighten weapons development program.

The design of what would become known as the Teller-Ulam design was ultimately straight forward from an engineering perspective. What materialized looked in simplest form something like this. It would remain the foundation for all thermonuclear weapons into the future.

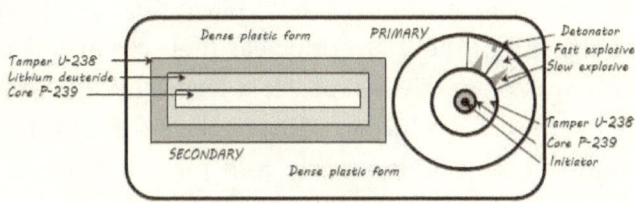

It was a given that for nuclear fusion to take place, it would take the enormous energy of a super-critical fission chain reaction as the primary event to create the necessary conditions.

Stanislaw Ulam's contribution was a different look at what happens within the early stages of the fission fireball which radiates most of its energy in the form of X-rays. Fusion takes place when the hydrogen isotope deuterium is heated to tens of millions of degrees thereby overcoming the positive electrical repulsion of the nuclei causing them to fuse into the next heaviest element helium. Hence the name hydrogen bomb, or thermonuclear bomb.

The previous designs, Teller's work principally, conceived of placing the thermonuclear fuel intended to undergo fusion spherically adjacent to the fission fuel. Such a design relied on heating the fusion fuel hydrodynamically. The result would be an unmanageable, an even fatter *Fat Man*. The mathematics further denied its workability. The device would simply blow apart before fusion occurred.

Ulam had the seemingly counterintuitive idea that if the fusion fuel were physically separated from the fission primary event, the enormous flux of X-rays could be made to start the thermonuclear fusion event. Since X-rays traveled at the speed of light it could reach the secondary fusion fuel assembly for that fraction of a second before the shock wave blew apart the assembly.

While the X-rays could heat the secondary assembly, that by itself would not cause fusion to take place. Compression to increase the density of the thermonuclear fuel was also necessary. The answer was elegantly simple. If a large flux of X-rays was discharged within a body of ordinary dense plastic form, the plastic would heat instantaneously to a plasma state. Wrapped around a cylinder of thermonuclear fuel, the super-heated plastic would exert a compressive force thousands of times more intense than the high-explosive lenses used in the primary fission detonation. The secondary fusion assembly turned out to be much easier to construct than the more precision primary fission bomb that acted as the trigger.

The resulting design could be contained within a cylindrical casing manageable in size for delivery by aircraft, although twice as heavy as the Nagasaki *Fat Man* bomb. At one end of the casing was a small version of the *Fat Man* implosion device. When it detonated, the X-rays radiated into the plastic surrounding the thermonuclear core, heating and compressing the core of lithium deuteride. When bombarded with sufficient neutrons, tritium, a heavy isotope of hydrogen is produced which is capable of undergoing nuclear fusion. Inside the lithium deuteride is a hollow cylinder of plutonium-239 or uranium-235. When compressed, it becomes super-critical and adds further to the complex process with a tertiary fission explosion.

The super fusion bomb was ultimately rather simple in construction once the extraordinary complex geometry of physical forces was worked out mathematically. So elegant was the design that it obviously would allow for future refinements for increasing yields and reducing physical size.

Stanislaw Ulam's contribution was the breakthrough to creating the thermonuclear bomb. Ulam was a pleasant engaging guy, while Edward Teller, the jerk, became known as the father of H-bomb. Ulam had as much claim to delivering both the A-bomb and the H-bomb as anyone, yet few would know his name today. Such are the distortions of popular history.

The Cold War took on the face of things to come on August 29, 1949 when the Soviet Union detonated its first nuclear bomb on the steppes of Kazakhstan. The United States was stunned. U.S. Intelligence had suggested the Soviets were still some years away. The bomb was remarkably like the Nagasaki *Fat Man* bomb, with a comparable yield.

From the President on down, a clear new challenge with a new enemy emerged to once again place United States nuclear weapons development as its singular strategic priority. The arms race erupted in full force. A renewed wartime-like urgency enveloped U.S. nuclear weapons development.

CHAPTER 35

"THINGS OF COURSE got much worse for the world in 1950 when North Korea invaded South Korea. With Korea, the Cold War almost became world war three. The face of Communism now had real weapons. American soldiers were dying at the hands of this new enemy," Voronin said.

"Before moving on with other things in 1950, tell me about what was going on in your mind with the disclosure that Klaus Fuchs was a Soviet spy," Victoria Prescott said. She knew the history of the period. Voronin's personal circumstances were more of interest.

"It was unsettling to say the least. Couldn't help wondering how safe I was."

"You know that Fuchs got caught from the same source that eventually led me to you," Prescott said.

"How's that? I don't recall the newspapers at the time saying how he was discovered."

"The GRU cipher clerk in Ottawa, Igor Gouzenko. When he defected in 1945, the intelligence materials he brought with him led to cracking Soviet transmissions. That led to Fuchs now in Great Britain. Fuchs gave up Harry Gold his courier. Gold led to

David Greenglass, which then led to Julius and Ethel Rosenberg. Gouzenko's intelligence documents also made mention of a Soviet agent code named PUPPETEER. PUPPETEER of course turned out to be Boris Ramazanov which eventually led me to you."

Voronin nodded.

"Those trials must have been even more unnerving for you. Especially the Rosenberg executions," Prescott said.

Voronin recalled those memories. It was indeed a terrible time. He was sure the FBI would eventually come for him.

"The heightened stress from those trials never did leave me. It was like living with a bad heart that might terminate you at any time. But what I recall most is the depth of guilt I felt at the time for exposing Teresa to the possibility of such a catastrophe."

"But it seems that the mechanism for transmitting your intelligence proved secure. This Colonel Kirilov running you from Moscow knew what he was doing. Kept your channel of communications out of the Soviet intelligence mainstream. So nothing ever led to Boris Ramazanov."

"Lucky for me. But then again you found me. I didn't beat out the throw to home plate."

"I don't know about that. You won't be hounded. You won't go to prison."

"Only because my mortality will beat you to it. What would you have done had I not been dying, Ms. Prescott?"

For a sick old man, Voronin still had all his wits. Too bad their time together was almost over. Too bad his life was almost over. Nothing personal, but she thought about what a sensation his exposure would make.

"You know the answer, Mr. Voronin. I would have gone public with my research. You would have been exposed. An extraordinary news sensation. You would probably have been arrested. Spent the rest of your days in prison. I'm glad that didn't happen. Better this way."

"Easy for you to say. You're not the one dying."

"Sorry. I didn't mean it the way it sounded."

Voronin smiled. "I know. Just being difficult. The preroga-
tive of an old man."

Prescott sighed and smiled. Time to wind this down. The rest
of Mikhail Voronin's life would be anticlimactic. Remarried. Retired from the Army. Taught engineering the remainder of his
working career. Second wife died of cancer. Retired to a pleasant
neighborhood in Southern California. That left only the indeli-
cate arrangements of how she was to inherit the various documents Voronin promised her after he died.

"I think we've come to the end of our journey into your
past, Mr. Voronin. Not to diminish the last fifty years of what
appears to be a productive life, but that's not compelling history
is it?"

"No. Only to me. So how will you summarize the importance
of my nefarious career as a Soviet World War Two spy?"

"Up to now, history suggests that the body of atomic intelligence secreted to the Soviets by Klaus Fuchs advanced their nuclear weapons program by years. Debates on that point are endless. The Soviets themselves contend it was of little significance.
Others say the Soviet program was already well advanced,
hampered only by access to natural uranium and the same problems of enriching sufficient quantities as experienced by the
Americans. But the prevailing wisdom was that it was enor-
mously helpful.

"Now add to that the parallel intelligence coming from you
from the highest level of access to the most secret of all U.S. activities. With your comprehensive understanding of every piece
of the Manhattan Project, organized into reports for Groves himself, the historical record will change. I suspect your intelligence
was perhaps much more helpful on the processes for producing
the fissile material. Fuchs material would have been more associated with the bomb design. While Fuchs provided technical

detail, you provided assessments of resources, people, capabilities, and even strategic thinking of the U.S. leadership. At the least, your intelligence would allow the Soviets to avoid the errors and unproductive paths encountered by the Americans.

"Together, this adds overwhelming weight to the success of the Soviet ENORMOZ penetration to advance the Soviet atomic bomb by many years. It wasn't a question of you *or* Fuchs being more damaging, it was you *and* Fuchs together. That in turn gave us the Cold War. Had the Soviets tested their own A-bomb much later than 1949, the world would have arguably been much different these last fifty years."

"So I will share the historical stage of this infamy with the shy Mr. Fuchs. If only it were so. It is not a boast when I say, that unfortunately I bear even more of the blame for the timing of Soviet nuclear parity with the United States."

"How is that? What makes your intelligence seemingly more important than Fuchs?"

"Because Fuchs left Los Alamos in 1946."

"I know that. But I still don't understand what you're getting at. You severed your spying activities with death of your wife and the Ramazanovs."

"My point is that Fuchs could have only passed on useful intelligence for the fission bomb design. The meaningful work on the *super*, the thermonuclear bomb, began after the War."

"But that's not actually correct as you know yourself, Mr. Voronin. Teller was working on this for years. Fuchs was doing calculations for Teller. So he would have passed that on to the Soviets."

"I'm sure he did. But that's my point. Teller promulgated the basic theory of a fusion-based weapon, but all his design concepts were unworkable. He got it all wrong. It wasn't until Stanislaw Ulam conceived his unique practical concept that meaningful development work moved forward. The mathematics was worked out after 1946. But all that was after Fuchs left the U.S.

program and returned to Great Britain. Fuchs didn't have access to anything of value related to thermonuclear bomb design after leaving. Worse yet for the Soviets, Fuchs earlier information would have caused delays had they actually pursued any of Teller's original work."

"Ok. So according to you, Fuchs' intelligence wouldn't have been helpful for developing thermonuclear weapons. Fuchs left Los Alamos and you severed your ties to the Soviets with the deaths of your wife and the Ramazanovs. So how would ....."

"You don't know do you?"

"Know what?"

"Your research was incomplete, Ms. Prescott. Your history, my story didn't end with the murders in 1945."

Prescott looked at Voronin wide-eyed. What was he getting at?

"You see, I resumed spying for the Soviets. That happened in 1949."

"What? Why in God's name would you do that? You hated the Soviets for everything they did to you. They killed your father. Sent your mother to die in a Siberian Gulag labor camp. You even committed a triple-murder to extricate yourself."

"It wasn't that simple. Nothing ever is of course. Let me tell you what happened."

ENIAC computer working on H-bomb calculations

CHAPTER 36

SANTA FE, NEW MEXICO – 1949

LIFE HAD TAKEN a decided turn for the better. The spying and the nightmare of the murders had receded to a manageable place in my mind after three years. I completed my master's degree, assuring me of a career when I retired from the Army after my twenty years. I was only thirty-four yet held the rank of lieutenant colonel. My Army job was rewarding with prestige. I could retire with a military pension and still pursue a second career in engineering.

I was happily married. Teresa and I were a good fit. Intellectually we shared each other's interests. I taught her chess. She taught me politics. We both read and enjoyed discussing literature. We loved the artistic atmosphere of Santa Fe. Both of us decided to try our hand at painting. Our lovemaking was frequent and fulfilling. While not the raw abandoned sex as with Elena, Teresa was every bit as enthusiastic.

Teresa graduated from law school and passed the bar the first time. She was now working in the New Mexico Governor's office in Santa Fe. She was excited about the prospects of her own career. Since I split my time between Los Alamos outside of Santa Fe, and Sandia Base outside of Albuquerque, a ninety-minute drive away, we could live conveniently in picturesque Santa Fe rather than boring Albuquerque. We bought a Spanish Southwestern-style house two miles outside of Santa Fe. It was tastefully decorated with local art. Great view of the mountains. For the first time in my life, we had a wide circle of friends and entertained frequently. Teresa's family warmly accepted me.

One remnant of the past however continued to torment me; the unknown fate of my poor mother. The terrible suffering inflicted on her. Was she still alive? No way to ever know unless by some miracle she could get another letter smuggled out of the labor camp. It had been three years since I had heard from her. This would now be her sixth year in the Gulag camp. Lurid accounts of conditions within Stalin's Siberian labor camps made their way into the western press. Difficult to see how anyone could survive such deprivations. I would never know. The Cold War effectively sealed off any communications of any sort with the Soviet Union. To my new family, I recounted the return of my parents to Russia only to have them die during the War.

Since my own life had turned so much for the better, there was a constant nagging horror imagining the fate of mother. I hoped she wasn't suffering, but that could only mean she was then dead.

Late one morning in March, I had driven back to Santa Fe from Sandia Base. I had been there for three days supervising the inventorying of bomb components. I was responsible for assessing how many functional nuclear bombs actually existed within the United States arsenal. Unfortunately, Teresa could not get away for lunch, so I planned a nice dinner out that evening. Free for the afternoon, I decided to relax by visiting a favorite Santa Fe art gallery.

After an hour browsing the galley, I decided I was hungry. A light snow had been falling all morning, accumulating to a couple of inches. I brushed off the car windows of my olive green army sedan. Backing out of the parking lot I felt the sickening sound and jolt of a light collision. In the mirror I could see I had hit another car. Shit. How did that happen? The parking lot was practically empty.

I got out. The other car's rear bumper was up against mine. Looked like we both backed out the same time from opposite directions. A well dressed woman got out of the other car.

"Oh my! I'm so sorry. It was probably my fault," the woman said.

I looked at the two bumpers. No real damage, just some scratches.

"Doesn't look like any real damage to either car actually. We should both be more careful," I said.

"I have a message for you, Colonel Voronin. Someone from Moscow wants to meet with you."

Her words paralyzed me. I suddenly felt light-headed. How could I have thought they were through with me?

"What did you say?"

The woman repeated the message.

"Who are you? What the hell are you talking about? I don't know anyone from Moscow. Furthermore, why would I want to meet with a stranger?"

"Because that person has news about your mother."

"My mother? What news?"

"I don't know. I'm just delivering the message. The person you're to see is at the La Fonda, in the dining room waiting for us."

I had no choice if this was about my mother. We both drove the few blocks and parked. The La Fonda Hotel on San Francisco Street had been a fixture in Santa Fe for generations. I followed the woman to a booth in the lounge where a man in a dark gray suit was seated. Seeing us, he rose and extended his hand. I did not take it. Whoever he was, this was a hostile encounter. The woman left us alone taking a seat at the bar.

"Please sit down, Colonel. I can image how you must feel right now," the man said.

He was trim, slender build, probably early forties. The suit and tie were good quality. He spoke excellent English but with a decided accent I recognized as Russian. Still, I did not know which side he was on. This could be an FBI subterfuge to make me incriminate myself.

"You can also address me as 'colonel'. We can therefore pursue our discussions as equals.

"Who are you really?

"For obvious reasons, it is better that my identity remains unknown. The code name COLONEL will suffice. Let us say I'm with Soviet intelligence. I have always been your Control. So I know you quite well, Mikhail Stefanovich."

The Russian proceeded to tell me particulars about Boris and Vanya Ramazanov, and Elena. He explained in detail how Boris transmitted my intelligence, including the mechanism for randomly identifying the Shakespearian sonnet to be used as the key for each one-time-pad cipher. If the Russian were really FBI, then they had me dead to rights. It wouldn't seem they'd need anything further to warrant my arrest. So he was a Soviet.

"Their deaths were a great tragedy to all of us. I understood you were very much in love with your late wife. My belated condolences. Your information was of great value. That was a great loss for your Motherland when the flow of information ceased. I assumed that you might leave the nuclear weapons program after the end of the War. Perhaps even leave the Army like so many others with the demobilization. To my surprise, you stayed on. And still involved at the center of the American bomb making effort. As this international contest between our two countries has escalated, you naturally became of great interest once again."

At least he didn't know I had murdered his agents.

"I have always been sensitive about protecting your identity. How to reestablish contact without involving others required careful planning. That is why it has taken a long time. That is why I have personally come here at great personal risk."

I wasn't buying any of this. My mother was the only reason for listening to him.

"You said you had news about my mother?"

"Very well. You of course have not heard from your parents for several years. I must sadly report that your father is dead. Some illness toward the end of the War. Unfortunately, your mother is in a labor camp in the East. For some reason she was declared an enemy of the state. I understand she is in reasonably good health. But of course, conditions there are hard, especially for a woman your mother's age."

The COLONEL was still playing out the Ramazanov subterfuge unaware that I knew the truth of my parents' fate years ago. I feigned shock as if hearing this for the first time.

"A Siberian labor camp? Enemy of the state? That's ridiculous bullshit. Russia is ruled by nothing more than a modern-day tsar. The Tsar's Okhrana of my parents' youth is now the NKVD. She was sent to the labor camps because of Stalin's megalomania. Stalin's a fucking monster no different than Hitler."

"I'm not with the NKVD. It is true they have committed many excesses. Finding a way to offer you the ability to save your mother was not easy. That is why it has taken so long to reestablish contact with you."

"To find the means to force my cooperation you mean."

"Nevertheless, that is your mother's unfortunate circumstance. Unless of course you help her," the Russian said, choosing not to engage me in argument. He then extracted a letter from his inside jacket pocket.

"Please read this. It's from your mother. From just two weeks ago. She was also asked to write some personal antidote in order for you to know it is really her writing this."

I opened the letter eagerly. A photograph fell out. I looked aghast at my mother's image. A tattered quilted coat with her head wrapped in a babushka made her look like a Russian peasant. She had aged beyond her years. This was the face of an old woman, but she was not yet sixty.

My Dear Misha,

I do not know what is going on, but some men came to see me. They said they were from Moscow. They told me of the death of your wife several years ago. I'm so sorry, my dear. They also said you were helping Russia during the War but they did not say how. Whatever that was, they want you to resume.

They apologized for what happened to your father and me. They explained that the Soviet Government was a very complex mechanism. Mistakes were sometimes made. I did not understand their meaning. They said they were not from that part of the government responsible for my imprisonment. That was the internal security organ. They worked for Soviet foreign intelligence. Because of your importance to the State, they said that they were authorized to have me released from this place and returned to Moscow. There I would be well cared for, given a small apartment, provided food and medical care. This in exchange for your helping them.

I beg you to resume whatever you were doing and save me from this place. I will not live long here. Please help your mother, Misha. I have lost everything else. I hope to survive and see you again one day.

They asked me to provide some antidote by which you will know that it is me writing this. I thought that odd, but so be it. I recall the time when shortly before you left for the university, you beat your father at chess for the first time. That ending was N–K6, KxN, Q–Q5ch, K–B3, Q–KB5. Your

father was checkmated. I remember the moves because your
father was so proud. He replayed me that ending many times.
  I love you my dearest,
  Mother

The Russian was who he said he was. I had almost wished he were FBI so this would end. The disease had only been in remission. False hope for the patient.

"So that's the deal. I give you secrets in exchange for my mother's release from your Siberian concentration camp. In effect she becomes a hostage," I said.

"A crude analogy, but essentially accurate, Mikhail Stefanovich. However, your mother is not the only one affected. Even assuming you care nothing for yourself, your new wife's life would be ruined if you were to be arrested as a spy. She would forever be marked as the wife of the celebrated spy, Mikhail Voronin."

"So you threaten me with exposure? Where's the profit in that for your side? I believe that is just a bluff."

"It would deter others from such rebellion. I assure you it is not an idle threat. We would have nothing to lose if you do not reengage with us. A great political victory would at least be salvaged. But I would hope it does not come to that, Colonel Voronin."

I looked at the Russian. He was immune to my hatred. This was just business and he held all the advantage. I knew I had no choice. How could I abandon my mother to die in such a place? I had already committed such terrible sins, what was lost in continuing for the sake of saving my mother? And saving myself.

"How will this work?" I was trapped. Reconciled into sinking back into this terrible alternative life, I wanted nothing more than to understand the procedures and get away from these people.

"Simply and securely. First of all, Jacqueline, the woman who brought you here shall be your conduit of communication. You will send your materials by microfilm photographs using this."

The Russian handed me a miniature camera under the table. I took a furtive look then put it in my pocket.

"Use of the camera is quite simple." The Russian passed me another packet under the table. "Here are several rolls of film. Now all you need to do is ....."

"I know how to use this. Then what?"

"Very well. You are to photograph your material and place the exposed film inside a package of cigarettes under the sealed portion of the pack and concealed from the light by the cigarettes. Do this in the dark. In this way, if someone...."

"If someone other than the intended person got hold of this, they would most likely destroy the film by exposing it to light. Boris Ramazanov explained the method."

"Of course. Now when you have information to pass on, you will call this number. Let it ring three times then hang up. No one will answer. The next day, place the cigarette package on the front seat of your car. The first time, leave the car unlocked and place a duplicate key under the passenger seat. From then on, Jacqueline will have the spare key."

"She is to be my only contact?"

"Yes. For your security, she is the only person other than me that knows your identity. She is an American citizen with a real job. She has no other assignment but you so there is no risk of her being discovered because of some other operation. Conveniently she lives in Albuquerque. It's her real identity. No need for a fabricated cover."

"And how does she get the information to Moscow?"

"She mails the microfilm to one of several people who do not know her. By the way, no fingerprints should be on the microfilm. Use surgical gloves. The microfilm is then hand-delivered to the Soviet Consulate in New York. From there it goes by diplomatic pouch to Moscow. No transmissions subject to American decryption efforts of signals traffic.

"Now as to how you will prepare your material. For added security it needs to be encrypted. You will use the same method that Ramazanov used. You are familiar with how that was done?"

"I am familiar with how that works. It's called a one-time-pad cipher. Boris explained how the key was based upon starting at a point within Shakespeare's sonnets based upon a mathematical algorithm. I did much of the encryption myself. So what algorithm applies here?"

The Russian looked at me with a slightly raised eyebrow.

"I'm impressed with your understanding of tradecraft, Colonel. In this case you will use the serial number on the cigarette package used to convey the microfilm. Here's how it works."

The Russian withdrew a pack of American cigarettes from his pocket. He then described how this would identify the Shakespearian sonnet number, the line, followed by the letter position where the cipher key would start.

The Russian continued the instructions. "From time to time, Jacqueline may need to meet face-to-face to pass instructions. Nothing is ever written to leave a trail. In that case she will leave a restaurant business card on your car seat indicating a meeting time. If ever questioned, you could claim an affair. Jacqueline lives in Albuquerque so this would be plausible with your work at Sandia. But of course it will never come to that."

"What if I need to meet with her? How do I contact her?"

"That should be very infrequently," the Russian said. "However, if that is ever necessary, dial the same telephone number and let it ring six times. Jacqueline will place a business card on your car seat with a rendezvous location and time."

This was a terrible nightmare. Everything I saw as hope for a normal future was shattered. In every way possible I hated the

Soviet Union. Now to save my mother I would have to again do the unthinkable. I remained silent for several moments just starring at the Russian.

He starred back expressionless, continuing to chain-smoke, making a ritual of lighting each cigarette with a gold lighter.

"Nothing happens until I know my mother has been removed from the camp. Back to Moscow."

"That will be arranged immediately upon my return to Moscow," the Russian said. "I assume then we have an understanding?"

"I have no choice do I? But I don't trust you bastards. I will need proof that my mother is being well treated. How do you suggest I can be satisfied on that account?"

The Russian thought for a moment while lighting another cigarette.

"Very well. What about each month you receive a photograph of your mother and a letter? You will see she her circumstances are as I have promised."

All sorts of scenarios occurred to me how the Soviets might manipulate the photography and force my mother to write what they told her. She could still be in Siberia for all I would know. There wasn't much I could do but I needed to assert some measure of control.

"Let's add a variation to that. The photograph each month is to be somewhere recognizable in Moscow. She will also be holding the front page of the New York Times which will validate the date."

Another idea came to me. Not perfect, but at least something. The Soviets could circumvent it but not without an unknown risk that I calculated they would not take.

"To know that my mother is being well treated, she and I will engage in a running chess match. My mother learned chess from my father as I did. She is a good player. You know that I am more than just a very good player. My mother could never beat me. I know her style of play. I suggest you do not try deceiving me and use some chess master to make her moves. I will know."

"How very clever, Colonel. Unnecessary, but we will do it your way. I will not deceive you. Do not deceive me. Understand that your mother's wellbeing is in your hands."

My expression was of undisguised hatred. The Russian was unaffected.

The Russian continued. "Now to specifics. We are interested in two areas of the United States weapons program. First, the status of the U.S. arsenal, how many weapons, where they can be deployed, production rates, that sort of information. The second concerns the work devoted to development of the next generation advanced nuclear weapon, the fusion-based bomb. This is the most important information we expect from you, Colonel Voronin. Or I should say FOUNTAIN."

First Thermonuclear Bomb Test
Enewetak Atoll, 1952

CHAPTER 37

LOS ALAMOS & SANDIA, NEW MEXICO – 1949-1954

L IFE WOULD NEVER be the same again. I was again trapped. It had been unrealistic to think I could escape the past. Would I do this? Continue to help these bastards? Of course I would. Abandoning my mother with the only chance to save her was unthinkable.

The obvious ploy would be to pass along misleading information. That idea was quickly dismissed as impractical. I simply did not know enough about the technology related to the super bomb to discriminate the value of the technology. The scientists themselves often had differing opinions. I was not remotely qualified to attempt any altering of the material.

The work was steeped in the most complex of mathematics to attempt understanding of how some condition never before created would performed in the smallest fraction of a second. It was all just theory, or more accurately, a compounding of related theoretical concepts. Mathematics well beyond my comprehension. There was little empirical data on which to build upon. Understanding how the physics in its most abstraction would behave in the physical realm could lead to a weapon of unimaginable destructive power. Or it might just be a scientific quest that proves unworkable in practical application. The *Fat Man* fission-implosion weapon had been an engineering feat in its final incarnation. The theoretical basis was well understood. *Little Boy* did not even need a validation test before it was successfully used against Hiroshima. The *super* was still a theoretical concept.

The mechanics of the forces that might instigate nuclear fusion, the process that powered the stars, was not well understood, nor subject to direct test. The mathematics had to unite various theoretical factors interacting under dynamic conditions. How did the various materials behave when heated to temperatures of tens of millions of degrees? How did the increasing density of neutrons of variable energies impact the reaction? What influence was exerted by the chemistry of the new elements formed by the fusion process? These and other problems required exceedingly complex mathematical solutions, much of which was founded on assumptions. If these abstract theoretical concepts could be successfully integrated, could it even be engineered into a workable weapon? Whoever solely possessed such a weapon would have unprecedented international political leverage.

With these stakes, my conscience should have rebelled at the thought of the Soviet Union ever possessing such a weapon. But I wasn't that strong. I simply could not cause my mother to die in abject suffering. I also realized I was still not willing to sacrifice my own life. I had another opportunity to do the right thing after my years of betraying my country. I chose the coward's option.

The world was clearly divided in a new contest of international antagonism. For the first time, there were two great contestants. The world had progressed to a point where international leverage could be exerted through a new generation of weapons. Nuclear weapons could destroy whole countries. In 1949, the world learned that the United States was not the lone possessor of this terrible new weapon. The Soviet Union detonated its first test. The bomb was similar in design as well as explosive yield to the *Trinity* and Nagasaki *Fat Man* bombs. President Truman moved development of the fusion bomb to a national priority.

My first act of renewed espionage was the recent work of Stanislaw Ulam. His approach was a wholesale rethinking of what happened in the initial stages of the unrestrained chain re-action of neutron bombardment of a critical mass of fissile mate-rial resulting in the enormous release of energy contained in the binding force of the atomic nucleus. That level of energy being essential for triggering the even greater release of energy when light element fuels undergo nuclear fusion, or the release of en-ergy when nuclei are forced to together to overcome the electri-cal repulsion of the positively charged protons. To initiate fusion required temperatures and physical forces that could only be created by nuclear fission in specific heavy elements. From the earliest work by Edward Teller, it was clear that the processes were linked. What Teller got wrong for years was how to con-nect the triggering event of a fission chain reaction to cause an-other fuel to undergo nuclear fusion. Ulam found the key.

Notes and strings of equations related to Ulam's work were spread out on my desk at Los Alamos. My own hand sketches graphically depicted Ulam's concept as it might apply to the ac-tual construction of a bomb. Two desk lamps bathed the papers on the desk with bright illumination. Focusing on one page per frame, I snapped twenty-one images.

I understood none of Ulam's calculations or the concepts they were meant to explain. The theoretical physics were of a whole new kind, attempting to understand processes never ex-perienced on earth. The mathematics was entirely original.

I possessed these papers since I was asked by Ulam to act as a courier to get these to John von Neumann at Princeton. The two great mathematicians had collaborated on the calculations for the explosive lenses of the implosion fission bomb. Von Neumann had been contributing to the vast body of calculations required for the fusion weapon using the world's first electronic computer, ENIAC at Aberdeen Proving Grounds in Maryland. Ulam now wanted von Neumann's opinion on this radical new approach.

I returned the papers to my safe. Tomorrow, they would accompany me on a priority flight in a briefcase handcuffed to my wrist. The miniature camera and its exposed film went home with me. As a deputy to the Commander of the AFSWP, my person was not subject to search as I left Los Alamos each day.

Arriving home, I dialed the prescribed telephone number, disconnecting after the third ring. It took two hours to encrypt the language portion of the material. Most of the package consisted of the many pages of calculations. No way to encrypt the mathematics or sketches. After Teresa was asleep, I locked myself in the bathroom. As Boris had instructed, I inserted a low-wattage red light bulb into the fixture. The wavelength of the red light would not ruin the exposed film but allowed enough light to remove it from the camera and secure it within the package of cigarettes.

At one of the prearranged coffee shops the following morning, I positioned myself to observe my car. I wanted to see the transfer. If it was anyone other than the woman called Jacqueline, then the Russian lied about my security. From the window I saw Jacqueline open my car door and leave immediately after retrieving the cigarette package.

And so began an infrequent routine for the next several years. Infrequent since I passed information no more than once a month. The process was simple. Much of the material was so sensitive that actually removing copies from either laboratory was more dangerous than simply photographing within my office. In those cases I at least was able to avoid the laborious task of encrypting the material. That probably placed me at greater risk but I gave it little thought.

Unfortunately, the spying took a toll. From that first day, I was never the same person again. Unaccounted bouts of sullen quiet would intrude for seemingly no reason. Poor Teresa suffered through these periods not knowing the cause, perhaps wondering if it wasn't somehow because of her. These depressions often accompanied the monthly letter from my mother.

Jacqueline would place the letter in my car under the driver's seat. Never knowing when it would come, I got in the habit of always checking each time I got into my car.

This was like living with a disease. Life was productive for the most part as long as I was able to compartmentalize my dark secret. The years ticked by. The Cold War became the new world reality. The hot war raging on the Korean Peninsula from 1950 to 1953, dominated American life. Communism in the form of the Soviet Union and China became the clearly defined enemy of the democratic West.

Nuclear weapons development therefore became all important. The collaborative effort of Teller and Ulam eventually yielded a workable design. The United States detonated the first thermonuclear explosion on a Pacific atoll named Enewetak. I was there along with thousands of other observers. The test was labeled *Ivy Mike.* At 10-12 megatons of TNT equivalent, the blast was 500 times more powerful than the Nagasaki *Fat Man.* The blast obliterated the island of Elugelab leaving a crater over a mile in diameter. The test incorporated what would become known as the Teller-Ulam design. It was a spectacular success. Only I knew that the Soviets had been receiving regular access to virtually all of the United State's scientific work for years.

There was great euphoria at Los Alamos and Sandia. Everyone felt we now had the edge on the Soviets. I knew otherwise. While the *Ivy Mike* test was intended to validate the design of a thermonuclear fusion secondary bomb, it was not a deployable weapon. *Ivy Mike* was actually an unwieldy device weighing 82 tons. It looked more like a building than a recognizable weapon. It was intended to validate the conceptual design. Of all the past nuclear bomb tests, this test of a second-stage fusion explosion had its basis solely in the unproven mathematics of barely understood physical phenomena. There was no practical way to conduct meaningful testing other than the real thing. So *Ivy Mike* was rigged to study the mechanics of this new device. It took another seventeen months for the *Castle Bravo* test to usher in the thermonuclear age for real. *Castle Bravo* was a 23,000 pound bomb that could be delivered by an aircraft. It was also more powerful than *Ivy Mike* with a yield of 15 megatons.

Not only were thermonuclear bombs more destructive by an order of magnitude compared to fission bombs, there was no limit to their destructive capability. Fission bombs functioned by achieving critical mass. Even with design features that boosted yields, the weapon disassembled that critical mass when exploded. This set a natural limit of yield at approximately one megaton. The secondary fusion detonation of the thermonuclear bomb was limited only by the amount of nuclear fuel that could be made to ignite and sustain fusion burning. There was no theoretical limit to destructive power.

Castle Bravo gave the dark vision that mankind had now created the means by which it could destroy itself. While the effects of residual radioactivity were known even with the *Trinity* test, the ramifications on this new scale made for a terrifying reality. *Castle Bravo* resulted in unanticipated radioactive contamination of naval personnel and ships. The prevailing winds also blew fallout eastward to other inhabited areas of the Marshall Islands. In this respect, it was the first nuclear disaster. This was a preview of the aftermath of a full nuclear exchange between the two super powers.

My personal circumstances took a decided downturn that same year. One Saturday evening on a pleasant summer night,

Teresa and I had left a restaurant in Santa Fe. After arriving home I realized that I had neglected to check under my seat earlier to see if I had a 'delivery'. Before going into the house I felt under the seat. Sure enough, there was an envelope.

After Teresa was asleep, I retrieved the envelope from the car. Locking myself in the bathroom, I extracted the expected letter and photograph. Unexpectedly, a business card for an Albuquerque restaurant also fell out. On the back was a scribbled note, saying, *'Need to meet any of these days and times.'*

The photograph jarred me. My mother was apparently in a hospital. The obligatory New York Times front page was from two weeks ago. My mother's letter went on to say that she had recently been diagnosed with tuberculosis. She was now in a sanitarium receiving good care. I wasn't to worry. She wrote that she should have suspected sooner. Her chronic cough only got worse. Once she began coughing up blood, she knew something was seriously wrong.

I was beside myself with anxiety as well as renewed rage. I couldn't wait to get to Albuquerque and hear details from my contact, Jacqueline. It took two days to find a reason to go to Sandia Base.

"How is my mother really? Her letter was vague on the seriousness of her condition," I asked Jacqueline. We were seated in an upscale hotel restaurant at lunchtime.

"I'm told it's quite serious. The disease is well advanced. I'm to assure you that she is getting the best medical care possible."

"What's that mean? Will she recover?"

Jacqueline averted her head. I knew what that meant.

"The prognosis is not encouraging. I was instructed to prepare you for the eventuality that your mother could die. She is seriously ill."

"And you people are the cause of this. She was placed in one of your concentration camps for no reason. It ruined her health. She was never an enemy of the state."

"That unfortunately was the work of Stalin. Thousands died unnecessarily because of his psychotic aberrations. But Stalin is now dead. Unfortunately all the harm he did cannot be undone," Jacqueline said. Obviously parroting the new party line; all the problems were the fault of Joseph Stalin, not the Communist government of the Soviet Union.

I wasn't listening to any of this crap.

"You people threw my parents into your Siberian shitholes. My father died early. He was lucky. You starved my mother and treated her no better than an animal. She contracted tuberculosis from her time in that place. I blame the Soviet government still in place. Stalin's fucking henchmen. Fuck all of them. Fuck the COLONEL."

Jacqueline was impassive at my outburst, muted as it was in volume so as not to create a scene.

"I'm instructed to remind you that your mother's medical care is contingent upon your continued cooperation. I'm sorry to have to remind you of this blunt reality."

I stood up and dropped my napkin on the table. "I know what I must do."

Late the following year, 1955, the Soviet Union detonated its own thermonuclear weapon. They had caught up to the United States. Perhaps in large measure because of me. For good or bad, the stalemate of mutually assured destruction would dominate the world for the next thirty-five years.

That year I received what was to be the last letter from my mother. For months her letters signaled a decline in her health. Her disease had now advanced to a point where death was imminent. The last picture was almost unrecognizable as my mother. Her cheeks were sunken. Her pallor was ghostly pale. The fire had left her eyes. I could already be looking at a cadaver.

Her short letter was scrawled in an unsteady hand.

Dear Misha,

I fear my time is ending very soon. I am so tired. They treat me well but there is little that can be done because of the advanced stage of my disease. They make me eat. I'm told I am being treated with newly developed drugs. It is alright. There is little to live for. With what I know is going on throughout the world, we are forever to be separated my son. Life holds nothing for me anymore. There is little more to say, only that I love you. Take care of yourself. Take care of your wife. I wish a long life for you. Do not grieve. I am at peace.

You learned chess well from your father. I could never beat you. Like your father, I delighted in your skill. I am in a difficult situation, even on the chess board. I move N-K6.

I love you,
Mother

I thought about her obligatory chess move. The layout of the board was imprinted in my mind. Her move was only a token defense. She could obviously see that I had mate in two moves. Her end was imminent.

Accompanying the letter was a typed note, no signature. It read briefly, '*I regret to inform you that your mother passed away on the 16th of May. She was comfortable in her last hours, sliding quietly into unconsciousness. I urge you not to do anything rash. Our arrangement must continue. Think of your future, think of your wife.*'

CHAPTER 38

VICTORIA PRESCOTT LET Voronin tell his story with little interruption. She made notes to come back to questions but didn't want to interrupt his narrative. This material was wholly unexpected. It was a goldmine. She had originally speculated he may have continued spying until learning he murdered his wife to sever his connection with Soviet intelligence. This gave weight to Mikhail Voronin as not just the other Soviet spy to Fuchs that advanced the Soviet's nuclear program, but perhaps the preeminent spy. It would force a reassessment of the importance of the Soviet intelligence penetration of the U.S. effort. Put simply, it could be argued that Mikhail Voronin was singularly instrumental in advancing the Soviet timetable for achieving thermonuclear weapons parity with the United States. That advanced timing prevented the United States from leveraging their early lead. This in turn solidified the Cold War, shaping the world for the second half of the twentieth century.

"That's quite a story, Mr. Voronin. There's nothing in the historic record to hint of a spy at your level in the years immediately following World War Two. Sakarov supports your view that Fuchs' intelligence related to the fusion thermonuclear bomb was not helpful. Wouldn't you expect him to at least reference this later intelligence you provided, even if nothing more than to diminish its importance?"

Andrei Sakarov was the Soviet nuclear physicist credited with design of the Soviet's thermonuclear bomb. He later re-nounced nuclear proliferation, becoming a vocal activist dissi-dent of international recognition.

"Who knows? Professional pride? Political pressure? Person-al survival even? What might a psychopath like Stalin do if his top scientists failed? Sakarov was the principle designer of the successful *Soviet Third Idea.* It was essentially the American Teller-Ulam design. It wasn't original work by Sakarov. The in-telligence I provided had to have been significantly useful."

Voronin was essentially correct from what was known of the Soviet program. But could he still just be embellishing his story? Even as the seemingly reluctant spy, was he making his story even more spectacular? The thought was only fleeting. She could sense the hatred as he recounted his mother's death. Yet she needed more than just his testimony.

For the next couple of hours Prescott looked to her notes and asked Voronin all sorts of questions. Her own intimate knowl-edge of that period in history allowed her to engage Voronin at a detailed level.

"I'm impressed with your knowledge of those times, Ms. Prescott. It's like talking to someone that shared that same expe-rience. Your book should be a success. It will certainly be pro-vocative."

"Thanks to you. My problem with all you've told me about your spying after World War Two relies only on your recollec-tion. There's no one that can corroborate any of this. In fact, it would be vigorously disputed. I don't recall anything I've ever read that would support your claim. I won't be able to use this other than attribute it solely to your unsubstantiated testimony.

Professionally, I'd have to retreat from placing any weight to how that affected world affairs. It's a hell of a story though."

Voronin studied Prescott for a few moments. "But you believe me?"

Prescott nodded firmly. "Yes I do. I've seen you tell me the details. I don't think you could make up such a story and populate it with all of these details. I wish I had even indirect corroborating information."

Voronin smiled. "What about direct corroboration? Actual real evidence, forensic evidence?"

Prescott caught her breath. What was the old man getting at?

"I told you once, when I kicked off, you would come into possession of certain documents. Documents that will support your work as academically worthy. I have no doubt that it will also prove to be a commercial success also. Undiscovered Soviet spy revealed. Cold War ghosts. John le Carré lookout.

"I would not have told you this tale had I not been able to back it up. Of all the materials you will get, the stuff you will inherit upon my death will be absolutely conclusive proof of my latter spying after the War."

"And what kind of evidence will do that?"

"Microfilms. Duplicates of all those I took and passed along to Moscow since 1948."

"My god! But are they still undeveloped? Are they still any good?"

"No they're developed. They wouldn't have survived all these years in just their exposed state. I learned how to do the developing myself. Not that complicated. Just a few chemicals and a makeshift darkroom. All I was doing was developing the exposed film into negatives, not actually making prints."

"But why were you making duplicates?"

"Not sure I can offer a rational explanation. Some crazy idea perhaps if I was ever caught. Maybe cut a deal. They might save me from a firing squad if I could at least show what was passed to the Soviets. At any rate, it became habit. Maybe I was expecting a time like this might arrive.

"A word of caution, Ms. Prescott. Many of these materials that will come into your possession will still be classified. Before you get yourself into trouble, I suggest you retain an attorney to negotiate with the Government. These revelations even after all of these years will upset a lot of Washington. I suspect some parts of the bureaucracy will feel threatened. Expect some blowback. But you'll certainly become the darling of the news talk shows."

Prescott was not qualified to explore Voronin's psychology with his extraordinary tale of espionage and murder. From a seemingly reluctant traitor, he appeared still concerned about his importance in history, as infamous as that would become. Validation of one's existence and all that psychological nonsense? Or maybe it was only the pragmatism of the engineer to get the record right. But she still must ask the obvious.

"In the end, how do you reconcile your spying for the Soviets?"

"Reconcile? How could I ever do that? It was simply an act of cowardice. In the beginning, I breached security by telling Elena things she had no need to know. My own inflated sense of worth to impress my lover. Once she revealed her treachery, it was too late. I was already hooked on Elena like a drug. The cure would have been fatal. So I took the path of least resistance. After that, my crimes became easier. Once the fate of my mother became an issue, I was too far gone to have moral qualms about what I was doing."

"Am I to explain nothing about your early political leanings as being a contributing factor to your.....?" Prescott said.

"Treason? No. Because in the end, none of that was a factor. All this about my Russian heritage, my parents returning to the Motherland, none of that really played into what I did. It was all for reasons of self-preservation. But in the end, did my passing information to the Soviets really change anything?"

"I believe it did. The Soviets would eventually have developed nuclear weapons without Fuchs, without you. The issue is the accelerated timing. That made all the difference in world events. The intelligence you provided in the post-war years would have been invaluable for their making an H-bomb."

"No matter. It will be quite a story however the facts are interpreted. Food for lots of argument," Voronin said.

Both Prescott and Voronin were silent for a time.

"Well. It would appear we are close to the end of your story," Prescott said. "With this last revelation of your continued spying in the post-war years, my original idea for the book has been hijacked by your compelling personal story. I believe there are two books here. Your story will read like a spy novel. I'm actually thinking of naming the title *Critical Mass*. The sequel will be the more studied historical academic work about the broader impact of early Soviet penetration into the United States nuclear program.

"So when did the spying end? You retired from the Army in 1959. Any involvement with nuclear weapons would have ended then. Did you stop before then? Colonel Kirilov, the control officer who ran you from Moscow, died in 1955. Since he ran you so close, did it just end with his death?"

"Yes it did. Something like that anyway. Less than a year after my mother died, I rid myself of Soviet intelligence."

"You were lucky Kirilov died. Otherwise the Soviets might have strong-armed you to continue indefinitely after the death of your mother."

Voronin smiled weakly. "Luck played no part in it. It was all about retaliation."

CHAPTER 39

Castle Bravo 15MT Thermonuclear Test
Bikini Atoll, 1954

LOS ALAMOS & SANDIA, NEW MEXICO – 1955

I T WAS A beautiful spring Saturday in early May. Teresa and I were strolling among vendors at a Santa Fe street festival. My life had fallen into patterns of habit. For the most part, life was rewarding. Teresa and I were a devoted couple. We had lots of friends. Yet I was still a spy for the Soviet Union. Surprising what human beings can live with and call normal. Typically I passed information at least once a month. That was fraught with a bout of guilt that made my stomach churn. The periodic bouts of depression eventually passed. I was like the serial killer that committed his terrible crimes then once sated, retreated back into normalcy. I loathed what I was doing but I didn't really loath myself. This was an aberration, a defect, a handicap. Something I had to live with.

Even the memory of my mother's suffering had receded. There was no overwhelming catalyst to suddenly provoke me into taking a stance that I had been incapable of for so many years. The feeling just came upon me with no particular provocation. *I simply decided not to continue spying.* Fatigue, anger, pride, revenge, duty, and whatever other emotions combined into a clear decision. Was I prepared to sacrifice my life, Teresa's happiness, if the Soviets exercised their threats? Not likely they would just let me walk away. But for whatever reason, I was now resolutely prepared to risk all that.

Yet I had no idea how I would approach this. It could not be just a passive jester of refusal. Not a sheep just refusing to go to slaughter. That would only provoke Soviet intelligence to respond harshly. The Soviets only respected strength. Actually they respected aggression even more. So how could I push back hard enough to maybe get free?

Even with no plan, nor even an idea, the thought that I could be free was liberating. The remainder of that day of decision passed with a renewed lightness of being. Teresa even noticed. We had plans to go out for a nice dinner. We would do that, but not before returning home and making love.

I had no practical solution to my problem. No reason to feel liberated. But I did. It only reinforced how much this thing had contorted my life. There was no turning back from the decision. I was skilled at analysis. This was simply another problem that had a solution, perhaps alternative solutions.

That initial euphoria passed over the next couple of weeks. My mind was still made up, but no clear solution presented itself. I simply had no leverage. The Soviets might choose not to retaliate immediately, but I could not live looking over my shoulder forever. They had not threatened direct harm to Teresa but it certainly was not beyond them. If they executed and imprisoned tens of thousands of their own citizenry, then nothing was beyond their brutality. If they played that card, then I would be back in the same situation as before. If nothing else, I would not go to prison without some act of rebellion toward the Soviets.

The only solution had always lurked there from the onset. It had worked before. Could I commit murder again? Would I get away with it? Would it end this nightmare for good?

Of course by murder, I meant killing the COLONEL. He was the architect of all this. It was his operation. By his own design I was a narrowly controlled source. He said that I was known by name to only him and Jacqueline. Probably not entirely true. Probably some staff in Moscow knew of me. Regardless, if the flow of my intelligence ceased, those higher up might still find a way of reestablishing the link. But the COLONEL was the key.

How could I even get the COLONEL to meet again face to face? It would be exceptionally dangerous for him to enter the United States under a false identity. How would I kill him? Could I do such a thing again? Depended on how probably. Might I be killed in the process? The COLONEL would probably not be alone. And what about Jacqueline? Would I have to kill her also? Not the perfect solution. Murder was decidedly crude. But if successful, my untenable situation would be dramatically altered one way or the other.

In the end, it was better to move forward. Only this course of action offered a chance at freedom. There was no return to the status quo. So I began to plan in earnest how I would kill the COLONEL. The options quickly narrowed to bad or uncertain.

A gun? Effective if I could pull the trigger. If I wasn't searched. If those with the COLONEL didn't then shoot me. A knife? No better than a gun. Worse. I couldn't plunge a knife into someone. Run him down in a car? How could I contrive the necessary circumstance? Poison? What kind? How would it work? How would I get him to ingest it?

The possible solution came to me as I was assessing capabilities of the military technical staff at Sandia Base. For the last several years there had been a push by the Army to shift nuclear bomb assembly work from the civilian dominated Los Alamos Laboratory to Sandia outside Albuquerque. The officer in charge of training at Sandia was a stickler for procedures and safety. I had contributed my experience to formulating the procedures, thereby becoming intimate with all phases of atomic bomb assembly.

Apart from the obvious radioactivity danger associated with the plutonium-239 and uranium-235 fissile materials, a lesser part of the bomb assembly was also a radiological hazard. This was the exceeding minute amounts of polonium used in the neutron initiator. While the plutonium and uranium threw off dangerous gamma radiation, polonium was a source of alpha particle radiation. Both are hazardous to human beings. Both result in radiation poisoning. For reasons I will explain, the thought immerged that polonium would make for the ideal murder weapon.

The polonium isotope used for initiating a burst of neutrons once the fissile shell has been compressed to a critical mass acts as one component of the bomb's spark plug called the initiator. The energetic decaying isotope polonium-210 radiates alpha particles at a high rate. When the explosive lenses detonate, compressing the fissile core, the polonium in the very center mixes with beryllium. When beryllium is bombarded with alpha particles, it releases a burst of neutrons. Those neutrons in turn boost the early stages of the chain reaction of uncontrolled neutron release within the super-critical mass of plutonium.

Polonium is a silvery-grey soft metal. Also known as radium F, it was originally discovered by Pierre and Marie Curie in 1898 by chemically extracting it from uranium-bearing ore called pitchblende. The earliest atomic bomb initiators employed the isotope polonium-210. It is created by irradiating bismuth with high energy neutrons in a reactor. Although highly radioactive, polonium-210 still can be handled easily using manageable precautions. Protection against gamma radiation requires very specific shielding. The alpha particle-emitting polonium-210 requires far less protection. The size of alpha particles does not allow for passage through human skin. Even paper is an effective barrier to the alpha radiation. However, if ingested or inhaled, it is incredibly deadly even with infinitesimal quantities. By mass, it is 250,000 times more deadly than hydrogen cyanide. As a murder weapon, polonium was comparatively safe to handle, offered options for delivery, and was exceeding lethal.

It was exceptionally rare and little known outside the scientific community. At the time, it had no other use than for the top secret bomb work. For my purpose, I might have access.

For use in atomic bomb code-named *Urchin* initiators, only eleven milligrams was used in the early *Fat Man* generation of weapons. With advances in the technology, this was reduced in the next generation *TOM* initiators introduced into bomb designs starting in 1952. Unfortunately, polonium had one problematic characteristic for bomb making; it had a half-life of only 138 days.

The decay rate of an isotope as it evolves into an isotope of lower atomic weight is called half-life. It is the exponential rate of the loss of neutrons. In practice this meant that one-half of the unstable portion of the isotope would decay within the half-life period. At two half-life periods, the remaining radiation capability would be reduced to 25% and so on as time progressed. For polonium, this meant that the initiator placed at the very center of the pit assembly of the bomb must be replaced often so that it retained sufficient active strength.

That presented a logistical problem for deploying the first nuclear weapons. The plutonium fissile fuel had a half-life of 24,000 *years*. Once constructed into a bomb assembly, it remained viable forever. These initiators required replacement on average every sixty days.

One of the earliest functions at Sandia became the replacement of initiators in bomb pits on a regular basis. It served as good training for Army technical staff to learn bomb assembly techniques.

I was familiar with the area of the laboratory devoted to initiator replacement. The small quantities of spent polonium were removed and placed in glass vials. Disposal protocols called for storage for a period of time to a point where the decay rate had rendered the polonium almost inertly radioactive. In less than three years, the radioactivity had dropped to less than one percent of the original at the time of its creation. Since it represented such a small physical volume of material, the spent material was capable of convenient storage. It took up little space. Sealed simply within glass vials, it required no elaborate shielding.

The larger objective of how to escape my circumstance now became a practical problem. How to obtain the polonium? How to administer it to the COLONEL?

This is not to say that I did not have moral qualms. Admittedly, since I had already murdered for much the same motivation, the thought of doing it again came easier. Perhaps more troubling was how I would do this. While I doubted I could kill with a gun point blank, I was still going to cause a death in the most horrible of ways. This was not carbon monoxide poisoning. I had read the medical reports of the deaths of Harry Daghlian, and later that of Louis Slotin from accidental releases of massive levels of gamma radiation. The mode of death read like something from a horror novel.

There is no cure nor counteracting of the effects of radiation poisoning. Ingesting or inhaling actively radioactive polonium-210 causes alpha particles to be absorbed by the body's major organs. The liver, the kidneys, the spleen, the bone marrow undergo massive functional degradation. Both red and white blood cell counts drop resulting in anemia, internal bleeding, and infection. The victim experiences vomiting, headaches, diarrhea, pain, and hair loss. Polonium poisoning looks like the end stage of cancer. Depending upon the level of poisoning, death may occur within a matter of days, or at most in a couple of weeks. Inhaling only a comparatively small amount of high energy alpha particles was absolutely fatal. There was no treatment. For my purpose, it became a close to perfect weapon.

Few doctors would recognize radiation poisoning as long as there were no overt signs of skin blistering and swelling as experienced in the Daghlian and Slotin gamma radiation accidents. Perhaps the COLONEL's case would be misdiagnosed if he succumbed before the telltale hair loss. Whatever happened, spying for the Soviets would be over for me one way or the other. There was comfort in that knowledge.

While radiated alpha particles could not penetrate the skin, extreme caution was still required. The removal process from the bomb's initiator was done in a glove box, a sealed glass enclosure with gloves extending into the chamber to isolate the technician. The danger was potentially breathing contaminated air even though the alpha particles lost energy after only a few centimeters from the source. I would still have to take precautions but that could be managed. I was confident in that part of the scheme. The remaining question was how to steal the polonium. Steal it and not have the theft discovered.

As a bomb component, polonium was on its way out because of its inherent short half-life. As Soviet-U.S. tensions continued to escalate, an expanded nuclear arsenal deployed for immediate use was hampered by the need to continually change the polonium charge of the neutron initiators. Within the arsenal, there were still weapons with the original *Urchin* initiators. The more advanced design *TOM* initiators were only replaced with the newer sealed neutron initiators in 1954 which had a longer shelf-life. Most of the arsenal however still had these older type initiators. It would be several years before all of the older generation initiators were phased-out.

The theft proved remarkably easy. I had legitimate access to the pit assembly area at Sandia Base. I routinely supervised inventory of viable bomb components so an accurate assessment of the nation's nuclear arsenal could be continually updated. The spent polonium was stored in glass vials placed in cardboard boxes with section dividers for the individual vials. Each box contained a variable number of vials since they were inventoried with each box representing the month of removal. After three years storage here, about three half-lives since the polonium was produced, the radiation had dissipated to such a low level that wholesale disposal was then possible. All this bred a relaxed concern for security. The boxes of spent polonium were kept in an unlocked steel storage cabinet with only a radiation hazard symbol to suggest its contents.

I now had a decision to make. Do I make my demand for a face-to-face meeting with the COLONEL before I stole the polonium? If I did the theft first, then the lethality of the polonium would diminish over the interval time. It could be months before a meeting might happen. Or, the COLONEL might refuse. No need to take the risk if the plan fell apart. But, what if I was not able to secure the polonium? What would I do at this meeting, resort to something desperate?

I decided I needed the polonium in hand before initiating the plan. Once back at Sandia Base I contrived a situation where I was alone in the storage room off the pit assembly area. I simply removed one vial from the newest dated box. There were unused sections within the selected box so visually it would not provoke any concern if someone were to look inside. No reason why anyone would for that matter. It would be three years time before that box would be removed for disposal. If reconciled with some inventory record from three years previous, the discrepancy would probably be attributed to administrative error. At the least it would be impossible to thoroughly investigate. No reason for particular concern after three years since any missing polonium would now be harmless.

I slipped one vial into my pocket. The theft took less than twenty seconds. I could feel the warmth generated by the radiation as I held the glass vial. As soon as I could, I washed my hands vigorously in case there was any polonium residue on the outside of the vial.

My whole plan was not perfect, but I had to admit it was elegant in an insidious way. After the last meeting with Jacqueline there were no qualms about killing the COLONEL.

If I was ever to rid myself of Soviet intelligence, I had to eliminate the COLONEL. He was the head of the snake. So I made the call. From a public telephone booth. I let it ring six times then disconnected. Jacqueline would know that I requested a meeting. The die was now cast.

Two days later, I left the house for Los Alamos. On the seat was a business card from a restaurant in Albuquerque with a date written for the day after tomorrow.

It was lunchtime at a popular Mexican restaurant frequented by a diverse clientele. Jacqueline was at a table in the back.

Without preamble, she said, "And the reason for this meeting?"

"To make a demand. I need to see the COLONEL. It's about my continued work."

"What about your work?"

"I'm not going to negotiate with you. You're a messenger. Just deliver the goddamn message. I want a meeting, here, somewhere in the United States. Somewhere I can travel to with a plausible reason. But it must be with the COLONEL personally. Anybody else shows then I quit. For good."

"Do I tell the COLONEL what this is about?"

"Not specifically. You can say that I want a new arrangement. You can also say that no further intelligence will be forthcoming until we meet."

"I don't have to remind you that you are still under a risk if you cease cooperating."

"Risk? Threat you mean. If I'm too valuable to lose, then I don't think the COLONEL will throw me to the FBI without doing everything possible to keep me in the fold. So pass the message. Remember, nothing more until I meet with the COLONEL."

"I'll pass the message," Jacqueline said. She got up to leave before we ordered. "Enjoy your lunch."

Then an odd expression came over her face, with a trace of a smile. "And good luck to you Colonel Voronin."

She walked away.

I expected that it might be weeks before I heard back. It was only five days.

Jacqueline had left another card on my car seat. This time it was a restaurant in Santa Fe. That irritated me since it was too close to home. Too many people knew me here. I might be seen. Seen with another woman.

"Why here?" I said angrily.

It was a cocktail lounge, fortunately one I did not frequent.

Jacqueline ignored my question. "I'm to tell you that a meeting is out of the question. I'm to remind you that Moscow is not without leverage. I represent just such leverage. I'm quoting directly now; *If you cease to be cooperative, then you risk your marriage. A way will be found for your wife to learn of your affair with one Jacqueline Landers of Albuquerque.*"

Jacqueline was clearly uncomfortable delivering the threat but that meant nothing to me. I could have strangled her on the spot had we not been in a public place. She might be only the messenger, but she was still the enemy.

Things had progressed to a place in my mind that turning back was unthinkable. The cloud over me would be removed or I would die in the process.

"You tell the fucking COLONEL that I call his bluff. If he does that, then there will never be anything further. He's not as smart as I thought he was. Just another asshole Russian thug. Tell him we meet or he sees nothing new ever again. And you can tell him if it isn't soon I'm moving forward to end it permanently. How? By simply resigning from the Army. Removing myself from access to the United States nuclear weapons program, that's how. I will submit my resignation papers in one week's time. That's what he risks. So I suggest he make the meeting very soon."

This time I got up abruptly and left her sitting.

Partially decayed polonium-210 from nuclear bomb initiator

CHAPTER 40

JUAREZ, MEXICO – 1955

THE METHOD OF delivering the lethal polonium to the COLONEL was evident from the onset. Cigarettes of course. The COLONEL chained smoked. He would not be able to resist my pack of American cigarettes. I recalled he was smoking Camels the first time we met, the same brand that I smoked. How to rig the cigarettes was not quite that simple.

While the polonium was harmless within the storage vial and would be effectively shielded by the cigarette paper as well as the outside package itself, I still had to assemble the weapon. It probably could be done in the open air because the alpha particles could not travel far before they lost energy and transformed into atoms of helium. The danger was inhalation if even a minute quantity of alpha radiated particles attached themselves to some airborne particle. I didn't understand the mechanics of the radiation sufficiently to risk inhalation. It only made sense to take extra precautions. My answer was to construct a makeshift glove box.

I found a clear plastic storage container at an Albuquerque department store, along with a wooden cutting board, and rubber kitchen gloves extending high on the wrist. At a hardware store I bought quick-drying glue and an assortment of hand tools. Needing a place to work uninterrupted, I rented a motel room for a night rather than stay at the officers' quarters on Sandia Base.

With a box-cutter, I cut two round holes on opposite sides of the plastic container. Into these I inserted the gloves, rolling back the tops. The tops were then cemented into place with the glue. I next prepared the cigarettes by carefully steaming open the cigarette package seal. The foil was carefully unfolded using a pen knife. I would need to reseal the package when completed.

I removed sixteen cigarettes, placing them on the cutting board. The vial, a piece of white paper, and a pair of fine-pointed tweezers from a pharmacy were placed alongside the cigarettes. Lastly, the glue was liberally applied to the plastic container edge which was securely placed on the cutting board to cure, thereby forming a sealed chamber.

Two hours later my glove box appeared to be adequately sealed. I began working. First I removed the fine polonium particles from the vial spreading them on the white toilet paper in order to see the small dark metal flecks. With tweezers, I first removed some of the tobacco from each cigarette. Into each I then inserted two particles of polonium about a half inch from the end of the cigarette. The tobacco was replaced. The process took an hour to rig all of the cigarettes.

I pried the assembly apart with a screw driver. Using surgical gloves, I delicately placed the sixteen cigarettes back into the package first. The four uncontaminated cigarettes were placed at one end of the pack. I resealed the foil carefully along with the cellophane wrapper using a touch of glue on the bottom.

I knew which end contained the four uncontaminated cigarettes. That was the part I was uncertain about. I would smoke no more than one cigarette from the package, but was it truly safe? Did the paper barriers form the contaminated cigarettes sufficiently shield the alpha particles?

The polonium vial was smashed and flushed down the toilet. The homemade glove box was thrown in a trash bin along with the tools. The cigarette package went into my overnight bag.

I had distributed eight milligrams of polonium among the sixteen cigarettes. If the COLONEL smoked only one, that would be sufficient to kill him.

The median lethal dose of polonium is as little as 50 billionths of a gram depending on its radioactivity at the time of ingestion. An amount of polonium smaller than a grain of salt could be lethal. The COLONEL would have received hundreds of times that amount if he smoked all of the contaminated cigarettes. I had distributed the entire quantity of one spent initiator consisting of about eight milligrams at something not much greater than one half-life. That meant it retained close to 50% of its original radioactive potency. The literature also spoke of the biological half-life, or the rate polonium was expelled from the human body. But that would not save the COLONEL. Regardless of the calculation, smoking even a single cigarette represented a massively lethal dose. I worried more that the COLONEL might succumb to the effects of the radiation before he left the United States. Better that he died elsewhere. Some place where the symptoms would not accurately be diagnosed.

Three weeks later, Jacqueline made contact. I was to meet her at a restaurant in Albuquerque. At least that was not provocative like the last meeting in Santa Fe.

"The COLONEL has agreed to meet with you. You can imagine that is very difficult. Precautions must be taken," Jacqueline said. "You are to meet me here Friday. Same time."

"Where are we going?"

"I can't say."

"How long will I be away?"

"No longer than the weekend."

Was this a set-up to create incriminating evidence of a contrived infidelity?

Four days later I returned to the same restaurant. Jacqueline was having coffee. Upon seeing me she got up, left money on the table and took my arm before I could even sit down.

"You will drive. Not far. To the Hilton Hotel on 2nd Street."

I parked the car and we both walked into the lobby. I followed Jacqueline directly to the elevator. She told the elevator operator the tenth floor. The operator gave us a curious once over. A well dressed, attractive woman with a good looking guy in a suit at midday in a hotel. I knew he thought this was a lover's assignation. The business man and his secretary.

Jacqueline unlocked the door to room 1023.

"We haven't much time. You are to undress. Completely," she said.

I looked at her with undisguised hatred. This was a trap to incriminate me.

"It's not what you think. I'm instructed to make sure you are not wired with a communications device. I'm sorry."

I disrobed. Once down to my undershorts I looked at Jacqueline. She nodded to remove everything.

I stood totally naked. Was I being secretly photographed? There was nothing sexual here for me. It was humiliating and served to fuel my resolve. Should I kill her also? It would not be beyond me in my present state of mind.

Jacqueline looked at me with a slight smile. She then searched my pockets, even the soles of my shoes, and then said, "You can get dressed now."

We drove to the airport in my car to a private executive service. We were escorted to a single-engine Cessna by the pilot. Once buckled in, the pilot said, "It'll be about a ninety minute flight to El Paso folks. Nice clear day. Good view of the spectacular Organ Mountains as we near Las Cruces, then heading down to El Paso. Enjoy the flight."

The plan was not surprising. The COLONEL would have to guard against a trap. The flight in a small private aircraft would thwart anyone following us. I could have turned. He would be a major bargaining chip, maybe even a get out of jail free card. I had never thought of that option. Something to think about if things turned out badly.

Landing in the backwater West Texas border town of El Paso, Jacqueline bundled us into a taxi.

"The Camino Real Hotel downtown, driver."

We exited the taxi at the hotel. Jacqueline checked us in.

"Room number 430 Mrs. Landers," the desk clerk said.

Out of earshot of the desk clerk, she turned to me and said, "You are to meet your party across the international border in Juarez. You walk south on this street for a few blocks. Once over the border into Mexico, just stand there. You will be met. You will answer to the name of Señor Jones. Carry this magazine showing the cover. When you return, come up to room 430."

I nodded my understanding and left. Mexico for the meeting was an added precaution for the COLONEL. My heart was pounding. The cigarette package was in my inside suit coat pocket.

I walked down South El Paso Street a half a mile to the international border crossing. Once into Mexico there was a beehive of activity with Mexican street vendors vying for American dollars. Americans frequently drove into Juarez for inexpensive goods and food. As instructed, I stood on the street, displaying the *Life* magazine cover. Ironically it was the January 17th issue featuring a scene in Russia.

Within a minute a beat-up twenty year old taxi pulled up. The middle-aged driver got out and inquired in accented English, "Señor Jones?" I nodded and got in. Ten minutes later we arrived at what appeared to be an upscale restaurant. The waiters were dressed in white jackets and ties.

The maître d' said, "Señor Jones? Please follow me."

He escorted me toward the table where I recognized the COLONEL. The Russian remained seated. No evidence of Russian bodyguards. Probably outside the restaurant.

"Please sit down Colonel Voronin."

The COLONEL was smoking. A pack of cigarettes was on the table. That could be a problem. They were even Camels. I needed him to smoke from my doctored pack.

"Cigarette?" The Colonel pushed the pack toward me. "Something to drink or eat?"

A half-finished glass of beer was in front of him. The waiters did not approach the table. I assumed he had instructed them not to disturb us unless signaled.

I shook my head no then picked up the pack of cigarettes. Only two cigarettes left. That was fortunate. Even opportune. I could smoke one of his. The idea of smoking one of my uncontaminated cigarettes placed next to the ones with polonium still made me uncomfortable. I wasn't at all sure that proximity to the other cigarettes would not also make them potentially dangerous.

I lit up the cigarette and feigned a cough. Reaching for a handkerchief, I blew my nose.

I commented tersely, "A cold." The ploy was to be my excuse for not repeatedly smoking more cigarettes.

The COLONEL took the last cigarette from the pack.

"Let me first offer my condolences for the death of your mother. I assure you that because of you her last years were spent in comfort. Even in the hospital, she was well cared for. I am told that tuberculosis is a wasting disease, not painful as with most other terminal diseases."

"I'm supposed to feel grateful for that? You put her in that stinking Siberian labor camp. My father too but he mercifully died soon after. My mother contracted tuberculosis because of conditions in your prison. You killed them both."

"I'm truly sorry. That was the excesses of the prior regime. Stalin was a madman. Unfortunately, thousands of innocent people suffered. That is all behind the Russian people now. But we've been over that before."

"Yes we have. And once my mother died, you were quick to threaten me with other leverage so I would continue working for you."

The COLONEL sighed. "Unfortunately that is necessary in my line of work. There are larger issues at stake that justify harsh actions even if I find them objectionable. Any apology would be hollow. Understand that you are of extraordinary importance as an intelligence source. I realize you find this distasteful, but in the end you have accomplished a great thing for world peace."

"What the fuck are you talking about? How the hell has feeding you Soviets secret U.S. intelligence helped world peace?"

"This so-called Cold War. It was bound to happen," the COLONEL said. "By your passing this information, the Soviet Union, your Motherland, Mother Russia, has been able to achieve something close to parity in nuclear weapons with the United States. That keeps the Cold War cold. If the United States had remained far ahead, then Washington would be tempted to use these new weapons. Mankind would be the real loser."

"That's bullshit convoluted logic. I'm long passed being persuaded by any self-serving ideological argument, especially Communist nonsense."

As his cigarette got toward the end, the COLONEL reached for the cigarette pack. Realizing it was empty, he crumpled the spent package. I used the opportunity to reach inside my jacket and throw my unopened pack across the table toward him.

"Be my guest," I said.

The COLONEL opened my cigarette pack and tapped out one cigarette offering it to me.

I shook my head and coughed. "They taste like shit with this cold. Makes me cough more."

The COLONEL laid the deadly pack of cigarettes down. He lit the first cigarette from my pack and inhaled deeply.

"As you Americans say, let's get down to business. Why have you caused me to come all this way?"

I fixated for a brief moment watching the COLONEL inhale the smoke. The deed had been done.

"I want a way out. I cannot live forever like this. The risk increases as I go on. How can I trust that there couldn't be some breakdown on your side? Look what happen to your other spies. Fuchs and Greenglass are in prison. The Rosenbergs were executed. I do not intend to end like that."

"Those were mistakes in tradecraft. A different intelligence directorate. You are far more secure. I've explained that."

"Not from where I'm sitting."

"So what are you suggesting?"

"My twenty years in the Army are up in 1959. Four years away. I want out then. To give you those extra years will cost you however. I want one hundred thousand dollars per year. That's a bargain for you and sets me up financially once I move on."

The COLONEL looked at me expressionless. He pulled another cigarette from the poison pack. He lit it savoring the smoke as he considered his response.

"Well. It has come to this. That can perhaps be arranged. However it will raise the expectations on our end. For that kind of money we may have other things we wish you to obtain. And how would this payment of such a large sum be made? You know you could not use it directly without attracting suspicion."

I glared at him. Coughing again for effect, I used the handkerchief again to cover my mouth and blow my nose again.

"Of course. I'm not stupid. The funds are to be deposited in a numbered Swiss bank account. You figure out the details. My guess you already have a procedure in place for this type of covert funding. I would not access the money while I was still in the Army. Then only over many years."

For the next two hours the COLONEL quizzed me on nuclear weapons. Taking this rare opportunity to talk directly with his most productive agent, he probed my duties, the potential for promotion, weapons production rates, deployment planning, and decision protocols for using nuclear weapons.

During this time, the COLONEL characteristically chain smoked continuously. I could not tell from which side of the pack he started. Regardless, he had now worked his way well into the polonium-laced cigarettes.

"Are we done?" I asked.

"I believe so."

I got up, the COLONEL did not. "So we understood one another, I expect to learn of the first deposit of money soon. That will show good faith. I'm afraid until that happens, I will not be sending any new information. Bear in mind I don't trust you, so satisfy that distrust by arranging a foolproof procedure for the money that is satisfactory to me."

The COLONEL gave a curt nod with a cold-eyed edge to his stare. I suspect he was seething at my ultimatum. He would not be accustomed to threats from a spy he was running.

"Good luck, FOUNTAIN. I suspect we shall not see each other again."

"I hope not. Keep the cigarettes. They're bad for your health," I said as I turned and walked out. Let him smoke the entire pack for good measure.

The COLONEL from Moscow was already a dead man walking when I left the restaurant.

I took a taxi to the border crossing. As I walked back into the United States, the thought struck me that if the COLONEL took ill immediately, it would be in Mexico. Unlikely any Mexican doctor would recognize the little known symptoms of acute radiation poisoning. If he made it back to Moscow, perhaps even those doctors would misdiagnose his condition. Shouldn't drink the water in Mexico.

Back at the Camino Real Hotel, I knocked on the door of room 430. Jacqueline opened the door and ushered me in.

I noticed an opened bottle of champagne in an ice bucket.

"Did your meeting go well?" she said.

"Let's say we have an understanding."

"I'll take that to mean we shall still be seeing each other occasionally. I thought we might enjoy ourselves before we returned to Albuquerque. Would you like some champagne, Colonel Voronin?"

"No thanks. I want to get going."

Jacqueline came up close to me placing her right hand on my chest. I noticed she had unbuttoned her blouse suggestively.

"You're a very good looking man, especially without your clothes. Shame to waste the hotel room. The plane leaves anytime we wish."

It was the first time she had made any advance toward me.

I removed her hand. "Listen to me. This is about business nothing else. I don't know what your deal is with the COLONEL but you're not on my side. Let's keep this a business relationship. Besides I'm happily married. Not interested in cheating on my wife. Now let's get the hell out of here. I need to be back in Albuquerque."

Jacqueline scowled then downed the remainder of the champagne in her glass. She knew she was attractive. She had not expected rejection.

"By the way, do you have any cigarettes? I'm all out," I said. I needed a smoke badly.

Less than three hours later, we were back in Albuquerque. I dropped Jacqueline off at a taxi stand downtown then set out for the drive north to Santa Fe. To home. To a new life I hoped. Whatever happened, things were now changed.

Unfortunately, I would still live in fear for some period. I would not know conclusively if my scheme had worked. There was no way to learn directly of the COLONEL's death. The ploy for the money arrangements was for the express purpose of knowing that I was successful. That of course assumed that the COLONEL had run me so tightly that I was unknown to other Soviet intelligence officers. Was that likely? Wouldn't my identity be somewhere in the Colonel's personal files? Hopefully he was sufficiently paranoid to have covered my identity. The best I could hope for was no further contact.

There was of course Jacqueline Landers. She knew who I was, what I did, while I knew nothing of her. I suspected she was American but who knows. Why was she working for the Soviets? Would some other Moscow intelligence officer reactivate her? What would she do when I never again made contact to hand over new material? She would remain a source of concern for some indefinite time.

CHAPTER 41

Oil on canvas paintings by Mikhail Voronin

CLAREMONT, CALIFORNIA – 1999

VICTORIA PRESCOTT HAD spent the last three weeks interviewing Mikhail Voronin. During that brief time, she could see his deterioration from the lung cancer. He was closer to the end than he thought.

He had given a firsthand account that reshaped her project. The fact that he was a previously unknown highly placed Soviet spy for twelve years would be a sensation. A spy that may have advanced Soviet H-bomb development by years. It would be an impressive professional accomplishment for Prescott, sure to also be a commercial success. When she set out on this investigation she never dreamed it would turn out to be so important. At best she expected to deliver professionally important work. But what she had would cause a rethinking of those early years as the United States and the Soviet Union developed nuclear weapons, laying the foundations for the Cold War.

Prescott was again taken back by Voronin's admission of having committed yet another murder.

"So now you know you were successful. Feliks Antonovich Kirilov, then a general in the Red Army GRU, died in 1955. Obviously not of natural causes. Apparently from this insidious polonium you gave him. Perhaps the Soviet doctors didn't even know what they were dealing with. Assuming he even made it back to Moscow. You have been a dangerous man to cross, Mr. Voronin. Was it all worth it?"

"Was what worth it? The spying or killing the people that entrapped me into doing it?"

"Both I guess. I'll include your thoughts as part of your final comments on your life."

"I've given you a lot of comments these last several weeks. There is no concise explanation, no acceptable rationalization, no excuse for anything I did. It was just a life. As it turns out, a life that effected lots of people, mostly in harmful ways. You can't claim to really justify murder. There were always other alternatives. For my own survival, I chose to react violently at what was done to me. So was it worth it? The murders? Yes, I'd say so. They accomplished the intended results didn't they? I'd say the victims deserved their fates.

"As to the spying, well that was a curse from the beginning. It was my fault for opening that door. I should have terminated that from the very beginning. For all these years, I have replayed all the possible scenarios that could have led elsewhere. For that failure, my guilt can never be expiated. Write it that way. Guilty as charged."

The remainder of Voronin's life story was unremarkable. He left the Army and nuclear weapons in 1959. Taught engineering at California State Polytechnic in Pomona, California until 1980. His second wife, Teresa died in 1978 of breast cancer. There were no children. Prescott asked a few questions to fill in the gaps of what she already knew from her research.

"One last thing, Mr. Voronin. With the death of General Kirilov in 1955, Soviet intelligence never attempted renewed contact?"

"No. The COLONEL, the general I guess, this Kirilov had apparently been true to his word. He ran me very tightly. No money was ever deposited anywhere so that was the first indicator my plan worked. No further communications after that meeting in Juarez. It was a year before I began to feel that I had perhaps successfully shed involvement with Soviet intelligence."

"And what about this intermediary, this Jacqueline Landers? You never heard from her again?"

Voronin didn't answer right away. He turned to look out the window of his living room and answered Prescott without turning back toward her. "No. I never heard from her again either."

VICTORIA PRESCOTT KEPT her word about not going public until Voronin passed on. Actually she was consumed with the work of writing. The finished manuscript was still not completed by the time Voronin died, so it was not like a death vigil for her. Voronin's revelations had reshaped her project into a whole new book. There were even new avenues of research suggested by what he revealed about his post-war activities.

Mikhail Stefanovich Voronin died at the Veterans Hospital in Loma Linda, California in March, 1999. His passing went unnoticed. There were no relatives. His attorney filed a will in probate. By Voronin's own instructions, he was cremated. No memorial service, no military funeral. As promised, the attorney arranged for delivery of a box of sealed records to Prescott in San Francisco. She was also given a letter with a key enclosed.

Dear Ms. Prescott,

It was an interesting time we spent together. Good luck with your book. I never harbored ill will toward you for discovering my past. Best perhaps that the truth becomes known. At least I get my say written into the history. My attorney should have given you the records I promised. In there you will also find the microfilms I referred to. Please

*remember to have these vetted before using them since many will still
be classified.*

*I suspect you will be quite the celebrity. By the way, the key you
were given was for my studio over the detached garage in the back of
the property. I told you I dabbled in painting. Oils. Teresa did also. Not
sure either of us were very good. We never showed them. It was just
our shared pleasure together. I'm sure you will be able to distinguish
hers from mine. As you well know, I had a particularly dark side. Obviously it is reflected in the tone of my paintings. I favored heavy tex-
tures using a lot of pallet knife. Do as you like with them. If they're
worth anything because of my impending notoriety, have the money
donated to a worthwhile charity.*

Good luck Victoria,
Mikhail Stefanovich Voronin

In the final stages of fact-checking the manuscript and recon-
ciling Voronin's chronology of events with the known historical
record, there remained one unanswered piece to his story. Whatever happened to Jacqueline Landers? Was she just a single-
purpose intermediary between Kirilov and Voronin? Did she
just resume whatever life she had other than being a part-time
Soviet agent? Was she married? Was that even her real name?
Voronin claimed never to know anything about who she really
was. It was a loose end that needed closure.

Prescott went to Santa Fe to look at old DMV records on mi-
crofilm from the mid-fifties. To her surprise she found her there.
There apparently was a real Jacqueline Landers, at least in name.
Prescott now had a photograph as well. She admonished herself
for not having done this while Voronin was still alive. Was
Landers still living? What if she could be interviewed?

There were five Landers in the Albuquerque telephone book
in 1999. None named Jacqueline. She called each one. The fourth
call was answered by an obviously elderly man.

"Jacqueline? Who did you say was calling again?"

"My name is Prescott. I'm doing some historical research from the 1950's. The name Jacqueline Landers came up."

"Came up how?"

"Do you know this Jacqueline, Sir?" It couldn't be this easy Prescott thought.

"You could say that if we're talking about the same person. That was the name of my first wife."

Prescott convinced the man to see her. She drove to Albuquerque in an hour.

"Yeah, that's Jacqueline. We separated in '53, divorced the following year," the man named John Landers said after Prescott showed him the old DMV photo. His current wife served them coffee. Both the Landers were in their eighties.

"Do you know what happened to her?" Prescott asked.

"No I don't. No one else does either as far as I know."

"What do you mean?" Prescott asked.

"Just went missing. 1955 it would have been. Police came around. Neighbors from our old house finally called the police after not seeing her for weeks. Her car was still parked in the driveway. Anyway, the police broke in. Her clothes were still there. Even some jewelry. No note or anything. Just vanished. As far as I know, she never turned up. One of those thousands that go missing and are never heard of again."

"Can you tell me something about her background, Mr. Landers?"

Landers told Prescott how they met. They married at the end of World War Two.

"Jacqueline worked as a civilian employee at Kirkland Air Base when I met her. She was Canadian you know. Came to Albuquerque during the War. Became a naturalized U.S. citizen. Liked the desert. Didn't like the Canadian winters she said. Parents were deceased in an auto accident in Canada so she had no family."

"I see. What was her maiden name?"

"Dashevsky. You see she was born in Russia. Parents were Jewish. They immigrated with her to Canada in 1925, fleeing the persecution of Jews by the Communists after the Revolution.

"Turned out we didn't get along that well," Landers said. Then after a moment's reflection, "No, that's not exactly why we split up. Truth was I suspected she was having an affair. Saw her twice with the same Army officer. Like I said, she worked out at the air base. Still, I wonder what ever happened to her."

Prescott's heart sank. This last piece of Mikhail Voronin's story suggested an uglier ending than she wished to consider. But it was the only conclusion that made sense. Even without the details, Victoria Prescott was sure she knew the fate of Jacqueline Dashevsky.

CHARACTER APPENDIX
Historical characters appearing in *CRITICAL MASS:*

Bacher, Robert: 1905-2004. American nuclear physicist. PhD University of Michigan, 1930. Taught physics at Cornell University prior to joining the Manhattan Project. Headed the Experimental Physics Division from March, 1943 to August, 1944. With reorganization of Los Alamos to development of the plutonium weapon implosion design, Bacher headed the Weapons Physics Division assigned to developing the functional designs for the explosive lenses, the initiator, and the detonation circuits. Personally assembled the plutonium core for the *Trinity* test bomb. Served on Atomic Energy Commission following WWII. Professor of Physics at Caltech, 1949. Testified on behalf of Robert Oppenheimer at the latter's high-profile security clearance hearing.

Beria, Lavrentiy Pavlovich: 1899-1953. Soviet political figure. Chief of the Soviet intelligence and security apparatus, the NKVD, during WWII. Beria was the longest lived and most influential of Stalin's secret police chiefs. Born in Georgia like Stalin, he joined the Bolsheviks in 1917 while a student. Joined the Bolshevik secret police, the Cheka, in 1921. Architected political purges in the Caucus region under Stalin's direction. Stalin brought Beria to Moscow in 1938 to shut down the Great Purge supervised by Nikolai Yezhov which had gotten out of hand. Beria had Yezhov executed and then purged half of the NKVD by 1940. Beria was assigned to supervise the Soviet atomic bomb development effort. Beria briefly held power as Soviet head of state after Stalin's death in 1953. Beria was executed that same year in a coup lead by Nikita Khrushchev.

Bethe, Hans: 1906-2005. German-American nuclear physicist. PhD University of Munich. Post-doctoral work at Cambridge and with Enrico Fermi in Rome. Since his mother was Jewish, he lost his position at the University of Tübingen in 1933 when the Nazis came to power. Moved to U.S. in 1935 and joined faculty at Cornell University. Joined the Manhattan Project as Director of the Theoretical Division. The Soviet spy, Klaus Fuchs worked in Bethe's section. Returned to Cornell after WWII for the remainder of his academic career. Bethe was heavy conflicted about the creation of the hydrogen bomb although he worked toward its creation. Testified on behalf of Robert Oppenheimer at the latter's security clearance hearing. Awarded Nobel Prize in Physics in 1967.

Bohr, Niels: 1885-1962. Danish physicist. PhD University of Copenhagen, 1911. Post-doctoral work at Trinity College, Cambridge and Cavendish Laboratory. Returned to University of Copenhagen in 1916 as Chair of Theoretical Physics, a position specifically created for him. Awarded Nobel Prize in Physics in 1922 for work in atomic structure and the emerging field of quantum mechanics.

German physicist Werner Heisenberg worked as an assistant under Bohr in 1926-1927. Heisenberg later became head of Germany's nuclear development program. In September, 1943, Bohr learned of his imminent arrest by German police in occupied Denmark because of his mother's Jewish background. Danish resistance managed his escape to neutral Sweden, then to Britain. Joined Manhattan Project as a senior consultant guiding discussions as the preeminent elder theoretical physicist of the time.

Bradbury, Norris: 1909-1997. American physicist and U.S. Naval officer. PhD University of California, Berkley. Supervised final assembly of the non-nuclear components of the first atomic bomb tested at *Trinity* in 1945. Succeeded J. Robert Oppenheimer as director of Los Alamos in 1945, serving in that capacity for 25 years.

Caincross, John: 1913-1995. British intelligence officer and Soviet spy. Code name LIST. Educated at the University of Glasgow, the Sorbonne in Paris, and Trinity College, Cambridge. Joined the British Foreign Office prior to WWII. Worked on the British ULTRA project to decode German ciphers at Bletchley Park, 1942-1943, and then joined the British Foreign Intelligence Service, MI6. Passed ULTRA transcripts to the Soviets including the German order of battle for Operation Citadel which led to the great tank battle, the Battle of Kirsk. The information provided the Red Army invaluable intelligence leading to stopping the German advance as the turning point on the Eastern Front. Caincross passed 5832 documents to the Soviets from 1941 to 1945. Fifth member of highly placed British officials spying for the Soviets known as the *Cambridge Five*, the others being Anthony Blount, Guy Burgess, Kim Philby, and Donald Maclean. Admitted to spying in 1951. Never prosecuted, the reason for which has remained controversial.

De Silva, Peer: 1917-1978. U.S. Army officer. Chief of security at Los Alamos, 1943-1945, also commanding the U.S. Army's Special Engineering Detachment of technicians at Los Alamos 1943-1944. Participated in Project Alberta to deliver atomic weapons on Japanese targets. Transferred to CIA in 1949. As CIA Station Chief in Saigon during the Vietnam War, de Silva implemented the infamous Phoenix Program whereby Vietcong and suspected sympathizers were tortured and executed as a means of counter-terror against North Vietnam. Retired from CIA in 1973.

Farrell, Thomas: 1891-1967. U.S. Army Brigadier General WWII. Civil engineering degree from Rensselaer Polytechnic Institute, 1912. Joined U.S. Army Corps of Engineers, 1916. Served in WWI earning a DSC and French Croix de Guerre decorations. Deputy Commander and Chief of Field Operations for the

Manhattan Project, January, 1945. Supervised bomb preparations on Tinian for
the bombings of Hiroshima and Nagasaki.

Fermi, Enrico: 1901-1954. Italian-American physicist. Educated at the Universities of Pisa, Leyden, and Gottingen. Professor of theoretical physics at the University of Rome, 1927. Accomplished in both theoretical and experimental
physics. Awarded Nobel Prize in Physics in 1938. Came to the United States in
1938 to Columbia University. His wife was Jewish, forcing them to leave Italy
because of anti-Semitic laws promulgated by Mussolini's fascist regime. Joined
the Manhattan Project in 1942 working at the University of Chicago under the
project code name Metallurgical Laboratory. Developed the first nuclear reactor designated the Chicago Pile-1. This led to the X-10 reactor at Oak Ridge and
eventually the reactors at Hanford, Washington for the production of plutonium. Testified on behalf of Robert Oppenheimer at the latter's security clearance
hearing. Died of stomach cancer at age 53.

Feynman, Richard: 1918-1988. American physicist. Undergraduate degree MIT,
PhD Princeton, 1942. Recruited to the Manhattan Project, 1943. Group leader
for diffusion problems in Hans Bethe's Theoretical Division. Youngest senior
physicist at Los Alamos. Applied early IBM computers to assist in the complex
mathematical calculations associated with the implosion explosive lenses.
Feynman was a noted prankster at Los Alamos. Professor at Caltech after
WWII. Awarded Nobel Prize in Physics, 1965. Popularizer of physics through
books and lectures. In 1986, served on panel investigating the *Challenger* shuttle
disaster and explained the origin of the problem as the primary O-ring.

Fuchs, Klaus: 1911-1988. German-British theoretical physicist and Soviet spy,
code named REST, later CHARLES. Joined Communist party in Germany in
1933. Immigrated to Great Britain after violent encounter with Nazis. PhD in
Physics from the University of Bristol and subsequently a D.Sc. from the University of Edinburgh under the renowned physicist Max Born. As a German
citizen, the British interned Fuchs on the Isle of Man and later in Quebec, Canada at the outbreak of war with Germany. Max Born interceded and Fuchs returned to Edinburgh in 1941. He was recruited for the British 'Tube Alloys'
atomic bomb development program. Recruited by the Soviet GRU in 1941. In
the joint American-British effort to develop an atomic bomb, he joined the Theoretical Physics Division at Los Alamos. Fuchs is considered to have provided
the Soviet Union with more sensitive atomic weapons secrets, including research on post-war thermonuclear weapons, than any other Soviet agent during the 1940's. The arrest and confession of Harry Gold in 1950, led directly to
Fuchs, then to David Greenglass, and subsequently to Julius and Ethel Rosenberg. In 1950, Fuchs was convicted in British court and sentenced to fourteen
years imprisonment. Released in 1959, he immigrated to East Germany.

Gouzenko, Igor: 1919-1982. Ukrainian. Soviet GRU cipher clerk for the Soviet Embassy in Ottawa, Canada. Notified of his recall to the Soviet Union in1945, Gouzenko defected along with his family taking with him 109 documents related to Soviet espionage in the West. His defection is believed to have been vital in the prosecution of Klaus Fuchs, and the investigation of David Greenglass, Julius and Ethel Rosenberg. Gouzenko likely assisted in the Venona transcripts which lead to the discovery of the high-ranking *Cambridge Five* Soviet spies within the British government. He was provided an assumed identity by the Canadian government and lived in Toronto until his death from a heart attack.

Greenglass, David: 1922-?? U.S. enlisted soldier and Soviet spy for the NKVD, code name CALIBER. He was recruited into Soviet espionage by his wife Ruth at the urging of his own brother-in-law, Julius Rosenberg. He was a machinist working first at Oak Ridge, then at Los Alamos as part of the U.S. Army's Special Engineering Detachment which provided technical manpower for the Manhattan Project. Klaus Fuchs' confession in 1950 identifying Harry Gold as a Soviet courier, led in turn to Greenglass. In 1951, under limited immunity and to save his wife, Ruth, Greenglass testified against his sister Ethel Rosenberg and her husband Julius. The Rosenbergs were executed by electrocution in 1953. Greenglass was released from prison in 1960. Ruth Greenglass died in 2008. David Greenglass may still be living under an assumed name.

Groves, Leslie R.: 1896-1970. U.S. Army Major General. Commanding Officer of the Manhattan Project, 1942-1946. Educated at the Massachusetts Institute of Technology and the U.S. Military Academy at West Point. Graduated in 1918, fourth in his class. Supervised construction of the Pentagon Building, 1942. Headed the Armed Forces Special Weapons Project created to control the military aspects of nuclear weapons at the end of WWII from 1947 to his retirement from the Army in 1948. Became an executive with the Sperry Rand Corporation until retiring in 1961.

Hall, Theodore: 1925-1999. American physicist and Soviet spy, code named YOUNG. Educated at Harvard, he was recruited at age 19 to join the Manhattan Project where he was the youngest scientist at Los Alamos. Volunteered to spy for the Soviets to counter a U.S. post-war monopoly on nuclear weapons. Hall switched careers to study biology at the University of Chicago after WWII. He began work at Cambridge University in 1962. In 1998, Hall provided a near-confession of his wartime espionage for the Soviets. He was never prosecuted.

Kistiakowsky, George: 1900-1982. Ukrainian-American chemist. PhD in Physical Chemistry University of Berlin, 1925. Fought with the White Army in the Russian Civil War after the 1917 Revolution. Escaped to Germany in 1920. Immigrated to the United States in 1926. Taught at Princeton then Harvard. Recruited to Manhattan Project in 1944. Deputy Division Leader of the Ordinance & Engineering Division heading the Implosion Program. Served the Eisenhower and Kennedy Administrations in various high-level capacities associated with nuclear arms controls as well as U.S. nuclear warfare planning. Professor of Chemistry at Harvard for remaining career.

Koval, George Abramovich: 1913-2006. American electrical engineer and Soviet GRU spy, code name DELMAR. Born to Jewish immigrants in Sioux City, Iowa, graduating from high school at age 15. Studied electrical engineering at the University of Iowa. In 1932, he traveled with his parents to the Soviet Union to settle in the Jewish Autonomous Region near the Chinese border. Recruited by the Soviet Main intelligence Directorate, the military GRU. Returned to the United States in 1940 and drafted into the US Army in early 1943. Continued engineering studies at the City College of New York. Worked at Oak Ridge and then at Dayton, Ohio, principally with polonium used in atomic bomb initiators. Koval left the U.S. in 1948 and settled in the Soviet Union. Koval's espionage activities only surfaced in a 2002 publication.

Landsdale, John: 1912-2003. American Army officer. Law degree from Harvard. Security officer for the Manhattan Project. Along with Col. Boris Pash, Col. Landsdale participated in Operations Alsos by leading a security team advancing with Allied forces after D-Day for the purpose of securing German uranium ore before the Soviet Red Army occupied the area. In 1995, he revealed that ten pounds of uranium oxide bound for Tokyo on German submarine U-234 was captured and subsequently sent to Los Alamos and probably used in the Hiroshima and Nagasaki bombs. Outraged by the revocation of Oppenheimer's security clearance in 1954, Landsdale ardently defended Oppenheimer as a loyal citizen at the hearings.

Lawrence, Ernest: 1901-1958. American experimental physicist. Educated at the University of Minnesota and the University of Chicago. PhD Yale University, 1925. One of the few physicists to have been wholly educated in the United States. Assistant Professor at Yale, then Associate Professor at the University of California, Berkley, 1928. Developed the cyclotron which produced high-energy particles for atomic disintegration research. Created the Radiation Laboratory at Berkley which became the world's foremost laboratory for nuclear physics research. Awarded Nobel Prize in Physics for his work on the cyclotron in 1939. One of the principle scientists at the inception of the Manhattan Project. Developed the large magnetic calutrons for the electromagnetic separation method to enrich uranium that became the massive Y-12 plant in Oak Ridge, TN. Died of chronic colitis at age 57.

Marshall, George C.: 1880-1959. U.S. Army General and Army Chief of Staff during WWII. Graduate of the Virginia Military Institute, 1901. Staff officer to General John Pershing in WWI. As Secretary of State after WWII, he architected the Marshall Plan to finance the rebuilding of Europe under the Truman Administration. Awarded Nobel Peace Prize in 1953.

Nichols, Kenneth: 1907-2000. U.S. Army officer. Chief Engineer for the Manhattan Engineering District, 1942-1945, headquartered at Oak Ridge, TN. Reported to Major General Groves. Graduate of West Point, 1929. Held two graduate degrees in engineering from Cornell and PhD in hydraulics engineering from the University of Iowa. Promoted to major general and command of the Armed Forces Special Weapons Project (AFSWP) in 1948, becoming the youngest major general in the Army at the time. Became General Manager of the Atomic Energy Commission in 1953.

Oppenheimer, Julius Robert: 1904-1967. American theoretical physicist. Scientific Director of Los Alamos known as Site Y, 1942-1945. Professor of Physics at the University of California, Berkeley. Educated at Harvard University, the University of Cambridge, and the University of Göttingen. Received doctorate in 1927 at age 23. Became Director of Institute for Advanced Studies at Princeton in 1947. In the wake of the Communist hysteria and the Joseph McCarthy era, the U.S. government revoked Oppenheimer's security clearance in 1953 because of his past associations with various Communists, including his brother and wife. Died of throat cancer at age 62.

Oppenheimer, Katherine (Kitty): 1911-1972. American. Educated at the Sorbonne and the University of California. Married J. Robert Oppenheimer in 1940, as her fourth husband. American Communist Party member along with husbands number two and three. She had two children with Oppenheimer.

Parsons, William (Deke): 1901-1953. U.S. Naval officer. Graduate of U.S. Naval Academy, 1922. Ordinance expert. Co-developer of the first radar-trigger proximity fuse used in naval anti-aircraft weaponry. Joined Manhattan Project as Associate Director and Leader of the Ordinance & Engineering Division. Personally armed the *Little Boy* nuclear weapon in flight on the B-29 *Enola Gay* for the bombing of Hiroshima. Died of a heart attack at age 52.

Pash, Boris (Pashkovsky): 1900-1995. U.S. Army officer. Father was Russian Orthodox priest, recalled to Russia in 1912. Graduated from seminary school,

1917. Pashkovsky fought with the White movement's navy in the Russian Civil War. Returned to U.S. as Bolsheviks began consolidating power. Shortened name to Pash. MA from University of Southern California. Became high school teacher. Called up as a reserve Army officer. Security Officer for the Manhattan Project with rank of colonel. Headed Operation Alsos, 1944-1945 to determine extent of Germany's nuclear weapons development, secure any nuclear materials, and to capture any German scientists to prevent them falling into the hands of the advancing Soviets. Always felt Robert Oppenheimer was a security risk, but overruled by General Groves. Pash testified against Oppenheimer at the latter's security clearance hearings.

Seaborg, Glenn: 1912-1999. American chemist. PhD in chemistry, University of California, Berkley, 1937. Did postdoctoral work with Ernest Lawrence's cyclotron studying artificial radioactivity. Assistant Professor of Chemistry at Berkley, 1941. Principle or co-discoverer of ten elements. Seaborg and his collaborators produced the first plutonium-239 through the bombardment of uranium. Demonstrated that the new element 94^{239} could be important as a fissile material for a bomb. Joined the Manhattan Project at the University of Chicago where Enrico Fermi's group would develop a reactor to produce plutonium as a by-product within a controlled uranium nuclear chain reaction. Seaborg developed the multi-stage chemical process that isolated and separated plutonium from the reactor output. Awarded Nobel Prize in Chemistry in 1951.

Segrè, Emilio: 1905-1989. Italian-American physicist. PhD University of Rome studying under Enrico Fermi. Professor of Physics at the University of Rome, 1932-1936. Director of the Physics Laboratory at the University of Palermo, 1936-1938. Born into a Jewish family, Segrè was in the United States in 1938 where he became an émigré with the passing of Mussolini's anti-Semitic laws barring Jews from university positions. Worked in the Manhattan Project at Los Alamos, 1943-1946. Awarded Nobel Prize in Physics, 1959. Professor of Physics at the University of California, Berkley until 1972. Professor of Nuclear Physics at the University of Rome, 1974.

Serber, Robert: 1909-1997. American theoretical physicist. Undergraduate studies at Lehigh University and PhD University of Wisconsin, 1934. Worked under J. Robert Oppenheimer at the University of California-Berkley. Recruited to Manhattan Project in 1941. Group leader for diffusion theory within the Theoretical Physics Division. Gave early overview lectures to the scientific staff at Los Alamos on the making of an atomic bomb which became known as the *Los Alamos Primer*. Created code names for the first atomic bomb designs. Serber was with the first American team to enter Hiroshima and Nagasaki to assess the results after the atomic bombings.

Serber, Charlotte Leof: 1911-1967. Married Robert Serber in 1933. Graduate of the University of Pennsylvania. Parents ran what amounted to a left-leaning political and artistic salon. She was a fervent activist of various left-wing causes during the 1930's. Former member of the Communist Party. Went to Los Alamos with her husband. She and her husband were personal friends of Oppenheimer prior to the Manhattan Project. She was appointed by Oppenheimer to head the technical library at Los Alamos where she was the only female section leader during wartime Los Alamos. She personally typed her husband's sensitive *Los Alamos Primer.*

Stalin, Joseph Vissarionovich: 1878-1953. Russian political figure. Born Iosif Vissarionovich Dzhugashvili in what is now the Republic of Georgia. General Secretary of the Communist Party of the Soviet Union's Central Committee from 1922-1953. Colleague of Vladimir Lenin and leader of the Bolshevik Revolution that toppled Russian Tsarist rule in 1917, leading to the modern Soviet state. Elevated himself to absolute dictatorial power and established the USSR as a police state. Attempting to eradicate potential opposition, Stalin caused 700,000 people in the government and military to be executed in the Great Purge of 1937-1938. A vast network of forced labor camps, the Gulag, was established in inhospitable Siberia as an instrument of repression. 3.3 million people were exiled to the region between 1941-1949, with 43% estimated to have died of disease and malnutrition. Hundreds of thousands of German prisoners of war from WWII died under Soviet imprisonment or execution.

Teller, Edward: 1908-2003. Hungarian-American theoretical physicist. Left Hungary for Germany in 1926 because of limitations on university enrollment for Jews. Chemical engineering degree University of Karlsruhe. PhD in physics University of Leipzig under Werner Heisenberg. Worked at the University of Göttingen, worked briefly with Enrico Fermi in Rome, and Niels Bohr in Copenhagen. Came to U.S. in 1935 as Professor of Physics at George Washington University. Recruited to the Manhattan Project in 1943 as part of the Theoretical Physics Division. Teller was an early advocate of research into a *super* fusion bomb, or thermonuclear bomb. Teller had a difficult and abrasive personality. He resented not being appointed head of Theoretical Physics. Shunted aside from the central work of the fission bombs because of disruptive conflicts, Teller was allowed to continue work on the fusion bomb. Left Los Alamos in 1946, for professorship at University of Chicago. Returned to Los Alamos in 1950. Teller and mathematician Stanislaw Ulam developed the design for the fusion thermonuclear bomb. After the first successful thermonuclear bomb test in the Pacific in 1952, Teller became known as 'the father of the hydrogen bomb'. He is also considered one of the inspirations for the character Dr. Stran-

gelove in the 1964 movie of the same name. Testified against Robert Oppenheimer in the latter's security clearance hearing.

Ulam, Stanislaw: 1909-1984. Polish-American mathematician. D.Sc. degree,
1933 from Lwów Polytechnic Institute. Studied at Harvard, 1936-1939. Escaped
Poland two weeks before German invasion. His Jewish family perished in the
Holocaust. Assistant Professor at the University of Wisconsin-Madison. Joined
Manhattan Project in late 1943. Worked on the complex hydrodynamical calculations with von Neumann to develop the explosive lenses for the implosion
design of the plutonium weapon. Associate Professor University of California
in Los Angeles after WWII. Returned to nuclear weapons development work in
1950 to pursue a thermonuclear fusion bomb in response to the Soviets detonation of a fission bomb in 1949. Developed the staged radiation implosion design known as the Teller-Ulam design with Edward Teller that became the
standard basis for thermonuclear weapons design. Instrumental in applying
early electronic computing to the mathematical problems of nuclear weapons
design. Returned to academia in 1967 as Professor & Chairman of the Department of Mathematics at the University of Colorado. Joint creator of the Monte
Carlo method of computational algorithms used in computer simulations of
physical and mathematical systems. Formulated the Fermi-Pasta-Ulam problem associated with the paradox of periodic behavior in chaos theory. Ulam's
name is mentioned in 697 scientific papers.

von Neumann, John: 1903-1957. Hungarian-American mathematician. PhD in
mathematics with minors in experimental physics and chemistry from
Pázmány Péter University in Budapest at the age of 22. Simultaneously earned
degree in chemical engineering from ETH Zurich in Switzerland. Known for 80
different mathematics related theorems, methods, equations, 26 of which are
identified with his name, he made significant contributions to a wide range of
mathematics including set theory, measure theory, ergodic theory, operator
theory, lattice theory, quantum logic, game theory, mathematical economics,
and linear programming. Regarded as the preeminent mathematician of his
time. Taught at University of Berlin, 1926-1930. Came to Princeton as one of the
original four members of the Institute for Advanced Study in 1930 at age 27.
Contributed to the mathematical work for the implosion design of the *Trinity*
and *Fat Man* bombs. Participated on the site selection committee for choosing
the Japanese target cities. Worked on thermonuclear bomb development after
1945. Credited with articulating the Cold War equilibrium strategy of mutually
assured destruction.

Weisskopf, Victor: 1908-2002. Austrian-American physicist. PhD University of
Gottingen, 1931. Postdoctoral work with Niels Bohr and Werner Heisenberg.
As a Jew, he was forced to leave Germany when the Nazis came to power. Pro-

fessor of Physics University of Rochester. Joined the Manhattan Project in 1943 as group leader of experiments, efficiency calculations, and radiation hydrodynamics under Hans Bethe's Theoretical Physics Division. After WWII, he joined the physics faculty at MIT.

Fictional characters appearing in CRITICAL MASS:

Voronin, Mikhail (Mike) Stefanovich: 1914-1999. U.S. Army officer and Soviet spy. Code name FOUNTAIN. Parents were Russian academics immigrating to the U.S. in 1913 to escape Tsarist secret police because of their Communist activities. Parents returned to Moscow in 1935 as a consequence of father losing his university position during the Depression. Civil engineering degree University of Southern California, 1936. Worked on Grand Coulee Dam as civil engineer with the Bureau of Reclamation. Commissioned in U.S. Army Corps of Engineers, 1938. Joined Manhattan Project as an aide to Brig. General Leslie Groves, 1942. Marries Elena Obolensky, 1943. Obolensky and her adoptive parents, Boris and Vanya Ramazanov, are Soviet agents. Voronin is co-opted to engage in espionage by his wife after she reveals that she is spying for the Soviets. Ceases espionage activities with death of wife in 1945. Receives master degree in civil engineering in 1947 from University of New Mexico while still in the Army. Remarries in 1948. Moscow re-engages him in 1949 by trading for his mother's release from a Siberian prison camp. Retires from Army in 1959 and moves to Southern California to teach at California State Polytechnic University, Pomona, CA. Second wife dies in 1978 of natural causes. Voronin dies of lung cancer in 1999. The story of his spying is revealed in a book by historian Victoria Prescott after his death.

Prescott, Victoria: 1965 - . American historian and academic. Masters and PhD Stanford University, 1990. Prior undergraduate work at Columbia University. Assistant Professor, Stanford faculty. Unmarried. Lives in San Francisco. Father is professor of political science at Columbia University and former State Department Undersecretary for Political Affairs and the ranking Soviet expert during the Reagan administrations. Mother is a partner in a law firm specializing in international business. Grandfather was a scientist at Los Alamos as part of the Manhattan Project during WWII. Her PhD thesis was titled *The Political Dynamics of the Manhattan Project & the Legacy Effects for Military & Foreign Policy*. Her academic specialty is U.S.-Soviet relations history of the early Cold War era. Author of the book *Critical Mass*, published in 2000 revealing her discovery of the previously unknown Soviet spy, Mikhail Voronin.

Obolensky, Elena Maximovna; 1919-1945, Canadian. Soviet GRU spy. Parents were Russian, immigrating to Canada in 1914. Orphaned at age five. Adopted by Boris and Vanya Ramazanov in 1926, retaining her birth surname. Under-graduate history degree from McGill University. Speaks Russian. Adopted parents recruit her into Soviet espionage. GRU code name DANCER. Married Mikhail Voronin in 1943 to gain access to the Manhattan Project.

Ramazanov, Boris Aleksandrovich (Boris Pavelovich Dmytryk): 1892-1945. Russian-Canadian. Chemical engineer. Soviet GRU spy. Code name PUPPET-EER. Chemical engineering degree from Moscow State University, 1913. Joins Tsar's Russian Army in 1914, mobilizing against Germany. Wounded in 1916 and returned to Moscow for convalescence. Meets future wife volunteering in the military hospital. She recruits him into the Bolshevik Party in early 1917. After the October, 1917 Revolution, joins Red Army military intelligence organ-ization, the GRU. Serves in Red Army intelligence during the Russian Civil War. Under pretext of fleeing anti-Semitic persecution, the GRU arranges his immigration to Canada in 1925 with employment by the chemical company E. I. du Pont. GRU constructs a 'legend' for him with the name Ramazanov, in-cluding a Jewish background, excising his past as a Bolshevik and Red Army intelligence officer. Receives PhD in chemical engineering from McGill Univer-sity, Montreal, 1927. Relocates to DuPont plant in the United States in 1942 with the assignment to infiltrate the Manhattan Project for Soviet intelligence.

Ramazanov, Vanya Ivanovna Durchenko (Dmytryk): 1895-1945. Russian-Canadian. Soviet GRU spy. Code name TRAVELER. Degree in classical studies Moscow State University, 1915. Active in Bolshevik Party since 1915. Recruits Boris Dmytryk into Bolshevik Party prior to the October, 1917 Revolution. Mar-ries Boris Dmytryk in 1918. Becomes a Soviet agent along with her husband, adopting the name Ramazanov and the constructed 'legend' excising her Bol-shevik past.

Kirilov, Feliks Antonovich: 1906-1955. Russian Soviet Red Army officer with the foreign military intelligence directorate, Glavnoye Razvedyvatel'noye Upravleniye, abbreviated GRU. Mathematics degree Moscow State University, 1927. Graduate of RKKA Military Academy, 1933. Assigned to intelligence di-rectorate. Fluent in English. Promoted to major in 1936. Avoids Great Purge of 1937-38 because of his middle-level rank. Promoted to lieutenant colonel in 1940. Becomes Moscow control of spies Klaus Fuchs and George Koval. In 1942, assigned mission of additional penetration the Manhattan Project at the highest level. Arranges transfer of agent team PUPPETEER, TRAVELER, and DANC-ER from Canada to the United States. Personally runs spy code named FOUN-TAIN identified in 2000 as U.S. Army officer Mikhail Voronin. FOUNTAIN remained the only undiscovered high-level Soviet espionage asset within the United States associated with the development of thermonuclear weapons. Kirilov died of unspecified causes in 1955.

Grigoryev, Anton Vladimirovich: 1955 - . Russian intelligence officer. Colonel and Deputy Director of the Sluzhba Vneshney Razvedki, or SVR, the principle foreign intelligence agency for the Russian Republic. The SVR is the successor of the First Chief Directorate (PGU) of the former KGB since its reorganization in December 1991. Career intelligence officer from 1979 with the KGB. Field officer for twelve years working in the West. Degree in political science. Fluent in English and French.

ILLUSTRATION CREDITS

- Cover: Castle Romeo test, 27 March, 1954, courtesy of National Nuclear Security Administration Nevada Site office.
- Back cover & title page: Operation Greenhouse, George Event, 8 May, 1951, courtesy of National Nuclear Security Administration/Nevada Site office.
- Page 24: Grand Coulee Dam construction 1937, courtesy of National Archives and Records Administration.
- Page 31: Franklin D. Roosevelt at the Grand Coulee Dam in Washington, 1937, courtesy of U.S. National Archives and Records Administration.
- Page 34: Downtown Washington D.C., 1940's, courtesy of www.imagesforfree.org.
- Page 39: Pentagon Building construction, 1942, courtesy of U.S. Army Corps of Engineers.
- Page 58: Road to Los Alamos Mesa, New Mexico, courtesy Los Alamos National Security, LLC, © Copyright 2011 Los Alamos National Security, LLC All rights reserved. Released into the public domain.
- Page 71: Major General Leslie R. Groves, courtesy of University of California, operator of the Los Alamos National Laboratory under contract W-7405-ENG-36 with the U.S. Department of Energy, © Copyright 2011 Los Alamos National Security, LLC All rights reserved, released into the public domain.
- Page 79: J. Robert Oppenheimer, courtesy of the University of California, operator of Los Alamos National Laboratory under contract W-7405-ENG-36 with the U.S. Department of Energy, © Copyright 2011 Los Alamos National Security, LLC All rights reserved. Released into the public domain.
- Page 108: K-25 Gaseous Diffusion Plant, Oak Ridge, Tennessee, courtesy of the American Museum of Science and Energy.
- Page 123: Earle Theater, Washington D.C., 1943, courtesy Office of the Chief Signals Officer, National Archives.
- Page 145: Joseph Stalin, 1943, courtesy of U.S. Army Signal Corps.
- Page 153: Los Alamos, 1944, courtesy of National Nuclear Security Administration.
- Page 171: U.S. Capital Building, courtesy of Ed Brown. Released into the public domain.
- Page 180: Soviet NKVD Headquarters, Lubyanka Square, Moscow, courtesy RIA Novosti archive, image #142949 / Vladimir Fedorenko / CC-BY-SA 3.0.
- Page 205: Y-12 Alpha Track, Oak Ridge, 1944-45, courtesy of U.S. Department of Energy.
- Page 221: X-10 graphite reactor, Oak Ridge TN, circa 1943, courtesy of U.S. Army Corps of Engineers.
- Page 254: B Reactor, Hanford, Washington, 1944, courtesy of U.S. Army Corps of Engineers.

- Page 275: Los Alamos colloquium, , courtesy of the University of California, operator of Los Alamos National Laboratory under contract W-7405-ENG-36 with the U.S. Department of Energy, © Copyright 2011 Los Alamos National Security, LLC All rights reserved, released into the public domain.
- Page 299: Goldmine at Kolyma Gulag, Siberia, courtesy of the Central Russian Film and Photo Archive, released into the public domain.
- Page 311: Trinity Test Site Base Camp, 1945, courtesy of National Nuclear Security Administration Nevada Site office.
- Page 322: Trinity Test Tower, courtesy of National Nuclear Security Administration Nevada Site office.
- Page 331: Trinity Gadget, 15 July, 1945, courtesy of U.S. Department of Energy.
- Page 342: Fat Man atomic bomb, Nagasaki, Japan, August 9, 1945, courtesy U.S. Department of Defense.
- Page 345: Little Boy atomic bomb, courtesy of the National Archives and Records Administration.
- Page 350: Fat Man atomic bomb, courtesy of the National Archives and Records Administration.
- Page 362: Oak Ridge, TN, 14 August, 1945, photo by Ed Westcott, courtesy of American Museum of Science and Energy.
- Page 380: Operations Crossroads, Baker Test, Bikini Atoll, Micronesia, July, 1946.
- Page 397: ENIAC Aberdeen, courtesy of U.S. Army.
- Page 408: Ivy Mike, First Thermonuclear Test, Enewetak, Marshall Islands, 1952, courtesy of the U.S. Government.
- Page 422: Castle Bravo 15MT Thermonuclear Test, Bikini Atoll, 1954, courtesy of the U.S. Government.